MURDER
TAKES A HOLIDAY

MURDER
TAKES A HOLIDAY

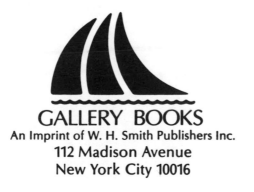

GALLERY BOOKS
An Imprint of W. H. Smith Publishers Inc.
112 Madison Avenue
New York City 10016

First published in the United States in 1991 by Gallery Books, an imprint of W.H. Smith Publishers, Inc., 112 Madison Avenue, New York, New York 10016 by arrangement with Michael O'Mara Books, London

Gallery Books are available for bulk purchase for sales promotions and premium use. For details write or telephone the Manager of Special Sales, W.H. Smith Publishers, Inc., 112 Madison Avenue, New York, New York 10016. (212) 532-6600

ISBN 0-8317-6157-1

Manufactured in the United States

CONTENTS

PERFECT HONEYMOON

by Robert Barnard

By the time Carol reached her unspoiled Greek honeymoon island, she was beginning to wish it could have been just that tiny bit spoiled. After the ceremony, and the wedding breakfast with the speeches, there had been the drive off, the wait at Manchester Airport, the flight, the coach ride from Athens airport, and now the long ferry trip to Mathos. As the island approached on the horizon Carol was inclining to the view that an airstrip would have improved the place enormously.

Of course David had been sweet through the entire trip. But then, knowing she had always been fascinated by the idea of Greece, this honeymoon trip had been his idea. So it was quite natural that he should keep her spirits up by little reminders of the romantic nature of the island, the exotic food, the excursions to Crete and Rhodes. And of course *the* pleasure of a honeymoon. David had always insisted that the first time would be in the luxury hotel on Mathos. David was old-fashioned. He didn't believe in anticipating marriage, and Carol thought it rather sweet of him. She had anticipated it all too often with other men.

Jutting up like a fairy cake in the middle of a brilliant blue tea-cloth, Mathos assumed more definite shape.

'It's beautiful,' said David. 'Just perfect.'

'It's all been just perfect,' said Carol dreamily. 'The wedding, the breakfast—everything.'

'Almost perfect,' responded David. 'I just wish Dad could have been there to share it.'

David had loved his father, who had died just before they had got engaged. He missed him, and found his new role as head of Lloyd-Jones Agricultural Estates burdensome and worrying. Carol put her hand over his on the prow of the boat.

'Almost perfect,' she agreed. 'As perfect as we could make it.'

As they neared the island, shapes began to appear. A ruined monastery on the hilltop, fishing-boats and a pleasure yacht in the harbour, a restaurant with tables outside, and red chequered table-cloths . . . people on the quayside.

'The local peasants, come to see us arrive,' said David. 'And a few tourists, I expect.'

'We needn't talk to any of them if we don't want to,' said Carol. 'We have each other.'

Suddenly, as the boat was approaching the quay, she was conscious of David's body stiffening.

'It can't be,' he muttered. 'It's just a . . . Oh my *God!*'

His face was purple with rage. Carol had never seen him like that. He was such a gentle soul. She looked up at him, with fear in her eyes.

'What is it, David?'

'The *swine!* The absolute swine. Don't you see who that is? It's that rotter Joshua Swayne.'

'Oh David, it *can't* be.'

But it did look very like him indeed. He was standing at the end of the quay, just where the ferry was to dock. He was wearing beautifully tailored white trousers, and a dashing shirt open to the waist and knotted at the navel. He was very tanned, very fit looking, so that even David's rural-proprietor complexion seemed beside his that of a country bumpkin. David, somehow, could never be said to look sexy.

'Take no notice of him,' said David, red and furious. 'He thinks we shall have to acknowledge him, standing there in the middle of the quay. Walk right past him. Ignore him. My God, what a diabolical liberty! Who does he think he is?'

There was not much doubt who Joshua Swayne was. Less than a year ago his . . . wooing of Carol had been the talk of Merioneth, staple gossip in pubs and tea-rooms around the county. Joshua Swayne was only a greengrocer's son, but he certainly knew how to cut a dash. And Carol had always resisted that 'only a greengrocer's son' formulation. Come to that, she was only a schoolteacher's daughter, wasn't she? And if anyone asked her *how* he cut the dash that he did, what he did it *on*, she merely shrugged and said it was none of her business. He was just a very entertaining companion, she said. Oh yes? said everyone else.

'Just don't look at him,' hissed David, as the boat docked. 'Walk off talking and don't acknowledge his existence. The cad!'

And that's what they did, though somehow it seemed terribly unnatural. They held hands, looked into each other's eyes, and walked straight past Joshua Swayne and on to the bus, where they sat, still talking in those unnaturally high voices, still looking anywhere but back to the quay, as the boot was loaded with their and the other tourists' luggage, and the bus began its steep ascent to the hotel.

Of course when they got out and walked into the hotel lobby, there he was again. Somehow David had expected it, since the ride had been so short, and Joshua was a notable mountaineer—'the mountain goat' he had been called, somewhat ambiguously, at home. Half expecting it didn't make it any easier for David to deal with. Carol went on ignoring him studiously, but as they marched up to the Reception Desk, and as he stood there in all his arrogant sexuality, David barked, 'Get out of my way,' and Joshua moved lithely aside with a pleasant smile.

They made their way to their room, watched from the open, sun-drenched doorway by Joshua, who seemed part, or product, of the sun itself. Once safely inside the bedroom, they sat on the bed and looked at each other.

'This is *dreadful*,' said Carol. 'Just unimaginable. He has no *right*.'

'Of course he has no right. You threw him over for me, and there's an end of it.'

'Actually I threw him over well be*fore* I got interested in you,' said Carol. And indeed there had been all of a fortnight's gap before she started going out with David. 'He acts as though he owns me.'

'I just can't see what's to be done.'

'We could move to another hotel.'

'And have him come after us? We'd become laughing-stocks.'

David was very conscious, always, of anybody laughing at him.

'But that means sticking it out here.' Carol giggled shyly. 'Of course we could stay in our room the whole time, and that would be nice. But we have to have meals.'

David looked around the room.

'No sign of room service. Anyway, I'm *damned* if I'm going to avoid the dining-room because he'll be there.'

'No. Why should we? Though it will be awkward . . . '

David looked very glum.

'He's spoilt everything. You know, what I'd like to do now is . . . well . . . you know. But I just don't want it to happen in this sort of atmosphere. We've got to get this sorted out, one way or the other.'

'Exactly. Because if we can't get it sorted out, we might as well go home and . . . start the marriage there.' Carol looked at her watch. 'Actually it's lunch-time now. And after all that travelling I *am* pretty hungry.'

They both showered, separately and modestly, and then they put on clean summer clothes, crisp and delightful on the body, clothes in which David looked *almost* handsome, Carol thought, and definitely better than presentable. Then they went, holding hands, down to lunch.

He wasn't there when they went in, and for that they were grateful. But they had hardly stewed over the menu and given their orders to the waiter when they saw him come in the door from the foyer. The waiter tried to steer him to what was obviously his usual table, but they saw something pass from hand to hand, and he came over and sat himself at the next table.

'Good *morning*, again,' he said cheerfully. 'You really have chosen well, you know. Mathos could hardly be bettered for a honeymoon island. You're going to be awfully happy here.'

David choked, and Carol managed a few reluctant murmurs of reply, for the benefit of other lunch-takers around them. Joshua had already turned to the waiter and begun ordering in what sounded like idiomatic Greek, to a non-Greek. He might have been the cookery correspondent of a glossy magazine.

It was a ghastly meal. Everything they said could be heard by him at the next table. They scampered through their three courses, and as they were getting up, Joshua said:

'Enjoy your afternoon. There are some quite fabulous walks around here, you know. Just give me the nod any time you feel like it, and I'll show you round.'

David and Carol choked with irritation. When they got to the door David made a decision. He left Carol there and marched back down the dining-room.

'Look here,' he said, 'just what is your game?'

'Game, old man? I don't quite understand you. I'm here on holiday like yourselves—well, *almost* like yourselves.'

'You're not going to tell me this is a coincidence.'

'All right. I won't try and tell you this is a coincidence.'

'You've come here deliberately, because you found out this was where we were coming.'

'This island has many attractions,' said Joshua, with a cat-like smile. 'And that, of course, was among them.'

'If you think you're going to make us turn tail and flee, you'll be disappointed.'

'On the contrary, I would be disappointed if you did. It would cause me so much hassle. But I know your sturdy Welsh stock, David, and I know you're not a quitter.'

'I knew you were a cad,' David said, his voice rising, so that people began to look at him from tables quite far away, and he blushed and reduced it to a hiss again, 'but I never thought you'd want to cause Carol this sort of distress.'

'Is she distressed? I don't know why she should be. Most women like having two men at their beck and call.'

'You are *not* at her beck and call.'

'I certainly am, supposing she decides to beck or call.'

'If you continue to force yourself on us in the way you have been doing today . . . '

'Yes?'

It was a thoroughly irritating question, and insolently delivered, the eyebrows raised quizzically. Because what, after all, could David threaten him with?

'I'll not answer for the consequences,' David spluttered, and marched out of the dining-room.

The consequences, unfortunately, were mostly on David and Carol's heads. David said he really didn't want to . . . start the honeymoon while all this was hanging over their heads, and Carol said that really she didn't want to either. They sat in their hotel room and talked things over, and Carol said that at least they did *have* each other to chew things over with, and that what they were really facing was the first crisis of their married life. If they could face up to all the others as calmly, things wouldn't work out too badly, would they?

The trouble was, thought David, that facing up to a marriage crisis was one thing, and that could be done calmly and with dignity; but facing up to Joshua Swayne was quite another matter. The mere thought of Joshua made him panic, as facing up to the farm workers had made him sweat in the first weeks of running the Estates after his father's death. It was the thought of him and Carol . . . Well, least said, soonest mended, but somehow David couldn't manage to put that thought out of his head.

They weren't going to be imprisoned in their room, that was for sure. About three o'clock they went out for a walk, and they probably would have enjoyed it if they hadn't constantly been glancing nervously around to see if they were being shadowed. The island was beautiful, with sloping, fertile pastures, and with cliffs stretching dazzlingly up skywards. Luckily they were young and fit, and David in particular was used to climbing. But as they approached their hotel, the inevitable happened. Joshua was suddenly to be found, insinuating himself beside them.

'Don't you agree it's a beautiful island?' he said. 'I thought I'd let you enjoy it on your own. Went down to Nimos, didn't you? And then up the hill to the coastguard station, then down the cliff path and back here?'

So he had been following them the whole time. David was livid. He drew Carol aside.

'You go on ahead, darling,' he said. 'I'm going to deal with this louse once and for all.'

It did not occur to David, in sending Carol on ahead, that really she had a lot more experience in dealing with that louse than he had. Probably even if it had occurred to him he would not have let her do the dealing.

'Now let's get this straight,' he said, turning to the imperturbably smiling and disgracefully tanned Joshua. 'This has got to stop.'

'Spoiling your honeymoon, is it?' asked Joshua.

There seemed nothing for it but to admit it.

'Yes.'

'That's tough. Carol being such a fun girl, and all. She gets whingy when things don't go as she wants them to. Have you found that out yet?'

'She does not get whingy. She is the sweetest girl on God's earth, and you're making her life a misery.'

'Now that I would hate to do. If only for old time's sake I'd like her to be happy. Just for her, David—just for her—I might be willing to come to an accommodation.'

David was bewildered. Was he offering to seek alternative lodgings?

'I don't get you.'

'I might, out of consideration for her, be open to an offer.'

David was outraged

'Do you mean you would accept money to go away?

Joshua shrugged, still smiling.

'Market forces rule. I'm sure you've always believed that. Voted for Thatcher last time, didn't you? The plain market fact is that you have money, and I want money. In addition, the service I can perform for that money is the service you want above all things: I can go away.'

'This is unbelievable!'

'You'd better believe it, boyo! I tell you what: you go back to your room and think it over. I can see it's a new idea for you. Never too quick to take in new ideas, are you, David? Then when you've thought it over, talked it over with Carol, you can come up with a sum, and we can talk it over. How about half past six, up near the coastguard station? There we'll be away from anyone English who might overhear. We wouldn't want either of us to be embarrassed, would we?'

David was, as Joshua implied, not the quickest thinker in the world. He thought over the proposal, and he talked it over with Carol; after all that he still found the idea utterly distasteful, but he couldn't think of any alternative to going along with it.

'I think we ought to agree,' he said finally. 'No—not *ought* to agree: it's a disgusting suggestion. But I think we simply have to.'

'I think we have to, too,' said Carol. 'If we don't, then the honeymoon is ruined, and that would be a terrible start to our marriage. And after all, it is only money. It's not nice to be swindled, that's for sure, but on the other hand I don't think we should make money some kind of god. We've got enough, heaven knows . . .'

So six-fifteen saw David toiling up the hill again, once more leaving Carol out of things, in that old-fashioned, gentlemanly way he had. Carol had been reluctant, in any case, to witness a transaction which might almost seem to an outsider to be a sale or auction of herself. David agreed with Carol that they should not make a god of money, but he determined not to offer at the start anything like the sum that he might be prepared to fork out after negotiation.

His heart leapt with justified outrage when he saw the figure of Joshua Swayne, on the top of the cliff, silhouetted against the setting sun. He was standing there, rather dejected-looking, and perhaps feeling in his heart the jerk his conduct was proving him to be.

'Well,' said David, a bit puffed, when he drew near to Joshua. 'I've thought it over.'

'Yes?' said Joshua, low. David modified his voice too.

'I think we might say three hundred pounds.'

'What?' shouted Joshua, suddenly raising his voice, and looking fiercely at David.

'I think we might say four hundred pounds,' yelled David in return.

'You swine!' shouted Joshua, in a voice that seemed to carry all over the island. 'My God, you're trying to *buy* me. You think I'm here to screw money out of you! I'm not going to stand for this!'

David did not sense the first blow coming. This was not at all what he had come prepared for. When Joshua engaged him in a close wrestling grip he was too breathless to put up more than a token resistance, and when further blows rained down on him, and they moved closer and closer to the cliff's edge, he could no more avoid the fate he saw coming than can a man in the maelstrom. As he was thrown, head first, over the cliff he knew his end was a second away, and yet he still did not understand. His overmastering emotion as he fell was bewilderment.

It had all worked out very nicely indeed, Carol considered, as she flew home, dressed in deep black (the Greeks were very good at black, they wore so much of it). She was accompanied by the coffin, but she thought very little of it. That part of her life was over and done with.

The coastguards whom Joshua had so cleverly ascertained spoke English had testified to the offer of money, and the sense of outrage felt by the accused. The Greek police, being natural romantics and admirers of Milord Byron, had felt considerable sympathy for the young man (did he not resemble in many ways the familiar features of the liberating English Milord?) who had suffered so much at being rejected by the woman he loved, and who was only making a desperate attempt at the very last moment to win her back. To be offered money to go away, this was the ultimate insult to his tender heart. The Greeks, in any case, take a very lenient view of crimes passionel. That, of course, was why she had manoeuvred David into choosing Greece. Carol had been assured by the Greek lawyer she had retained for herself (though she had been very cunning about not seeming to ask for any reason beyond indignation and pity for the fate of her husband) that Joshua Swayne was unlikely to serve more than five years ('Alas, Madame, but that is how we regard these things in this country!')

Five years! It seemed a lifetime. But her heart swelled with pride as she thought what Joshua was willing to suffer, for her, and for the money. For money there would be now, in abundance. She did not expect to be well received by David's mother, or his sister, but really there was nothing whatsoever that they could do. From now on she was effective head of Lloyd-Jones Agricultural Estates. She had always fancied herself running a big business enterprise. When Joshua got out, they would either marry in North Wales and outface the talk, or she would sell up and they would branch out into something more glamorous than large-scale farming. The world was all before them.

Joshua was worth waiting for. That she knew for certain. It was unlikely that she would meet anybody in the next five years that would force her to break her compact with Joshua. She was quite certain she would keep faith with him. Almost a hundred per cent certain. It was more than probable that she would.

And if she didn't, of course, there was nothing whatsoever that *he* could do either.

THE SUMMER HOLIDAY MURDERS

by Julian Symons

1

'It's rather steep, this path,' said Miss Penny. 'And a little bit slippery.'

'You'll be all right,' said her companion reassuringly. 'Just hold on to the rail.'

'Oh, don't worry about me. I haven't enjoyed myself so much for years. It was such a wonderful idea, the coach tour. Everybody seems so nice. And the weather.' Miss Penny looked up, a little old birdlike woman wearing a mauve silk frock, a hat with a great deal of fruit on it, and dazzlingly ornamental dark glasses. The cliff rose up, as it seemed, a long way above her, overhanging so that the top was invisible. She saw sky and sea that, through her glasses, was not dazzling but muted blue. She saw the face of her companion, smiling. And below, quite near now, was a rocky cove hollowed out of the cliff, with little pools between the rocks.

'Rather a sharp turn,' said her companion. A hand was laid upon her arm, upon the arm that held the handrail.

'This is really a great adventure,' Miss Penny said gaily.

Quite gently the hand lifted her arm from the rail, a knee pushed her less gently in the back. Miss Penny fell helter-skelter down the last few steps, squawking like a duck. She caught her head nastily upon a rock, and before she could get up, before she really knew what was happening at all, hard hands gripped her shoulders and forced her resistlessly down so that her face touched the salt and slimy water in one of the pools. Miss Penny struggled then, and tried to speak, but when she opened her mouth water filled it. She did not struggle for long. It was the end of her great adventure.

Her hat floated on the pool, like a toy boat laden with cherries and strawberries. Her body lay face down in the water.

There was one more thing to do, and her companion did it. The time was just after six o'clock in the evening.

The Top-Grade Coaches Luxury Tour party sat in the lounge of the Barkbeck Hotel and waited for dinner. The Barkbeck was not the best hotel in Eastbourne, but it justified well enough, Gilbert Langham thought, the brochure's claim: '*The hotels specially selected by our experts offer THE BEST OF EVERYTHING—food prepared by Continental chefs, smiling service, and rooms with a view of the sea.*' The room was comfortable, the service was quick, and there were pleasant smells coming from the dining-room.

But back to duty. This was really a piece of field research for Gil Langham, whose fifth detective novel was to be about a murder committed on a coach tour in Southern England. With a plot sketched out he found himself at a loss to imagine what sort of people actually went on such a tour. What could be simpler than to go on one himself, and find out?

He took a small black notebook from his pocket and studied what he had already written, after the trip down from London with its break for a 'surprise' lunch (which proved to be a picnic), and a visit to Arundel Castle.

Wiliam and Mary Blake. Married couple. Husband much older than wife. Wandered off on their own this afternoon.

Gil Langham looked at them now, sitting on a window seat with hands touching, and wondered if they were honeymooners. At a table nearby sat the handsome grey-haired old man named Antrobus, and on a sofa Mrs Williams, Elaine Williams, lay back studying her blood-red nails and looking bored. He read what he had written:

—*Antrobus*. Retired businessman? Made a fuss when we stopped for drinks, said he'd been charged twopence too much for tomato juice.

But looks prosperous. Doesn't seem really to be enjoying himself.

Elaine Williams. Merry Widow spider? Looking for husband-fly to walk into her parlour?

A hand was placed upon his shoulder, and a voice boomed in his ear. 'Hallo, hallo! This won't do. Settling down to work while you're on holiday isn't allowed. Have a drink, old man.'

Tompkins was fortyish, almost bald, and obviously destined for the part of bore of the tour. But very likely his book would have a bore in it, Gilbert Langham thought with a mental sigh as he said that he would like a drink. As they passed the Merry Widow she looked up. Her eyes telegraphed an invitation which he ignored.

'Not a bad piece that,' Tompkins said when they had their whiskies at the bar. 'Did you notice her giving me the eye? But I always say, take it easy. You don't want to start anything you can't finish on a holiday like this.'

'You've been on tours like this before?'

'I get around,' Tompkins said vaguely. 'Now, don't think I'm nosey, old man, but I always flatter myself I can spot a man's occupation. You're a schoolmaster, right?'

Gilbert had been prepared for this. 'No, I'm a journalist, a free-lance.'

'Looking for copy, eh? Writing us up?'

'Of course not!' But he felt uncomfortable. The look in Tompkins's eye had been remarkably shrewd. He might be a bore, but he was far from a fool.

A young man came into the lounge, a young man with a brown face, dark hair carefully parted, and teeth that showed dazzlingly white when he smiled. This was Jerry Benton, the tour guide, who seemed to Gilbert Langham rather too much of a good thing. One couldn't make him a murderer in a story because it would be too obvious, but all the same —

'Don't like that chap,' Tompkins said, cutting into and confirming his thoughts. 'Don't trust him. "Call me Jerry," he says. I'll call him—' And he made a coarse joke.

Benton was going round from table to table, talking to all the members of the party, many of whom Gilbert Langham did not know. He chatted for a minute with Mr Antrobus and then stopped beside the Merry Widow. They came over to the bar together. Benton performed introductions in a low voice.

'There is a dance this evening at the Winter Garden. For those on the tour there is no charge.'

'Don't dance,' Tompkins snapped.

'And a concert at the Pavilion. Again no charge. Tomorrow morning at ten-thirty there is a mystery tour that will last the morning.'

'Same old South Downs mystery, I suppose,' Tompkins said.

Benton was imperturbable. 'Those who wish to stay here of course may do so. We leave the hotel after lunch.'

The Merry Widow smiled at him. 'Are you going to the dance?'

Benton smiled back. 'Of course!'

The dinner gong sounded, and at the same moment the manager came into the lounge with a tall, hard-faced man wearing a blue serge suit. They came up to Benton together.

'Mr Benton?' the man in the blue suit said. 'My name is Lake. Detective-Superintendent Lake.'

For a moment there seemed to be a break in Benton's perfect composure, then his smile was in place again. 'Yes, Superintendent. What can I do for you?'

'You have a Miss Penny in your coach party?'

'That's right. But she's not here at the moment. She is a little late for dinner.'

'Miss Penny won't want dinner. She's dead.'

Mrs Williams gave a little scream. Tompkins said, 'An accident?'

'It seems that she fell down by some rocks, caught her head and drowned in a pool.' The superintendent spoke with deliberate slowness. 'But there's one odd thing. A book, with all the pages torn out, was by her side. The pages were scattered around.'

'What was the book?' Gil Langham asked.

Superintendent Lake stared at him. 'The Adventures of Sherlock Holmes.'

Langham stared, and said with a gulp when asked his occupation: 'I write detective stories.'

A sergeant in the corner of the manager's office, where this interrogation was taking place, snorted slightly. Gilbert Langham gulped again, and decided that he might as well go on. 'I'm here to get background material for a new book.'

'You've been very successful.' With the same grim sarcasm Lake said, 'Using your no doubt exceptional faculties of observation, have you noticed anything odd on this coach tour so far?'

'I can't think of anything.'

'Or about Miss Penny?'

Miss Penny, Miss Penny? They had hardly spoken. She was a face to him, no more than that, an old face inquisitive and perhaps vain, topped by a ridiculous hat. 'I remember the fruit on her hat more than the face under it. Wasn't it an accident, then, Superintendent?'

'This is a queer business.' Lake stared hard at him. 'A crime writer might have thought it up.' Langham flinched. 'This little old woman goes off for a walk, climbs down some steps, slips—we can see the mark—falls, hits her head, and drowns in a pool of water. That's the way it looks. I think we might accept it as an accident. But then someone—someone, Mr Langham—tears the pages out of a crime story, throws them all over the place, and leaves the gutted book by her body. If she was murdered, why should the murderer do that, after arranging things to look like a neat little accident? Or why should anybody else do it? This is the kind of thing that should appeal to a writer of crime stories.'

The way in which these last words were spoken made Gilbert Langham gulp again. 'Have you found out anything about Miss Penny? I mean, why should anybody want to kill her?'

The sergeant in the corner said: 'Evelyn Penny. Spinster. Lived at 18 Cotes Avenue, Turnham Green, London. Told other members of party that she had retired from work in a drapery store, had small private income, went away somewhere every year. Did not appear to know anyone else in coach party.'

'And her movements, Sergeant?'

'Coach arrived Barkbeck Hotel, Eastbourne, about three-thirty. Miss Penny had tea in lounge, then said she was going for a stroll. Was seen by Mr Tompkins on front, later by Mr and Mrs Blake having photograph taken at the Nu-Stile-Picksher stall also on the front. This was about four-forty-five. Not seen afterwards until discovery of body just before seven o'clock. Purse appeared not to have been touched, no sign of bodily violence.'

'There's nothing to connect this with the coach,' the superintendent said. 'But still, I'd like to keep what you might call an unofficial sort of an eye on your party. With your powers of observation, Mr Langham, you could be a help to us in that way if you cared to.' The superintendent smiled now. It made the request sound like an order.

'All right! But I don't really see what you want me to do.'

'Just keep your eyes and ears open. We'll get in touch with you in a day or two.'

Dinner was late, but it could not be said that Miss Penny's death cast a shadow over the coach party. Rather it provided a ready-made subject of conversation which could be added to weather and food. Gilbert Langham sat afterwards at a table with the Blakes and listened to them talking about it.

'Honestly, you know, Mr Langham, I don't think the poor thing was quite all there,' Mary Blake said. 'I mean, we saw her having her photograph taken on the parade by those people who give away prizes every day—

'Nu-Stile-Pickshers,' her husband said. He was a hearty, tweed-jacketed, pipe-smoking man in his early thirties, perhaps ten years older than his birdlike wife. 'Advertising stunt, you know. As a matter of fact we had our own pictures taken.'

'But no luck with a prize,' Mary Blake said. 'Anyway, when the young man asked if she wanted her picture taken, she was primping and blushing like a girl of fifteen.'

Mr Blake puffed at his pipe, rustled the evening paper. 'I reckon some man got hold of her, sex maniac.'

'But Bill,' his wife said with ghoulish eagerness, 'there wasn't—I mean, she wasn't *interfered with*, was she?'

Bill Blake was having trouble with his pipe. He tapped out the dottle in an ashtray. 'The superintendent didn't say so. If we're going to this dance, my girl, you ought to get ready.'

Mary Blake excused herself. Her husband began to read the paper.

Gilbert Langham also went to the dance at the Winter Garden. The unattached women in the party, he saw, were beginning to pair with men. He found himself asking the Merry Widow to dance. They talked, as seemed inevitable about Miss Penny.

'I'm so glad it hasn't been allowed to spoil the tour,' she said. 'Jerry has been simply marvellous about it. You know how silly people are, they get worried, but Jerry's told them all it was just an accident.'

'That was good of him.'

'Yes, wasn't it? But he must have had a lot of experience in handling awkward situations. He was some sort of courier in the Middle East at one time. And then he was a smuggler.'

'Really? What did he smuggle, Mrs Williams?'

'My name's Elaine.' She came close to him. The bloom of youth, he saw, had been replaced by the enamel of middle age, but she was still an attractive woman. She whispered in his ear: 'Diamonds.'

[15]

He wanted to ask why, if Jerry Benton was a diamond smuggler, he had this humble job of guide to a coach party, but after all it was none of his business if the guide liked to tell fairy stories to impressionable women. Instead he said, 'Who was particularly worried about Miss Penny?'

'That's a funny thing. It was a man who keeps himself to himself. Mr Antrobus.'

Mr Antrobus, grey-haired and really remarkably handsome, sat in the lounge drinking coffee when the party from the Winter Garden returned, gay and chattering. Tompkins also was in the lounge. He made a bee-line for Gilbert Langham.

'I've had a word with the super and told him my theory about the Penny murder—'

Jerry Benton interrupted him. 'It was an accident. And anyway it's rather a gloomy subject, old man. I think it should be declared closed.'

Tompkins glared at him. 'It's a free country. This is my theory. That old girl, Miss Penny, had somehow got the wrong side of a chap who's a maniac about books, see. And this chap did for her, and then left the book by her side. What you might call symbolic.'

There was a clatter from the other side of the lounge. Mr Antrobus had knocked his coffee cup to the floor. He did not pick it up, but slowly rose and walked over to the lift.

'Good night,' Tompkins said cheerfully.

Mr Antrobus did not reply.

2

A man who is tired of Brighton is tired of life, Gilbert Langham said to himself, bringing Dr Johnson up to date. He walked from the lawns of Hove to the Palace Pier in a trance of pleasure, leaving the promenade as he passed the Metropole to walk down beside the beach. Here children shrieked happily, their parents bought tea trays and sticky cakes, young men in vivid shirts left the sunlight to play earnestly on pin-tables in amusement arcades.

Behind this popular, vulgar Brighton lay the solid hotels full of money, behind them again the appropriately artificial glamour of the Prince Regent's onion domes. He stopped before a little hut that said Nu-Stile-Pickshers. Underneath was a sign in dashing scarlet

calligraphy: '*Have Yore Foto Takn and Win Wun of Our Munny Prizes.*'
A curly-haired young man with an engaging smile was in charge.

'Step right up now, and take advantage of this stupendous offer. Three postcard size pictures for a bob, and a money prize if you get one of today's lucky numbers.'

A chord was struck in Gilbert Langham's mind. 'Haven't you got a place in Eastbourne?'

'Eastbourne, Littlehampton, Brighton, Worthing, Folkestone, a dozen places along the coast,' the young man said. 'But only one set of prizes each day, and each day at a different town. Today it's Brighton. Come along, you lucky people, we're offering you twenty-five quid to nothing.'

'You were offering prizes in Eastbourne yesterday,' Langham said. 'Did you happen to see an old lady named Miss Penny?'

The young man looked at him sharply, shouted inside the hut, 'Just going out for a cuppa,' and led the way to a self-service café twenty yards away from the hut. He put three spoonfuls of sugar in his tea, stirred and said, 'The name's Wilson, Charlie Wilson. What's yours?'

'Gilbert Langham.'

'So now we know each other's monicker. I like to know who I'm talking to. Now, what's your interest?'

There was something a shade odd about the young man, Langham thought, as though he knew that working for Nu-Stile-Pickshers demanded a front of brass that was not natural to him. A university graduate seeing the other side of life?

'I'm one of the coach party she was with. I write crime stories and her death roused — you might call it my professional curiosity.'

'Fair enough! She came along yesterday, had her picture taken. Funny old girl! I remember the way she mucked around with her hat, trying it this way and that for effect. Then she went off. I told the police.' He hesitated.

'You've remembered something else.' Gilbert Langham was careful not to sound too eager.

'Not exactly. It's just that they were only trying to fix a time, and I told them she came along at a quarter to five. They didn't want anything else, so I didn't tell them.'

'Tell them what?'

'She seemed a bit excited, as if she was going to meet someone. And after she left the hut she did meet someone. I saw her.'

'What did he look like?'

'I only caught a glimpse, mind. And side face. I'm not sure I could identify him. But he was a good-looking sort of a chap, about her own age I should say. And he had a fine crop of iron grey hair.'

Mr Antrobus.

'Superintendent Lake, please.' he said into the receiver. 'Tell him it's Gilbert Langham. About Miss Penny.'

There was a click and he heard Lake's voice, with its faint undertone of sarcasm. 'Yes, Mr Langham?'

With attempted casualness he said, 'I've been talking to a man named Wilson, who works for those Nu-Stile-Pickshers people. He saw Miss Penny walking with somebody after she had her photograph taken yesterday.'

'Why didn't he tell us?'

'You were concentrating on the time,' he said with a touch of complacency. 'Wilson's not sure that he could identify the man, but says he had a fine crop of grey hair. From the description it might be a man on the tour named Antrobus.'

There was silence. Then Lake said: 'Miss Penny died between six and six-thirty. Antrobus was in the hotel lounge a minute or two after six o'clock. Three or four people saw him.'

'Alibis have been broken before now,' Gilbert Langham said. He put down the receiver.

The telephone box was opposite the Palace Pier. When he came out of it he hesitated. The coach party had split up, some of them going on a tour of the Royal Pavilion, and others preferring what was rather oddly called 'Free Time'. They were all to meet back at the Packham Hotel at half past six. With an hour to fill, Gilbert Langham went on to the Palace Pier.

He strolled idly, sniffing the salt air, until he saw ahead of him the grey hair and slightly shuffling walk of Mr Antrobus. It was with a feeling that he was about to make a discovery of vital importance that he cautiously followed the grey head up the pier, and with some disappointment that he saw Mr Antrobus turn into the Palace of Pleasure and settle down to play a game called Cup and Ball, at which he proved to be rather skilful.

He went up behind Antrobus and said, 'Hallo!'

The grey-haired man turned round with what might have been a look of alarm but was certainly, when he recognized Langham, one of annoyance. 'Good afternoon!'

[18]

'You didn't go to the Pavilion?'

'Evidently not.'

'You're not forced to do anything on this sort of tour, that's what I like about it.'

Mr Antrobus did not reply. He shot up a small silver ball and dexterously caught it in the cup.

'Where did you go with Miss Penny, when you met her yesterday afternoon?'

Mr Antrobus was about to catch another ball. His hand jerked, and he dropped it. He turned round and said very decidedly, 'I did not meet Miss Penny. I did not even know her. You are being a nuisance. Will you please go away?'

Gilbert Langham went away.

When the tour of the Pavilion was over the Blakes and the tour guide, Jerry Benton, went down to the beach.

'Have you made up your minds?' Jerry Benton asked.

'Let me see it again.' There was something greedy in Bill Blake's voice.

They sat down. Jerry drew from an inside pocket something wrapped in tissue. As he unwrapped it, the white stone sparkled in the sunlight.

'Oh Bill,' Mary Blake breathed, 'it's lovely, lovely!'

'You're asking a hundred,' her husband said. 'That's a lot of money.'

'A quarter of what it's worth.' Jerry Benton began to wrap the stone.

'Don't put it away. I told you, I don't know anything about diamonds. I'd need to have it examined by a jeweller.'

'And have him asking where it came from? Not likely! I risked a five-year sentence to bring this in. I'm not having any jeweller poking his nose in.'

'Bill,' said Mary Blake in a small voice, 'Mr Tompkins said last night that he knew a lot about jewellery. Supposing he looked at it for us, would that—?' she left the sentence unfinished.

'That would suit me.' Blake looked at Benton.

Benton hesitated, then shrugged. 'Tompkins doesn't love me much. But all right. You can show it to him tonight.'

He let the stone rest in his palm. Blake could not take his eyes off it.

'Another whisky?' Bill Blake said.

'I don't mind if I do.' Tompkins was wearing a powerfully checked shirt, open to reveal his boiled red neck, and purplish linen trousers. He downed half the whisky at a gulp and sighed with pleasure. 'This is the life.'

'Mr Tompkins.' Mary Blake put her pretty arms on the bar counter and looked at him with her birdlike head on one side. 'You said you used to be an agent for a firm of jewellers.'

'Correct, my dear lady. Brant and Boulting, Hatton Garden, dealers in precious stones.'

'Would you look at a stone for us?'

Tompkins frowned. 'Mixing business and pleasure, don't like that. Why d'you want me to look at it?'

'We'd pay you—' Bill Blake began, but his wife interrupted.

'We're thinking of buying it, wondered how much we should pay. And we're awfully stupid about these things. We thought we'd come to an expert.'

The frown changed to a leer. 'Anything to oblige a charming lady,' Tompkins said.

Upstairs in Tompkins's room, Bill Blake took out of his pocket the stone wrapped in tissue which Jerry Benton had given him, with the remark that nobody could say he didn't trust his fellow men. Tompkins glanced at it, raised his thick eyebrows, and then took from his suitcase a jeweller's glass which he put into his eye. He examined the stone carefully, turning it this way and that, for perhaps half a minute. When he spoke his tone was professional.

'It's a diamond, and quite a fine one. Not cut as well as it might be, but still a very nice stone.'

'How much is it worth?'

Tompkins took the glass out of his eye, and grinned at them conspiratorially. 'You notice I haven't asked where it came from, and I don't want to know. But if you were asking me to buy it, that's the first question I'd ask.'

'I'm not asking you to buy it. What's it worth to me?'

'I'm telling you the difficulty about selling it is that any honest jeweller will ask the same question. He'll want to be sure it came into this country legally.' Now Tompkins winked.

'We shouldn't want to sell it,' Mary Blake said excitedly. 'It's to make into a ring for me.'

Tompkins rubbed his chin. 'Hard to put a value on it. Wouldn't be dear at two hundred quid.'

'Oh, you darling man,' Mary Blake said. She kissed Tompkins on the cheek.

The Merry Widow was telling Gilbert Langham the story of her life, as they sat in deckchairs on the front. Her husband, a colonel in the Engineers, had gone through the war unscratched, and had then died in a yachting accident shortly after his retirement, three years ago. 'No children,' she said, turning upon him the full force of still-lustrous eyes. 'And this rambling old house in Shropshire to look after. I'm a lonely woman, Gil.'

Gilbert Langham was not much interested in her past. 'You remember that yesterday evening we were sitting in the lounge of that hotel at Eastbourne. Did you happen to notice what time that man Antrobus came into the lounge?'

'I already told the police that as far as I could remember it was about six o'clock,' Elaine Williams said coldly.

'You couldn't be more exact?'

'No. I must be going back to the hotel.' As she got up she said, 'I detest snoopers.' Gilbert Langham sighed. The way of an amateur detective is hard.

That night there was a firework display at the end of the Palace Pier, and tickets were free for those who wanted them. 'I must say,' said Mr Portingale, a self-important, pigeon-chested man who went about with a limp, long-nosed wife apparently permanently attached to his arm, 'that young chap Benton knows how to manage things. As a businessman myself I respect efficiency.'

'He's very good,' Gilbert Langham agreed. He was watching Mr Antrobus to see if he took one of the tickets. He did, after asking whether they were free.

'My husband had thirty men under him at his retirement,' Mrs Portingale said in a melancholy voice.

'A versatile young fellow, too,' Portingale resumed. 'Used to be in the diamond trade, I understand. Adventurous.'

'It takes all sorts to make a world,' Mrs Portingale said sadly.

'Yes, indeed.' Langham took one of the tickets. The Portingales took them, too.

The night was hot, the sea still. Rockets swished up skywards, burst into patterns of stars. A set piece slowly made the pattern WELCOME TO BRIGHTON. There was a burst of clapping.

'It's simply gorgeous,' Mary Blake said. 'Perfect. I want it to last for ever. Have you told Jerry about the ring, darling?'

'A hundred pounds is okay,' her husband said. 'I'll give you a cheque tomorrow.' He produced the stone in its tissue and Benton took it.

'No cheques, old man. Strictly cash. If you can let me have the money at the end of the tour I'll hand over the stone then.' His teeth gleamed in a smile. 'You can ask Tompkins to vet it for you again then, if you like. See you later.' He waved a graceful hand.

'I wonder why he insists on cash.' Blake took out his pipe and tapped it thoughtfully on the rail.

'He's just being careful, silly. Ooh!' A cascade of coloured lights exploded just above their heads. The hand that she had placed over her husband's clutched at him, the nails dug gently into his palm.

'I want some cigarettes,' Elaine Williams said, and opened her bag. 'Oh, damn! I've forgotten my purse.'

Portingale, who was sitting just behind her, took out his case. She murmured her thanks, lighted the cigarette, took a few puffs, then murmured something about going back to the hotel, and got up.

It was a few minutes afterwards that Langham, who had been temporarily enthralled by a set piece depicting the battle of Trafalgar, with the *Victory's* guns magnificently firing, noticed that Antrobus was not in his place. He got up and walked down the pier to look for him. But the man with grey hair had vanished.

Elaine Williams did not go back to the hotel. An hour later she was walking by the cliffs near Rottingdean, talking about her husband's death and the big house in Shropshire.

'Yes,' her companion said. 'Yes. Yes.'

'The truth is I am a very lonely woman.'

'We are all lonely.' Her companion took her hand and led her nearer to the cliff top.

'Sometimes—you'll think it foolish—my heart really aches.' She guided her hand to her aching heart.

'You're not foolish at all.' Another hand encircled her shoulder. She held up her face to be kissed. Then she felt herself being forced backwards, and opened her lips to scream, but the hand that had been on her heart quickly covered them. Her high heels scrabbled at the cliff edge before she went over.

4

It was no more than eleven o'clock in the morning, but already a fierce sun shone into the little room. The sandy sergeant he had seen before waved Gilbert Langham into a seat directly facing the window and the glare. Superintendent Lake sat in the shade.

'Now, Mr Langham, I shall value your skilled observation. What have you got to tell me?'

'I still don't know exactly what's happened,' Gilbert Langham said. 'There are all sorts of rumours. Nobody knew that Mrs Williams hadn't come back to the hotel until this morning. Your people haven't really told us much.'

'She's dead,' Lake said. 'She fell, or was pushed, off the cliffs near Rottingdean some time yesterday evening. There's a drop of about eighty feet and she was probably killed at once. She'd been dead several hours when she was found, early this morning.' Lake paused and then said, 'There was a book found near the body, looked as if it had been thrown from the cliff top.'

He held up a book on the desk before him, its cover spotted with damp. Gilbert Langham read the title on the back. It was *The Suicide's Grave* by James Hogg.

'That's not been gutted.'

'Not this time. But the queer thing is that it should have been there at all. What sort of woman was Mrs Williams?'

'I thought of her as the Merry Widow. She was flirtatious, particularly with young men.'

'With you, for instance?'

'Yes. Though I lost favour because I didn't react properly when she said she was lonely. She seemed to like Jerry Benton, the guide. But it didn't mean anything. She'd have behaved in the same way with any other young man.'

'Mr Langham.' Lake leaned forward. The outlines of his face were harsh. 'It seems likely that Mrs Williams died through what you call her flirtatiousness with a young man—or an old one. And since whoever killed her left a book, as he did with Miss Penny, it's a fair assumption that the murderer is linked with your coach party. I want you to tell me exactly what you saw and heard after going out to watch the fireworks.'

'At about nine o'clock or a little after, Mrs Williams left us, saying she was going to the hotel. She'd left her purse there, had no money to buy cigarettes—'

Lake interrupted. 'She said she had no money, you're sure of that?'

'Yes. A man named Portingale was sitting just behind her, offered her a cigarette.'

'Her handbag went over the cliff with her. There was a five-pound note in it, loose.'

'No purse?'

'Her purse was in the hotel. But a five-pound note is money. Why didn't she use it?'

A bluebottle buzzed on the window pane. The glare of sunlight was hot on Gilbert Langham's body. He felt slightly damp. Lake went on:

'She didn't go back to the hotel, she went to meet somebody. It must all have been arranged in advance.' He said sharply to Langham, 'What happened after she left?'

Langham told him of Antrobus's disappearance, and his own movements.

'You say you got back to the hotel just after eleven. Nobody saw you?'

'No.'

'You didn't go out again?'

'Of course not.'

'I'm keeping the coach party here for the moment. Let me know if you have any intention of leaving Brighton, won't you?'

Gilbert Langham got up and said incredulously, 'You mean you suspect *me*?'

'I suspect everybody.' Lake smiled. 'I'm still in need of suggestions, even from amateur criminologists.'

'There ought to be some sort of clue in that book.'

'There are no prints on it, if that's what you mean.'

'No.' Langham picked it up. 'You see, this book is usually called *The Memoirs of a Justified Sinner*. This is a special edition, published in 1895, and it just might be possible to trace it.'

'Nothing on the fly-leaf, sir,' said the sergeant.

'No, but—' Langham leafed through the pages, and gave an exclamation.

'What is it?' Lake came round the table, and Langham pointed out

[24]

what he had found. At the bottom of a page in the middle of the book, very small and faint, was a circular die-stamped mark. It said: '*Charles Antrobus. Dealer in Rare Books. Specialist in Crime and the Occult.*'

Lake said to the sergeant, 'Duff, I think we'll have a word with Mr Antrobus. No, hang on a minute. Ask Benton to come in for a minute first. I'd like to know whether he's got any details of when and how Antrobus booked for this coach tour, whether his bookings were linked with Miss Penny's and Mrs Williams's, for instance. That might help.'

'Yes, sir.'

'You're thinking we were stupid to have missed that,' Lake said to Langham when the sergeant had left them.

'Why, no. This is a favourite book of mine. I happened to know it was an unusual edition—'

'It was careless. Two of us have looked through the book and we ought to have seen it. We've been doing fifty different things since the body was found this morning, but that's no excuse.' He crossed to the window and stood looking out. The street was shimmering with heat. 'I don't know why people go abroad when we have weather like this in England.'

'Have you found out anything more about Miss Penny?'

'Yes. It confirms that she was just what she seemed to be, a nice old lady who hadn't got much money and lived a quiet life. There's no motive. Whoever did all this is slightly crazy. Duff's taking his time.' He rattled money in his pocket.

The door opened, and the sergeant came in, breathing hard. 'He's not there, sir.'

'Antrobus?'

'No, Benton.'

Lake's face went very red. 'I thought I gave instructions that nobody in the party was to leave the hotel until I'd talked to them.'

'Yes, sir.' The sergeant said stolidly, 'We had men at the front door. Reckon he skipped down the fire escape. There are some people called Portingale looking for him, say he was in the hotel ten minutes ago.'

'Right,' Lake said. 'Let's get up to his room.'

5

Mr Portingale, wife connected to him like a broken-down car being towed by a van, was waiting for them in the passage. 'Inspector, I have something I want to report to you—'

'Superintendent,' Lake snapped. 'It will have to wait.' He turned to the sergeant. 'Duff, he'll reckon on having at least half an hour's start. Chances are he'll take a train for London. Go to the station. Take someone with you who knows him by sight.'

'I'll go along,' Gilbert Langham said. In the car Sergeant Duff expressed himself rather scornfully about the likelihood of Benton catching a train.

'One of the super's not so bright ideas,' he said. 'There's more ways out of Brighton than out of a rabbit's burrow. If he tries the train he wants his brains tested.'

'It's the quickest way of getting up to London,' Langham said absently. He was astonished by the turn of events. If Benton was the murderer, what was the meaning of the books placed by the bodies? He was pondering this problem when the police car pulled up outside Brighton station with a screech of brakes. The station, clean and bright, was comparatively empty at this time of the morning and Duff, who had been so sceptical in the car, was full of energy in action. Within no time at all, as it seemed, he had learned that the last train for London had gone half an hour back, and that the next one left in ten minutes' time from platform three.

'Wouldn't have had time for the last one,' Duff said as they walked along the train corridor. 'Now, you look out for him. Brown face, medium height, good looking, bit film starish, you said. Might apply to me, eh?' He was in his forties and looked like a sandy-haired monkey.

Benton was not on the train. 'Didn't suppose he would be,' Duff said as they went back along the platform. 'Knew it was a wild-goose chase. We'll just stay around until the train goes. You get over by the departure board there and make yourself inconspicuous. I'll stay by the entrance. Give me the office if you spot him.'

Langham nodded. The train left at twelve-fifteen. At exactly thirteen minutes past twelve Jerry Benton walked briskly out of the station lavatory with an attaché case in his hand, looked once round the station, and began to walk over to platform three. Gilbert Langham raised his hand and Duff nodded.

Perhaps it was this gesture that made Benton look towards the departure board. He saw Langham, changed direction and began to run out of the station. Duff and Gilbert Langham ran after him. Benton had several yards start. He was almost out of the station when

[26]

a family consisting of father, mother, babe-in-arms and a screaming small boy wearing a cowboy hat and carrying spade and bucket entered it. The small boy stuck the spade between Benton's legs and he went down with a crash. Before he could get up Duff and Langham were on him.

The small boy had stopped screaming, and looked slightly awestruck at the effect of his work. 'Now, Bertie,' said his mother, 'you didn't ought to have done that.'

'Oh yes, he did,' said Duff, holding Benton's arm in a lock. 'He's helped to make an important arrest. Are you Wyatt Earp?' he asked.

'Nah, I'm Matt Dillon.'

'Well, buy yourself another gun, Matt, will you?' He gave the boy half a crown.

'Can't buy much of a gun for 'alf a crown,' the boy said.

The last words they heard as they got into the police car were his mother's. 'There you are, Bertie. I told you you should have left the gentleman alone.'

'She's got the right idea,' Benton said, and grinned.

He did not look like a murderer, Gilbert Langham thought. But then, had he any idea at all what this particular murderer looked like?

They went back to the hotel room where Lake had conducted his interrogations. There Mr Portingale stood, indignation filling his pigeon chest. There also, Langham saw with surprise, were the Blakes.

'All right, Benton. What have you got to say?' Lake's tone was rough.

'I don't know what this is all about.' Benton smiled. 'I just got fed up with the job and decided to chuck it.'

Lake sighed. 'Mr Portingale.'

Mr Portingale took from his pocket something wrapped in tissue. When he unwrapped the tissue a stone gleamed in the sunlight.

'You offered me this for a hundred pounds, said it was a diamond. Then this morning you asked me for twenty pounds cash deposit, which I gave you, and handed me the stone. Later on I happened to be speaking to Mr Blake—'

'Just the same story,' Blake said. He produced another stone. 'We took them to a jeweller. They're not diamonds, they're quartz.'

'How many more have you got in that case?' Lake asked.

'Six,' Benton said calmly. 'I don't know what they're moaning about. I never guaranteed the stones. They were sold to me as diamonds. I suggested they should contact somebody who would check on them.'

'It's no good, Benton.' Lake nodded to Duff.

The sergeant went outside. When the door reopened it revealed to Gilbert Langham's astonishment, the bald head, puce face and check shirt of Tompkins. The back-slapping geniality was gone, however. Tompkins had no eyes for anybody but Benton.

'You rat,' he said. 'skipping and leaving me to carry the baby. Did you think I'd wear that?'

'All right,' Benton said. 'It's a cop. But I had nothing to do with those two women getting done. That put the wind up me, I don't mind telling you.'

'If I'm not much mistaken we shall find that both these boys have got records as long as my arm,' Lake said. He addressed himself to the Portingales and the Blakes. 'A nice little racket they ran together. You see how it worked. Benton spread a rumour about smuggling diamonds, then showed you the stone. He couldn't let you take it away and show it to a jeweller, so Tompkins meanwhile makes it known that he's an expert, and also that he dislikes Benton. He certifies the stone as genuine. If everything had gone as planned, you'd have handed over a hundred pounds each at the end of the tour and never seen either of them again. You're lucky that Benton got the wind up, took part of the money from you, and tried to skip.'

'We had nothing to do with the other business,' Tompkins said. 'You can see it queered our pitch, the police coming in.'

'I believe you,' Lake said, and sighed again. 'Take them away.'

'That leaves Mr Antrobus,' Gilbert Langham said. It was one o'clock, just two hours since he had made that momentous discovery about the book.

'Yes. We've delayed our talk with him long enough. What's his room number, Duff?'

'Second floor. Two fourteen. But he may have come down to the lounge.'

The lounge was buzzing with excited members of the coach party who had seen Benton and Tompkins taken away by the police, but Antrobus was not among them. They took the lift up. Duff strode along the corridor.

'Here we are. Two-ten, two-twelve.' He stopped abruptly, sniffing.

'Gas.' Lake put a handkerchief round his mouth and nose, and turned the door-handle of room two-fourteen. The room was not locked, the blinds were drawn. The smell of gas rushed out at them.

6

Lake rushed across the room, pulled aside the curtains, opened the window wide, turned off the gas tap, and came out coughing. 'Doctor,' he said to Duff. The sergeant ran down the corridor.

Looking over Lake's shoulder Gilbert Langham could see the body of Mr Antrobus lying on the floor, his head near to, but not quite resting on, a pillow. The hose connecting the gas tap to a fire set into the wall had been pulled away and lay just by the man's mouth. Lake drummed on the wall with his fingers while they waited for the gas to clear. 'This looks like the end of the road.'

'I suppose so.' Langham felt queerly disappointed.

When they were able to enter the room they found further evidence. At a little writing-desk in one corner of the room was a scrap of paper pencilled in a fine, thin, clerkly hand: 'I feel the bitterest regret for what has happened. I cannot go on.'

Langham bent down to look at the note, and Lake said quickly: 'Don't touch it.'

'That paper has been torn off a larger sheet. I wonder why he was so parsimonious.' The superintendent was kneeling by the body, extracting a wallet from the jacket. There was a pencil beside the note, a yellow Venus 3B. Langham opened his mouth to say something else, then closed it again. Lake was going through the wallet.

'Pound notes, a wad of them. Membership cards of various societies. Cheque book. Nothing personal. Ah, this is interesting. Membership of the Antiquarian Booksellers' Association in the name of Charles Antrobus. He simply told me he'd retired from business. Ah, hullo, Doctor.'

The doctor examined the body briefly, then shook his head. 'No hope, I'm afraid. He's had the gas tube very nearly in his mouth for hours.'

'How many hours?'

'I wouldn't like to say. *Some time last night, certainly.*' The doctor said with a slight note of surprise, 'He's had a knock on the head at some time. Not very long ago, either.'

'Enough to stun him?' Gilbert Langham asked.

'Possibly.'

'Supposing he'd turned on the gas tap and sat down to write his suicide note,' Lake suggested. 'He might have been overcome by the gas, fallen and struck his head on the gas fire. Could that have happened?'

'I suppose so,' the doctor said, without much conviction.

'And that would explain why his head wasn't on the pillow but beside it. Suicides generally like to make themselves comfortable. But why didn't somebody find him earlier this morning? I think we might ask the reception desk. Then I suppose I should have a word with the rest of the tour party. Duff, will you get them together for me in one of the lounges?'

When they left the bedroom the photographers and fingerprint men were at work. Downstairs, Lake said to the young receptionist, 'Did Mr Antrobus in room two-fourteen leave any sort of message last night?'

'I'll find out for you, sir. Edward, the night porter, would have taken any message at that time.'

Edward was old and gnarled as a tree trunk. 'Mr Antrobus? Yes, sir. He rang about eleven o'clock last night and said he had a migraine headache, didn't want to be disturbed until after lunchtime today.'

'Do you know Mr Antrobus?' Langham asked: 'Would you recognise his voice?'

The porter shook his head. 'Why, no, sir. He was one of those on the coach tour, that's all I know. Wouldn't know him to speak to at all.'

'You're hard to satisfy, Langham,' Lake said. 'You put us on to Antrobus in the first place, Now when you're proved right you're still unhappy.'

'Somebody else could have been in that room, hit Antrobus on the head, put the gas tube in his mouth, and rung down to the porter.'

'In theory, yes. In practice the obvious explanation is the right one ninety-nine times in every hundred. Just wait till we dig into Antrobus's background. You'll find he's a psycho all right, and that he killed those two women for some reason that doesn't make sense to you or me then committed suicide. Now I'm going to break the news to the rest of them. If I'm not much mistaken, with three casualties and two arrests in the party, they'll want to go home. Are you coming?'

Langham shook his head. He walked moodily towards the potted palms at the hotel entrance. The name 'Antrobus' spoken behind him, made him turn. A blonde girl wearing a dark blue frock stood by the reception desk.

'Were you asking for Mr Antrobus?' Langham said.

'Why, yes. I'm Sheila Antrobus. He's my uncle.'

'I'll handle this,' he said to the receptionist. And then to the girl: 'You must be prepared for a shock.'

She was shocked, certainly, but she did not seem deeply surprised. 'Uncle Charles had been getting odder and odder ever since his wife died two years ago. It made things a bit difficult for me, because he was my guardian.'

'Odd in what way?'

'He was a dealer in rare books, crime books especially. Soon after Aunt Rose died he gave all that up, and in the last few months it's sometimes seemed to me that he really hated books.'

'There's something else. You'll have to know about it soon. I may as well tell you.' He told her about Miss Penny and Elaine Williams. 'Do you think he might have done that?'

She said in a subdued voice, 'I don't know. I'd like to see him, please.'

They went up to the room. She looked at the figure on the floor, shivered and turned away.

'There's something I want you to see.' He led her over to the desk and showed her the note. 'Is that your uncle's writing?'

'His prints are on it,' one of the fingerprint men said. 'And on the pencil.'

'Poor uncle,' the girl said. Her face was very pale.

They walked out of the hotel, along the Marine Parade and into the Old Steine. 'There's something I want to ask you,' Gilbert Langham said. 'Did your uncle draw?'

'Sometimes. He wasn't very good, but he liked to sketch.' She looked surprised. 'Why?'

'I know something about pencils. That note on the desk—the one that's supposed to be a suicide note—was written with a thin fine pencil, probably 2H. The pencil on the desk is a 3B, a drawing pencil.'

She said nothing. They walked round into Church Street. The North Gate to the Royal Pavilion was in front of them. 'Shall we go in?'

'All right.' She stopped and faced him. 'What does it mean, about the pencils?'

'I believe your uncle was murdered. And if he was, then everything that has happened has been planned, with him as the final victim. You said he made things difficult for you. How?'

'I want to get married. I'm only twenty. Uncle Charles didn't approve of Chris. In fact he very much disapproved. So we agreed to wait.'

'Chris?'

'Chris Watling. The man I'm going to marry.'

They stood in the Pavilion gardens, with the statue of George IV on one side and the cupola of the dome on the other, together with those fragments of the eccentric architectural past now transformed to respectable library and art gallery. She opened her bag and took out a photograph. He looked at it, and felt as though he had been struck between the eyes. The photograph told him almost the whole of the story.

7

'Tell me about Chris.'

There was some unfathomable expression in her blue eyes. 'You wanted to go into the Pavilion. Let's go, then.'

He waved a hand at the onion domes. 'Do you know Sydney Smith's joke about the Pavilion architecture? That the dome of St. Paul's must have come down to Brighton and pupped? But I like it.'

She made no reply. They walked in silence through the Octagon Hall and the entrance hall. In the Chinese Corridor she said, staring intently at one of the bamboo plants on the wall. 'What do you want to know?'

'About Chris.'

'You've seen his photograph. He doesn't find it easy to settle in a job. That's what Uncle didn't like.'

'He's been in trouble?'

'His father lost all his money when Chris was about thirteen. There was trouble about a couple of years ago over some cheques.' She turned to face him, her face desperate. 'But he's awfully nice — Chris — he's such fun to be with. He's always wanting to do something dashing, something that will get his photograph in the papers. He makes a joke of it, he's full of jokes. There's nothing bad about him really. You've got to believe that.'

'It might be easier for you if I guessed some of the story and you filled in the details. Your uncle was quite rich, and most of the money comes to you.'

'All of it. He's got no other close relations and he is—was—very fond of me.'

'He disapproved of Chris, more strongly than you said. He blamed himself for letting you go about with Chris, told you to stop seeing him, threatened in a good Victorian way to cut you out of his will. Right?'

'I told you I'm not twenty-one yet and I didn't want to upset uncle. Do you think I cared about the money?'

'Chris cared about it, though. Didn't he?'

She turned and ran from him, ran back through the halls, while shocked respectable holiday-goers, wearing sleeveless shirts and with shorts above sun-reddened knees, looked after her. He found her in the garden. 'If your uncle died the money would come to you, and there would be no obstacle to your marriage. Uncle Charles was eccentric, he did odd things like coming on this coach tour. Why did he do that, by the way?'

'He always went on tours. He was awfully mean in little ways, said they were wonderful value for money. And this one attracted him because of going to different places each day. All the places had piers. He loved playing on the slot machines.' She smiled faintly.

'Yes. Uncle Charles was eccentric, but he wasn't crazy. If Chris murdered him and tried to make it look like suicide, questions would be asked. But supposing it could be shown that Uncle Charles had really gone round the bend—supposing he'd killed two people and left the books he hated beside his victims—then his suicide wouldn't be questioned. Superintendent Lake is prepared to accept it now.'

'You mean that those two people, Miss Penny and Mrs Williams, were murdered just to show—'

'To convince people that your Uncle Charles was a psychopathic killer? I'm afraid so.' He paused, said abruptly: 'You recognised that so-called suicide note, didn't you? It was part of a letter from your Uncle to Chris.'

'I don't know. There *was* a letter in which uncle said something like that, about blaming himself for letting me go around with Chris. but I still can't believe it was the same. What makes you so sure?'

'Why, you see,' Gilbert Langham said, 'I know Chris.'

When they got back to the hotel Mr Portingale stood in the doorway beside the potted palms. 'Have you heard the news?' he asked eagerly.

'Do you know that we have been nursing a pair of scoundrelly tricksters in our midst?'

Langham had almost forgotten about Benton and Tompkins. 'The superintendent has got them under lock and key, though, hasn't he?'

'Would you believe it, my dear sir, they tried to practise their arts on me. I'm afraid they picked the wrong person there, eh, Mrs P.?' Mrs Portingale, firmly attached to one arm, smiled and nodded. 'But as a result our happy little party is broken up. The coach company is making a very handsome refund, and Mrs P. and I are departing for fresh fields and pastures new.'

To call the party a happy one seemed to Langham an overstatement. 'Where are you going?'

Mr Portingale beamed. 'We are lucky enough to have been able to book with another coach tour. We are off to the New Forest. I believe that there are still one or two vacancies if you would care to—'

'No, thank you,' he said hurriedly.

Sergeant Duff said cheerfully, 'Where have you been? The super's been looking for you, wants to pin a medal on your chest, I shouldn't wonder.'

He said a little pompously, 'This is Mr Antrobus's niece, Sheila. We've got to see the superintendent urgently. Some fresh information about the case.'

Duff scratched his sandy head. 'The trouble with you amateurs is you can never let well alone. The super's round at the station.'

They went round to the station and saw Lake. He listened impatiently, until Sheila Antrobus produced the photograph.

'That's Chris Watling.' Gilbert Langham said.

Lake gasped. Then he said, 'This seems to be an occasion for a little telephoning.' When he put down the receiver after a telephone call to London he said, 'He's in Folkestone.'

'What are we waiting for?' Langham asked.

From the promenade at Folkestone you can reach the beach either by way of the two lifts that go up and down together, working in series, or more circuitously, by the famous zig-zag with its right-angled paths separated by banks of shrubs. Or you can get to the beach by going through the Old Town, emerging near the harbour. The police car came round there and stopped.

They began to walk across the shingle, past the children's playground.

'You understand what to do, Miss Antrobus?' Lake said. 'If you don't feel up to it, say so now.'

'I'm up to it.'

'Good.' Lake was brisk. 'We'll follow you slowly as you walk along the lower promenade. We shan't be more than a few yards away.'

The lower promenade was full of people buying sweets, ice-cream and cups of tea. Children were crowded round a Punch and Judy show. Langham jumped down to the pebbled beach and watched. Sheila Antrobus threaded her way along through the people, putting one foot precisely before another, unhurried and cool-looking in her dark blue dress.

8

She stopped in front of a hut that stood beside an ice cream stall, and said: 'Hullo, Chris.'

The young man who had called himself Charlie Wilson was talking earnestly to a prospective customer for Nu-Stile-Pickshers. He stopped speaking, and the look on his face was for a moment that of one who wakes to find that some private nightmare, the death of a loved child or an ordeal by fire, has come true. Then his engagingly boyish smile was in place again, and he said: 'Why, Sheila ducks, whatever are you doing in Folkestone?'

'You didn't tell me you were doing this sort of thing.'

'I said I was doing a job for a few weeks that was great fun. Don't you call this fun?' He said to the customer, 'Do go in, madam, you'll find the photographer inside. And don't forget, if you get a lucky number you win one of today's cash prizes.'

'Chris, I want to talk to you.'

'Of course, ducks.' He shouted—and how well Gilbert Langham, who heard it, remembered his shouting the same words before—'Just going for a cuppa.' He fell into step with her and said, 'There's a little place along here with an old lady running it who just loves me.'

'They all love you, don't they?' Sheila Antrobus said. 'I mean the ladies.'

He stared at her with what seemed unaffected surprise. 'I just don't know what you mean. If you don't like my doing this job, all right. you're always saying I ought to work, and there aren't so many jobs that fit my peculiar talents.'

[35]

Sheila Antrobus went on talking, slowly and without expression, as though some sort of machine had been wound up inside her. 'Especially the ladies who got the prizes. That was the way it happened, wasn't it? You found out the people who were on the coach tour, got into conversation as they passed you, had their photographs taken or took them yourself, and then told the ones you picked, the unattached women, that their number had come up and they'd won a prize. After that, naturally they were delighted to meet such a charming young man a little later on to receive the prize. That was where the five-pound note came from that was in Mrs Williams's handbag, wasn't it? Careless, Chris.'

'Sheila.' He jumped back as though she had jabbed him with a needle.

'And it wasn't really a clever idea to leave that note, out of the letter he wrote you. If I came down there was a good chance I'd recognise it. But I suppose you thought I'd marry you anyway.' Very slowly now, the record dying down, she said: 'After we'd married, Chris, what would have happened to me?'

He made an ineffectual gesture with his hand, still backing away. Langham began to move up the shingle and at the same time Lake and Duff, behind Sheila, quickened their steps. Chris Watling turned, bolted for the nearest entrance to the zig-zag and began to run up it.

Lake and Duff went after him. Langham paused beside the girl who stood, looking upwards, with no expression at all on her face.

'That must have been terrible for you.'

Her voice was harsh. 'I've done what you asked, haven't I? You said I could break him down, while the police might not be able to. Now he's running. That's what you all wanted.'

'You talk as though you didn't want him to be caught. He's killed three people.'

'I love him.' She said flatly. They watched the figures running up the paths between the shrubs. 'He's gaining on them.'

'Lake's got a man waiting at the top.'

For a few moments Watling was out of sight, hidden by a turn in the path. Then he emerged, and they could see the man who stood solidly blocking the exit. Watling took something from his pocket, and ran towards the man at the top.

'He's got a gun,' Langham said. They heard two small sharp cracks, and the man went down. They could see Watling now, far above, running along the front, firing backwards at Lake and Duff. He reached the entrance to the lift leading down to the beach, and paused.

'He's coming down.' Langham began to run towards the red-brick Victorian lift house. The girl followed him.

When they reached it, Langham said to the attendant, 'There's a man coming down in that lift who's wanted for murder. Can you stop him?'

'No, sir. He can't get out though. Door's bolted outside.' They stared up and saw the great wooden cage on wheels descending. Above it was a sign: 'The Lift. Fare 3d. One Minute to Centre of Town.' The two lifts moving up and down worked together, and as the wooden cage from the top descended they could see some sort of confused activity inside it. There was a crash of glass, and they saw Watling climbing out of the window, still holding the revolver. He swung out and up on to the curved lift roof.

'He's going to jump over to the other one,' Langham said. No doubt Lake and Duff were now running down the slope and Watling thought he might get away at the top. It was almost certainly hopeless—the crowd would never let him off the lift, revolver or no revolver—but he was going to try it. They watched him poised on the top of the sloping cage as it slowly descended and the other lift rose to meet it. When the two cages were almost level, he jumped easily from one to the other.

'He's done it,' the attendant said.

But Watling had failed to get a proper purchase on the lift's curved top. They could see him desperately trying to get a grip with hands and feet. Like a figure in a slow motion film his body slipped away from the lift roof. Then suddenly he dropped, limp as a puppet.

Sheila Antrobus turned away her head and screamed.

The broken thing that had caught in the cable at the bottom was not quite dead when Gilbert Langham reached it. The lips moved, whispered, 'Sheila.'

'Yes?'

The smile was engaging as ever. 'Tell her I shall have my picture in the papers.'

TRIANGLE AT SEA

by Anna Clarke

I first saw them in the Floral Lounge, the coolest and most comfortable part of the ship.

The elderly man had a fine head of white hair, good features, and a very courteous manner. The two old women appeared to complement each other. One of them was large and commanding and had one of those upper-class English voices that seem to penetrate everywhere. The other was tall and thin with a long melancholy face and a voice that was equally irritating in a different way: a gentle nagging voice, the sort that drives a patient husband to drink or desperation. I judged her to be either the paid companion or a poor relation of the aristocratic lady.

My book lay open on my lap. I raised my eyes from its pages and stared with great concentration at an indigo sea and a spectacular orange sunset while I listened to the little drama. I am an unobtrusive sort of person and have often been criticized by my friends for not making the most of myself. But this is what an 'observer' ought to be. People smile at me and ask me if I am enjoying the cruise, and I say I am, and they immediately start telling me about themselves, which I find very fascinating and also very useful material for my stories.

'Now, Frederick,' said the lady-of-the-manor, 'I am going to make you a little present.'

'That's very kind of you, Julia,' was the reply.

The old man had an attractive voice. It was measured, cultivated, but not too posh. Retired lawyer? Doctor? Or some sort of scholar?

'I have it here,' said Julia. 'At least I thought I did. It was wrapped in tissue paper. Nellie—' very accusing '—did you take that little parcel out of my handbag?'

The last word was pronounced in true Lady Bracknell style. I ventured to glance across at the three of them. They took not the slightest notice of me. An enormous black-leather bag lay on the seat between the two ladies and both of them were scrabbling about in it, as if trying to find the prize in the lucky dip. The old man seemed to be watching them with as much curiosity as I was myself.

'You carry too much about with you, Julia,' said the nagging voice. 'Why don't you leave valuables with the purser?'

Not a paid companion, I thought. Calls her 'Julia.' Friend or relation. Maybe not so downtrodden, after all.

'Because I don't trust these Germans one inch,' cried the loud voice at the very moment that the chief officer, a handsome Bavarian, happened to be walking through the lounge. I looked up and caught his eye and received a cheerful wink.

'It's perfectly disgraceful,' continued Julia, 'that there is no British ship cruising to this part of the world.'

'But the purser has to be honest,' protested Nellie. 'I really do think you could trust him.'

'Ah! I've got it.' Julia's voice triumphed over all opposition. Nellie was silenced. Frederick leaned forward in his chair opposite the two women. The chief officer paused and turned his reddish-gold head, and several people at nearby tables turned their heads, too. The three main actors still appeared to be blissfully unaware that we were all of us holding our breaths with curiosity and suspense.

I had the best vantage point. The white wrapping paper was laid on the knees of Julia's lemon-colored trousers and her plump fingers, generously splashed with rings, unfolded the paper. The chief officer, under pretext of checking a fire hydrant, actually took a step back toward the group. At least half a dozen pairs of eyes watched with the intensity of fascination normally only accorded to a conjuror.

The object was produced at last.

It was a little piece of soft material, shining and scarlet.

'A cravat!' exclaimed Frederick. 'How very delightful!'

'It belonged to my husband,' boomed Julia. 'He always liked to wear a cravat. I have a number of them remaining, although it's six years since he died. I always take some of his possessions with me when I go on a cruise in case I should have the opportunity of making somebody a little gift.'

'That is a very charming and friendly thing to do,' said Frederick.

I admired his composure. It was all I could do not to laugh out loud. I could hear the chief officer still fiddling around with the fire hydrant behind me and I knew that if I were to catch his eye we should both explode. But a moment later it no longer seemed so funny. Julia was leaning back in her seat and I suddenly found myself looking beyond all the jewelry and the smart cruising clothes to the tired and perhaps lonely old lady beneath. Was she looking for another husband? Or just short-term companionship? And what part did Nellie play?

'I'm so glad you like it.' The voice was slightly muted.

'I like it very much,' said Frederick, folding up the cravat and slipping it into the pocket of his safari shirt. 'Thank you very much indeed.' There was a moment's silence. The chief officer went on his way at last and the other viewers returned to their own affairs. I alone continued to listen and observe.

Nellie was the next to speak. 'I think he would have preferred the gold cufflinks,' she said.

'Would you, Frederick?' Julia actually sounded quite anxious. 'Would you rather have had a gift of jewelry?'

'My dear lady,' he replied, 'there is absolutely no reason why you should make me a present of any sort at all, but you have done me that kindness, and I find the gift very much to my taste.'

Oh, thank you, Frederick, I found myself mentally exclaiming, for the little scene now appeared to me as almost unbearably pathetic, with the commanding Julia at the heart of the pathos. As for Nellie, I could have hit her.

When the bell sounded for luncheon, we all trooped into the dining room like ravenous school children, although it was barely two hours since we had had our midmorning refreshments and in another couple of hours there would be afternoon tea. We helped ourselves and I deserted my usual quiet corner table and followed the three old people to the center of the room, where I seated myself behind the old man and listened shamelessly to their conversation.

This time it was dominated by Nellie's thin monotone. She was telling Frederick about Julia's home and possessions. I learned that Nellie was Julia's cousin and lived with her in what sounded like an exceedingly luxurious mansion. Frederick, permitted a few sentences occasionally, identified himself as a retired actor.

I was disappointed. I had hoped he was genuine, but found his account of himself rather suspicious and wondered what he was up to. Nellie's object appeared plain enough: to impress this agreeable and personable old man with Julia's wealth and social position.

But to what end? To find Julia another husband? Perhaps the whole business had been gone through before, on earlier cruises. There are, of course, far more lone old women than old men in the world, but with so much on offer surely one of the latter could be bought. It was all most intriguing, and strangest of all was the part played by Nellie. If Julia hooked Frederick, surely Nellie would lose her home and inheritance? Unless, of course, she was being paid to do the hooking.

In which case, she was in an excellent position to try some double-crossing. Oh, Julia, I thought, I do hope you will take care. This is a dangerous game you are playing and you'd do better to play it alone.

During the next couple of days I found myself surprisingly worried about Julia and I kept a close watch on the trio. Frederick appeared to be well and truly caught.

'Why aren't you wearing the cravat?' I heard Julia demand in her most imperious manner one morning in the Floral Lounge.

'I will fetch it at once, dear lady,' he replied, getting up from his seat.

'No, no—don't go now. I only want to be reassured that you like it.'

'I'm sure he'd prefer the diamond tiepin,' put in Nellie.

'I didn't bring it,' retorted Julia almost snappishly.

'Yes, you did.' said Nellie. 'I saw you put it in myself, together with the cufflinks and several other pieces.'

She's crazy, I said to myself. They both are. These women positively deserve to lose their valuables.

That evening Frederick was wearing not only the cravat, but the pin and the cufflinks as well. On anybody else it would have looked most peculiar, but he had an air about him that could carry off anything. After dinner they settled themselves in deckchairs to enjoy the moonlight on the water and I leaned over the rail a few feet away.

The first officer, doing his social rounds, stopped to speak to them.

'I want you to put on a play during the cruise,' boomed Julia, 'so that Frederick can take a leading part.'

'You might suggest it to the entertainments director,' replied my

Bavarian friend tactfully. 'He is always pleased to make use of the talents of passengers.'

'I must decline the honor, dear Julia,' said Frederick in the smooth tone that had at first attracted me but that I was now beginning to find rather nauseating. 'After all, I'm on holiday.'

'That's true. Oh, well. Later on, perhaps. When we get home.'

'Ah. When we get home. Great things will happen. That's right, isn't it, Julia?'

'I hope you will feel much the better for your holiday,' said the first officer, 'and I hope we shall have the pleasure of welcoming you aboard next winter.'

'Thank you, sir.' It was Frederick's voice again. 'But I think we will probably have other plans. Eh, Julia?'

The next thing I heard was a little laugh. It had to come from Julia, but it really was the most extraordinary sound and it added to my sense of unease. A young courting couple came and leaned on the rail near me, and to get away from them I moved farther along the deck to a quiet spot behind a lifeboat. After a minute or two, I heard and felt somebody come and stand beside me. I had no need to glance at the gold braid to know who it was.

'Is it true,' I asked in German, 'that the captain of a vessel at sea is authorized to perform a marriage ceremony?'

'Perfectly true.' The first officer laughed. 'When shall it be, Liebling?'

'You're going too fast, Willy. I'm thinking of the lady-of-the-manor and her conquest.'

'Oh, yes.' He was immediately serious. 'That is a very different matter. I've spoken to the captain and it's as I feared.'

'The old man? Frederick?'

'Yes. He was on our sister ship last year. An elderly lady lost some very valuable possessions. Oh, no—nothing so crude as theft. They were freely given to the charming old gentleman whom she expected to marry. No charges were made—there was no crime after all—and for the old lady's sake it was all kept quiet.'

'And now he is at it again.'

'It seems so. It's very sad, but there is nothing we can do to stop it. He has committed no offense, not even impersonation. He really is a retired actor. If rich old ladies choose to behave in this way—'

The first officer shrugged and started to move away.

'I'm still not satisfied,' I said. 'I think Julia may be in danger.'

'How so?'

'How easy is it for someone to disappear on board ship?' I countered.

'Now, Liebling—'

'Don't tell me it can't happen. I don't believe it.'

'Of course it can happen, but it's not so easy. She is a big lady. She is not weak and small like a child. And why should he wish to get rid of the goose who lays the golden eggs?'

'He may not want to, but the other lady might.'

'The cousin who inherits? She is aiming for both the man and the money? You are full of ideas, Marianne.'

'I have to be,' I retorted. 'I make my living by writing stories.'

'And don't you think you may be making up a little story now?'

'There's something behind it,' I said obstinately. 'It isn't just an old woman handing over jewelry to a smart con man.'

'All right,' he said resignedly. 'I will keep watch. And I will tell the stewards to keep watch, too. Attempted murder at sea—oh, no, that won't do our business any good at all.'

He did his best, and I know the stewards did, too, but I was the one who actually saw it happen.

We were anchored at one of our tropical ports of call and most of the passengers had gone ashore. A small group, mostly elderly, lay dozing around the swimming pool on the lido deck after luncheon. Siesta time. All very lazy. My sunhat covered my face. I was still as the tomb on my sunlounger. A faint splash told me that someone had got into the pool. I shifted very slightly. From under my hat I could see them. Nellie was in the water, swimming quite competently. Julia, in the lemon-yellow cruising suit, stood at the very edge of the pool. Beside her, with a hand resting on her shoulder, stood Frederick.

I glanced around. All the other bodies on deck, if they looked anywhere at all, were looking in a different direction. This was the ideal moment. Julia probably could not swim, and in any case if she tried to climb out there was Nellie, down in the pool, to hold her under water.

An accident, of course. Nellie's story would be that she had been trying to rescue her.

But what should I do? Jump up and make my presence known? That would stop anything happening now, but it would not stop them trying again later on. Wait and see, so that if anything happened there would be at least one witness that it was no accident? But that might be too late to save Julia.

[43]

While I was hesitating, the decision was made for me. There was a loud splash. I had been looking straight at Julia and Frederick, but even so I couldn't have sworn that she had been pushed, so neatly and quickly was it done. I found myself at the edge of the pool without any consciousness of how I had got there and I slithered into the water.

'Take her arms!' cried Nellie, panting and struggling with Julia's weight.

I began to struggle, too. She really was a very big woman indeed and her attempts to help herself only impeded us.

We got her out at last. Frederick was nowhere to be seen, and a couple of sunbathers who had woken up sufficiently to come and investigate told me they thought he had gone to fetch the ship's doctor.

'I don't want the doctor!' cried Julia, sitting up suddenly. 'I want the captain! This wasn't an accident! I was pushed!'

The sunbathing couple exchanged glances and moved away. They had no desire to be involved in any sort of scene. I caught Nellie's eye and she nodded. It occurred to me then, for the first time, that Nellie really had been trying to save Julia from drowning even before I came on the scene. This did not fit with the role I had devised for her. Had I been wrong about everything else as well?

'Would you mind fetching the captain?' said Nellie. 'I don't think I'd better leave her.'

'I think he's ashore,' I replied, 'but I'll fetch the first officer.'

And so my friend Willy took over and the whole story came out at last. I had been right in supposing that two of the trio were plotting against the third, but it was Julia and Nellie who were the schemers and Frederick who was to be trapped.

Oh, no—not into marriage. That was all put on for his benefit. The true aim was to get him to show himself up as the villain he was and to have him punished for it. Nellie was to implant in his mind the idea that if Julia were out of the way, he could have Nellie and her inherited fortune as well. She played her part to perfection. He fell for it completely.

'An exceedingly clever lady,' said the chief officer. 'And devoted to her cousin.'

I said that I hoped she didn't realize I had been suspecting her.

'She will have forgiven you,' he replied. 'She doubts if she could have managed the rescue without your help.'

'But what a risk to take.' I shuddered. 'Why did they do it? They'd never even met Frederick before.'

'They had not met him, but Julia's sister had. I told you about the wealthy old lady on our sister ship.'

Enlightenment came to me. 'The one Frederick treated so badly? That was Julia's sister?'

'It was. And they were determined to get their own back. A very devoted family. Sisters and cousins and all.'

'So what happens to Frederick? Can he be convicted of anything?'

'He certainly can,' said the first officer grimly. 'But first we've got to find him.'

'You don't mean—'

Yes. He did mean that. Frederick had gone ashore. Run away. And with him had gone all the rest of Julia's valuables and loose money. He'd got hold of the key to her cabin and had taken the risk of collecting the lot while Nellie and I were by the pool deciding what was to be done.

We were in the harbor of a town where it was all too easy to hide and where one could live for a long time on very little money. No doubt Frederick would manage very well.

The two old ladies took his disappearance philosophically. They were delighted with what they regarded as the success of their scheme. The villain had been faced and challenged. Family honor had been upheld.

I listened to their tale of triumph and was inclined to sympathize with their desire that the matter should now be allowed to rest.

But it was the chief officer who felt personally affronted by the whole affair. He set inquiries going in the port, and he went on and on about Frederick all the way back to Europe. I tried to protest.

'But Willy, he's done you no harm. If the ladies are prepared to make no charge—'

'Right under my nose!' he cried. 'How's that for impudence?'

In the end, I just tried to avoid the subject completely.

And I am avoiding it still. Apart from this one topic, my husband is the kindest and most compassionate of men, and our wandering life suits me admirably. But I always feel slightly anxious when we come to that port again. Supposing Frederick is still there and should take it into his head to stowaway on a cruise liner? We always carry a good quota of gullible old ladies. Supposing he should get hold of one of them and spin her a hard-luck story? I think I would rather not try to imagine how that particular tale might end.

[45]

THE ADVENTURE OF THE DEVIL'S FOOT

by Arthur Conan Doyle

I n recording from time to time some of the curious experiences and interesting recollections which I associate with my long and intimate friendship with Mr Sherlock Holmes, I have continually been faced by difficulties caused by his own aversion to publicity. To his sombre and cynical spirit all popular applause was always abhorrent, and nothing amused him more at the end of a successful case than to hand over the actual exposure to some orthodox official, and to listen with a mocking smile to the general chorus of misplaced congratulation. It was indeed this attitude upon the part of my friend, and certainly not any lack of interesting material, which had caused me of late years to lay very few of my records before the public. My participation in some of his adventures was always a privilege which entailed discretion and reticence upon me.

It was, then, with considerable surprise that I received a telegram from Holmes last Tuesday—he has never been known to write where a telegram would serve—in the following terms: 'Why not tell them of the Cornish horror—strangest case I have handled.' I have no idea what backward sweep of memory had brought the matter fresh to his mind, or what freak had caused him to desire that I should recount it. But I hasten, before another cancelling telegram may arrive, to hunt out the notes which give me the exact details of the case, and to lay the narrative before my readers.

It was, then, in the spring of the year 1897 that Holmes's iron constitution showed some symptoms of giving way in the face of constant hard work of a most exacting kind, aggravated, perhaps, by occasional indiscretions of his own. In March of that year Dr Moore Agar, of Harley Street, whose dramatic introduction to Holmes I may some day recount, gave positive injunctions that the famous private agent should lay aside all his cases and surrender himself to complete rest if he wished to avert an absolute breakdown. The state of his health was not a matter in which he himself took the faintest interest, for his mental detachment was absolute, but he was induced at last, on the threat of being permanently disqualified from work, to give himself a complete change of scene and air. Thus it was that in the early spring of that year we found ourselves together in a small cottage near Poldhu Bay, at the farther extremity of the Cornish peninsula.

It was a singular spot, and one peculiarly suited to the grim humour of my patient. From the windows of our little whitewashed house, which stood high upon a grassy headland, we looked down upon the whole sinister semicircle of Mounts Bay, that old deathtrap of sailing vessels, with its fringe of black cliffs and surge-swept reefs on which innumerable seamen have met their end. With a northerly breeze it lies placid and sheltered, inviting the storm-tossed craft to tack into it for rest and protection. Then comes the sudden swirl round of the wind, the blustering gale from the south-west, the dragging anchor, the lee shore, and the last battle in the creaming breakers. The wise mariner stands far out from that evil place.

On the land side our surroundings were as sombre as on the sea. It was a country of rolling moors, lonely and dun-coloured, with an occasional church tower to mark the site of some old-world village. In every direction upon these moors there were traces of some vanished race which had passed utterly away, and left as its sole record strange monuments of stone, irregular mounds which contained the burned ashes of the dead, and curious earthworks which hinted at prehistoric strife. The glamour and mystery of the place, with its sinister atmosphere of forgotten nations, appealed to the imagination of my friend, and he spent much of his time in long walks and solitary meditations upon the moor. The ancient Cornish language had also arrested his attention, and he had, I remember, conceived the idea that it was akin to the Chaldean, and had been largely derived from the Phoenician traders in tin. He had received a consignment of books upon philology and was settling down to develop this thesis, when suddenly to my sorrow, and to his unfeigned delight, we found ourselves, even in that land of dreams, plunged into a problem at our very doors which was more intense, more engrossing, and infinitely more mysterious than any of those which had driven us from London. Our simple life and peaceful, healthy routine were violently inter-rupted, and we were precipitated into the midst of a series of events which caused the utmost excitement not only in Cornwall, but throughout the West of England. Many of my readers may retain some recollection of what was called at the time 'The Cornish Horror', though a most imperfect account of the matter reached the London Press. Now, after thirteen years, I will give the true details of this inconceivable affair to the public.

I have said that scattered towers marked the villages which dotted this part of Cornwall. The nearest of these was the hamlet of Tredannick Wollas, where the cottages of a couple of hundred inhabitants clustered round an ancient, moss-grown church. The vicar of the parish, Mr Roundhay, was something of an archæologist, and as such Holmes had made his acquaintance. He was a middle-aged man, portly and affable, with a considerable fund of local lore. At his invitation we had taken tea at the vicarage, and had come to know, also, Mr Mortimer Tregennis, an independent gentleman, who increased the clergyman's scanty resources by taking rooms in his large, straggling house. The vicar, being a bachelor, was glad to come to such an arrangement, though he had little in common with his lodger, who was a thin, dark, spectacled man, with a stoop which gave the impression of actual physical deformity. I remember that during our short visit we found the vicar garrulous, but his lodger strangely reticent, a sad-faced, introspective man, sitting with averted eyes, brooding apparently upon his own affairs.

These were the two men who entered abruptly into our little sitting-room on Tuesday, March 16th, shortly after our breakfast hour, as we were smoking together, preparatory to our daily excursion upon the moors.

'Mr Holmes,' said the vicar, in an agitated voice, 'the most extraordinary and tragic affair has occurred during the night. It is the most unheard-of business. We can only regard it as a special Providence that you should chance to be here at the time, for in all England you are the one man we need.'

I glared at the intrusive vicar with no very friendly eyes; but Holmes took his pipe from his lips and sat up in his chair like an old hound who hears the view-hallo. He waved his hand to the sofa, and our palpitating visitor with his agitated companion sat side by side upon it. Mr Mortimer Tregennis was more self-contained than the clergyman, but the twitching of his thin hands and the brightness of his dark eyes showed that they shared a common emotion.

'Shall I speak or you?' he asked of the vicar.

'Well, as you seem to have made the discovery, whatever it may be, and the vicar to have had it at second hand, perhaps you had better do the speaking,' said Holmes.

I glanced at the hastily-clad clergyman, with the formally dressed lodger seated beside him, and was amused at the surprise which Holmes's simple deduction had brought to their faces.

'Perhaps I had best say a few words first,' said the vicar, 'and then you can judge if you will listen to the details from Mr Tregennis, or whether we should not hasten at once to the scene of this mysterious affair. I may explain, then, that our friend here spent last evening in the company of his two brothers, Owen and George, and of his sister Brenda, at their house of Tredannick Wartha, which is near the old stone cross upon the moor. He left them shortly after ten o'clock, playing cards round the dining-room table, in excellent health and spirits. This morning, being an early riser, he walked in that direction before breakfast, and was overtaken by the carriage of Dr Richards, who explained that he had just been sent for on a most urgent call to Tredannick Wartha. Mr Mortimer Tregennis naturally went with him. When he arrived at Tredannick Wartha he found an extra-ordinary state of things. His two brothers and his sister were seated round the table exactly as he had left them, the cards still spread in front of them and the candles burned down to their sockets. The sister lay back stone-dead in her chair, while the two brothers sat on each side of her laughing, shouting, and singing, the senses stricken clean out of them. All three of them, the dead woman and the two demented men, retained upon their faces an expression of the utmost horror—a convulsion of terror which was dreadful to look upon. There was no sign of the presence of anyone in the house, except Mrs Porter, the old cook and housekeeper, who declared that she had slept deeply and heard no sound during the night. Nothing had been stolen or dis-arranged, and there is absolutely no explanation of what the horror can be which has frightened a woman to death and two strong men out of their senses. There is the situation, Mr Holmes, in a nutshell, and if you can help us to clear it up you will have done a great work.'

I had hoped that in some way I could coax my companion back into the quiet which had been the object of our journey; but one glance at his intense face and contracted eyebrows told me how vain was now the expectation. He sat for some little time in silence, absorbed in the strange drama which had broken in upon our peace.

'I will look into this matter,' he said at last. 'On the face of it, it would appear to be a case of a very exceptional nature. Have you been there yourself, Mr Roundhay?'

'No, Mr Holmes. Mr Tregennis brought back the account to the vicarage, and I at once hurried over with him to consult you.'

'How far is it to the house where this singular tragedy occurred?'

'About a mile inland.'

'Then we shall walk over together. But, before we start, I must ask you a few questions, Mr Mortimer Tregennis.'

The other had been silent all this time, but I had observed that his more controlled excitement was even greater than the obtrusive emotion of the clergyman. He sat with a pale, drawn face, his anxious gaze fixed upon Holmes, and his thin hands clasped convulsively together. His pale lips quivered as he listened to the dreadful experience which had befallen his family, and his dark eyes seemed to reflect something of the horror of the scene.

'Ask what you like, Mr Holmes,' said he, eagerly. 'It is a bad thing to speak of, but I will answer you the truth.'

'Tell me about last night.'

'Well, Mr Holmes, I supped there, as the vicar has said, and my elder brother George proposed a game of whist afterwards. We sat down about nine o'clock. It was a quarter-past ten when I moved to go. I left them all round the table, as merry as could be.'

'Who let you out?'

'Mrs Porter had gone to bed, so I let myself out. I shut the hall door behind me. The window of the room in which they sat was closed, but the blind was not drawn down. There was no change in door or window this morning, nor any reason to think that any stranger had been to the house. Yet there they sat, driven clean mad with terror, and Brenda lying dead of fright, with her head hanging over the arm of the chair. I'll never get the sight of that room out of my mind so long as I live.'

'The facts, as you state them, are certainly most remarkable,' said

Holmes. 'I take it that you have no theory yourself which can in any way account for them?'

'It's devilish, Mr Holmes; devilish!' cried Mortimer Tregennis. 'It is not of this world. Something has come into that room which has dashed the light of reason from their minds. What human contrivance could do that?'

'I fear,' said Holmes, 'that if the matter is beyond humanity it is certainly beyond me. Yet we must exhaust all natural explanations before we fall back upon such a theory as this. As to yourself, Mr Tregennis, I take it you were divided in some way from your family, since they lived together and you had rooms apart?'

'That is so, Mr Holmes, though the matter is past and done with. We were a family of tin-miners at Redruth, but we sold out our venture to a company, and so retired with enough to keep us. I won't deny that there was some feeling about the division of the money and it stood between us for a time, but it was all forgiven and forgotten, and we were the best of friends together.'

'Looking back at the evening which you spent together, does anything stand out in your memory as throwing any possible light upon the tragedy? Think carefully, Mr Tregennis, for any clue which can help me.'

'There is nothing at all, sir.'

'Your people were in their usual spirits?'

'Never better.'

'Were they nervous people? Did they ever show any apprehension of coming danger?'

'Nothing of the kind.'

'You have nothing to add, then, which could assist me?'

Mortimer Tregennis considered earnestly for a moment.

'There is one thing that occurs to me,' said he at last. 'As we sat at the table my back was to the window, and my brother George, he being my partner at cards, was facing it. I saw him once look hard over my shoulder, so I turned round and looked also. The blind was up and the window shut, but I could just make out the bushes on the lawn, and it seemed to me for a moment that I saw something moving among them. I couldn't even say if it were man or animal, but I just thought there was something there. When I asked him what he was looking at, he told me that he had the same feeling. That is all that I can say.'

'Did you not investigate?'

'No; the matter passed as unimportant.'

'You left them, then, without any premonition of evil?'

'None at all.'

'I am not clear how you came to hear the news so early this morning.'

'I am an early riser, and generally take a walk before breakfast. This morning I had hardly started when the doctor in his carriage overtook me. He told me that old Mrs Porter had sent a boy down with an urgent message. I sprang in beside him and we drove on. When we got there we looked into that dreadful room. The candles and the fire must have burned down hours before, and they had been sitting there in the dark until dawn broke. The doctor said Brenda must have been dead at least six hours. There were no signs of violence. She just lay across the arm of the chair with that look on her face. George and Owen were singing snatches of songs and gibbering like two great apes. Oh, it was awful to see! I couldn't stand it, and the doctor was as white as a sheet. Indeed, he fell into a chair in a sort of faint, and we nearly had him on our hands as well.'

'Remarkable—most remarkable!' said Holmes, rising and taking his hat. 'I think perhaps we had better go down to Tredannick Wartha without further delay. I confess that I have seldom known a case which at first sight presented a more singular problem.'

Our proceedings of that first morning did little to advance the investigation. It was marked, however, at the outset by an incident which left the most sinister impression upon my mind. The approach to the spot at which the tragedy occurred is down a narrow, winding country lane. While we made our way along it we heard the rattle of a carriage coming towards us, and stood aside to let it pass. As it drove by us I caught a glimpse through the closed window of a horribly-contorted, grinning face glaring out at us. Those staring eyes and gnashing teeth flashed past us like a dreadful vision.

'My brothers!' cried Mortimer Tregennis, white to his lips. 'They are taking them to Helston.'

We looked with horror after the black carriage, lumbering upon its way. Then we turned our steps towards this ill-omened house in which they had met their strange fate.

It was a large and bright dwelling, rather a villa than a cottage, with a considerable garden which was already, in that Cornish air, well filled with spring flowers. Towards this garden the window of the sitting-room fronted, and from it, according to Mortimer Tregennis, must have come that thing of evil which had by sheer horror in a single instant blasted their minds. Holmes walked slowly and thought-fully among the flowerpots and along the path before we entered the porch. So absorbed was he in his thoughts, I remember, that he stumbled over the watering-pot, upset its contents, and deluged both our feet and the garden path. Inside the house we were met by the elderly Cornish housekeeper, Mrs Porter, who, with the aid of a young girl, looked after the wants of the family. She readily answered all Holmes's questions. She had heard nothing in the night. Her employers had all been in excellent spirits lately, and she had never known them more cheerful and prosperous. She had fainted with horror upon entering the room in the morning and seeing that dreadful company round the table. She had, when she recovered, thrown open the window to let the morning air in, and had run down to the lane, whence she sent a farm-lad for the doctor. The lady was on her bed upstairs, if we cared to see her. It took four strong men to get the brothers into the asylum carriage. She would not herself stay in the house another day, and was starting that very afternoon to rejoin her family at St Ives.

We ascended the stairs and viewed the body. Miss Brenda Tregennis had been a very beautiful girl, though now verging upon middle age. Her dark, clear-cut face was handsome, even in death, but there still lingered upon it something of that convulsion of horror which had been her last human emotion. From her bedroom we descended to the sitting-room where this strange tragedy had actually occurred. The charred ashes of the overnight fire lay in the grate. On the table were the four guttered and burned-out candles, with the cards scattered over its surface. The chairs had been moved back against the walls, but all else was as it had been the night before. Holmes paced with light, swift steps about the room; he sat in the various chairs, drawing them up and reconstructing their positions. He tested how much of the garden was visible; he examined the floor, the ceiling, and the fireplace; but never once did I see that sudden brightening of his eyes and tightening of his lips which would have told me that he saw some gleam of light in this utter darkness.

'Why a fire?' he asked once. 'Had they always a fire in this small room on a spring evening?

Mortimer Tregennis explained that the night was cold and damp. For that reason, after his arrival, the fire was lit. 'What are you going to do now, Mr Holmes?' he asked.

My friend smiled and laid his hand upon my arm. 'I think, Watson, that I shall resume that course of tobacco-poisoning which you have so often and so justly condemned,' said he. 'With your permission, gentlemen, we will now return to our cottage, for I am not aware that any new factor is likely to come to our notice here. I will turn the facts over in my mind, Mr Tregennis, and should anything occur to me I will certainly communicate with you and the vicar. In the meantime I wish you both good morning.'

It was not until long after we were back in Poldhu Cottage that Holmes broke his complete and absorbed silence. He sat coiled in his arm-chair, his haggard and ascetic face hardly visible amid the blue swirl of his tobacco smoke, his black brows drawn down, his forehead contracted, his eyes vacant and far away. Finally, he laid down his pipe and sprang to his feet.

'It won't do, Watson!' said he, with a laugh. 'Let us walk along the cliffs together and search for flint arrows. We are more likely to find them than clues to this problem. To let the brain work without sufficient material is like racing an engine. It racks itself to pieces. The sea-air, sunshine, and patience, Watson—all else will come.

'Now, let us calmly define our position, Watson,' he continued, as we skirted the cliffs together. 'Let us get a firm grip of the very little which we *do* know, so that when fresh facts arise we may be ready to fit them into their places. I take it, in the first place, that neither of us is prepared to admit diabolical intrusions into the affairs of men. Let us begin by ruling that entirely out of our minds. Very good. There remain three persons who have been grievously stricken by some conscious or unconscious human agency. That is firm ground. Now, when did this occur? Evidently, assuming his narrative to be true, it was immediately after Mr Mortimer Tregennis left the room. That is a very important point. The presumption is that it was within a few minutes afterwards. The cards still lay upon the table. It was already past their usual hour for bed. Yet they had not changed their position or pushed back their chairs. I repeat, then, that the occurrence was immediately after his departure, and not later than eleven o'clock last night.

'Our next obvious step is to check, so far as we can, the movements of Mortimer Tregennis after he left the room. In this there is no difficulty, and they seem to be above suspicion. Knowing my methods as you do, you were, of course, conscious of the somewhat clumsy water-pot expedient by which I obtained a clearer impress of his foot than might otherwise have been possible. The wet, sandy path took it admirably. Last night was also wet, you will remember, and it was not difficult—having obtained a sample print—to pick out his track among others and to follow his movements. He appears to have walked away swiftly in the direction of the vicarage.

'If, then, Mortimer Tregennis disappeared from the scene, and yet some outside person affected the card-players, how can we reconstruct that person, and how was such an impression of horror conveyed? Mrs Porter may be eliminated. She is evidently harmless. Is there any evidence that someone crept up to the garden window and in some manner produced so terrific an effect that he drove those who saw it out of their senses? The only suggestion in this direction comes from Mortimer Tregennis himself, who says that his brother spoke about some movement in the garden. That is certainly remarkable, as the night was rainy, cloudy, and dark. Anyone who had the design to alarm these people would be compelled to place his very face against the glass before he could be seen. There is a three-foot flower-border outside this window, but no indication of a footmark. It is difficult to imagine, then, how an outsider could have made so terrible an impression upon the company, nor have we found any possible motive for so strange and elaborate an attempt. You perceive our difficulties, Watson?'

'They are only too clear,' I answered, with conviction.

'And yet, with a little more material, we may prove that they are not insurmountable,' said Holmes. 'I fancy that among your extensive archives, Watson, you may find some which were nearly as obscure. Meanwhile, we shall put the case aside until more accurate data are available, and devote the rest of our morning to the pursuit of neolithic man.'

I may have commented upon my friend's power of mental detachment, but never have I wondered at it more than upon that spring morning in Cornwall when for two hours he discoursed upon celts, arrowheads, and shards as lightly as if no sinister mystery was waiting for his solution. It was not until we had returned in the afternoon to our cottage that we found a visitor awaiting us, who soon brought our minds back to the matter in hand. Neither of us needed to be told who that visitor was. The huge body, the craggy and deeply seamed face with the fierce eyes and hawk-like nose, the grizzled hair which nearly brushed our cottage ceiling, the beard—golden at the fringes and white near the lips, save for the nicotine stain from his perpetual cigar—all these were as well known in London as in Africa, and could only be associated with the tremendous personality of Dr Leon Sterndale, the great lion-hunter and explorer.

We had heard of his presence in the district, and had once or twice caught sight of his tall figure upon the moorland paths. He made no advances to us, however, nor would we have dreamed of doing so to him, as it was well known that it was his love of seclusion which caused him to spend the greater part of the intervals between his journeys in a small bungalow buried in the lonely wood of Beauchamp Arriance. Here amid his books and his maps, he lived an absolutely lonely life, attending to his own simple wants, and paying little apparent heed to the affairs of his neighbours. It was a surprise to me, therefore, to hear him asking Holmes, in eager voice, whether he had made any advance in his reconstruction of this mysterious episode. 'The county police are utterly at fault,' said he; 'but perhaps your wider experience has suggested some conceivable explanation. My only claim to being taken into your confidence is that during my many residences here I have come to know this family of Tregennis very well—indeed upon my Cornish mother's side I could call them cousins —and their strange fate has naturally been a great shock to me. I may tell you that I had got as far as Plymouth upon my way to Africa, but the news reached me this morning, and I came straight back again to help in the inquiry.'

Holmes raised his eyebrows.

'Did you lose your boat through it?'

'I will take the next.'

'Dear me! That is friendship indeed.'

'I tell you they were relatives.'

'Quite so—cousins of your mother. Was your baggage aboard the ship?'

'Some of it, but the main part at the hotel.'

'I see. But surely this event could not have found its way into the Plymouth morning papers?'

'No, sir; I had a telegram.'

'Might I ask from whom?'

A shadow passed over the gaunt face of the explorer.

'You are very inquisitive, Mr Holmes.'

'It is my business.'

With an effort, Dr Sterndale recovered his ruffled composure.

'I have no objection to telling you,' he said. 'It was Mr Roundhay, the vicar, who sent me the telegram which recalled me.'

'Thank you,' said Holmes. 'I may say, in answer to your original question, that I have not cleared my mind entirely on the subject of this case, but that I have every hope of reaching some conclusion. It would be premature to say more.'

'Perhaps you would not mind telling me if your suspicions point in any particular direction?'

'No, I can hardly answer that.'

'Then I have wasted my time, and need not prolong my visit.' The famous doctor strode out of our cottage in considerable ill-humour, and within five minutes Holmes had followed him. I saw him no more until the evening, when he returned with a slow step and haggard face which assured me that he had made no great progress with his investigation. He glanced at a telegram which awaited him, and threw it into the grate.

'From the Plymouth hotel, Watson,' he said. 'I learned the name of it from the vicar and I wired to make certain that Dr Leon Sterndale's account was true. It appears that he did indeed spend last night there, and that he has actually allowed some of his baggage to go on to Africa, while he returned to be present at this investigation. What do you make of that, Watson?'

'He is deeply interested.'

'Deeply interested—yes. There is a thread here which we have not yet grasped, and which might lead us through the tangle. Cheer up, Watson, for I am very sure that our material has not yet come to hand. When it does, we may soon leave our difficulties behind us.'

Little did I think how soon the words of Holmes would be realized, or how strange and sinister would be the new development which opened up an entirely fresh line of investigation. I was shaving at my window in the morning when I heard the rattle of hoofs, and, looking up, saw a dogcart coming at a gallop down the road. It pulled up at our door, and our friend the vicar sprang from it and rushed up our garden path. Holmes was already dressed, and we hastened down to meet him.

Our visitor was so excited that he could hardly articulate, but at last in gasps and bursts his tragic story came out of him.

'We are devil-ridden, Mr Holmes! My poor parish is devil-ridden!' he cried. 'Satan himself is loose in it! We are given over into his hands!' He danced about in his agitation, a ludicrous object if it were not for his ashy face and startled eyes. Finally he shot out his terrible news.

'Mr Mortimer Tregennis has died during the night, and with exactly the same symptoms as the rest of his family.'

Holmes sprang to his feet, all energy in an instant.

'Can you fit us both into your dogcart?'

'Yes, I can.'

'Then, Watson, we will postpone our breakfast. Mr Roundhay, we are entirely at your disposal. Hurry—hurry, before things get disarranged.'

The lodger occupied two rooms at the vicarage, which were in an angle by themselves, the one above the other. Below was a large sitting-room; above, his bedroom. They looked out upon the croquet-lawn which came up to the windows. We had arrived before the doctor or the police, so that everything was absolutely undisturbed. Let me describe exactly the scene as we saw it upon that misty March morning. It has left an impression which can never be effaced from my mind.

The atmosphere of the room was of a horrible and depressing stuffiness. The servant who had first entered had thrown up the window, or it would have been even more intolerable. This might partly be due to the fact that a lamp stood flaring and smoking on the centre table. Beside it sat the dead man, leaning back in his chair, his thin beard projecting, his spectacles pushed up on to his forehead, and his lean, dark face turned towards the window and twisted into the same distortion of terror which had marked the features of his dead sister. His limbs were convulsed and his fingers contorted, as though he had died in a very paroxysm of fear. He was fully clothed, though there were signs that his dressing had been done in a hurry. We had already learned that his bed had been slept in, and that the tragic end had come to him in the early morning.

One realized the red hot energy which underlay Holme's phlegmatic exterior when one saw the sudden change which came over him from the moment that he entered the fatal apartment. In an instant he was tense and alert, his eyes shining, his face set, his limbs quivering with eager activity. He was out on the lawn, in through the window, round the room, and up into the bedroom, for all the world like a dashing foxhound drawing a cover. In the bedroom he made a rapid cast around, and ended by throwing open the window, which appeared to give him some fresh cause for excitement, for he leaned out of it with loud ejaculations of interest and delight. Then he rushed down the stair, out through the open window, threw himself upon his face on the lawn, sprang up and into the room once more, all with the energy of the hunter who is at the very heels of his quarry. The lamp, which was an ordinary standard, he examined with minute care, making certain measurements upon its bowl. He carefully scrutinized with his lens the talc shield which covered the top of the chimney, and scraped off some ashes which adhered to its upper surface, putting some of them into an envelope, which he placed in his pocket-book. Finally, just as the doctor and the official police put in an appearance, he beckoned to the vicar and we all three went out upon the lawn.

'I am glad to say that my investigation has not been entirely barren,' he remarked. 'I cannot remain to discuss the matter with the police, but I should be exceedingly obliged, Mr Roundhay, if you would give the inspector my compliments and direct his attention to the bedroom window and to the sitting-room lamp. Each is suggestive, and together they are almost conclusive. If the police would desire further information I shall be happy to see any of them at the cottage. And now, Watson, I think that perhaps we shall be better employed elsewhere.'

It may be that the police resented the intrusion of an amateur, or that they imagined themselves to be upon some hopeful line of investigation; but it is certain that we heard nothing from them for the next two days. During this time Holmes spent some of his time smoking and dreaming in the cottage; but a greater portion in country walks which he undertook alone, returning after many hours without remark as to where he had been. One experiment served to show me the line of his investigation. He had bought a lamp which was the duplicate of the one which had been burned in the room of Mortimer Tregennis on the morning of the tragedy. This he filled with the same oil as that used at the vicarage, and he carefully timed the period which it would take to be exhausted. Another experiment which he made was of a more unpleasant nature, and one which I am not likely ever to forget.

'You will remember, Watson,' he remarked one afternoon, 'that there is a single common point of resemblance in the varying reports which have reached us. This concerns the effect of the atmosphere of the room in each case upon those who have first entered it. You will recollect that Mortimer Tregennis, in describing the episode of his last visit to his brother's house, remarked that the doctor on entering the room fell into a chair? You had forgotten? Well, I can answer for it that it was so. Now, you will remember also that Mrs Porter, the housekeeper, told us that she herself fainted upon entering the room and had afterwards opened the window. In the second case—that of

Mortimer Tregennis himself—you cannot have forgotten the horrible stuffiness of the room when we arrived, though the servant had thrown open the window. That servant, I found upon inquiry, was so ill that she had gone to her bed. You will admit, Watson, that these facts are very suggestive. In each case there is evidence of a poisonous atmosphere. In each case, also, there is combustion going on in the room-in the one case a fire, in the other a lamp. The fire was needed, but the lamp was lit—as a comparison of the oil consumed will show—long after it was broad daylight. Why? Surely because there is some connection between three things—the burning, the stuffy atmosphere, and, finally, the madness or death of those unfortunate people. That is clear, is it not?'

'It would appear so.'

'At least we may accept it as a working hypothesis. We will suppose, then, that something was burned in each case which produced an atmosphere causing strange toxic effects. Very good. In the first instance—that of the Tregennis family—this substance was placed in the fire. Now, the window was shut, but the fire would naturally carry fumes to some extent up the chimney. Hence, one would expect the effects of the poison to be less than in the second case, where there was less escape for the vapour. The result seems to indicate that it was so, since in the first case only the woman, who had presumably the more sensitive organism, was killed, the others exhibiting that temporary or permanent lunacy which is evidently the first effect of the drug. In the second case the result was complete. The facts, therefore, seem to bear out the theory of a poison which worked by combustion.'

'With this train of reasoning in my head I naturally looked about in Mortimer Tregennis's room to find some remains of this substance. The obvious place to look was the talc shield or smoke-guard of the lamp. There, sure enough, I perceived a number of flaky ashes, and round the edges a fringe of brownish powder, which had not yet been consumed. Half of this I took, as you saw, and I placed it in an envelope.'

'Why half, Holmes?'

'It is not for me, my dear Watson, to stand in the way of the official police force. I leave them all the evidence which I found. The poison still remained upon the talc, had they the wit to find it. Now, Watson, we will light our lamp; we will, however, take the precaution to open our window to avoid the premature decease of two deserving members of society, and you will seat yourself near that open window in an arm-chair—unless, like a sensible man, you determine to have nothing to do with the affair. Oh, you will see it out, will you? I thought I knew my Watson. This chair I will place opposite yours, so that we may be the same distance from the poison, and face to face. The door we will leave ajar. Each is now in a position to watch the other and to bring the experiment to an end should the symptoms seem alarming. Is that all clear? Well, then, I take our powder—or what remains of it—from the envelope, and I lay it above the burning lamp. So! Now, Watson, let us sit down and await developments.'

They were not long in coming. I had hardly settled in my chair before I was conscious of a thick, musky odour, subtle and nauseous. At the very first whiff of it my brain and my imagination were beyond all control. A thick black cloud swirled before my eyes, and my mind told me that in this cloud, unseen as yet, but about to spring out upon my appalled senses, lurked all that was vaguely horrible, all that was monstrous and inconceivably wicked in the universe. Vague shapes swirled and swam amid the dark cloud-bank, each a menace and a warning of something coming, the advent of some unspeakable dweller upon the threshold, whose very shadow would blast my soul. A freezing horror took possession of me. I felt that my hair was rising, that my eyes were protruding, that my mouth was opened, and my tongue like leather. The turmoil within my brain was such that something must surely snap. I tried to scream, and was vaguely aware of some hoarse croak which was my own voice, but distant and detached from myself. At the same moment, in some effort of escape, I broke through that cloud of despair, and had a glimpse of Holmes's face, white, rigid, and drawn with horror—the very look which I had seen upon the features of the dead. It was that vision which gave me an instant of sanity and of strength. I dashed from my chair, threw my arms round Holmes, and together we lurched through the door, and an instant afterwards had thrown ourselves down upon the grass plot and were lying side by side, conscious only of the glorious sunshine which was bursting its way through the hellish cloud of terror which had girt us in. Slowly it rose from our souls like the mists from a landscape, until peace and reason had returned, and we were sitting up on the grass, wiping our clammy foreheads, and looking with apprehension at each other to mark the last traces of that terrific experience which we had undergone.

'Upon my word, Watson!' said Holmes at last, with an unsteady voice, 'I owe you both my thanks and an apology. It was an unjustifiable experiment even for oneself, and doubly so for a friend. I am really very sorry.'

'You know,' I answered, with some emotion, for I had never seen so much of Holmes's heart before, 'that it is my greatest joy and privilege to help you.'

He relapsed at once into the half-humorous, half-cynical vein which was his habitual attitude to those about him. 'It would be superfluous to drive us mad, my dear Watson,' said he. 'A candid observer would certainly declare that we were so already before we embarked upon so wild an experiment. I confess that I never imagined that the effect would be so sudden and so severe.' He dashed into the cottage, and, reappearing with the burning lamp held at full arm's length, he threw it among a bank of brambles. 'We must give the room a little time to clear. I take it, Watson, that you have no longer a shadow of a doubt as to how these tragedies were produced?'

'None whatever.'

'But the cause remains as obscure as before. Come into the arbour here, and let us discuss it together. That villainous stuff seems still to linger round my throat. I think we must admit that all the evidence points to this man, Mortimer Tregennis, having been the criminal in the first tragedy, though he was the victim in the second one. We must remember, in the first place, that there is some story of a family quarrel, followed by a reconciliation. How bitter that quarrel may have been, or how hollow the reconciliation, we cannot tell. When I think of Mortimer Tregennis, with the foxy face and the small, shrewd, beady eyes behind the spectacles, he is not a man whom I should judge to be of a particularly forgiving disposition. Well, in the next place, you will remember that this idea of someone moving in the garden, which took our attention for a moment from the real cause of the tragedy, emanated from him. He had a motive in misleading us. Finally, if he did not throw this substance into the fire at the moment of leaving the room, who did do so? The affair happened immediately after his departure. Had anyone else come in the family would certainly have risen from the table. Besides, in peaceful Cornwall, visitors do not arrive after ten o'clock at night. We may take it, then, that all the evidence points to Mortimer Tregennis as the culprit.'

'Then his own death was suicide!'

'Well, Watson, it is on the face of it a not impossible supposition. The man who had the guilt upon his soul of having brought such a fate upon his own family might well be driven by remorse to inflict it upon himself. There are, however, some cogent reasons against it, and I have made arrangements by which we shall hear the facts this afternoon from his own lips. Ah! he is a little before his time. Perhaps you would kindly step this way, Dr Leon Sterndale. We have been conducting a chemical experiment indoors which has left our little room hardly fit for the reception of so distinguished a visitor.'

I had heard the click of the garden gate, and now the majestic figure of the great African explorer appeared upon the path, He turned in some surprise towards the rustic arbour in which we sat.

'You sent for me, Mr Holmes. I had your note about an hour ago, and I have come, though I really do not know why I should obey your summons.'

'Perhaps we can clear the point up before we separate,' said Holmes. 'Meanwhile, I am much obliged to you for your courteous acquiescence. you will excuse this informal reception in the open air, but my friend Watson and I have nearly furnished an additional chapter to what the papers call the Cornish Horror, and we prefer a clear atmosphere for the present. Perhaps, since the matters which we have to discuss will affect you personally in a very intimate fashion, it is as well that we should talk where there can be no eavesdropping.'

The explorer took his cigar from his lips and gazed sternly at my companion.

'I am at a loss to know, sir,' he said, 'what you can have to speak about which affects me personally in a very intimate fashion.'

'The killing of Mortimer Tregennis,' said Holmes.

For a moment I wished that I were armed. Sterndale's fierce face turned to a dusky red, his eyes glared, and the knotted, passionate veins started out in his forehead, while he sprang forward with clenched hands towards my companion. Then he stopped, and with a violent effort resumed a cold, rigid calmness which was, perhaps, more suggestive of danger than his hot-headed outburst.

'I have lived so long among savages and beyond the law,' said he, 'that I have got into the way of being a law unto myself. You would do well, Mr Holmes, not to forget it, for I have no desire to do you an injury.'

'Nor have I any desire to do you an injury, Dr Sterndale. Surely the clearest proof of it is that, knowing what I know, I have sent for you and not for the police.'

[63]

Sterndale sat down with a gasp, overawed for, perhaps, the first time in his adventurous life. There was a calm assurance of power in Holmes's manner which could not be withstood. Our visitor stammered for a moment, his great hands opening and shutting in his agitation.

'What do you mean?' he asked, at last. 'If this is a bluff upon your part, Mr Holmes, you have chosen a bad man for your experiment. Let us have no more beating about the bush. What *do* you mean?'

'I will tell you,' said Holmes, 'and the reason why I tell you is that I hope frankness may beget frankness. What my next step may be will depend entirely upon the nature of your own defence.'

'My defence?'

'Yes, sir.'

'My defence against what?'

'Against the charge of killing Mortimer Tregennis.'

Sterndale mopped his forehead with his handkerchief. 'Upon my word, you are getting on,' said he. 'Do all your successes depend upon this prodigious power of bluff?'

'The bluff,' said Holmes, sternly, 'is upon your side, Dr Leon Sterndale, and not upon mine. As a proof I will tell you some of the facts upon which my conclusions are based. Of your return from Plymouth, allowing much of your property to go on to Africa, I will say nothing save that it first informed me that you were one of the factors which had to be taken into account in reconstructing this drama—'

'I came back—'

'I have heard your reasons and regard them as unconvincing and inadequate. We will pass that. You came down here to ask me whom I suspected. I refused to answer you. You then went to the vicarage, waited outside it for some time, and finally returned to your cottage.'

'How do you know that?'

'I followed you.'

'I saw no one.'

'That is what you may expect to see when I follow you. You spent a restless night at your cottage, and you formed certain plans, which in the early morning you proceeded to put into execution. Leaving your door just as day was breaking, you filled your pocket with some reddish gravel which was lying heaped beside your gate.'

Sterndale gave a violent start and looked at Holmes in amazement.

'You then walked swiftly for the mile which separated you from the vicarage. You were wearing, I may remark, the same pair of ribbed tennis shoes which are at the present moment upon your feet. At the vicarage you passed through the orchard and the side hedge, coming out under the window of the lodger, Tregennis. It was now daylight, but the household was not yet stirring. You drew some of the gravel from your pocket, and you threw it up at the window above you—'

Sterndale sprang to his feet.

'I believe that you are the devil himself!' he cried.

Holmes smiled at the compliment. 'It took two, or possibly three, handfuls before the lodger came to the window. You beckoned him to come down. He dressed hurriedly and descended to his sitting-room. You entered by the window. There was an interview—a short one—during which you walked up and down the room. Then you passed out and closed the window, standing on the lawn outside smoking a cigar and watching what occurred. Finally, after the death of Mr Tregennis, you withdrew as you had come. Now, Dr Sterndale, how do you justify such conduct, and what were the motives for your actions? If you prevaricate or trifle with me, I give you my assurance that the matter will pass out of my hands for ever.'

Our visitor's face had turned ashen grey as he listened to the words of his accuser. Now he sat for some time in thought with his face sunk in his hands. Then, with a sudden impulsive gesture, he plucked a photograph from his breast-pocket and threw it on the rustic table before us.

'That is why I have done it,' said he.

It showed the bust and face of a very beautiful woman. Holmes stooped over it.

'Brenda Tregennis,' said he.

'Yes, Brenda Tregennis,' repeated our visitor. 'For years I have loved her. For years she has loved me. There is the secret of that Cornish seclusion which people have marvelled at. It has brought me close to the one thing on earth that was dear to me. I could not marry her, for I have a wife who has left me for years, and yet whom, by the deplorable laws of England, I could not divorce. For years Brenda waited. For years I waited. And this is what we have waited for.' A terrible sob shook his great frame, and he clutched his throat under his brindled beard. Then with an effort he mastered himself and spoke on.

'The vicar knew. He was in our confidence. He would tell you that she was an angel upon earth. That was why he telegraphed to me and I returned. What was my baggage or Africa to me when I learned that such a fate had come upon my darling? There you have the missing clue to my action, Mr Holmes.'

'Proceed,' said my friend.

Dr Sterndale drew from his pocket a paper packet and laid it upon the table. On the outside was written, '*Radix pedis diaboli*,' with a red poison label beneath it. He pushed it towards me. 'I understand that you are a doctor, sir. Have you ever heard of this preparation?'

'Devil's-foot root! No, I have never heard of it.'

'It is no reflection upon your professional knowledge,' said he, 'for I believe that, save for one sample in a laboratory at Buda, there is no other specimen in Europe. It has not yet found its way either into the pharmacopoeia or into the literature of toxicology. The root is shaped like a foot, half human, half goatlike; hence the fanciful name given by a botanical missionary. It is used as an ordeal poison by the medicine-men in certain districts of West Africa, and is kept as a secret among them. This particular specimen I obtained under very extraordinary circumstances in the Ubanghi country.' He opened the paper as he spoke, and disclosed a heap of reddish-brown, snuff-like powder.

'Well, sir?' asked Holmes sternly.

'I am about to tell you, Mr Holmes, all that actually occurred, for you already know so much that it is clearly to my interest that you should know all. I have already explained the relationship in which I stood to the Tregennis family. For the sake of the sister I was friendly with the brothers. There was a family quarrel about money which estranged this man Mortimer, but it was supposed to be made up, and I afterwards met him as I did the others. He was a sly, subtle, scheming man, and several things arose which gave me a suspicion of him, but I had no cause for any positive quarrel.

'One day, only a couple of weeks ago, he came down to my cottage and I showed him some of my African curiosities. Among other things, I exhibited this powder, and I told him of its strange properties, how it stimulates those brain centres which control the emotion of fear, and how either madness or death is the fate of the unhappy native who is subjected to the ordeal by the priest of his tribe. I told him also how powerless European science would be to detect it. How he took it I cannot say, for I never left the room, but there is no doubt that it was then, while I was opening cabinets and stooping to boxes, that he managed to abstract some of the devil's-foot root. I well remember how he plied me with questions as to the amount and the time that was needed for its effect, but I little dreamed that he could have a personal reason for asking.

'I thought no more of the matter until the vicar's telegram reached me at Plymouth. This villain had thought that I would be at sea before the news could reach me, and that I should be lost for years in Africa. But I returned at once. Of course, I could not listen to the details without feeling assured that my poison had been used. I came round to see you on the chance that some other explanation had suggested itself to you. But there could be none. I was convinced that Mortimer Tregennis was the murderer; that for the sake of money, and with the idea, perhaps, that if the other members of his family were all insane he would be the sole guardian of their joint property, he had used the devil's-foot powder upon them, driven two of them out of their senses, and killed his sister Brenda, the one human being whom I have ever loved or who has ever loved me. There was his crime; what was to be his punishment?

'Should I appeal to the law? Where were my proofs? I knew that the facts were true, but could I help to make a jury of countrymen believe so fantastic a story? I might or I might not. But I could not afford to fail. My soul cried out for revenge. I have said to you once before, Mr Holmes, that I have spent much of my life outside the law, and that I have come at last to be a law unto myself. So it was now. I determined that the fate which he had given to others should be shared by himself. Either that, or I would do justice upon him with my own hand. In all England there can be no man who sets less value upon his own life than I do at the present moment.

'Now I have told you all. You have yourself supplied the rest. I did, as you say, after a restless night, set off early from my cottage. I foresaw the difficulty of arousing him, so I gathered some gravel from the pile which you have mentioned, and I used it to throw up to his window. He came down and admitted me through the window of the sitting-room. I laid his offence before him. I told him that I had come both as judge and executioner. The wretch sank into a chair paralyzed at the sight of my revolver. I lit the lamp, put the powder above it, and stood outside the window, ready to carry out my threat to shoot him should he try to leave the room. In five minutes he died. My God, how he died! But my heart was flint, for he endured nothing which my innocent darling had not felt before him. There is my story, Mr Holmes. Perhaps, if you loved a woman, you would have done as much yourself. At any rate, I am in your hands. You can take what steps you like. As I have already said, there is no man living who can fear death less than I do.'

[67]

Holmes sat for some little time in silence.

'What were your plans?' he asked, at last.

'I had intended to bury myself in Central Africa. My work there is but half finished.'

'Go and do the other half,' said Holmes. 'I, at least, am not prepared to prevent you.'

Dr Sterndale raised his giant figure, bowed gravely, and walked from the arbour. Holmes lit his pipe and handed me his pouch.

'Some fumes which are not poisonous would be a welcome change,' said he. 'I think you must agree, Watson, that it is not a case in which we are called upon to interfere. Our investigation has been independent, and our action shall be so also. You would not denounce the man?'

'Certainly not,' I answered.

'I have never loved, Watson, but if I did, and·if the woman I loved had met such an end, I might act even as our lawless lion-hunter has done. Who knows? Well, Watson, I will not offend your intelligence by explaining what is obvious. The gravel upon the window-sill was, of course, the starting-point of my research. It was unlike anything in the vicarage garden. Only when my attention had been drawn to Dr Sterndale and his cottage did I find its counterpart. The lamp shining in broad daylight and the remains of powder upon the shield were successive links in a fairly obvious chain. And now, my dear Watson, I think we may dismiss the matter from our mind, and go back with a clear conscience to the study of those Chaldean roots which are surely to be traced in the Cornish branch of the great Celtic speech.'

KILL AND CURE

by Guy Cullingford

'As I see it, we shall have plenty of time to kill,' said a prim female voice.

A pair of masculine hands twitched convulsively upon the papery edges of *The Times* outspread for cover.

'Then I suggest,' said the second female voice, 'a brisk walk to the end of the esplanade and back. After that perhaps we might buy a few little souvenirs before taking our letter of introduction to the vicar.'

The hands relaxed.

Just what the doctor ordered, thought Rex Burnham with a wry grin.

Although an acknowledged master of the cliché, even he sometimes thought literally. Two days ago he had been huddling on his clothes in the doctor's consulting room with that sheepish yet relieved feeling which accompanies a thorough medical examination.

Nervously he had asked: 'Well?'

The doctor, who was also a personal friend, was scribbling away merrily at a small pad. He tore off a sheet and replied with an absent air:

'Eh? Oh! There's nothing wrong organically. As sound as a bell, my dear fellow! As to these other symptoms . . . these nightmares and—um—hallucinations, hah! In my opinion'—he looked extremely grave—'you are being slowly and systematically poisoned.'

To say that the patient was thoroughly alarmed at this verdict is putting it mildly. He wouldn't have looked out of place on one of his own book-jackets.

'Yes,' said the doctor with a wicked gleam, 'you're suffering from an overdose of sensationalism, self-administered. How many of these shockers have you written during the last six months?'

'I prefer to call them crime novels,' remarked Rex, cut to the quick.

'I don't care what you call the darned things. I want to know how many.'

'Five or six, I suppose.'

'Ye gods, man! You're turning yourself into a murder factory.'

'I have to live,' Rex reminded him sulkily.

'I see no signs of malnutrition. In my considered opinion yours is a fairly advanced case of an enlarged imagination—not necessarily fatal. Mind you, it won't do to neglect it. Could develop into a nervous breakdown. We don't want to rob the public of one of its favourite authors even in the interests of mental health. Well, I've written you out a prescription. Here you are, but for heaven's sake don't take it to a chemist!'

He passed the prescription form, folded in half, across the top of the desk. Rex opened it. He read the name of a private hotel at Bunmouth. '*Dose: One fortnight.*'

Rex glared at him.

'You're joking.'

'Indeed I'm not! Never been more serious in my life.'

'I thought you'd give me a course of tablets—some sort of sedative.'

'Maybe I'm old-fashioned. I'm not so keen on experiment, not on friends, anyway. I've never stayed in a dump like that for years.'

'That's half the trouble.'

'How on earth did you come by the address?'

'I stayed there myself. I ran down to Bunmouth in the car for a breath of sea air and couldn't get into the Royal Bun. There was a golf tournament on, and I had to take what I could get. I made a mental note of it. I've just been waiting for the right patient to send there.'

'There may not be a tournament on now,' said Rex, brightening up. 'I wouldn't mind the Royal Bun so much.'

'I dare say you wouldn't! That's not the cure. You want somewhere unlicensed, with a well-balanced diet. Just teetering on the edge of starvation.'

'You think this would put me right?'

'I'll bet you my next salary increase.'

'It will be most inconvenient for me to get away.'

'It will be most inconvenient for you to spend three months in a nursing-home. But you needn't take my advice. I'm used to people who don't.'

'I always take advice—when I have to pay for it,' admitted Rex.

So here he was in the private hotel, his first morning, after a breakfast more smell than substance, sitting in a room called the lounge on a chair which had the appearance of comfort, but felt like something out of a geometry book.

He was not reading *The Times*, as he normally did, but was listening unashamedly to the conversation around him, a natural defect in those who strive after realistic dialogue. Although Rex couldn't exactly imagine Larry the Eye saying to Slasher Green: 'Another lovely morning! We must make the most of it while it lasts!', doubtless he would have shared the sentiment—perhaps even Larry the Eye had a maiden aunt who could, at a pinch, be used as padding.

It is a marvellous thing to come out of one world and discover the co-existence of others as round, as compact and exclusive as one's own. To name a few: the horse world, the yacht world, the golf professionals' world. This obviously was the maiden ladies' world. Apart from the casual coming and going of middle-aged couples, pottering over the countryside in their tiny cars before the seasonal high prices drove them back to their own gardens, anyone else who booked at Baxter's had got in by mistake.

These dear souls mostly went about in pairs; yet, as Mr Burnham's shrewd eye observed, each twin had a distinct personality and was as often bound by animosity as love.

These two must be Miss Meadows and Miss Faraday; he could detect London suburban in their voices under the gentility, and he had tracked them down in the register. Nosey Parker was Mr Burnham, it was part of his stock-in-trade, and he was a dab hand at remembering names. He risked a glance over the top of his newspaper. Caught in the act by Miss Meadows, the lean and stringy one, he gave her a smile of disarming simplicity, which she returned with caution.

Rex was feeling a lot better already and even in a strange bed had slept tolerably well with only one bad dream, which he put down to the curry at dinner rather than to the state of his nerves. From his bedroom window he had an unlimited view of the ocean, the sound of it sucking upon stones had lulled him to sleep.

He put down *The Times* and frankly stared about him. Now, that was an interesting old dame—sorry, lady—sitting there in the corner. Stiff with character; he must find out all about her. Later, he would establish relations with the Meadows-Faraday combine and pump them for information; he could see that it wouldn't do to approach her direct and invite a snub. She had the unmistakable aura of breeding and he christened her Lady Rag-Bag. Her dress deserved it. She was also, he decided, deaf; her voice at table, when complaining of stewed figs, was authoritative and harsh. You might have thought from what she said to her companion that the pips had been put in personally to spite her.

Presently, the companion came bustling into the room and hurried over to close the window.

'Oh, Miss Ives, you shouldn't be sitting there in a draught. You know how susceptible you are to colds.'

That placed her—the paid attendant—the dogsbody.

Miss Ives lifted her patrician but repulsive head and said harshly: 'Open the window again, Bates. At once. Can't you see that I'm enjoying the fresh air?'

Bates cast a despairing glance around the assembled company and said weakly, 'Oh, but—Miss Ives—'

'Open the window, Bates!'

The unfortunate Bates did as she was told, then said in as firm a tone as she could muster, 'I shall fetch your shawl. Yes, whatever you say, I shall fetch your shawl!'

She hurried out again, face taut and anxious. Rex felt an instinctive sympathy; she looked like he had been feeling latterly. He thought he recognised the end of a tether when he saw it.

'The old Tartar,' he thought. 'Now there's a ripe subject for murder. I daresay there's a little legacy attached to it as well. It's not much in my line but perhaps if I jerked it up a bit—holy smoke, there I go again! I'm not fit for polite society. No wonder Doc advised me to get right away!'

Conscience-smitten, he marched out of the lounge, past the dining-room door, the letter-rack and the consistently unattended reception counter and found himself on the esplanade.

He helped himself to a lungful of the health-giving ozone and set off at a brisk pace in the direction of the cliffs. The pace soon slackened to a stroll and when he reached the bottom of the cliffs he decided to put off the ascent until tomorrow. He sank down on a slatted seat in the sun.

Maybe I am a little out of condition, he admitted with reluctance, Glancing down, he was aware of a switchback contour starting from his waistline which he hurriedly corrected. Perhaps a few exercises? Meanwhile, how pleasant it was to sit without a typewriter in front of him; he had quite forgotten the sensation.

He was still sitting there when the redoubtable Miss Ives passed him, shepherded by her companion. Miss Ives had on a straw hat which was obviously brought out every year to confront the summer. She also carried what she no doubt called a parasol, whether to protect the garden in her hat or her leathery cheeks was open to question. As the two passed without acknowledgment of his presence, the companion was saying: 'But I really don't think you should tax your strength with the climb this warm weather.'

In answer to which the harsh voice was borne gratingly back to him: 'Allow me to know best, Bates. There is always a good breeze at the top.'

Two days later, Rex had ingratiated himself sufficiently with Miss Meadows and Miss Faraday to learn all he wanted to know about Miss Ives. These ladies knew all about everybody and he, too, had not been absent from their innocent speculations.

'I should put him down as something scholastic,' hazarded Miss Meadows. 'Did you notice how quickly he did the *Telegraph* crossword? The big one, you know, not the little one.'

'Schoolteachers are not on holiday now,' pointed out Miss Faraday. 'He is not quite — *quite*' — she hesitated — 'I think he might be someone rather important in a big store. He has the figure for it.'

Neither of these guesses would have pleased Mr Burnham, although he had long passed the stage where he wanted to tell everyone he met that he was an author.

'She comes from an extremely old family,' explained Miss Meadows in a carefully lowered voice. 'Miss Bates tells me that the Ives have been established in this part of the country for eight hundred years at least.'

'I shouldn't have put her age down as quite as much as that,' said Rex solemnly. 'But then I suppose that she's what you ladies would describe as well-preserved?'

'Oh, Mr Burnham, you will have your joke! But, of course, it is because of her great age that she is here with Bates — Miss Bates — to look after her. Her own beautiful home is sold up. She couldn't keep it up, you know, partly through lack of staff and partly' — her voice was dropped to the pitch suitable for a cathedral — 'through lack of money.'

'In a way you disappoint me,' commented Rex. 'I thought that at least she would have had some sort of title. At least an "hon".'

'Oh dear me no! She wouldn't like that idea at all. To be Miss Ives—that is really something.'

'And to be Miss Bates is to be a feudal retainer. I wonder how she sticks it!'

'There is not much opening for the post of paid companion in these democratic days, is there, Mr Burnham? Who else would employ her?'

Who else, thought Mr Burnham at dinner, searching for the one edible mouthful in his cutlet. Yet he was beginning to feel marvellously fit. A low diet and no work were doing wonders to his constitution. He had promised the doctor not to write a word, but the truth was that, in this atmosphere, he couldn't have done so if he had wished. The place was far too quiet; he simply couldn't concentrate.

But his imagination still roved. He couldn't contemplate the spectacle of Miss Ives and her companion for long without thinking how dead easy it would be for Miss Bates to cut her bonds and come into her inheritance. He barely stopped himself from giving her a hint. Strive as he might to repress his professional enthusiasm, at least a dozen gallows-proof ways of dealing with female dragons suggested themselves to his fertile mind. Miss Ives' chief sport was to send that wretched woman scampering up to their joint room to fetch small articles. No sooner did Miss Bates show her face in the lounge with the required object than she was despatched again on another errand.

'And their bedroom is right at the top,' breathed Miss Meadows into his ear. 'For reasons of economy, you understand. Of course, I know why she does it—' But a belated discretion sealed her mouth.

'And I know why she does it, too,' said Mr Burnham grimly. The old devil, he thought, must have someone to boss around. Her lot had been doing it for generations.

That night he had a return of his old trouble. Miss Bates was impaling her employer on a long sword and he wanted to help her but couldn't move an inch. Luckily, this was an isolated instance.

He was becoming more mobile. Twice he had been half way up the cliffs. At last, one day, he made the top. Miss Ives had been right—that was the devil of it, she often was—and on that exposed height there was quite a stiffish breeze. But he found a sheltered nook a good way back from the cliff edge and sat there at peace with himself and this new curious world. It was deserted. The sun shone in a cloudless sky. He was quite alone. But was he?

A hat he knew rose above the steep, a hat he readily recognised.

Miss Ives and her companion breasted the top, rising like two resurrected ghosts from churchyard mould. Miss Ives was on the side nearest to him; but if she hadn't learned to recognise him across the width of the dining-room she was not likely to recognise him at this distance. Besides, he was hidden by two bushes rampant.

Then something totally unexpected happened—at least to him.

The hat, the celebrated hat, was caught by a gust of wind. It sailed off its owner's head and was borne past Miss Bates right over the unprotected edge. Both ladies started after it, Miss Bates in the lead and, as her agitation took her to a point beyond caution, the redoubtable Miss Ives put forth her parasol and, with its long, pointed ferrule in the small of her companion's back, firmly propelled her over the top. It was all over in the twinkling of a second.

The despairing cry dissolved into the original quiet in which nothing obtruded but the song of a lark. Rex Burnham sat pinned to his seat; no nightmare had ever held him so secure.

Miss Ives turned and without further ado, without a glance either backwards or roundabout, disappeared in the same manner as she had arisen. In the instantaneous glimpse Rex had of her face he could detect no change of expression; she had looked neither pleased nor sorry.

As for Rex himself, he was in a state of shock. The sun still shone but not for him. He was in an arctic region where no sun could penetrate. For a time he sat entirely motionless except for the trembling of his limbs. A drop of eighty feet terminated by rocks did not suggest to him that he wanted to make reacquaintance with Miss Bates. But what to do—that was the problem.

Had he seen it? He was sure that he had seen Miss Bates go over the top; there wasn't the shadow of a doubt about that. But had he really seen Miss Ives send her over with the tip of that incredibly ancient sunshade? Was it only one more of his—well—his hallucinations?

How could he prove it, even if he wanted to do so? It would be simply Miss Ives' word against his—and who was he? If the police ever came to inquire into his antecedents, he was a thriller-writer suffering from mental strain. And Miss Ives was—Miss Ives. There was absolutely nothing for him to do but to get back to the town, if his legs would take him there.

He staggered to his feet, and went tottering down the path like an old man. He didn't catch up with Miss Ives, not he! Thank God, there was no sign of her! All Lombard Street to a China orange she had gone to report the matter at the police station.

He went straight to the Royal Bun, where he drank three double whiskies and finally returned to something like normal. Nor did he return for his luncheon to the private hotel, not even though they liked to be notified of absences well in advance. Anyone was welcome to his share of the cold ham and salad. It would remind him too much of a funeral feast.

But he had to go back, in the end. He must not draw attention to himself in too obvious a manner. He crept in to the sound of the dinner gong, smelling furiously of strong drink.

He was relieved to find that Miss Ives was taking her evening meal in her room.

He ate with his eyes fixed glumly on his plate. He chewed away morosely and he couldn't have told anyone what he was eating—which was not altogether a dead loss as the chef had been experimenting with corned beef.

He couldn't hope to escape altogether. For the sake of appearances he had to drink his coffee in the lounge, where Miss Meadows and Miss Faraday pounced upon him with the tale of disaster. They didn't mean to be unkind, but they couldn't help enjoying it. The body of poor Miss Bates had been recovered, also the hat, both battered beyond recognition.

'And the funeral is to be held as soon as the inquest is over,' said Miss Faraday. 'Do you think we should all go as a sign of respect, Mr Burnham? We should so like your advice.'

'I shan't be here,' said Mr Burnham gruffly. 'I'm leaving tomorrow morning—by the first train.'

'Oh now, what a pity! I though you were staying for the full fortnight. Is it a sudden decision? I do hope that this tragedy hasn't caused you to alter your plans!'

'He had been drinking—he wasn't at all himself,' Miss Meadows informed her friend afterwards.

'Business reasons,' mumbled Mr Burnham.

'What did I tell you?' said Miss Faraday later. 'I knew he was something in a shop!'

'Who knows?' she went on. 'Perhaps it is all for the best. Miss Ives was nearly desperate. Poor Miss Bates fussed so, you know. Miss Ives told me the other day that she would have to get rid of her. But she has such a kind heart under that somewhat forbidding exterior. She couldn't bear the idea of giving her notice.'

Rex didn't feel safe until he was settled in his first-class compartment, rattling away to London.

Then and then only was he able to relax.

Oh, what bliss to be going back to the company of Spike O'Harrigan, Larry the Eye, Slasher Green and all those violent characters who sprang to life at the touch of his typewriter.

Never again would any of that fraternity be capable of giving him a nightmare. Now, if he ever saw something which shouldn't be there out of the corner of his eye, he would invite it to join him in a drink.

He was cured, all right.

And if he met a fellow-author in a similar plight, over-writing himself in a vain attempt to keep body and soul together, he would willingly hand on the address.

Miss Ives would still be there for the next hundred years.

THE BEACH HOUSE

by Norman Daniels

F ourteen miles north of Ventura, where the San Buenaventura
Mission stands, the California coastline is rugged, rocky, eroded,
but here and there, the forbidding, wind-washed, rock-bound
coast is broken by a small beach. Most are unapproachable, so they are
little used, even during the vacation season.

The beach house was located on one of those rare and deserted bits
of sandy shore. It stood a hundred yards back from where the sea rolled
at high tide. A similar distance to the rear of the house were the cliffs
that seemed to rise up out of the sand. There was a tortuous foot trail
half a mile north; otherwise, the beach house could be approached
only from the sea.

It had one asset—surf fishing from this point was excellent, for the
beach dived sharply behind the tide, and created a deep pool where
good-sized fish congregated. Also in its favour was the fact that it was
quiet here. Nobody ever came to the spot except to fish and those who
did, wanted it that way.

Orlando Sims owned the beach house, a sprawling two-storey,
eight-bedroom frame structure some recluse had once built many years
ago and promptly abandoned because the seclusion was too great.
Orlando Sims had bought it for a song and moved in, and spread the
word that rooms and meals were ready for any fisherman who wanted a
vacation in solitude. It was quite surprising how many people came,

Orlando Sims . . . nobody knew his real first name was Orlando
. . . was known only by the name he fought under in the ring. Pogo

Sims, because he hopped around so much, his opponent could never reach him. That had been a few years ago. Pogo suddenly gave up the fight game and came to this tiny beach to live and set about luring paying guests there.

Pogo had long since gone to fat and no one cared less than he. His sole interest these days revolved around the welfare of his guests. Just now, there were four guests in the beach house. Oddly enough, all four had come independently and were not known to one another until Pogo introduced them.

Ed Morton had started the poker game right after breakfast because there was fog and a heavy mist almost resembling rain, so that surf fishing would be unpleasant. It had been a good poker game, nobody won or lost much, and now the sun was beginning to burn away the fog and the men were restlessly glancing at the windows to see when the weather was completely cleared.

Ed Morton was a real estate broker in one of the coast towns, fifty miles away. A bulky, thick-necked loud mouth in Pogo's book of personal estimations.

Bill Heath, not quite forty, was a successful dentist who deserted his practice as often as possible so he could fish. He had a cheerful personality and his hearty laugh would rise above the others whenever a joke was told. He could lose a poker hand with an enviable aplomb. Everybody liked him. Ron Chaffee was a feature reporter on one of the large newspapers, so he conducted himself with an overrated air of importance, as if he knew where all the bodies were buried and he'd never be treated with respect. Like Dr Heath, he was about thirty-eight.

The youngest member of the group was Charley Scott. He was an aeronautical engineer working at Hartley Think Plant just above Malibu. The Think Plant was an isolated, glass and steel structure devoted to scientists who thought deeply about space problems and defence and conducted complicated experiments.

Charley Scott broke the game up by throwing in his hand and getting up to look out of the window. He said, 'Clearing well now. I think I'll take a walk along the beach and see how it is.'

'Better wear something warm,' Dr Heath suggested. 'This raw air can give you a lot of lung trouble at this time of year.'

Charley's bag and clothes were upstairs, but a black-and-white checked, mackinaw-type coat hung over the back of a chair. Charley picked it up. 'Would the owner of this coat mind if I wear if for a few minutes?'

Pogo came out of the kitchen where he'd just set another pot of coffee on the stove. 'O.K., Mr Scott . . . you go ahead and use it.'

'Thanks Pogo, Nice coat. You can see it ten miles away, but I like it.'

He swung into the jacket, put on his long-peaked Tojo cap and opened the beach house door. It faced the cliff. Charley took a deep breath of the fog and salt-laden air, but it felt good in his lungs. He stepped to the sand, kicked it experimentally and then took six steps towards the side of the house on his way to the beach.

He felt the sting first. It was as if someone had drawn an exceedingly sharp blade along his neck. He was already raising a hand to investigate the sudden pain, when the shot rang out. The bullet had travelled a lot faster than the sound of the charge which had exploded behind it.

For a moment, Charley just stood there, looking at the blood on his fingers, still hearing the sharp crack of the rifle. Then realization of danger hit him and he reacted promptly. He gave a wild shout of warning and practically flew over the sand to the still-open door of the beach house. He dived in, head first, and the men at the table jumped to their feet. Pogo rushed to the door, slammed it shut and then helped Charley to his feet.

'I heard that shot,' Pogo said. 'Couldn't believe my ears. Hey . . . you been hurt, Mr Scott!'

'What the hell's going on?' Ed Morton demanded loudly.

Dr Heath moved up to Charley's side and studied the crease along his neck. 'I'm no M.D.,' he said, 'but I've had enough medical school training to handle that. Pogo, got a first-aid kit?'

'Bring it right here.' Pogo hurried to the kitchen. Ron Chaffee, his reportorial nose already twitching with excitement, took a quick look out of the window.

'I don't know what happened.' Charley was finally getting his breath back. 'I just started to walk down the beach and this bullet sliced my neck.'

Chaffee looked around from his position at the window. 'Somebody must be up on that cliff with a high-powered rifle,' he said. 'Probably has telescopic sights on it. Looks like he was making you his target for today, Charley.'

Pogo returned with a metal first-aid kit that contained everything Dr Heath needed. The dentist did a very good job of cleaning and bandaging the wound.

'It's a bit deep,' he said, 'but not dangerous. However, if it had hit one inch further to your right, old boy, you'd be out there on the sand, not caring if anybody rescued you or not. That was a close one.'

Charley nodded. 'Frankly, I like my bullets ten miles away from my head. What gets me, however, is why anybody should take a shot at me. I haven't any enemies.'

'Maybe,' Dr Heath said thoughtfully, 'it wasn't meant for you, but for one of us. That sniper has to be very high up on that cliff unless he's hanging by his toes. Even with a telescopic sight, he might find it hard to identify his victim.'

Charley went over to the buffet which had been turned into a bar the day before. He poured himself a stiff hooker of bourbon and drank it swiftly, though he didn't drink much and rarely this fast.

'I tell you, no matter how hard I try, I can't think of anybody sitting up there, just waiting to shoot me.'

'Well, you're lucky,' Chaffee grumbled. 'I've been a reporter— crime mostly—so long, I must have a thousand enemies.' He frowned deeply. 'Still, I can't think of any who'd risk a murder rap for knocking me off. And, at the moment, I'm not working on anything so important, that someone might like to have it stopped. No . . . that bullet wasn't meant for me, I'm sure. How about you, Morton?

'What about me?' Morton asked harshly.

'You're a pretty good prospect,' Chaffee said, 'Way I heard it told, you've made a profitable success out of cheating.'

'Listen, you big mouth . . .'

'Hold it,' Chaffee said. 'I know all about your many deals, my friend. I don't say I'm against what you've been doing, I don't even say you're fool enough to risk jail by an out-an-out swindle, but you have pulled some fast ones and a victim might possibly be thinking it's time to even things up.'

'You're out of your so-called mind,' Morton said loudly. 'I don't have enemies with the guts to kill me.'

Chaffee glanced at Dr Heath. 'How about you, Doc? Pulled the wrong tooth lately?'

'Listen,' Dr Heath said, 'we're all probably getting excited over nothing. That shot could have been an accident. People are always shooting deer out of season here and three-fourths of them are lousy shots. They kill one another as if they were on the freeway.'

'Pogo?' Chaffee asked the owner with the broken, twisted nose, the perpetually lopsided jaw and the swollen ear. 'I bet you took more than one dive and maybe just one wasn't made at the right time. How about it, Pogo?'

'I kinda wish you guys would clear outa here and go home,' Pogo said suddenly. 'I got nothing but trouble now. Guy out there, tryin' to shoot us up. If he gets one, he's gotto go for the others, so we can't get any help.'

Charley looked over the group. They were trying to retain a carefree composure, but he could see that they were frightened. He didn't blame them.

'Well, who's right?' he asked. 'Chaffee's theory that somebody on that cliff hates one of us? Or Dr Heath's, which says it could have been an accident?'

'I know a way to find out,' Morton said.

'I think I know what your idea is, but say it out loud anyway,' Chaffee invited.

'Let one of us step outside the door and see what happens?'

'Yeah . . . not a bad idea, but who's going to be the sucker?' Chaffee asked. 'Me, I don't know if I've got that kind of guts.'

Charley said, 'We have to find out. I've been studying the topography out there and it's not to our benefit, I can tell you. There's only this one door facing the cliff. To go anywhere, a man has to leave by that door and the sharpshooter must have his telescopic lens pointed right at it with his finger hard on the trigger.'

'How about the windows overlooking the beach?' Dr Heath asked.

'O.K.,' Charley said. 'We could get out that way, but where do we go? To the cliff? Where'd you go when you got there? If you got there. To the beach? Same problem, and either way you'd be wide open to that rifle. My friends, we are sitting ducks.'

'Somebody has to make the test,' Morton said. 'One of us has to stick his nose out the door.'

'I had first crack at it,' Charley said. 'Don't count on me. My heart won't stop pounding for three days.'

'The cards,' Ed Morton said. 'Let's cut and low man takes a walk.'

Nobody argued the point. It made sense, this experiment. They had to know if that shot had been deliberate, and if the gunman was still waiting somewhere up there on the cliff overlooking the beach house and the beach itself. There was no escape from that sniper, no chance to send for any help. No phone . . . nothing. Just the isolation each man had sought and now roundly cursed.

'O.K. with me,' Dr Heath said.

[82]

'Not me,' Chaffee told them. 'No, sir.'

Morton walked up to him. He outweighed the reporter by sixty or seventy pounds, had a three-inch-reach advantage and a belligerence to match his physical superiority.

'Now you understand this, Chaffee. We're a rather select group of men here. We're all successful and well-educated and we should pride ourselves on having a certain amount of courage. So — we cut and low man takes a walk. Low man . . . or the man who refuses to play the game. You cut and take your chances or we'll throw you out.'

'That's fair enough,' Dr Heath said. 'We're in this together.'

'What about Pogo?' Charley asked.

'He's a slob,' Morton said. 'Who'd want to knock him off? How about it, Pogo?'

Pogo's expression was as morose as ever. 'Like you said, Mr Morton, I'm a slob and slobs don't have enemies. But I'll cut the deck along with the rest of you.'

'Good for you,' Charley said. 'Let's get at it.'

Morton shuffled the cards, the cuts were made swiftly and there was no question about the loser. Dr Heath had drawn a deuce.

'Well,' he said, 'in words I helped make famous, this won't hurt much.'

He opened the door. The others ducked away from the door and the windows. Dr Heath stood in the doorway a few seconds, feeling his knees begin to waver and his nerve to weaken. He wanted to dive back inside, no matter how ignominious the act might be, but he knew there was no chance of escape that way. They'd only throw him bodily out on to the sand. He took half a dozen quick steps. Nothing happened. There was no sharp, distant crack of a rifle, no smashing drive of a slug into his body. He looked over his shoulder and grinned, while his courage flowed back into his veins.

The first bullet hit the sand about two feet in front of him. The second one inch from his right foot, extended to take a step. The third hit the beach ten inches to his left, sending a spurt of sand high enough so he felt it sting his cheek.

He spun around, as quickly as the sand would permit, and covered the six steps he'd taken, in two long strides. He dived headlong through the door, just as Charley had done. They helped him up quickly. Someone closed the door. Heath made his way to the table and sank into one of the chairs. He was visibly shaking.

'I've never been shot at before,' he said. 'I don't like it. I almost got killed.'

'I don't think so, Doc,' Charley said musingly. 'That guy could have just as easily put any or all of those slugs in your hide, as miss you. My guess is, he doesn't want to kill you, and he missed on purpose. But if you'd disregarded those warnings, I'll give odds he'd have dropped you with the next one.'

'Well, what the hell is it all about?' Morton asked in a hollow voice. 'I don't get it.'

'Out there,' Charley waved vaguely at the cliff, 'a man is waiting to kill one of us. He must have a very good reason. He'll wait until the person he wants, walks out of here. Anyone else who tries to leave, will be warned—as I was and as Doc was.'

'What do you mean, you were warned?' Dr Heath said, in a sudden burst of belligerence. 'He didn't miss you, Charley.'

'He could have killed me,' Charley argued. 'We saw an example of his marksmanship. He's a whiz with a rifle. He creased me, but he didn't mean to because that sniper doesn't shoot just to crease a man. He shoots for two reasons—to warn or kill. Nothing in between.'

Chaffee sat down heavily at the table. 'Maybe you're right, Charley. But . . . what can we do about it? It's impossible to pop out of here and make a run for it in any direction. He has us covered, no matter which way we turn.'

'We can stay here . . . outlast him,' Pogo said suddenly. 'I got food and stuff.'

'It won't work,' Charley argued. 'In the first place, there was a full moon last night and there'll be another tonight. Remember how we wondered if we should try moonlight surfing tonight?'

'Then maybe the fog . . .' Pogo began.

'At this season of the year, there's no guarantee of fog, even in the morning,' Charley argued.

Morton picked up the deck of cards and began to shuffle them automatically, as a nervous gesture, with no thought of dealing them.

'We got us a problem,' he said. 'Far as I can see, there's only one way out of this. We have to figure who that guy is after.'

'What do you mean,' Chaffee asked sarcastically, 'turn the joint into a confessional?'

'We have to know who that guy wants dead,' Morton insisted. 'It might be me and I'm not ashamed to tell you why. Not at this point, where we all may get it if that guy grows impatient. Or he mistakes one of us for the guy he really wants.'

'We'll be here all day if we have to listen to your sins,' Chaffee said.

'You're a louse, Chaffee,' Morton told him bluntly, 'and I imagine you got quite a string of names forming in your head. Me . . . I got enemies. Plenty of 'em, but only one who'd take a chance to kill me. That'd be Miles Stanton. Any of you know him?'

'I do,' Heath said.

'O.K. —well, Miles and I bought up a big tract. We got it cheap and we invested a mint in landscaping and promoting it. But we just didn't make the deadline on the payments and the original owners took the land back—after we'd built seventy-three houses on it. Took the whole kit and caboodle back and Miles went into bankruptcy. I almost did, but not quite.'

'I know about that dirty deal,' Dr Heath said, 'The people who foreclosed were working with you, Morton. It was a trick to get Miles to invest everything he owned and then get rid of him.'

'It was a legitimate business deal,' Morton protested. 'If it wasn't, Miles could have sued. He didn't, did he?'

'Miles had no money to sue. But I can tell you something about Miles that maybe you don't know, Morton. Miles and I served in the same Marine company. He has a couple of sharpshooter medals and I watched him pick off Japs so well hidden in the trees, I couldn't even see them.'

Morton paled and dashed to the buffet for a drink. In his nervousness, he forgot he was tightly gripping the deck of cards. As his fingers relaxed, the cards dribbled to the worn rug, making a trail behind him.

Dr Heath had the floor and the others let him keep it because they could sense he had more to say. Heath sat down slowly.

'Seeing it's time for confession,' he said, 'I have my own. A friend of mine . . . he was a friend of mine . . . was sent abroad for a year. I'm not married and he was gone a long time. His wife got the idea she wasn't married either. My friend came home unexpectedly, day before yesterday. He's the reason I cancelled every appointment in my book for two weeks. I intended to hole up here until it blew over. My friend knows how to use a rifle too.'

'O.K.,' Chaffee said. 'But why did he just warn you with those shots then? Not kill you as we know he could have.'

Dr Heath looked down at the surface of the table. 'He'd want me to live awhile, to suffer awhile. I know him so well. If I don't make a run for it, he'll come after me. Sooner or later, he'll come here.'

'Anybody in this gang got a gun?' Charley asked quickly.

'I got me a .30–.30 I used to use deer-hunting,' Pogo offered.

'Wonderful,' Charley said. 'you fetch that gun, Pogo, and all the rounds of ammo you've got. We may need it. Now where do we stand? Morton could be the victim. No question about it. And so could Dr Heath. We'll get around to me in a minute. How about you, Chaffee? You're the boy with the answers.'

Chaffee glared at him. 'Who hasn't got enemies these days? If you don't claw your way up, you never get there. Some guys can't claw as hard, and get left behind. I passed plenty on my way up to feature-writer on my paper.'

'Chaffee wrote some pretty rough articles on Brady Smith's gambling setup,' Dr Heath offered. 'I happen to know Chaffee got his dope first-hand—by making Smith think he was on the side of the gamblers. After he milked Smith dry, he published everything . . . lambasting the man who gave him the information in confidence.'

'Brady Smith's a punk, a small-timer,' Chaffee said. 'Who pays attention to him?'

'I'd pay attention to the combine that backs him,' Morton put in angrily. 'There are no independent gamblers these days. They're all backed up by much bigger people. The kind who don't stand for any of the nonsense you pulled on Smith. People who don't think twice about ordering some paid hood to go out and make a "hit" on somebody they don't like. Somebody . . . like you, Chaffee.'

Chaffee nodded. 'I grant that. Could be too . . . the boys who are hired to make a hit are sharpshooters. Yeah . . . could be . . . and if that's who's out there, I'm a dead man if I stick my nose out that door. What'll we do?'

Charley considered the problem for a moment. 'Now what have we got? You three men have enemies who would kill and who know how to handle a gun as well. I'm going to be frank with you now. I'm younger than any of you and maybe that's the reason why I don't have any enemies. I came to California less than a year ago. I work at the Think Shop. I don't have time for fooling around. No women, no card-cheating, no enemies. I'm a scientist and I haven't had time to get into any trouble. I swear to all of you that the man out there isn't after me.'

'Well, good for good old Charley,' Morton grumbled. 'Where does that leave the rest of us?' His lids suddenly narrowed, shading his sharp eyes. 'Wait a minute. We four men have considered ourselves only. But what about Pogo. Eh, Pogo? What about you?'

'I dunno what you're talkin' about,' Pogo shouted, but there was a touch of frenzy in his voice. Morton either knew something or had hit a raw nerve purely by accident.

Morton knew what he was talking about. 'Pogo, you quit the fight game all of a sudden. You quit because . . .'

A bullet smashed through one of the front windows. Everyone in the beach house hit the floor. A second bullet broke another window and then a third. After that, there was no more shooting.

Slowly, they arose crouching, slipped on to chairs and huddled close around the table. Dr Heath shook his head energetically.

'I don't think we have much time left. That was a warning. He'll start picking us off pretty soon.'

'O.K. . . . O.K. and maybe you got an idea what we better do,' Morton snapped.

'I did have,' Heath admitted. 'I figured if we could determine whose enemy is outside, that man could either step out and face it—or we'd throw him out. The sniper would then go away.'

'We didn't finish with Pogo,' Morton recalled. 'Listen—it's getting mighty clear now. Pogo left the ring after a particularly lousy fight. Most of his fights were setups anyway, but this last one—the betting was on him and he didn't come through. How about it, Pogo? Right afterwards, you ran away and bought this place. Nobody knew you'd done that. It cost you a lot of money, so I figure you bet against yourself, took a dive when you weren't supposed to and cost a lot of fancy boys their shirts. Now we've been talking about characters who make "hits". The boys Pogo would have to tangle with, are experts at this. And they never forget and never forgive. I think Pogo's got the mark of death on him.'

'Let's throw him out,' Chaffee urged.

'Hold it,' Charley argued. 'I admit that Morton makes a lot of sense, but we're talking about putting a man out to die.'

Chaffee broke in again. 'He's right about that fight. I remember it now—sure it was fixed somehow. Pogo's the man. He has to be.'

'I agree, in all likelihood, he is,' Charley said. 'My main reason for that, is the fact I was shot at as if the gunman meant it. I was wearing that loud jacket of Pogo's, remember?'

'That's right,' Dr Heath exclaimed. 'He didn't intend to miss with you, but you must have moved just as he fired.'

'And moved too fast afterwards for him to draw a bead,' Charley added. 'Pogo, are we right?'

Pogo sat down heavily. 'O.K. . . . so it could be me. But it could be one of you guys too. There're lots of jackets like mine around.'

'They'd know exactly what you were accustomed to wear,' Chaffee put in. 'Those boys operate as perfectionists. My suggestion is, we put that jacket on Pogo and throw him out. If he's the guy, he'll get it, but the rest of us will be safe. Pogo, either you walk out or we'll throw you out.'

'But that ain't fair,' Pogo complained loudly. 'The rest of you guys got enemies too.'

'All except me,' Charley said slowly. 'If he's after Pogo, or any of the rest of you, he wouldn't mistake me for you. I'm a little guy . . . smaller and skinnier than any of the rest of you. A half-blind man wouldn't mistake me for Pogo. I still say I was creased by accident, and I'm willing to take a chance that's how it happened.'

'I don't get this,' Dr Heath said. 'What are you driving at?'

Charley tapped his fingertips on the table as he spoke, frowning deeply as his scientifically trained mind sought the right answers.

'We're faced with two possible ways out of this. We can throw Pogo out and see what happens.'

'I'm all for it,' Chaffee said. 'And right now, before our friend up on the cliff starts shooting the whole place up.'

'All right,' Charley said. 'But if he misses Pogo on purpose, some one of you will have to be next.'

'We got to think of a better idea,' Morton said quickly.

'There's an alternative. Now listen, gentlemen, because we're all involved in this and we don't have much time left. In a little while, the sun is going to strike that cliff. Our friend up there may have a smoked lens on his rifle, but even so, he is at least going to be partly blinded. Do you agree?'

'Sun's awful bright against that cliff at four o'clock, for about twenty minutes.'

'A man with his eye glued to a telescopic sight will have a hard time adjusting to strong sunlight if he takes his eye off the 'scope for even a second or two. That's where we find our advantage.'

'Just how?' Chaffee wanted to know.

'I'll take Pogo's rifle. When the sun is just right, one of you will make a fast pass at going out a rear window and sprinting for the beach. At the identical moment, I'll go charging out the front door and head for the bottom of the cliff where he can't nail me. Whoever hits the beach, will draw his attention and maybe his fire so he'll have to move fast. But by the time the sniper realizes it's a trick and switches his sight to the front door, I should have made it. He'll be blind for a second or two. That's all I need to make the cliff.'

'Might work,' Chaffee admitted. 'And after that, what?'

'This is where my proposition involves all of us,' Charley said. 'I'll reach the trail and go up as fast as I can. Maybe our friend up there won't even know one of us has escaped. At any rate, I'll get to the top. I'll slip up behind the man and . . . I'll take him.'

'You mean . . . kill him?' Dr Heath asked, in sudden awe.

'We're all gentlemen here,' Charley said. 'All civilized, intelligent men. Even Pogo, I suspect. At any rate, he's one of us and we have to protect one another. If I don't kill that man up there and we simply let him go, he'll just do this all over again and the next time, the man he's after, might not be so lucky.'

'But I thought . . . if we could take him prisoner . . .' Dr Heath said.

'He'd have to tell the authorities why he was after whichever of you he is after. According to the reasons you have given me, not one of you can stand the publicity he'd bring down on you.'

'You'll . . . just kill him . . . like that . . . for one of us?' Morton asked.

'As I said, we're all in this together.'

'But what about . . . him?' Chaffee waved a hand at the cliff.

'When he is dead,' Charley said, 'all of us will bury him. All of us will agree never to mention this to another soul. And—to insure the silence of each of you, I shall take steps so that not one of you can recognize him. We'll bury an unidentified man. And remember, he tried to kill you.'

It took them half a minute to agree. Charley picked up Pogo's gun and examined it. It was a fine rifle, heavy and deadly. Charley took his place at a window facing west and watched the sun.

As the shadows on the cliff were slowly wiped out by the bright sunlight, they got ready. Dr Heath, being slim, and having already been fired upon—perhaps as a warning—might again escape being hit. He consented to chance it. He opened the window and clambered out. All he could do now was streak for the water's edge. Running in either direction along the beach would be fatal.

Pogo knew the sunlight here so he was to give the word, Pogo watched intently, without exposing himself at the window. The sunlight passed down along the face of the cliff and it was time.

[89]

Dr Heath started running. There were two quick shots from the cliff. Charley couldn't tell exactly where they came from, but there wasn't time to wait until the sniper fired again.

He raced out the front door, held open by Chaffee. There was another shot, but the sand didn't spurt near him. The man was still shooting at Dr Heath who had now doubled back as fast as he could run.

Perhaps the sharpshooter realized this was some sort of a trick because as Charley reached the bottom of the cliff, the man began shooting blindly at the front of the house, sending the bullets smashing through the walls and the open door which Chaffee had abandoned the moment the first shot was heard.

Charley ran lightly in the direction of the trail. It took him ten minutes and then twenty more to make his way along it to the top of the cliff. Now he could peer down. The sun was low enough so its rays didn't bother him, though there was still a great deal of light. He flattened himself behind a round rock and waited, gripping Pogo's rifle in a sweaty hand.

Then he saw the momentary glint of sunlight against polished steel. The sniper was about a hundred feet below and two hundred to the left. A vantage point from which he could see everything below, except that portion of the beach directly under the cliff. It was a long drop on to jagged rocks from where the sniper lay prone, waiting and watching.

Charley backed up, moving very slowly. He had no desire to find himself faced by the muzzle of the rifle. In his opinion, a sniper should expect to be sniped upon. Nothing was fair in this game of life and death.

Charley spent fifteen minutes getting into position. He was now above the man and he could see him spread out full length with the rifle nestled against his shoulder.

Charley aimed Pogo's deer rifle, drew a bead on the middle of the sniper's back. Down below, the others were still probably wondering which of them this man was after. Charley knew. Charley had known for some time.

Charley said, in a crisp, clear voice. 'Don't move a muscle, George. Don't even shiver.'

The man below him froze. Charley spoke again, taking his time about it.

'I thought you'd catch up with me, Georgie boy. Where'd you get

[90]

the nerve to kill me? And how come you missed? By the way, I have a nasty deer rifle aimed at your back.'

'Go ahead and shoot,' Georgie called, without moving. 'If you don't, I'll kill you. I swear it.'

'I know that very well indeed, but I've outthought you again, George. I'm going to get away with this. You set it up perfectly for me. You see, I'll have four conspirators helping me. I made them think you were after one of them and only I was innocent. They're going to help me bury you somewhere along these old rocks where you'll never be found. They think I'm doing them a favour and by the time I get through with you, they won't know who you are because you won't have a face left. However, they'll never be able to talk about this because you might be their enemy. Or someone their enemy sent. They'll never be sure, George.'

'I didn't think I'd get away with it,' George called back. 'I know how resourceful you are. How deceptive . . . how crooked. I hope the honours they shower on you for the work I did and you stole, chokes you. Slowly and thoroughly.'

Charley said, 'I can't delay this, George. I don't want a thing about this to be suspicious to those people down there. I'm just a very brave man, fighting their battle.'

George said, 'I'm going to get up, turn around and try to kill you. I . . . won't make you wait.'

He rolled over, tried to raise his rifle and Charley shot him through the chest. George let go of the rifle and lay very still. Charley crept down to him, gun ready. George moved a little and Charley aimed at his head.

George opened his eyes. It was for the last time and he knew it, but he laughed weakly. 'Your mistake, Charley, old boy. I came prepared for this. In my pocket . . . copy of a letter I mailed to six different people. I wrote . . . if I didn't come back, it meant you'd killed me. Your friends down there will find that out. They won't hold back, Charley. You're a dead man too. You're as much dead as I . . .'

Charley fired three shots into him, silencing the laughter, but when the echo of the last shot died away, the fear came. The utter and complete terror.

He found the letter, saw the list of people who had a copy, who would read the indisputable proof of his guilt. He suddenly hurled the rifle off the cliff and walked to the edge. He looked down at the rocks against which he had intended to throw the body. He took a long breath . . . but it was no use. He sank down to his knees and finally buried his face against the ground.

They found him that way, an hour later. He didn't offer any resistance. He didn't even look at the four men who regarded him, without a word.

Ed Morton, Dr Heath, Ron Chaffee and Pogo Sims. . . .

A SCHOOLMASTER
ABROAD

by E. W. Hornung

I

It is a small world that flocks to Switzerland for the Christmas holidays. It is also a world largely composed of that particular class which really did provide Dr Dollar with the majority of his cases. He was therefore not surprised, on the night of his arrival at the great Excelsior Hotel, in Winterwald, to feel a diffident touch on the shoulder, and to look round upon the sunburnt blushes of a quite recent patient.

George Edenborough had taken Winterwald on his wedding trip, and nothing would suit him and his nut-brown bride but for the doctor to join them at their table. It was a slightly embarrassing invitation, but there was good reason for not persisting in a first refusal. And the bride carried the situation with a breezy vitality, while her groom chose a wine worthy of the occasion, and the newcomer explained that he had arrived by the afternoon train, but had not come straight to the hotel.

'Then you won't have heard of our great excitement,' said Mrs Edenborough, 'and I'm afraid you won't like it when you do.'

'If you mean the strychnine affair,' returned Dollar, with a certain deliberation, 'I heard one version before I had been in the place an hour. I can't say that I did like it. But I should be interested to know what you both think about it all.'

Edenborough returned the wine-list to the waiter with sepulchral injunctions.

'Are you telling him about our medical scandal?' he inquired briskly of the bride. 'My dear doctor, it'll make your professional hair stand on end! Here's the local practitioner been prescribing strychnine pills warranted to kill in twenty minutes!'

'So I hear,' said the crime doctor, dryly.

'The poor brute has been frightfully overworked,' continued Edenborough, in deference to a more phlegmatic front than he had expected of the British faculty. 'They say he was up two whole nights last week; he seems to be the only doctor in the place, and the hotels are full of fellows doing their level best to lay themselves out. We've had two concussions of the brain and one complicated fracture this week. Still, to go and give your patient a hundred times more strychnine than you intended—'

And he stopped himself, as though the subject, which he had taken up with a purely nervous zest, was rather near home after all.

'But what about his patient?' adroitly inquired the doctor. 'If half that one hears is true, he wouldn't have been much loss.'

'Not much, I'm afraid,' said Lucy Edenborough, with the air of a Roman matron turning down her thumbs.

'He's a fellow who was at my private school, just barely twenty-one, and making an absolute fool of himself,' explained Edenborough, touching his wine-glass. 'It's an awful pity. He used to be such a nice little chap, Jack Laverick.'

'He was nice enough when he was out here a year ago,' the bride admitted, 'and he's still a sportsman. He won half the toboggan races last season, and took it all delightfully; he's quite another person now, and gives himself absurd airs on top of everything else. Still, I shall expect Mr Laverick either to sweep the board or break his neck. He evidently wasn't born to be poisoned.'

'Did he come to grief last year, Mrs Edenborough?'

'He only nearly had one of his ears cut off, in a spill on the ice-run. So they said; but he was tobogganing again the next day.'

'Dr Alt looked after him all right then, I hear,' added Edenborough, as the champagne arrived. 'But I only *you* could take the fellow in hand! He really used to be a decent chap, but it would take even you all your time to make him one again, Dr Dollar.'

The crime doctor smiled as he raised his glass and returned compliments across the bubbles. It was the smile of a man with bigger fish to fry. Yet it was he who came back to the subject of young Laverick, asking if he had not a tutor or somebody to look after him, and what the man meant by not doing his job.

In an instant both the Edenboroughs had turned upon their friend. Poor Mr Scarth was not to blame! Poor Mr Scarth, it appeared, had been a master at the preparatory school at which Jack Laverick and George Edenborough had been boys. He was a splendid fellow, and very popular in the hotel, but there was nothing but sympathy with him in the matter under discussion. His charge was of age, and in a position to send him off at any moment, as indeed he was always threatening in his cups. But there again there was a special difficulty: one cup was more than enough for Jack Laverick, whose weak head for wine was the only excuse for him.

'Yet there was nothing of the kind last year,' said Mrs Edenborough, in a reversionary voice, 'at least, one never heard of it. And that makes it all the harder on poor Mr Scarth.'

Dollar declared that he was burning to meet the unfortunate gentleman; the couple exchanged glances, and he was told to wait till after the concert, at which he had better sit with them. Was there a concert? His face lengthened at the prospect, and the bride's eyes sparkled at his expense. She would not hear of his shirking it, but went so far as to cut dinner short in order to obtain good seats. She was one of those young women who have both a will and a way with them, and Dollar soon found himself securely penned in the gallery of an ambitious ball-room with a stage at the other end.

The concert came up to his most sardonic expectations, and he resigned himself to a boredom only intensified by the behaviour of some crude humorists in the rows behind. Indifferent song followed indifferent song, and each earned a more vociferous encore from those gay young gods. A not unknown novelist told dialect stories of purely territorial interest; a lady recited with astounding spirit; another fiddled, no less courageously; but the back rows of the gallery were quite out of hand when a black-avised gentleman took the stage, and had not opened his mouth before those back rows were rows of Satan reproving sin and clapping with unsophisticated gusto.

'Who's this?' asked Dollar, instantly aware of the change behind

[95]

him; but even Lucy Edenborough would only answer, 'Hush, doctor!' as she bent forward with shining eyes. And certainly a hairpin could not have dropped unheard before the dark performer relieved the tension by plunging into a scene from *Pickwick*.

It was the scene of Mr Jingle's monologue on the Rochester coach—and the immortal nonsense was inimitably given. Yet nobody could have been less like the emaciated prototype than this tall tanned man, with the short black moustache, and the flashing teeth that bit off every word with ineffable snap and point.

'Mother—tall lady, eating sandwiches—forgot the arch—crash—knock—children look round—mother's head off—sandwich in her hand—no mouth to put it in—' and his own grim one only added to the fun and swelled the roar.

He waited darkly for them to stop, the wilful absence of any amusement on his side enormously increasing that of the audience. But when it came to the episode of Donna Christina and the stomach-pump, with the culminating discovery of Don Bolaro Fizzgig in the main pipe of the public fountain, the guffaws of half the house eventually drew from the other half the supreme compliment of exasperated demands for silence. Mrs George Edenborough was one of the loudest offenders. George himself had to wipe his eyes. And the crime doctor had forgotten that there was such a thing as crime.

'That chap's a genius!' he exclaimed, when a double encore had been satisfied by further and smaller doses of Mr Jingle, artfully held in reserve. 'But who is he, Mrs Edenborough?'

'Poor Mr Scarth!' crowed the bride, brimming over with triumphant fun.

But the doctor's mirth was at an end.

'That the fellow who can't manage a bit of a boy, when he can hold an audience like this in the hollow of his hand?'

And at first he looked as though he could not believe it, and then all at once as though he could. But by this time the Edenboroughs were urging Scarth's poverty in earnest, and Dollar could only say that he wanted to meet him more than ever.

The wish was not to be gratified without a further sidelight and a fresh surprise. As George and the doctor were repairing to the billiard-room, before the conclusion of the lengthy programme, they found a group of backs upon the threshold, and a ribald uproar in full swing within. One voice was in the ascendant, and it was sadly indistinct; but it was also the voice of the vanquished, belching querulous futilities. The cold steel thrusts of an autocratic Jingle cut it shorter and shorter. It ceased altogether, and the men in the doorway made way for Mr Scarth, as he hurried a dishevelled youth off the scene in the most approved constabulary manner.

'Does it often happen, George?' Dollar's arm had slipped through his former patient's as they slowly followed at their distance.

'Most nights, I'm afraid.'

'And does Scarth always do what he likes with him—afterwards?'

'Always; he's the sort of fellow who can do what he likes with most people,' declared the young man, missing the point. 'You should have seen him at the last concert, when those fools behind us behaved even worse than tonight! It wasn't his turn, but he came out and put them right in about a second, and had us all laughing the next! It was just the same at school; everybody was afraid of Mostyn Scarth, boys and men alike; and so is Jack Laverick still—in spite of being of age and having the money-bags—as you saw for yourself just now.'

'Yet he lets this sort of thing happen continually?'

'It's pretty difficult to prevent. A glass about does it, as I told you, and you can't be at a fellow's elbow all the time in a place like this. But some of Jack's old pals have had a go at him. Do you know what they've done? They've taken away his Old Etonian tie, and quite right too!'

'And there was nothing of all this last year?'

'So Lucy says. I wasn't here. Mrs Laverick was, by the way; she may have made the difference. But being his own master seems to have sent him to the dogs altogether. Scarth's the only person to pull him up, unless—unless you'd take him on, doctor! You—you've pulled harder cases out of the fire, you know!'

They had been sitting a few minutes in the lounge. Nobody was very near them; the young man's face was alight and his eyes shining. Dollar took him by the arm once more, and they went together to the lift.

'In any case I must make friends with your friend Scarth,' said he. 'Do you happen to know his number?'

Edenborough did—it was 144—but he seemed dubious as to another doctor's reception after the tragedy that might have happened in the adjoining room.

'Hadn't I better introduce you in the morning?' he suggested with much deference in the lift. 'I—I hate repeating things—but I want you to like each other, and I heard Scarth say he was fed up with doctors!'

This one smiled.

'I don't wonder at it.'

'Yet it wasn't Mostyn Scarth who gave Dr Alt away.'

'No?'

Edenborough shook his head as they left the lift together. 'No, doctor. It was the chemist here, a chap called Schickel; but for him, Jack Laverick would be a dead man; and but for him again, nobody need ever have heard of his narrow shave. He spotted the mistake, and then started all the gossip.'

'I know,' said the doctor, nodding.

'But it was a terrible mistake! Decigrams instead of milligrams, so I heard. Just a hundred times too much strychnine in each pill.'

'You are quite right,' said John Dollar quietly. 'I have the prescription in my pocket.'

'You have, doctor?'

'Don't be angry with me, dear fellow! I told you I had heard one version of the whole thing. It was Alt's. He's an old friend—but you wouldn't have said a word about him if I had told you that at first— and I still don't want it generally known.'

'You can trust me, doctor, after all you've done for me.'

'Well, Alt once did more for me. I want to do something for him, that's all.'

And his knuckles still ached from the young man's grip as they rapped smartly at the door of No. 144.

II

It was opened a few inches by Mostyn Scarth. His raiment was still at concert pitch, but his face even darker than it had been when the crime doctor saw it last.

'May I ask who you are and what you want?' he demanded—not at all in the manner of Mr Jingle—rather in the voice that most people would have raised.

'My name's Dollar and I'm a doctor.'

The self-announcement, pat as a poly-syllable, had a foreseen effect only minimised by the precautionary confidence of Dr Dollar's manner.

'Thanks very much. I've had about enough of doctors.'

And the door was shutting when the intruder got in a word like a wedge.

[98]

'Exactly!'

Scarth frowned through a chink just wide enough to show both his eyes. It was the intruder's tone that held his hand.

'What does that mean?' he demanded with more control.

'That I want to see you about the other doctor—this German fellow,' returned Dollar, against the grain. But the studious phrase admitted him.

'Well, don't raise your voice,' said Scarth, lowering his own as he shut the door softly behind them. 'I believe I saw you downstairs outside the bar. So I need only explain that I've just got my bright young man off to sleep, on the other side of those folding doors.'

Dollar could not help wondering whether the other room was as good as Scarth's which was much bigger and better appointed than his own. But he sat down at the oval table under the electrolier, and came abruptly to his point.

'About that prescription,' he began, and straightaway produced it from his pocket.

'Well, what about it?' the other queried, but only keenly, as he sat down at the table too.

'Dr Alt is a very old friend of mine, Mr Scarth.'

Mostyn Scarth exhibited the slight but immediate change of front due from gentleman to gentleman on the strength of such a statement. His grim eyes softened with a certain sympathy; but the accession left his gravity the more pronounced.

'He is not only a friend,' continued Dollar, 'but the cleverest and best man I know in my profession. I don't speak from mere loyalty; he was my own doctor before he was my friend. Mr Scarth, he saved more than my life when every head in Harley Street had been shaken over my case. All the baronets gave me up; but chance or fate brought me here, and this little unknown man performed the miracle they shirked, and made a new man of me off his own bat. I wanted him to come to London and make his fortune; but his work was here, he wouldn't leave it; and here I find him under this sorry cloud. Can you wonder at my wanting to step in and speak up for him, Mr Scarth?'

'On the contrary, I know exactly how you must feel, and am very glad you have spoken,' rejoined Mostyn Scarth, cordially enough in all the circumstances of the case. 'But the cloud is none of my making, Dr Dollar, though I naturally feel rather strongly about the matter. But for Schickel, the chemist, I might be seeing a coffin to England at this moment! He's the man who found out the mistake, and has since made all the mischief.'

'Are you sure it was a mistake, Mr Scarth?' asked Dollar quietly.

'What else?' cried the other, in blank astonishment. 'Even Schickel has never suggested that Dr Alt was trying to commit a murder!'

'Even Schickel!' repeated Dollar, with a sharp significance. 'Are you suggesting that there's no love lost between him and Alt?'

'I was not, indeed!' Scarth seemed still more astonished. 'No. That never occurred to me for a moment.'

'Yet it's a small place, and you know what small places are. Would one man be likely to spread a thing like this against another if there were no bad blood between them?'

Scarth could not say. The thing happened to be true, and it made such a justifiable sensation. He was none the less frankly interested in the suggestion. It was as though he had a tantalising glimmer of the crime doctor's meaning. Their heads were closer together across the end of the table, their eyes joined in mutual probation.

'Can I trust you with my own idea, Mr Scarth?'

'That's for you to decide, Dr Dollar.'

'I shall not breathe it to another soul—not even to Alt himself—till I am sure.'

'You may trust me, doctor. I don't know what's coming, but I sha'n't give it away.'

'Then I shall trust you even to the extent of contradicting what I just said. I *am* sure—between ourselves—that the prescription now in my hands is a clever forgery.'

Scarth held out his hand for it. A less deliberate announcement might have given him a more satisfactory surprise; but he could not have looked more incredulous than he did, or subjected Dollar to a cooler scrutiny.

'A forgery with what object, Dr Dollar?'

'That I don't pretend to say. I merely state the fact—in confidence. You have your eyes upon a flagrant forgery.'

Scarth raised them twinkling. 'My dear Dr Dollar, I saw him write it out myself!'

'Are you quite sure?'

'Absolutely, doctor. This lad, Jack Laverick, is a pretty handful; without a doctor to frighten him from time to time, I couldn't cope with him at all. His people are in despair about him—but that's another matter. I was only going to say that I took him to Dr Alt myself, and this is the prescription they refused to make up. Schickel may have a spite against Alt, as you suggest, but if he's a forger I can only say he doesn't look the part.'

'The only looks I go by,' said the crime doctor, 'are those of the little document in your hand.'

'It's on Alt's paper.'

'Anybody could get hold of that.'

'But you suggest that Alt and Schickel have been on bad terms?'

'That's a better point, Mr Scarth, that's a much better point,' said Dollar, smiling and then ceasing to smile as he produced a magnifying lens. 'Allow me to switch on the electric standard, and do me the favour of examining that handwriting with this loop; it's not very strong, but the best I could get here at the photographer's shop.'

'It's certainly not strong enough to show anything fishy, to my inexperience,' said Scarth, on a sufficiently close inspection.

'Now look at this one.'

Dollar had produced a second prescription from the same pocket as before. At first sight they seemed identical.

'Is this another forgery?' inquired Scarth, with a first faint trace of irony.

'No. That's the correct prescription, rewritten by Alt, at my request, as he is positive he wrote it originally.'

'I see now. There are two more noughts mixed up with the other hieroglyphs.'

'They happen to make all the difference between life and death,' said Dollar, gravely. 'Yet they are not by any means the only difference here.'

'I can see no other, I must confess.' And Scarth raised stolid eyes to meet Dollar's steady gaze.

'The other difference is, Mr Scarth, that the prescription with the strychnine in deadly decigrams has been drawn backwards instead of being written forwards.'

Scarth's stare ended in a smile.

'Do you mind saying all that again, Dr Dollar?'

'I'll elaborate it. The genuine prescription has been written in the ordinary way—*currente calamo*. But forgeries are not written in the ordinary way, much less with running pens; the best of them are written backwards, or rather they are *drawn upside down*. Try to copy writing *as* writing, and your own will automatically creep in and spoil it; draw it upside down and wrong way on, as a mere meaningless scroll, and your own formation of the letters doesn't influence you, because you are not forming letters at all. You are drawing from a copy, Mr Scarth.'

'You mean that I'm deriving valuable information from a hand-writing expert,' cried Scarth, with another laugh.

'There are no such experts,' returned Dollar, a little coldly. 'It's all a mere matter of observation, open to everybody with eyes to see. But this happens to be an old forger's trick; try it for yourself, as I have, and you'll be surprised to see how much there is in it.'

'I must,' said Scarth. 'But I can't conceive how you can tell that it has been played in this case.'

'No? Look at the start, "Herr Laverick," and at the finish, "Dr Alt". You would expect to see plenty of ink in the "Herr", wouldn't you? Still plenty in the "Laverick", I think, but now less and less until the pen is filled again. In the correct prescription, written at my request to-day, you will find that this is so. In the forgery the progression is precisely the reverse; the *t* in "Alt" is full of ink, but you will find less and less till the next dip in the middle of the world "Mahlzeit" in the line above. The forger, of course, dips oftener than the man with the running pen.'

Scarth bent in silence over the lens, his dark face screwed awry. Suddenly he pushed back his chair.

'It's wonderful!' he cried softly. 'I see everything you say. Dr Dollar, you have converted me to your view. I should like you to allow me to convert the hotel.'

'Not yet,' said Dollar, rising, 'if at all as to the actual facts of the case. It's no use making bad worse, Mr Scarth, or taking a dirty trick too seriously. It isn't as though the forgery had been committed with a view to murdering your young Laverick.'

'I never dreamt of thinking that it was!'

'You are quite right, Mr Scarth. It doesn't bear thinking about. Of course, any murderer ingenious enough to concoct such a thing would have been far too clever to drop out *two* noughts; he would have been content to change the milligrams into centigrams, and risk a recovery. No sane chemist would have dispensed the pills in decigrams. But we are getting off the facts, and I promised to meet Dr Alt on his last round. If I may tell him, in vague terms, that you at least think there may have been some mistake, other than the culpable one that has been laid at his door, I shall go away less uneasy about my unwarrantable intrusion than I can assure you I was in making it.'

It was strange how the balance of personality had shifted during an interview which Scarth himself was now eager to extend. He was no longer the mesmeric martinet who had tamed an unruly audience at sight; the last of Mr Jingle's snap had long been in abeyance. And yet there was just one more suggestion of that immortal, in the rather dilapidated trunk from which the swarthy exquisite now produced a bottle of whisky, very properly locked up out of Laverick's reach. And weakness of will could not be imputed to the young man who induced John Dollar to cement their acquaintance with a thimbleful.

III

It was early morning in the same week; the crime doctor lay brooding over the most complicated case that had yet come his way. More precisely it was two cases, but so closely related that it took a strong mind to consider them apart, a stronger will to confine each to the solitary brain-cell that it deserved. Yet the case of young Laverick was not only much the simpler of the two, but infinitely the more congenial to John Dollar, and not the one most on his nerves.

It was too simple altogether. A year ago the boy had been all right, wild only as a tobogganer, lucky to have got off with a few stitches in his ear. Dollar heard all about that business from Dr Alt, and only too much about Jack Laverick's subsequent record from other informants. It was worthy of the Welbeck Street confessional. His career at Oxford had come to a sudden ignominious end. He had forfeited his motoring licence for habitually driving to the public danger, and on the last occasion had barely escaped imprisonment for his condition at the wheel. He had caused his own mother to say advisedly that she would 'sooner see him in his coffin than going on in this dreadful way'; in writing she had said it, for Scarth had shown the letter addressed to him as her 'last and only hope' for Jack; and yet even Scarth was powerless to prevent that son of Belial from getting 'flown with insolence and wine' more nights than not. Even last night it had happened, at the masked ball, on the eve of this morning's races! Whose fault would it be if he killed himself on the ice-run after all?

Dollar writhed as he thought upon this case; yet it was not the case that had brought him out from England, not the reason of his staying out longer than he had dreamt of doing when Alt's telegram arrived. It was not, indeed, about Jack Laverick that poor Alt had telegraphed at all. And yet between them what a job they could have made of the unfortunate youth!

[103]

It was Dollar's own case over again—yet he had not been called in—neither of them had!

Nevertheless, when all was said that could be said to himself, or even to Alt—who did not quite agree—Laverick's was much the less serious matter; and John Dollar had turned upon the other side, and was grappling afresh with the other case, when his door opened violently without a knock, and an agitated voice spoke his name.

'It's me—Edenborough,' it continued in a hurried whisper. 'I want you to get into some clothes and come up to the ice-run as quick as possible!'

'Why? What has happened?' asked the doctor, jumping out of bed as Edenborough drew the curtains.

'Nothing yet. I hope nothing will—'

'But something has!' interrupted the doctor. 'What's the matter with your eye?'

'I'll tell you as you dress, only be as quick as you can. Did you forget it was the toboggan races this morning? They're having them at eight instead of nine, because of the sun, and it's ten to eight now. Couldn't you get into some knickerbockers and stick a sweater over all the rest? That's what I've done—wish I'd come to you first! They'll *want* a doctor if we don't make haste!'

'I wish you'd tell me about your eye,' said Dollar, already in his stockings.

'My eye's all right,' returned Edenborough, going to the glass. 'No, by Jove, it's blacker than I thought, and my head's still singing like a kettle. I shouldn't have thought Laverick could hit so hard—drunk *or* sober.'

'That madman?' cried Dollar, looking up from his laces. 'I thought he turned in early for once?'

'He was up early, anyhow,' said Edenborough, grimly; 'but I'll tell you the whole thing as we go up to the run, and I don't much mind who hears me. He's a worse hat even than we thought. I caught him tampering with the toboggans at five o'clock this morning!'

'Which toboggans?'

'One of the lot they keep in a shed just under our window, at the back of the hotel. I was lying awake and I heard something. It was like a sort of filing, as if somebody was breaking in somewhere. I got up and looked out, and thought I saw a light. Lucy was fast asleep; she is still, by the way, and doesn't know a thing.'

'I'm ready,' said Dollar. 'Go on when we get outside.'

It was a very pale blue morning, not a scintilla of sunlight in the valley, neither shine nor shadow upon clambering forest or overhanging rocks. Somewhere behind their jagged peaks the sun must have risen, but as yet no snowy facet winked the news to Winterwald, and the softer summits lost all character against a sky only less white than themselves.

The village street presented no difficulties to Edenborough's gouties and the doctor's hobnails; but there were other people in it, and voices travel in a frost over silent snow. On the frozen path between the snowfields, beyond the village, nails were not enough, and the novice depending upon them stumbled and slid as the elaborated climax of Edenborough's experience induced even more speed.

'It was him all right—try the edge, doctor, it's less slippy. It was that little brute in his domino, as if he'd never been to bed at all, and me in my dressing-gown not properly awake. We should have looked a funny pair in—have my arm, doctor.'

'Thanks, George.'

'But his electric lamp was the only light. He didn't attempt to put it out. "Just tuning up my toboggan," he whispered. "Come and have a look." I didn't and don't believe it was his own toboggan; it was probably that Captain Strong's, he's his most dangerous rival; but, as I tell you, I was just going to look when the young brute hit me full in the face without a moment's warning. I went over like an ox, but I think the back of my head must have hit something. There was daylight in the place when I opened the only eye I could.'

'Had he locked you in?'

'No; he was too fly for that; but I simply couldn't move till I heard voices coming, and then I only crawled behind a stack of garden chairs and things. It was Strong and another fellow—they did curse to find the whole place open! I nearly showed up and told my tale, only I wanted to tell you first.'

'I'm glad you have, George.'

'I knew your interest in the fellow—besides, I thought it was a case for you,' said George Edenborough simply. 'But it kept me prisoner till the last of the toboggans had been taken out—I only hope it hasn't made us too late!'

His next breath was a devout thanksgiving, as a fold in the glistening slopes showed the top of the ice-run, and a group of men in sweaters standing out against the fir-trees on the crest. They seemed to be standing very still. Some had their padded elbows lifted as though they were shading their eyes. But there was no sign of a toboggan starting, no sound of one in the invisible crevice of the run. And now man after man detached himself from the group, and came leaping down the subsidiary snow-track meant only for ascent.

But John Dollar and George Edenborough did not see all of this. A yet more ominous figure had appeared in their own path, had grown into Mostyn Scarth, and stood wildly beckoning to them both.

'It's Jack!' he shouted across the snow. 'He's had a smash—self and toboggan—flaw in a runner. I'm afraid he's broken his leg.'

'Only his leg!' cried Dollar, but not with the least accent of relief. The tone made Edenborough wince behind him, and Scarth in front look round. It was as though even the crime doctor thought Jack Laverick better dead.

He lay on a litter of overcoats, the hub of a wheel of men that broke of itself before the first doctor on the scene. He was not even insensible, neither was he uttering moan or groan; but his white lips were drawn away from his set teeth, and his left leg had an odd look of being no more a part of him than its envelope of knickerbocker and stocking.

'It's a bu'st, doctor, I'm afraid,' the boy ground out as Dollar knelt in the snow. 'Hurting? A bit—but I can stick it.'

Courage was the one quality he had not lost during the last year; nobody could have shown more during the slow and excruciating progress to the village, on a bobsleigh carried by four stumbling men; everybody was whispering about it. Everybody but the crime doctor, who headed the little procession with a face in keeping with the tone which had made Edenborough wince and Scarth look round.

The complex case of the night—this urgent one—both were forgotten for Dollar's own case of years ago. He was back again in another Winterwald, another world. It was no longer a land of Christmas-trees growing out of mountains of Christmas cake; the snow melted before his mind's eye; he was hugging the shadows in a street of toy-houses yielding resin to an August sun, between green slopes combed with dark pines, under a sky of intolerable blue. And he was in despair; all Harley Street could or would do nothing for him. And then—and then—some forgotten ache or pain had taken him to the little man—the great man—down this very turning to the left, in the little wooden house tucked away behind the shops.

How he remembered every landmark—the handrail down the slope—the little porch—the bare stairs, his own ladder between death and life—the stark surgery with its uncompromising appliances in full view! And now at last he was there with such another case as his own— with the minor case that he had yet burned to bring there— and there was Alt to receive them in the same white jacket and with the same simple countenance as of old!

They might have taken him on to the hotel, as Scarth indeed urged strongly; but the boy himself was against another yard, though otherwise a hero to the end.

'Chloroform?' he cried faintly. 'Can't I have my beastly leg set without chloroform? You're not going to have it off, are you? I can stick anything short of that.'

The two doctors retired for the further consideration of a point on which they themselves were not of one mind.

'It's the chance of our lives, and the one chance for him,' urged Dollar vehemently. 'It isn't as if it were such a dangerous operation, and I'll take sole responsibility.'

'But I am not sure you have been right,' demurred the other. 'He has not even had concussion, a year ago. It has been only the ear.'

'There's a lump behind it still. Everything dates from when it happened; there's some pressure somewhere that has made another being of him. It's a much simpler case than mine, and you cured me. Alt, if you had seen how his own mother wrote about him you would be the very last man to hesitate!'

'It's better to have her consent.'

'No—nobody's—the boy himself need never know. There's a young bride here who'll nurse him like an angel and hold her tongue till doomsday. She and her husband may be in the secret, but not another soul!'

And when Jack Laverick came out of chloroform, to feel a frosty tickling under the tabernacle of bed-clothes in which his broken bone was as the Ark, the sensation was less uncomfortable than he expected. But that of a dull deep pain in the head drew his first complaint, as an item not in the estimate.

'What's my head all bandaged up for?' he demanded, fingering the turban on the pillow.

'Didn't you know it was broken, too?' said Lucy Edenborough gravely. 'I expect your leg hurt so much more that you never noticed it.'

IV

Ten days later Mostyn Scarth called at Doctor Alt's, to ask if he mightn't see Jack at last. He had behaved extremely well about the whole affair; others in his position might easily have made trouble. But there had been no concealment of the fact that injuries were not confined to the broken leg, and the mere seat of the additional mischief was enough for a man of sense. It is not the really strong who love to display their power. Scarth not only accepted the situation, but voluntarily conducted the correspondence which kept poor Mrs Laverick at half Europe's length over the critical period. He had merely stipulated to be the first to see the convalescent, and he took it as well as ever when Dollar shook his head once more.

'It's not our fault this time, Mr Scarth. You must blame the sex that is privileged to change its mind. Mrs Laverick has arrived without a word of warning. She is with her son at this moment, and you'll be glad to hear that she thinks she finds him an absolutely changed character—or, rather, what he was before he ever saw Winterwald a year ago. I may say that this seems more or less the patient's own impression about himself.'

'Glad!' cried Scarth, who for the moment had seemed rather staggered. 'I'm more than glad, I'm profoundly relieved! It doesn't matter now whether I see Jack or not. Do you mind giving him these magazines and papers, with my love? I am thankful that my responsibility's at an end.'

'The same with me,' returned the crime doctor. 'I shall go back to my work in London with a better conscience than I had when I left it—with something accomplished—something undone that wanted undoing.'

He smiled at Scarth across the flap of an unpretentious table, on which lay the literary offering in all its glory of green and yellow wrappers; and Scarth looked up without a trace of pique, but with an answering twinkle in his own dark eyes.

'Alt exalted—restored to favour—Jack reformed character—born again—forger forgotten—forging ahead, eh?'

It was his best Mr Jingle manner; indeed, a wonderfully ready and ruthless travesty of his own performance on the night of Dollar's arrival. And that kindred critic enjoyed it none the less for a second strain of irony, which he could not but take to himself.

'I have not forgotten anybody, Mr Scarth.'

[108]

'But have you discovered who did the forgery?'

'I always knew.'

'Have you tackled him?'

'Days ago!'

Scarth looked astounded. 'And what's to happen to him, doctor?'

'I don't know.' The doctor gave a characteristic shrug. 'It's not my job; as it was I'd done all the detective business, which I loathe.'

'I remember,' cried Scarth. 'I shall never forget the way you went through that prescription, as though you had been looking over the blighter's shoulder! Not an expert—modest fellow—pride that apes!'

And again Dollar had to laugh at the way Mr Jingle wagged his head, in spite of the same slightly caustic undercurrent as before.

'That was the easiest part of it,' he answered, 'although you make me blush to say so. The hard part was what reviewers of novels call the "motivation".'

'But you had that in Schickel's spite against Alt.'

'It was never quite strong enough to please me.'

'Then what was the motive, doctor?'

'Young Laverick's death.'

'Nonsense!'

'I wish it were, Mr Scarth.'

'But who is there in Winterwald who could wish to compass such a thing?'

'There were more than two thousand visitors over Christmas, I understand,' was the only reply.

It would not do for Mostyn Scarth. He looked less than politely incredulous, if not less shocked and rather more indignant than he need have looked. But the whole idea was a reflection upon his care of the unhappy youth. And he said so in other words, which resembled those of Mr Jingle only in their stiff staccato brevity.

'Talk about "motivation"!—I thank you, doctor, for that word—but I should thank you even more to show me the thing itself in your theory. And what a way to kill a fellow! What a roundabout, risky way!'

'It was such a good forgery,' observed the doctor, 'that even Alt himself could hardly swear that it was one.'

'Is *he* your man?' asked Scarth, in a sudden whisper, leaning forward with lighted eyes.

The crime doctor smiled enigmatically. 'It's perhaps just as lucky for him, Scarth, that at least he could have had nothing to do with the second attempt upon his patient's life.'

'What second attempt?'

'The hand that forged the prescription, Scarth, with intent to poison young Laverick, was the one that also filed the flaw in his toboggan, in the hopes of breaking his neck.'

'My dear doctor,' exclaimed Mostyn Scarth, with a pained shake of the head, 'this is stark, staring madness!'

'I only hope it was—in the would-be murderer,' rejoined Dollar gravely. 'But he had a lot of method: he even did his bit of filing—a burglar couldn't have done it better—in the domino Jack Laverick had just taken off!'

'How do you know he had taken it off? How do you know the whole job wasn't one of Jack's drunken tricks?'

'What whole job?'

'The one you're talking about—the alleged tampering with his toboggan,' replied Scarth, impatiently.

'Oh! I only thought you meant something more.' Dollar made a pause. 'Don't you feel it rather hot in here, Scarth?'

'Do you know, I do!' confessed the visitor, as though it were Dollar's house and breeding had forbidden him to volunteer the remark. 'It's the heat of this stove, with the window shut. Thanks so much, doctor!'

And he wiped his strong, brown, beautifully shaven face; it was one of those that require shaving more than once a day, yet it was always glossy from the razor; and he burnished it afresh with a silk handkerchief that would have passed through a packing-needle's eye.

'And what are you really doing about this—monster?' he resumed, as who should accept the monster's existence for the sake of argument.

'Nothing, Scarth.'

'Nothing? You intend to do nothing at all?'

Scarth had started, for the first time; but he started to his feet, while he was about it, as though in overpowering disgust.

'Not if he keeps out of England,' replied the crime doctor, who had also risen. 'I wonder if he's sane enough for that?'

Their four eyes met in a protracted scrutiny, without a flicker on either side.

'What I am wondering,' said Scarth deliberately, 'is whether this Frankenstein effort of yours exists outside your own imagination, Dr Dollar.'

'Oh! he exists all right,' declared the doctor. 'But I am charitable enought to suppose him mad—in spite of his method *and* his motive.'

[110]

'Did he tell you what that was?' asked Scarth with a sneer.

'No; but Jack did. He seems to have been in the man's power—under his influence—to an extraordinary degree. He had even left him a wicked sum in a will made since he came of age. I needn't tell you that he has now made another, revoking—'

'No, you need not!' cried Mostyn Scarth, turning livid at the last moment. 'I've heard about enough of your mares' nests and mythical monsters. I wish you good morning, and a more credulous audience next time.'

'That I can count upon,' returned the doctor at the door. 'There's no saying what they won't believe—at Scotland Yard!'

THE OLD SHELL COLLECTOR

by H. R. F. Keating

T hey made their presence felt down there on the beach from the moment they arrived. Not that it was a scene of intense solitude and quiet beforehand. There were children running up and down the dark wet sand shouting and calling. More than one mother was trying to make some toddler return to the family encampment without herself getting up off the beach towel spread over the pebbles which the now receding tide had not reached; and all this required a good deal of increasingly irritated yelling. There was also a game of cricket being played, a tense affair in which a boy of seven or eight was standing worriedly in front of a set of bright yellow plastic stumps while his thick-waisted father strove at the bowling end to revive younger days; and this naturally resulted in more and more sharply uttered words floating up into the August air. So it was not really a tranquil scene.

But there were areas of comparative quiet. There was, for instance, a row of deck chairs drawn up just underneath the rust-stained concrete wall of the promenade where it was thought the sharp breeze would not strike with quite as much force as elsewhere; and here a number of elderly citizens grimly sat, the men wrestling with wind-teased newspapers, their spouses mostly knitting away for dear life, one or two determined souls actually succeeding in dozing in the illusory warmth of the sun.

It was one of these half-sleeping gentlemen, the oldest probably of the whole deck-chair row, who received the brunt of the arrival.

With a wild outburst of whooping they came tearing along the half-deserted front, sending the staid gulls wheeling and crying; and, for some reason or other, when they got to the exact point underneath which the old gentleman was letting the late hours of his life glide harmlessly away, the girl who happened to be in front of the racing, jostling mob elected to jump down onto the beach. She gave a piercing shriek, echoing out even above the noise the rest of them were making, and took off with long slim legs held together aiming for some point on the stony beach below.

And the tips of her outstretched toes just brushed against the flat white cap that protected the old man's head from the sun. They sent the incongruously jaunty piece of headgear spinning and rolling over the pebbles and put the old boy into a state of alarm which the sight of the rest of the crowd jumping one by one onto the beach on either side of him did nothing to dispel.

The girl who had landed first took a look at the flinching octogenarian and turned quickly away. Evidently she was not the type to brazen out any such accident that occurred in her rackety progress about her world. But others of the party—there were no more than eight of them in fact, though to the quiet folk on the beach it must have seemed as if scores of the vandals had descended—were more hard-faced. Another of the girls, a pert-figured redhead in a saucily diminutive green bikini, turned to the boy beside her and commented on the incident in a voice which rang round the whole beach.

'They shouldn't let 'em out that old,' she shouted cheerfully. 'It's enough to make you sick just seeing them.'

And then with a renewed full-throated whoop she set off leaping over the pebbles toward the somewhat more inviting area of the dark water-gleaming sand.

Once down on the sand, the newcomers proceeded brazenly to take over the whole area. They ran races from end to end of the level stretch, and woe betide anyone foolish enough to remain in their way. They indulged in short games sessions with an enormous brightly coloured rubber ball they had brought with them, bouncing it once right onto the carefully laid-out sandwich boxes and thermos bottles of a family eating an early lunch. And all the while they kept up a running commentary on their own activities delivered at the tops of their voices and interspersed with braying inconsequential laughter.

[113]

So bit by bit the whole of the sand was given over to them, mothers sharply calling their children back onto the pebbles, middle-aged fathers darting furious glances at the mob but equally withdrawing to places that were safer, if a good deal more uncomfortable.

Only one determined parent, father of two small boys and a girl, resolutely refused to budge. He was engaged on serious business. From the moment the sea had retreated beyond the pebbles he had been busy constructing an immensely elaborate sand castle. With the aid of their little pails his children had been dragooned into amassing a sufficient quantity of sand while he himself, equipped, not with any plastic seaside spade, but with a proper no-nonsense garden tool, had toiled manfully to dig out a foot-deep trench all round the area of his proposed edifice. Once or twice as the crowd of newcomers had run whooping and shrieking past he had looked up briefly and a quick frown of annoyance had shown itself on his dedicatedly intense face above the sober pair of spectacles which rested as firmly on the bridge of his nose here on the beach as they did at his office desk.

And as was almost inevitable, before long, these two parties staking claim to the sand, each determined in a different way, came into conflict.

It was the girl who had first jumped down onto the beach who was responsible. Jacky they called her, yelling insults at her in their friendly and thoroughly uninhibited way. She must have been about seventeen by the look of her, certainly no more. And it was in the course of one of their brief but violent games with the big rubber ball—a heavy object of some two feet in diameter—that the incident occurred.

Jacky was standing just above the newly built sand castle, which its architect was busy giving a final shaping to, not without sharply reproving advice to his underlings, and the ball had come bouncing along toward her. She made a dash for it, swerved when it bounced askew, and went sprawling frankly spread-eagled right over the delicate structure. In an instant it was reduced from fantasy to flattened nothingness.

She heaved herself up on her elbows and looked across at her companions.

'Oh, God,' she shouted, 'I've got sand all down inside my bikini!'

And since this time she could hardly pretend she had not been responsible for the damage, she entirely ignored it. She pushed herself to her knees, digging two deep pits in the soft sand by way of final insult added to injury, then staggered upright and ran down toward

[114]

the sea, pulling the bikini top away from her body and shimmying wildly to get rid of the sand.

'You've spoiled our castle,' exclaimed its builder, looking at her retreating back. 'You've made a complete mess of it!'

None of the group paid the least attention to him. Jacky was for the time being the focus of their interest. The four boys rushed up and eagerly surrounded her, beginning vigorous and by no means disinterested efforts to help her get rid of more sand.

This activity, as might have been expected, drew a great deal of covert interest from the holidaymakers on the pebbly area. They had all been pretending to ignore the usurpers, but nonetheless they had kept a constant eye on their activities; and by now they had some idea of their different personalities and which name to attach to each of them. And they watched with relished disapproval while Mike, the blatantly handsome and self-assured one; Bob, the blond muscle-boy; the serious-looking Herbert, who had already raised more than one chorus of strident booing by perpetrating frightful puns; and the smallest of the bunch, little bespectacled Dickie, all set upon the shrieking Jacky and pulled and tugged at her bikini and patted und brushed her body, pretending, with enough shouting to encourage a football team, that she was still thickly sand-covered.

But this was hardly to the liking of the other girls, especially—it looked to the greedy censorious eyes watching from the pebbles—of the pert redhead (was her name Jo?), who had been noted as showing a particular interest in the handsome Mike.

And so—with a great deal of 'Hey, leave the silly twit alone' and 'What do you want to go and knock over the poor old man's sand castle for?'—they succeeded at last in diverting the boys' attention from little Jacky into a sprint across the sand ('First to touch the breakwater' and 'Last there's a sissy'), in which, as usual, the muscular, and proud of it, Bob was first home.

When they had all arrived at the breakwater and had begun a new outburst of shouting, arguing, and minor horseplay, the first heavy drops of rain began to fall from a suddenly clouded-over sky. The noisy group took no notice, except that the girl in the white swimsuit with the deep, deep tan complained in a loud voice that she would not be able 'to get even five minutes of sunbathing'. But the rest of the beach, of course, promptly retreated in face of this unpleasant manifestation of unfair Nature. Towels were hastily folded and draped over husbandly arms, sandwiches were stuffed, sand-speckled as they were, back into

[115]

their plastic boxes, children were summoned, spades and pails were frantically gathered, and small procession after small procession made its way back to the cheerless prospect of boarding-house bedrooms.

When the invaders noticed this sensible mass retreat it seemed only to heighten their spirits, and they set off on a monster leapfrog chase all the way across to the other side of the beach, still ignoring the progressively heavier raindrops. Then the boys began a game of stone throwing, aiming first at one object until it had been hit and then moving on to something else, a discarded beach shoe, a seaweed-draped spur of rock, a soggy ice-cream carton.

The girls made bets on their prowess.

'Hit it, hit it, Mike,' screeched Jacky. 'I'll give you such a kiss if you do.'

'You'll keep your thieving little hands off him,' Jo, the pert redhead, yelled almost as loudly.

'I'll bet Bob gets it, I bet he does,' shouted Christine, who was blond and wore her hair piled high on her head.

'Bob,' the punster Herbert boomed out, 'I'll bet a bob he can't.'

'Darling Bob, hit it for God's sake, this rain's getting cold,' the white-swimsuited well-tanned Liz begged, her voice not much less strident than the others'.

And at that moment the rain abruptly came down in sheets.

The group looked wildly round for shelter. And there not fifty yards away was the old Shell Museum.

The words were painted out on a long sun-bleached board running all the way across the front of the single-storied barnlike building just at the edge of the beach. A broad flight of sea-smoothed wooden steps led up to its veranda and the open double-doors beyond.

The group set off like a stampede of horses toward it, the girls screaming as the cold rain struck them, the boys shouting in sheer animal spirits.

And that was when they met old Mr Peduncle.

He was sitting just inside the doors at a small oilcloth-covered table on which were scattered dozens of little shells, sitting where he had been all morning in his old brown-varnished wheelchair with the mottled brown leatherette seat and back. He was a big man, filling the chair like a great mound of wheat in his old shabby check suit, and he had a large head, deep pink in hue and mound-shaped, descending from a round skull covered with sparse white hairs to two big cheeks. He sat almost immobile only his hands moving restlessly but with method among the shells on the table, sorting and shifting, and his eyes, bright and beady behind a tiny pair of gold-rimmed pince-nez in the middle of that big expressionless face, darting quickly here and there.

'Hey,' demanded Mike, the handsome one, as they all crowded up into the shelter of the veranda, 'is this place open? Can we come in like?'

Mr Peduncle looked up at the white-painted board beside the open doors, its black letters fretted by the sea winds.

'Admission three pence,' he said in a voice that was quiet but plainly audible. 'Children, one penny.'

'That'll be a penny for this one then,' said the boy with the glasses, Dickie, pushing Jacky sharply forward.

Mr Peduncle took no notice. He slipped open the drawer in the table in front of him and brought out two rolls of cardboard tickets, one pink, one blue, a tall black leather-bound book and a small bottle of India ink with a steel-nibbed pen.

'There is also a two-and-sixpenny season ticket,' he said. 'Or life membership at three guineas.'

He turned back the cover of the big black book. Its paper, once white, had faded to a uniform shade of buff, but the ink of the entries on the first page stood out still bold and black. There were only seven names. The first of them had next to it the date: August 12, 1910.

Liz, the suntanned one in the white swimsuit, spoke sharply from outside on the veranda.

'For God's sake,' she said, 'pay him somebody, will you? I'm freezing.'

But she was to wait before she got into the comparative warmth of the sea-battered building. Her remark produced, as all remarks made in that company tended to, a whole minor outbreak of noisy verbal warfare.

The redhead, Jo, was first in with a crack.

'Freezing?' she called out cheerfully. 'Some people are never happy unless they're lying there baking in the sun.'

'Yes,' little Jacky came yelling in. 'And with half a dozen boys dangling round too.'

And then the blond muscular Bob came roaring to Liz's rescue.

'And who's never happy unless she's lying there doing something else? Eh, Jo girl, eh?'

'Nothing wrong with a bit of that,' Jo shouted back, perfectly unabashed.

'All right, all right,' Bob yelled, 'I'm queuing up, old Jo.'

'When you like, boy, when you like.'

'Hey, Mike, you hear that?' little Dickie called out, though the handsome Mike, or anybody, would have had to be deaf not to have heard.

However, Mike took no notice of the crack, smiling noncommittally and busying himself with fishing in an inner pocket of his bathing trunks and producing a handful of half-crowns. He sprawled them thunderingly onto Mr Peduncle's table, displacing two or three of the neatly ranged little shells.

'Make it season tickets for one and all,' he said. 'You never know, this old place might come in useful.'

Without a word Mr Peduncle brought out from his drawer eight green cards and handed one to each of them as they stepped past his table and into the dark of the museum itself.

'I'll switch on the electric light for you,' he said when they were all in. 'If it's overcast outside, it's difficult to see the specimens properly.'

'There's nothing wrong with a bit of dark,' said the blond Christine, seizing the muscular Bob's arm with one hand and the handsome Mike's with the other.

But Mr Peduncle was not to be put off. With surprising speed and dexterity he manoeuvered his wheelchair round, shot down the alleyway between the two rows of glass-topped showcases that ran the length of the big room, and came to rest beside a small door marked 'Private.' There he reached up to a pair of switches and clicked one of them on.

It was not a particularly strong light that hung on a chain from one of the wooden beams across the ceiling, but it did serve to show the accumulated specimens moderately well. There were hundreds of them. All the walls right up to the high windows were lined with them, hung in thin wire frames and each carefully labelled with its Latin name, its common name, and its place of origin. There were the pink and yellow and brown-spotted tapering cylinders of the volutes: the prickly murexes in an infinity of rock-coloured shades; the mitres, fit headgear for miniature bishops, darkly red in the interior or vividly orange-splotched; the augers, wickedly pointed and delicately spotted, the many cones with their extraordinary variety of pattern; the wide-spreading scallops, the rapas, the chanks, and the turrids.

And in the two long rows of glass cases were the prize specimens, big and small—the Chambered Nautilus, the golden cowries, little

Aristotle's Lanterns, a big startingly pink Queen Conch, the Lace-edged Strombus, the Wrinkled Scorpion, the Striped Helmet with its alternate lines of white and golden-yellow, and the delicately cross-hatched Dunker's Triton.

Mr Peduncle swished his old chair back to the table by the entrance, from which he could look out over the rain-beaten beach, and returned to his minute examination of the pile of shells he had been working on, apparently ignoring his visitors. The group wandered aimlessly round, with the solemn-faced Herbert the only one to pay much attention to the exhibits, and then only to read out an occasional label with the object of perpetrating one of his terrible puns, a diversion which did little to raise the spirits of the others, who seemed suddenly to have run out of steam.

But it was not long until the provocative redhead, Jo, always somewhat of a pioneer, hit on something a little more to the taste of her friends. She reached up and pretended to put her ear to a wide-mouthed conch hanging on the wall and then exclaimed in a loud voice, 'What are the wild waves saying?'

She pretended to listen more intently.

'Oh,' she shouted, 'there's a little murmur in here says someone in this room's going to get married before they're much older.'

She glanced significantly over at the handsome and moneyed Mike.

'Mind you,' she bawled, 'you never can tell with a boy.'

Roars of laughter. And all the girls now must reach up and listen to shells of their own. Impudent Dickie joined them.

'Listen to this, listen to this,' he shouted above the general hubbub. 'I've news here from the wild waves that an engagement broken by mutual consent may be renewed before long.'

Christine, the girl with the piled-up blond hair, stepped backward from the shell she had her ear to.

'Cut it out, Dickie,' she said, cold anger showing in her eyes and the taut line of her neck.

But Dickie was not one to learn.

'In spite of many and varied adventures,' he intoned, 'a certain person is confidently expected to return before long to her first and true love.'

And now Mike intervened. He came rapidly up behind little Dickie and seized his arms in a swift lock.

'Whatever there was between Chris and me,' he said, 'is over, and I'll thank you not to make any cracks.'

[119]

He stood holding the helpless Dickie, and began slowly and painfully twisting Dickie's arms behind his back. There was a smile on his handsome mouth.

'Hey, let go,' Dickie exlaimed, the pain putting an undertow of anxiety into his voice.

'When you've been taught your lesson,' Mike replied.

Little Dickie gave a sudden sharp gasp.

'Let him go, you great big bully,' young Jacky jumped in, loud as ever.

'When I'm ready to,' Mike replied.

Dickie let out a long whimper. The others stood round watching. It was an unpleasant moment. Then an unexpected voice broke in.

'Perhaps I can tell you something of the history of the museum?'

It was Mr Peduncle, swiftly and silently beside them in his dark wheelchair.

'I've been here thirty years, you know,' he said in those quiet but carrying tones of his. 'I've not actually left the place in all that time. It wouldn't be possible. They'd have to bring along a crane for my chair.'

Curly-haired, straight-nosed, cleft-chinned Mike, let little Dickie go. They stood looking at Mr Peduncle, uneasily suspicious.

'Yes,' he said, 'I just have a red flag I can hoist as a signal if anything should happen to go wrong, but otherwise I'm perfectly content. I have my work, you see.'

'Work?' said the pert Jo.

She glanced round at the yellowy varnished wooden walls with their rows and rows of shells, at the heavy old-fashioned display cases, at the table by the entrance doors with its scattering of black mussel shells and the little tiny white whorls of other British molluscs.

'Oh, yes,' said Mr Peduncle, 'this is my work. The study and comparison of shells. I pay the children on the beach a penny a bucket for them, and in summer it takes me all my time to go through what they bring in. And every now and again in a moment of discovery I hit on some difference in one particular shell that is significant, something that adds a drop to the ocean of knowledge. That makes it all worthwhile.'

It was at this point that Jacky began to laugh. She put back her seventeen-year-old head and laughed and laughed.

'Shells,' she gurgled out. 'Spending a lifetime going over and over a lot of mouldy old shells.'

'You think it humorous,' said the old man, unruffled. 'Well, let me

[120]

tell you that systematic study in any field of knowledge is always worthwhile. The making of observations, the carrying out of comparisons. They pay in the end. Sometimes in quite unexpected ways.'

A ray of pale sunlight came suddenly in through the high windows above his head, effacing the pale glare of the light.

'Hey, the rain's stopped,' shouted Bob, the muscle-boy.

He gave the pertly provocative Jo a friendly slap.

'Race you to the sea, Jo girl,' he yelled.

And in less than ten seconds the whole group were out.

While the sun shone they continued to sport on the beach, and the more timid holidaymakers, creeping out again with the better weather, once more were forced to give up most of the flat area of the sand to their activities. They ran races, jumping over any obstacles and careless of whom they bumped into. They played with the big rubber ball. They grabbed a child's plastic pail and started throwing water over each other, as well as over a good many onlookers.

Only the already deep-brown Liz dropped out after a while to take advantage of the shining sun and lie full length on the sand, improving on an unimprovable tan. For a little she succeeded in securing the muscular Bob as an attendant, but before long red-headed Jo, never content for anyone to be doing nothing if she could help it, came up and started whispering into Bob's ear, and he leaped to his feet and began discussing some sort of handicap race from one seaworn breakwater all the way across to the other.

They ran it too. Bob gave Jo a short start, and she won by a yard. And this, of course, in its turn started a series of other races between girls and boys. Jacky against Bob, squealing all over the beach when he outdistanced her. Jo with the same handicap against first Herbert, who dead-heated with her, and then Mike, whom she failed to beat and ended up tussling with, to the great disgust of a group of old biddies up in deck-chair row.

And eventually even Liz, deprived of any sort of male attention, got to her feet and issued a challenge to Jo. She nearly beat her too, for all the sultry laziness of her appearance; but at the last moment up by the edge of the pebbles Liz's breath gave out and she collapsed moodily onto the scuffed sand.

And shortly after this, as suddenly as they had come, the whole group disappeared. They made for the promenade, still talking at the tops of their voices, laughing and shrieking. And then came the roar of the engine of young Mike's sports car, and they were gone.

'Good riddance,' came the mutters from the staid row of deck chairs, also beginning to break up as the sun dipped toward the distant sea horizon.

But they came back again late in the evening. The noise of the car was heard coming to a squealing halt somewhere at the far end of the promenade, and some of them came down to the beach again in the soft light of the very last of the long day.

Old Mr Peduncle was taking the air on his veranda. When Jo and Bob glanced back at the wooden structure of the Shell Museum, after they had climbed over the long weed-decked breakwater and dropped down into the darkness on the far side, a tiny glitter of light struck off from the little pair of pince-nez that Mr Peduncle wore perched on his broad pink-coloured nose. It sent a brief flash out into the oncoming night. . . .

The group did not visit the museum at all the next day. Mr Peduncle saw them, of course. Anyone keeping even half an eye on the beach could not have failed to see them. They made, if possible, even more of a nuisance of themselves than they had the day before. From morning till dusk it was nothing but shouting. 'Hey, Mike.' 'Hey, Dickie.' 'Watch it, Herbert.' 'Go on, Jo.'

Mr Peduncle noted the facts, as he noted all the facts that came his way. He saw how friendly the redheaded Jo and the handsome, moneyed Mike seemed to be. He saw Dickie going to immense pains while the serious castle-building father was away at lunchtime to undermine the new and even more elaborate structure he had built that day, so that when the poor man came back ready to add a few last refinements, the whole thing collapsed as soon as he knelt in front of it.

He noted that the blond Christine had succeeded in playing off Herbert against Dickie most of the morning, to her visible satisfaction. He saw that in the afternoon Liz, who had actually managed to sunbathe all morning and was doing the same thing now, had persuaded both Herbert and Bob to sit beside her.

He saw all this, and he sorted through some two hundred shells that the penny-a-bucket children had brought him.

And on the next day, when naturally enough it did rain, the group burst into museum once more. None of them had kept the green season ticket, but Mr Peduncle did not mind.

'I remember you,' he said.

Again there was no one else in the big beam-crossed room, and again the group made a fair nuisance of themselves, here as elsewhere.

They had not been inside long, and the rain was still beating down on the black-tarred roof in a steady thrumming when the redheaded Jo announced that she must have a drink.

'Bob,' she proclaimed, 'you're the fastest on your feet, sprint along to the stand and get us all something to drink. I'm parched.'

'Yes, Joanna,' Bob said with unexpected acquiescence, considering how hard the rain was coming down.

He squared his shoulders at the entrance doors and in a moment was off, pounding over the pebbles below at a tremendous rate.

He must have kept it up all the way to the ice-cream stand and all the way back with his big paws wrapped round eight cartons of orange drink. But when he handed them over—'Here you are, Joanna'—he got little thanks.

She took one long suck through her pair of plastic straws and jerked her head up in disgust.

'Nuts,' she said. 'It's not cold, it's hot. Who the hell wants a drink of tepid orange?'

She flung her carton down in a corner.

'Tepid, is it?' shouted Herbert, the punmaker. 'When the chap at the stand poured it out he didn't look which *tep h'ed* used.'

The others were prepared to accord him the customary noisy groan, but Jo thought differently.

'Did you think your drink was cold, then?' she snapped at him.

He blinked. 'Well,' he said, 'I did think it was coolish, as a matter of fact.'

'Then you're as big a fool as you look.'

And then little Dickie caught the rough edge of her tongue. The rain had slackened, and he was the first to notice it.

'Hey, Jo,' he called. 'Sun's coming out. How about I race you to the sea? Same prize as Bob got the first day?'

Jo looked at him. 'No, thank you,' she said bluntly.

They left then, as noisily as they had come. And Mr Peduncle took his chair across to his private quarters at the back, fetched a walking stick, and used it upside down to jockey Jo's drink carton laboriously across the floor, out onto the veranda, and down onto the pebbles of the beach.

Then he went back to sorting shells . . . .

The next day was brilliantly sunny, for once really hot. And Jo died.

[123]

They had been playing the burying-in-the-sand game. Each of them in turn had volunteered or been noisily cajoled into lying in the soft dry sand just beside one of the high breakwaters and been covered all over by the others, with eventually only two plastic straws from an orange-drink carton left to breathe through. A sort of competition had evolved out of the game: it was a matter of completing the burial and then leaving the victim deserted for as long as possible.

It had begun as a practical joke and developed into a cruel-edged test of endurance. The rules seemed to be that each one of the party went off in a different direction, and the one whose nerve broke first and who came back to release the victim from the heavy covering of sand was the next to be buried.

More or less everybody on the beach was aware of the rules. The loud shouts in which they had been arrived at ensured this.

Jo, bright red hair encased in a bathing cap that matched the vivid green of her minimal bikini, was the last of them to submit to the burying process, and, so it appeared later, she had been covered up a little more deeply than any of the others so that it had really been impossible for her to have kicked her way to freedom.

However, she had her two straws to breathe through, and they were well clear of the sand over her. So she had been in no real danger. Until somehow a pail of sand had been tipped over the place where the straws pointed up to the serenely blue sky. The police surgeon gave it as his opinion that death would have come very quickly.

Of course, when the tragedy was discovered—little Dicky had been the one whose nerve had broken this time and who had come back to find the brazenly noisy Jo no longer alive—there was a tremendous fuss. The local constable had been summoned by Bob, who had run in his bathing trunks all the way through the little town looking for him, and in his turn the constable had sent for his superior officers from farther along the coast. Then the various auxiliaries had been brought in—the police surgeon, the ambulance men, the shirt-sleeved detectives with measuring tapes and elaborately operated cameras.

And the local C.I.D. Chief, glaringly incongruous on the beach in his heavy dark-brown suit, frequently removing his battered soft hat to wipe a sweaty forehead, had questioned at length each of the individuals of the group. And, for all that the town constable prowled stolidly in a sort of invisible circle round the spot where the interrogations took place, the main outlines of the matter percolated quickly enough to the remaining holidaymakers on the beach, all studiously pretending not to notice the activity going on near the breakwater.

It seemed that each member of the group had wandered far from the place they had buried Jo, in an attempt to hold out longest from rescuing her, and that none of them had seen any of the others after a couple of minutes from their simultaneous departure. Nor had any of them kept much of an eye on the time. They were all totally vague about everything. None seemed to have been back before any of the others, though they were all converging on the spot again when little Dickie had made his discovery. None certainly had been near enough, so they said, to have seen whether anybody else had chanced to go near Jo's recumbent body.

Much the same result came out of the slow inquiries which half a dozen detectives, sand trickling into their solid shoes, made among the other holidaymakers. Nobody had taken much notice when the noisy little group had moved away. They had got on thankfully with their own affairs, reading the newspapers, knitting, cricket playing, sand-castle building.

So at the end of an investigation that had taken almost the rest of the day, the C.I.D. Chief's final word to the remaining seven had been taken everywhere as the official verdict. 'Of course,' he had said, 'there'll have to be an inquest, though I don't see that it'll really get us much forrader.' And he had added a request that the group did not leave the district until after the inquest had been held.

The next day, which was also brilliantly sunny, the reduced group made a much-muted appearance, contenting themselves with sitting along the top of the wall overlooking the beach, and wearing reasonable clothes in spite of the heat.

But the day after, when massively building-up clouds threatened thunder and it seemed hotter than ever, their attitude was not so decorous. They continued to sit on the sea wall just above the black-tarred roof of the Shell Museum, but they were by no means as quiet as they had been the day before. They were, in fact, decidedly quarrel-some, and not at all careful to keep their voices down.

Little waves of shock ran all the way along the row of deck chairs at the foot of the wall, back and forth with each new outbreak from above.

Then the storm came. There was one eerie flash of purplish lightning which seemed to illuminate and transform the whole beach, and almost simultaneously a single peal of thunder cracked out from directly overhead. And then the rain began, pelting down with tropical violence.

The group got inside the museum in seconds.

Mr Peduncle was seated as always in his battered old wheelchair at the table by the entrance doors, his huge body still and mound-shaped, his hands moving over the shells spread out in front of him, his little bright-blue eyes sharp behind the tiny gold-rimmed pince-nez that seemed almost lost on his large face. He watched the seven of them push their way past into the dim interior of the shell-surrounded room and offered no comment.

The talk now was all of 'getting out of this bloody place' and 'to hell with telling that idiot Inspector'. They spoke to each other in sharp biting phrases, which echoed and clashed noisily in shadowy confines of the museum.

Bob, with his body almost bursting the blue T-shirt and white cotton trousers he wore, came and stood for a moment at the open doors, looking impatiently at the thundering rain. He seemed half-determined to repeat his dash through the downpour of three days earlier.

'Damn it,' he said to no one in particular. 'Jo was a nice kid, but she's dead, and there's nothing we can do for her.'

The declaration appeared to strike Mr Peduncle with particular force. His fingers abruptly stopped moving over the shells on his table as Bob pronounced the dead girl's name. He looked up at Bob intently.

'You will tell me it's not my business,' the old shell collector said, 'but you ought to wait a little longer.'

Christine, the blond with the high-piled hair, swung round.

'No,' she said loudly, 'it isn't any of your business. And when we're ready to go, we'll go.'

Mike glared out at the rain.

'Just as soon as this stops,' he promised. 'I'm off. The car's just at the end of the prom, and you won't see me for dust.'

Curiously, Mr Peduncle did not at that moment repeat his advice. Instead he opened the drawer at his table and felt about inside it. Apparently he could not find what he wanted, because after half a minute he brought out the tall black book, opened it with a little sigh which might have been audible to some of them had they not gone back to their noisy bickering, and tore out a sheet from the back. He then uncapped his bottle of India ink and with the steel-nibbed pen wrote a few words on the torn-out page, folded it over, wrote again, and finally tucked the whole into a pocket of his old check suit.

Little Dickie was now looking out at the rain.

'I think it's not so bad now,' he announced. 'Let's go.'

The statuesque Liz glanced through the open doors.

'Go out in this?' she said. 'You have to be crazy.'

And certainly the rain was still beating down with considerable force.

'Well, I'm not staying cooped up here more than another few minutes,' Dickie, once so cheerful, announced with distinct viciousness.

Mr Peduncle abruptly swung his chair along the sand-scattered floor of the museum and stopped it by the door at the back marked 'Private'. Here there was a lanyard running up through a little hole in the roof. Mr Peduncle untwisted the thin rope and pulled it energetically.

Herbert, the serious, saw him.

'What the hell are you doing?' he demanded.

Mr Peduncle looked at him through his tiny glasses.

'I was pulling up my red signal flag,' he replied tranquilly. 'There's something I want.'

He wheeled his chair back to the entrance doors but stopped now in front of his table instead of behind it so that he almost completely blocked the exit.

'There is something I ought to tell you,' he announced. 'I know which one of you killed Jo.'

They all turned to face him. He sat there in the doorway, the hands which had moved rapidly over the shells on the table, sorting and shifting, lying quite still now on the arms of the chair. For a long moment they looked steadily at him, and then, as though on a given signal, their glances flickered from one to the other, as if a wordless conspiracy was beginning to form.

'I mentioned the other day,' Mr Peduncle remarked steadily, 'that I have a mind accustomed by long training to observe first and then to classify. You were disparaging about that process. Yet observation and comparison have led me to my answer.'

The self-assured Mike gave a little twist of a smile.

'The armchair detective, eh?' he said. 'Well, name your name.'

'Certainly,' said Mr Peduncle.

At the placid conviction in his voice the unity of the group inside the dim museum visibly shivered. The glances that were exchanged now were no longer conspiratorial but probing.

'I have had a good deal of opportunity of observing you all since you came to the beach,' Mr Peduncle said. 'Both here in the museum and outside as you played at your various games. So when I learned how Jo died, I asked myself if one of you might be responsible. Certainly no one else was going to murder her. It is hardly likely that the gentleman whose sand castle you destroyed would go to such lengths for revenge. No, I had only to look among the seven of you.'

Again a flicker of uneasiness passed round the group. Only Mike resisted it.

'You said you could name a name,' he challenged.

'So I can,' replied Mr Peduncle. 'You see, when I asked myself who among you had reason to hate that girl enough to kill her but was concealing that hatred—and one of you was—the answer came to me soon enough. As I sifted over the facts about you, I hit on one quite evident thing standing out as decidedly out of the ordinary.'

'Here, let's just go,' Herbert broke in, looking not quite as sedately serious as usual.

'No,' said Mike, 'I want to hear the man.'

'No, don't go,' Mr Peduncle said firmly. 'Not until I've told you about the races you ran. And the one that had an unexpected winner.'

His big head moved suddenly, and the twinkling little eye-glasses were focused sharply on the muscle-boy, Bob.

'Yes,' said Mr Peduncle; 'you, Bob, are the fastest runner of the lot—even the girl Jo said so. Yet when you ran against her, she won.'

It was little Dickie who broke in here, staring insolently down at Mr Peduncle.

'You big goop,' he said. 'That was a handicap race.'

'Oh, yes, I know Jo had a head start,' Mr Peduncle replied, unperturbed. 'But she had exactly the same start over Mike a few minutes later, and Mike beat her easily.'

He let the silence fall over them. His eyes were fixed on Bob.

Bob took a step forward.

And at that moment there came the sound of rapidly running feet mounting the steps outside. Everybody wheeled.

A curious headless figure in bright red mackintosh shot up onto the veranda. Once under the shelter, it flipped back the plastic raincoat it had been wearing over its head to reveal itself as a boy of about ten.

'Hello, Mr Peduncle,' he said. 'I saw your flag up, and Mum said I'd better run over and see if you were in trouble.'

'Oh, no,' Mr Peduncle answered. 'No trouble. Just a note I wanted delivered.'

And he pulled the little folded slip of paper out of his pocket, leaned forward, and thrust it into the boy's hand. The boy took a look at what had been written on the outside. His eyes widened.

'Right ho,' he said, and instantly vanished from the veranda.

Mr Peduncle turned back to Bob.

'I think,' he said, 'you were just going to tell me that you lost that race on purpose. It was a bet between you and Jo, wasn't it? Rather a secret kind of bet, of course. But one which brought you your reward later that night. Isn't that so?'

Bob tilted up his smooth face. 'Yes, it did, if you want to know,' he said.

'Yes,' said Mr Peduncle. 'I simply used that instance as an illustration of the sort of unusual thing I was looking for, and of the danger of not taking all the associated facts into consideration. I might just as well have chosen to consider the race that Liz ran.'

He gave a flick to the wheel at his side, and the old brown chair swung round so that he was directly facing the dark-tanned sun-worshipping Liz.

'If the evident thing about Bob was that he could run faster than any of you,' he said, 'the evident thing about Liz is that she does not like running at all, and whenever the sun shines, she simply lies there enjoying it. But then on one occasion she challenged Jo to a race.'

They were all looking at Liz now, even Mike, and with a degree of accusation in all their looks. Here was one of them who had been a bit of an 'odd girl out'.

'Yes,' Mr Peduncle went on, 'and one could easily imagine a motive for Liz. Jo had taken the boys away from her. I mean simply that she had just taken Bob, who was sitting by her, off to play beach games. But I am sure Jo could have taken boys away in the long term too.'

Mr Peduncle's gaze moved quietly over the shells in their wire holders on the wall all round.

'You see,' he went on, 'there was another example of the small variation that seems to mean a great deal. But, of course, you have to look at all the facts. Some variations are significant, others are just accidental. And plainly this instance of Liz getting to her feet and running a race was just accidental. She had been deprived of her temporary escort, she hoped she could gain a victory over Jo, she failed. Not exactly a reason for murder.'

'Hey,' said little Dickie to the rest of them, 'you know what the old fool's going to do? He's going to cook up some sort of story about each one of us, and none of them's going to mean any more than any of the others. Look, the rain's definitely got less now. Let's get out of here.'

There was a chorus of agreement. The group began coming toward Mr Peduncle.

He made no attempt to move.

'I see,' he said, 'that I must admit I have been keeping you under false pretences.

'Then you don't know who it was,' Christine said sharply.

'Oh, yes, I know. But I was, I confess, a trifle unsure how the rest of you would take what I had to tell you. Suppose, I said to myself, they feel their loyalty to their dead companion is greater than any loyalty to society. They might combine to attack me and help the guilty one escape.'

It was Mike who laughed. 'You know, we might,' he said.

'That is why I tried to detain you with suppositions,' Mr Peduncle explained gravely.

'So we'll be off then,' Herbert said, recovering his assurance.

'You'll go, and six of you will never know who killed her?' Mr Peduncle asked with a flash of his beady blue eyes behind the gold-rimmed pince-nez.

Their steps slowed. They came to a halt.

'Oh, all right, tell us,' Mike said.

Mr Peduncle looked out of the open doors of the museum. It was still raining though not as torrentially as before. And the wet and dreary beach appeared totally deserted.

'Well,' he said, 'I told you that I was on the lookout for slight but significant variations in behaviour. And something that was said shortly after you came in here just now gave it to me. "Jo was a nice kid, but she's dead." Those were the words. And at once they put me in mind of something. Something curious.'

They were paying him an almost awed attention now.

'You all,' he continued, 'used to call her Jo. All except one of you. And he only started to call her Joanna after the first evening you were here.'

The gaze behind the tiny pince-nez traveled slowly round.

[130]

'Didn't you, Bob?' said Mr Peduncle. 'And didn't you switch back to calling her Jo after she was dead?'

Bob did not reply.

'Now, why does a young man suddenly take to calling a girl by her formal name?' Mr Peduncle resumed. 'Is this a significant variation? Well, coupled with the bet that Bob won, the bet that entitled him to that evening walk to a secluded spot behind the breakwater, undoubtedly it was significant. What was the somewhat coarse expression that Jo herself used? Yes: you never can tell with a boy. No, Bob, you didn't come up to expectations, did you? And Jo, when she was disappointed in her little treats, whether it was a boy or a carton of orangeade, could be unpleasantly spiteful, bitterly wounding, couldn't she?'

Suddenly Bob moved. He took one long bound across the width of the room, and from the shell-covered wall he snatched one particular shell. Mr Peduncle knew what it was at once. It was his prize specimen of Terebra Maculata, commonly known as the Marlin Spike, a sharp-pointed auger almost nine inches long, tough as steel, and no mean weapon.

'All right,' Bob shouted. 'You know a hell of a lot, don't you? Well, if you're silenced, I'll take a risk with my friends.'

And he launched himself with bunched athlete's muscles at the chair-bound Mr Peduncle.

Chair-bound, but wheelchaired. Mr Peduncle's big hands flicked hard at the wheels beside him. His chair shot forward at a sharp angle. Bob tried to turn to catch him, skidded on the sand-dusted floor, and crashed heavily to his side.

Before he even had time to get up, the local constable was thumping up the stairs of the veranda, in answer to Mr Peduncle's summons.

COTTAGE FOR AUGUST

by Thomas Kyd

Professor Hinman (mathematics) joined his colleagues in the Wurzhaus booth, and signalled for a sandwich and beer.

'You, too, I presume,' said Professor Parks (English), 'have looked on Beauty bare.'

'True,' said Professor Hinman, 'but less frequently than I should wish.'

There was an approving chuckle from Professor Mendel (Romance Languages).

'The phrase,' said Parks, 'was originally applied to Euclid. I wasn't thinking of you as lover-manqué.'

Mendel defrothed his moustache with a paper napkin. 'It's an odd thing. At faculty meetings we twitter. In class we drone. Here we talk like professors. Probably it's the beer.'

'We've been discussing absolutes,' explained Parks. 'What would you say? Is it possible to produce samples of pure beauty, pure love, pure evil, and so on?—like samples of pure sulphur or copper?'

Hinman looked thirstily toward the counter. He was slight and unimposing, but people liked to hear his opinions. 'There's no such thing as pure sulphur or copper. We call things *chemically* pure when they meet certain practical tests. I should say we might treat your absolutes in somewhat the same way.'

'Precisely,' said Parks. He tapped a column in his *Times*. 'And here's "chemically" pure evil. It meets any test.'

'Test? What test?' This from Professor Katz (Social Sciences). He lifted his thin, dedicated shoulders.

'Katz has been telling us,' said Parks, 'that this incident reported in the *Times* should be thought of as an explosion of social tension. Three New York urchins attacked a Columbia freshman for his pocket money—exactly one dollar and fifty-five cents. Then they calmly clubbed him to death.'

'I didn't say it was pretty!' Katz's voice rose several decibels. 'It's hideous, it's terrifying. But so is the sight of a python swallowng a sheep.'

Hinman received his beer with thanks, and took a reflective sip. 'You mean that clubbing a Columbia freshman is only natural?'

'In a sense, yes—for those particular boys. You've seen Morningside Heights, and how its grandeur rises on the edge of Harlem. Just take a look some time from below on 116th Street.'

'I have. When I taught there, I used to forget the switch on the subway at 96th.'

'Those boys weren't just clubbing another boy. They were clubbing the University and the Heights. In a way, they were clubbing their own ignorance and confusion.'

'But they took the dollar fifty-five.'

'Plus,' said Mendel fairly, 'one nickel-plated wrist watch.'

Hinman worked on his sandwich for a moment.

'I think Katz has a point.'

Parks sighed. 'Here we go! You science people can analyse good and evil out of existence.'

'Not at all,' said Hinman. He nodded at the paper. 'That's evil, but not *pure* evil—not so long as there's an explanation, even a bad explanation like Katz's.'

Parks was silent, suspecting a trick.

'My point's simple enough,' Hinman went on. 'How can you have pure evil so long as you can imagine worse? What if that freshman had been clubbed by a fellow-freshman? The evil of the act would have been less divisible by Katz's social factor, or any other factor. Pure evil should be indivisible.'

Mendel nodded. 'I get it—a moving scale, determined by the increasing stature of the evil doer and the decreasing size of his prize. It would be purer evil if he had been clubbed by a freshman, still purer if he had been clubbed by a sophomore, and so on up the line—

[133]

until he's clubbed by the Dean for half a buck, or by the Provost just for fun.'

Park's expression showed that he considered this levity in poor taste, but Hinman put it to use.

'Killing for fun, or for no reason at all, takes us out of the realm of evil into that of mental disease. The motive must be inadequate but understandable. Katz could put this better than I can, but how's this for a test? It approaches pure evil if some fortunate and intelligent human being, of recognisably normal tastes, is willing to deprive another human being of life for the sake of a petty personal convenience.'

They thought this over a moment, then Mendel spoke with unusual seriousness. 'I don't like your word "willing". Last summer I worked at the Huntingdon Library, and rented one of the little twin villas they have out there, perched on the edge of a canyon. Everything was fine except that the old lady next door had a queer little cough. It was like popping bubble-gum, and it came every fifteen seconds on the second. Our two places had a common drive along the ledge of the canyon, and soon I was calculating the chances of her car plunging over. My God, gentlemen, she was just a nice little old lady, but in my mind I was murdering her every day!'

'But you took no action.'

'The devil I didn't! I began pestering her with warnings about that drive as much as she pestered me with her cough. Bad conscience.'

Even Parks grinned, and Hinman nodded affectionately. 'You're in the clear, Mendel. I think evil impulses must be what is meant by "Original Sin". Acting on them in reverse is "Salvation by Grace".'

He paused in sudden recollection, his lips compressed. Then he spoke in a new tone.

'Still, a mere thought *can* be a sample of pure evil. So can an act of omission. Do you men have two o'clock classes?'

'Why?' asked Katz, glancing at his watch.

'I have an experience to tell you about. Mendel's story reminded me of it. An encounter with pure evil. I think it meets the test.'

Their reply was to order more beer.

'I warn you this is unpleasant—so much so that my mind had almost ploughed it under. Then a moment ago it came through clear again, as if it had happened yesterday. You're sure you want to hear it?'

They nodded.

'It was seven years ago, during the summer of 1949. That was my first year here, and the only time I've taught the summer session. It was hot, even for Cambridge, and Martha and the children almost perished. We had a top-floor apartment on Walker Street. It came to a boil when the sun hit the roof, and kept simmering all night long. We had been spending summers at a South Jersey beach, and scarcely knew what hot spells meant. The two girls were eight and nine. They and Martha just panted, and looked at me reproachfully. The boy cried. He was two, and had prickly heat that had become infected.'

Parks, who was a bachelor, stirred uneasily. Hinman reassured him. 'This isn't a tale of domestic squalor. That part's already over . . . At the beginning of August I knew we couldn't take it any longer, but the session had the full month more to run. I had to wait until the week's classes were over then on a Saturday, August third, I made an expedition to Cape Anne. Martha had a doctor's appointment for the baby, so I couldn't use the car. I arrived on the earliest train, and began phoning real estate offices from the Gloucester station. If I could rent a cottage for August, the family could get out of Walker Street, and I could come up week-ends.

'My chances, I knew, were dim. The heat had been driving people to the shore in droves, and this was past the mid-season rental period. My best bet, I had been told, was Annisquam, since it was slightly off the tourist track. I kept dropping nickels in the phone, and kept being told that I was wasting my time. The last office on my list gave me the usual answer, but with one slight addition. I might try the Annisquam antique dealer, a man named Mr Potts. I called up Mr Potts. There was no answer, but I got a taxi to his shop and finally tracked him down.

'Potts looked like a kindly old uncle. He was a typical Yankee trader—all homespun simplicity on the outside, and solid granite inside. He might have something, but then again he might not—he wasn't exactly sure. When he learned I was a professor, he seemed more inclined to think he might have something. He had a nephew at the University. Did I know him? I didn't, but we discussed his nephew at considerable length. There we sat among his dusty antiques, me eyeing him like a spaniel.

'At last he came to the point. Actually there *was* an empty cottage, a nice one at a reasonable figure, but in a sort of way it was already rented. A young couple had left a deposit in early June, but they hadn't appeared on August first to pay the balance and take possession. Time was a-passing by, and it didn't seem exactly right to take the risk that they wouldn't show up, and thus make the owner take a loss. I agreed fervently that it didn't seem right at all. But on the other hand, he said, it didn't seem right to risk arrangements with a brand-new person either—unless that person paid cash on the nail.

'I fairly lunged for my wallet. I hadn't seen the cottage, but I paid the rental in full. I also paid the telephone deposit, ditto gas, ditto electricity, ditto water. I also signed a number of documents in triplicate. When we were through, never had rights of occupancy been more firmly secured—nor the cash considerations.

'Potts then drove me to the cottage. It wasn't simply nice, it was perfect. It was completely isolated at the edge of a big estate on a crescent of water called Sapphire Cove. It faced west, so that you would get sunsets over the vast blue sweep of Ipswich Bay. Most wonderful of all, it was at least thirty degrees cooler than Walker Street, and within twenty feet of deep water.

'The granite in Potts had receded the moment the money changed hands. He showed me around like a friendly neighbour—four airy bedrooms, a neat kitchen, a huge living room, even a little country garden. We walked to the water.'

Hinman drew out a pencil and reached for a paper napkin.

'This is the part you must follow carefully. Here's the porch of the cottage. You walk over twenty feet of lawn, and you're on this level outcropping of brown rock. Ten feet below—just a nice dive—is the surface of the water, about twelve feet deep and so clear that you can see bottom. Alongside the rock is a tier of natural stone steps, leading to a bit of steep shingle with a rowboat beached on its edge. You get the picture? In ten seconds a person on the rock could get to that boat, and in ten more seconds could be out in the water. From the cottage itself the operation might take ten to fifteen seconds more.'

They nodded their understanding.

'When I asked Potts what the water was like, I got the usual New England joke. He winked and said it was "bracing". He also said there was a beach at the far end of the cove that would be safer bathing for the children. Since my girls were like little seals, I told him I wasn't worried. Then he went off in his car.'

Parks interrupted. 'You mean Potts isn't the villain of this piece?'

'Lord, no! Just a man who rented me a cottage.'

Mendel protested. 'Look, Hinman. In the annals of evil the miscreant is supposed to appear early and often. You're the only character left.'

[136]

A curious look flickered over Hinman's face. He seemed about to say something, then switched to something else. 'Two more "characters" as you call them are about to appear. Just let me go on. I went back to the cottage to wait for Martha and the children. I had called her as soon as the deal was closed. The plan was for her to drive up and inquire for Potts' antique shop, then he would guide her to the cottage. She was due to arrive about two o'clock. I decided to make up some of the sleep I had been losing, and stretched out on the porch swing.

'It was after one when I woke up, and of course I was feeling logy. When it dawned on me where I was, the thought of that water out front came to me like a blessing. I stripped to my underpants and stepped out to the rock. But before I could dive, I heard a motor and watched a car rounding the drive. It wasn't Martha.'

'Enter the miscreants,' whispered Mendel.

'It was a Mr and Mrs Durham.' Hinman paused, concentrating. 'I wish I could make you see them. We've spoken of fortunate, intelligent people. Add youth—they were still in their twenties or very early thirties—complete ease of manner and remarkable good looks. He was built like a decathlon competitor, and had the appropriately crisp light hair and classic features. She was a quite lovely brunette, with a stunning figure. Her shorts and striped basque shirt let you see her perfect tan, and let you guess at all the rest.'

Mendel murmured appreciatively. 'Noble man and nubile lady. I see them—or at least her.'

Hinman's failure to respond to this sally was the measure of his present dead-seriousness. His mood communicated itself to them, and they stirred a little uneasily.

'They were quite cultivated people and expert dispensers of charm —as I realised the moment they joined me on the rock. Sorry to inconvenience me, they said after introducing themselves, but they had just arrived, and Mr Potts had sent them to explain. By the way, it turned out that this wasn't so—the visit was their own idea. Explain what? I asked, although I had already guessed. On the drive was their sports car, top down, and back seat piled high with luggage, including golf bags and painting easels. Their explanation came with easy fluency. They were the couple who had originally rented the cottage. They had arrived a few days after the beginning of their month because this was the first weekend and Mr Durham's vacation had just begun.

[137]

'I realised I had a mean situation on my hands. In a sense, of course, they were in the right. All ten points of the law were with me, but that scarcely cancelled their claim. If a third party had been considering who should have that cottage—the Hinmans or the Durhams—his decision would depend entirely on whether he was their friend or ours.'

It was Katz's turn to interrupt. 'You say Potts isn't the villain of this piece. I'm not so sure. What about his purely mercenary ethics— minimise your own risks regardless of the other fellow's?'

Hinman waited patiently until Katz had finished. Then he held out his two palms like the pans of a set of scales. 'There were two factors that governed my reaction. I'll try to describe them as objectively as I can. First of all, the Durhams' approach was wrong. If they had been just a little shy and uncertain, discouraged but desperately hopeful, I might still have held on to the cottage as a family obligation, but I would have felt bad about it. But they didn't act that way. They were almost jolly about it. They either felt, or pretended to feel, complete assurance that I would just move over. They may have been using this technique—getting something by taking it for granted that it would be given—or they may just have been acting in character. Their whole attitude suggested that they were used to having their way. The world was their oyster, and bits of shell like myself could be casually flicked away. Behind their superficial graciousness, you could detect the hard core of egotism and the absolute conviction of superiority.

'The other factor is less creditable to myself. I was *feeling* their superiority and resenting it like the devil. There they were in all their handsome elegance, and there was I in my underpants. They were tanned, and I was the colour of a flounder's belly. He was big and I was small. She was fresh as morning, and Martha, after a month in Cambridge, was looking as if she had been through a mangle. In the back of their car were golf clubs and easels, not babies with prickly heat. Need I say more?

'I was scrupulously polite, but I am sure I wasn't quite able to keep surliness out of my voice. My dealings, I said, had been with Mr Potts, not with them. I had rented and paid for the cottage in good faith. My wife and children were on their way now. We needed the cottage, we had it, and we intended to keep it. I added that I was sorry and was sure Mr Potts would return their deposit.

'One thing about my remarks, they were conclusive. Their effect upon Mr and Mrs Durham was remarkable. They didn't argue and

[138]

they didn't scowl. Of course they didn't smile any longer either. It was as if they had suddenly turned into superlatively well-formed zombies. They still looked at me, but it was obvious that they no longer saw me. I felt extremely uncomfortable, especially since they made no move to leave. It's hard for a man to take even passive hostility from a beautiful woman, however little he may admire her, and I wanted an end of it. I mumbled a few more words of regret, made the obvious point that I had come out to swim, and then dived off the rock.

'Now this is bound to sound like an anti-climax. The moment I hit the water I understood why Annisquam was so cool. It was refrigerated by Ipswich Bay. I have felt cold water before—at Cape Cod and occasionally in South Jersey—but never anything like this. The July temperature in Massachusetts that year must have averaged ninety, but the water in that cove was nearer forty-five. I struck out in a hurry, hoping to warm up by activity. When I was about fifty yards offshore, I realised this was a mistake, I wasn't getting warm, I was getting numb. As I turned to hustle back to the rock, it occurred to me for the first time that it was just as well that someone was on it. The Durhams were there all right, in exactly their former positions, still silently watching me.'

Hinman paused as he drank the last of his beer.

'Have any of you ever had a stomach cramp?'

They shook their heads.

'But you've had a leg cramp?'

They nodded.

'Well just imagine the same kind of thing extending from your groin to your solar plexus and right through to your spine. Your body becomes one knot of pain, and your legs seem to disappear. I had intimations on the way in, while the Durhams were still above my line of vision, but the thing struck squarely after I had come under the lee of the rock—when I was only eight or ten feet from safety. I went under, but I flailed my arms and came up again. I let out a scream for help. Now you may not think I would be conscious of this, but I was— my scream sounded dreadful, hoarse and animal-like. One other thing about it: it was loud—loud enough to be heard on the rock, in the cottage, anywhere about the cove. Then I went under again.

'You've heard of the mental processes of drowning men—the flashing pictures of past events, and so on. With me everything was strictly contemporary and, believe it or not, there was room in a corner of my mind for embarrassment. I was going to be fished out by the Durhams. How could I hang on to the cottage after that? When I came up the second time, my eyes went to the boat on the shingle. The Durhams weren't there. I didn't yell again. The truth came to me like a revelation. They weren't going to be there.

'I'll have to take this up now from Martha's angle. After she got my call, she still had to take the baby to the doctor, and to stock up at the supermarket since I would have the car in Cambridge during the week. But with relief from the heat in sight, the two girls were co-operative and even the baby was less irritable. By eleven thirty she was packed up and away, and by one thirty she was in Potts' antique shop in Annisquam. They chatted a little, then he got in the car to guide her to the cottage.

'They were both surprised to see the Durhams sitting on the porch steps. Mr Potts had told her of the mix-up, but had assured her there was nothing to worry about. They hadn't kept their contract, so the cottage was ours. Still the sight of them rising politely as the car pulled up was rather disturbing. Both proved to be models of graciousness and charm. They helped unload the children and kept up a light banter about coming in second best for the prize. Where was I? I had gone in the water about fifteen minutes ago and was probably swimming around in the cove. They were wondering if it would be all right if they took a dip themselves before leaving.

'Then Martha saw me. As I emerged up those stone steps and weaved towards the cottage, I must have looked like a walking bundle of seaweed, but she said that all she could see were my black eye-sockets in my dead-white face. That, and the fact that I wasn't even looking at her. I was looking at the Durhams.

'Rage is supposed to release adrenalin. Maybe that's what got me ashore. I had gone under again after I saw there was to be no rescue, and somehow I must have scrabbled my way to the slope. I remember dragging myself out along the gunwhale of the boat. The cramp left the moment I was on the shingle, almost like a leg cramp when you step out of bed. But then I got sick. I retched everything out of my stomach, then lay exhausted on the stones. After five to ten minutes I heard the car pull up and the sound of voices.

'As Martha noticed, I didn't even see her. I didn't see Potts or the children. I saw only the Durhams. He had seen me as soon as Martha, and watched my approach with a complete poker-face—he was leaning nonchalantly against the rail of the porch. She was kneeling at the steps, her back toward me, playing with my little boy. I stopped behind her and said, "Mrs Durham." She looked up over her shoulder, and I caught her expression. What do you suppose it was?'

Katz and Mendel shook their heads. Parks cleared his throat to speak, then decided against it.

'Well, what would you think? Fear? Guilt? Shame?'

They waited.

'No,' said Hinman, 'none of those things. Just disappointment. Just plain, ordinary disappointment.'

His listeners lifted their empty glasses to their lips like synchronised marionettes.

'I told her to take her hands off the child and get up. Then I told both of them to start moving. I lost control as they climbed into their car and I began to yell "Murderers" at them. I kept it up until they had backed up out of the drive, then I passed out. It was all right. I met my classes on Monday.'

Hinman had known all three of his listeners for at least five years. Now they sat immobile, avoiding his eyes and each other's.

'Well, that's the story. I don't want you to comment on it because I know the spot you're in. You can't quite believe it. For one thing the setting is all wrong—atmospherically impossible. A summer rental at Annisquam. Popsicles and sand-in-the-shoes—of course. Pure evil—no. Furthermore, my facts may not be quite so reliable as I think they are. What if the Durhams didn't realise I was in trouble in that water?'

Hinman rubbed his hands over his eyes.

'In that case, you still have your sample of pure evil. Imagine *them* telling this story to *their* friends—about that ghastly little reptile who swiped their cottage from under their nose, then accused them of wanting to let him drown and his children become orphans. How could any human being think such a thing of other human beings! And all over what? Over nothing—over a cottage for August!'

DEATH IN
GUATEMALA

by Frances Crane

I t was Evelyn Proctor's idea. Charles, she said, let's take Ada
Peevyhouse with us this trip. Charlie Proctor asked who the devil
was Ada Peevyhouse. Why, don't you remember, dear? She was
one of my maids of honour when I was Miss Magnolia. That had been,
Charlie thought but never said, twenty years ago. Miss Magnolia had
been very beautiful. Charlie had plummeted for her sparkling blue
eyes, rosy little mouth, and curly brown hair. At thirty-eight Miss
Magnolia had put on considerable weight but she was still beautiful
and Charlie was content. They were ideally suited to one another
because Charlie loved to make money and Evelyn adored spending it.

'The poor thing has never been anywhere, Charles. She supports
her old mother. Teaches sixth grade. Always will. She's as thin as a
slat. Homely. Nose too long. Mouth too big. Hair in a bun. Nice
brown eyes and that's all. This will be a break for poor Ada.'

For me, too, Charlie thought. His reason for visiting Guatemala
was to invest. He was forty-five, one of those square-faced, short-
nosed blond Americans who age so agreeably. He was stocky but not
paunchy, self-made, rich and retired.

To fill in his time he invested or sought ways to invest. Evelyn
shopped. When outside her own country she went into perfect frenzies
of shopping and their home, especially the attic and basement, was
crammed with things she expected to have some use for some day.

[142]

The truth was, Evelyn hoarded. Nobody called it that. There was plenty of money, so why not? Charlie disliked shopping with his wife, so having the old-maid teacher along meant that he would be free to delve unhampered into oil, timber, and coffee in Guatemala.

Before their departure, Evelyn shopped, got fitted and permed, read up on what to wear at this season in Guatemala and what to buy there. The girls gave her going-away parties. She called the party-givers her p.g.s. —pronounced peegees. She kept a list of the peegees and promised to bring them gifts of woven cloth, for which Guatemala is famous. Evelyn always made the peegees her excuse for high-powered buying in far places, but had she ferreted into herself, she would have found that the peegees were incidental: she simply loved buying and owning.

Miss Peevyhouse also shopped—in a little ready-to-wear place—and acquired a perky suit with a short narrow skirt, a blue cotton dress with frisky ruffles climbing from the hem into a sort of bustle, and her very first cocktail outfit, a black taffeta, also bustley, with a bolero. She went quite overboard and had her hair cut.

Evelyn was exhausted when they took off. She sank down by a window and told Ada to sit beside her and keep an eye on her minks. Charlie sat behind them looking at oil maps. Evelyn yanked the shade down. Ada saw nothing all the way to Mexico City. Evelyn said there was nothing to see and since Evelyn was a seasoned traveller, Ada knew she was right.

In the Mexican capital Evelyn over-ate and suffered that well-known malaise, and Ada was able to show her gratitude by waiting on her hand and foot.

In the Guatemala plane Evelyn again pulled the shade down and Ada, too timid to crane through other people's windows, missed seeing the famous Mexican volcanoes. She didn't mind. She was too wonder-struck.

In Guatemala City there were more volcanoes in view from the airport taxi, but Charlie was scrutinising another map and Evelyn was saying she must rest up at once to be ready for tomorrow's markets. So Ada kept to herself the rapture inspired in her breast by the fairy-tale peaks.

At the hotel she unzipped Evelyn, helped her feel comfortable, and at last could go along to her own room. It was small, stuffy, and without a view, but there were flowers on the night-stand and a desk just as in the Proctors' de-luxe suite.

[143]

Breathless, Ada showered, changed to the blue cotton dress, and set out to explore the hotel. It was lovely. Now and then the corridors widened into glass-roofed patios filled with tropical flowers. There was a gorgeous lounge and, one floor up, a roof garden. There, Ada saw many mountains rising from the plain around the city. Their beauty was fantastic, unreal. Tears filled her eyes. Oh, what wonder! How lucky she was! How many people ever had the privilege of seeing something like this? She felt humble, blessed, and she loved Evelyn.

Charlie spoke twice before she heard him. He was with two Texas oilmen. One was grey, the other pink. He introduced them.

'Hi, honey!' the pink one cried. 'Peevyhouse? We can't have that. Ada? Now that's cute. Buy you a drink, Ada, honey?'

The grey oilman said, 'As I was saying when interrupted, Charlie, we can charter a plane and wrap this little country up in two or three days.'

Ada, blushing, went back downstairs, bought coloured post cards at the porter's desk and in a flowery nook wrote messages to her mother and her girl friends, all teachers like herself. She wrote out of a brimming heart. Believe it or not, this scene is even more breath-taking than in this picture. Wish you were here. Going back for stamps, she came on Evelyn at a table in the lounge drinking tea and eating sandwiches and cakes.

'Wherever have you been, Ada? I had to call a maid to help me dress. She had bare feet! They all have.' She frowned. 'My dear, that dress is *cotton*. This is their *winter* season.' She gobbled a sandwich. 'It's too short. The skirt is too tight. You really must watch that wiggle, Ada. You're not Marilyn Monroe, you know.' She ate some more cake. 'Why didn't you go to Neiman's? Even in their thrift departments the vendeuses have taste. I hate to speak about the raggedy haircut, but that style is for *girls*.' Another sandwich. 'Did you bring any of the clothes you usually wear?' Ada nodded. 'Good! That dress and your suit are suggestive. *Their* men aren't like *ours*, you know.'

Evelyn was so right. You've got a darling figure, honey, that salesgirl at the cheap shop had said. Skirts are short and tight. You've got the sweetest legs. Take a tip, dear. Don't be mad, but do get yourself a gamin haircut. Money in the bank, honey. Ada had studied up on geography, topography, Indian legens, and archaeology including the Mayan ruins, and here she was ignorant, not even knowing the proper thing to wear—or that *their* men were different.

They dined with the two oilmen at the American Club. Ada wore her black taffeta, and, as Evelyn advised, kept the jacket on. You've got darling shoulders, honey, that girl had said; but Evelyn whispered in Ada's ear that up to now she had supposed Ada wore falsies.

The grey oilman wolfed his food in order to have more time to talk about the oil business. The pink man loved to dance. Ada explained to suspicious Evelyn that the reason she knew the new steps, even the cha-cha, was because the teachers danced with the students in the gym and at evening school parties. After a sort of pavane around the room with his wife, Charlie wanted to learn the gay steps, too, but Evelyn said it was time to go to the hotel, what with the men taking off at five a.m. and a morning market ahead for herself. A night club, baby? the pink man murmured to Ada alone. She was shocked.

They made the first market while the vendors were still setting up stalls and laying out their wares. Ada wore a loose old blouse and an old skirt which hung straight down from the waist. Not a curve or wiggle could possibly show as she trailed after Evelyn and took charge of the newspaper-wrapped loot.

Evelyn haggled in one of her expensive outfits, including a costly hat and fifty-dollar shoes, which she planted in the market mire as she skilfully brought a $3 item down to $1.50.

She always settled for quantity, not quality. The battle itself was the thing. Hers was a tournament. Armed only with rudimentary market Spanish and an elemental knowledge of the Guatemalan currency, she made her jousts and tilts with gestures, grimaces, disdainful shrugs, and pretended walking-aways, which eventually mowed the very toughest down.

She bought goods. Yard goods. Tablecloths. Lunch cloths. Napkins. Masks? Too ugly. Baskets? Better in Mexico. Flowers? Ada suggested once. What for?

The markets closed for the siesta. As soon as they were open again, Evelyn was back. They dined evenings as they were and afterwards, in the Proctors' sitting-room, Evelyn gloated over her purchases.

The little country wrapped up, Charlie came back and for a wonder made no objection to accompanying them in a rented car to the famous Sunday market at Chicastenango. He had seen colourful Lake Atitlan from the air and though scenery is corny he wanted to see that lake close up. On the way to the great Sunday market they would spend Saturday night by the lake.

They arrived near sundown at a hotel directly on the lake. Evelyn retired at once, had her dinner set up on a tray, and had Ada close the French doors on the balcony and also the curtains to shut out the sheen of the water.

By the time Ada stepped onto her own balcony, twilight was almost at hand. The pearl-blue lake lay like a magic mirror within a fringe of purple volcanoes. A crescent moon hung above one ancient crater. Her throat tightened. Tears ran down her cheeks. No matter what lies ahead, I've seen this. Who am I, that God has granted me this?

'Hey, there!' Charlie called from across an inlet. 'Look out for that balcony—ours is shaky. Bridge is yonder. Restaurant's over here, Miss Ada.' When she joined him, 'This sure is some lake. Why don't you tell me about it, Miss Ada?'

Ada said that the lake was so deep it had never been plumbed, that the Indians were superstitious about it, and yes, a volcano did erupt now and then.

At dinner she got to speak of some of the things she had studied up on, including facts about the town with the famous market. After dinner they had nightcaps on the hotel veranda. Didn't you bring that blue dress, Ada? Finally and reluctantly, Ada, honey, we got to turn in—two more hours and we've got to be on our way again to that damn market.

What a market! Pretty much the same things, but more of them. Oddly enough the savage-looking Indian vendors usually spoke English, but they were combatants who called for every whit of Evelyn's boldness, prowess, ruthlessness, and guile.

Evelyn was magnificent. Ada was filled with awe. Charlie soon wandered off and found the Mayan Inn. If he could persuade Evelyn to lunch here—doubtful because she planned to be back in Guatemala City for the Monday morning market—it would mean another night by that mysterious lake. Just in case, he telephoned for the same rooms and was delighted when Evelyn proved amenable, because she was excited about something she'd bought, which she couldn't even whisper about because the Indians all around them had sharp ears. Ada was staying with it in the car. No, it couldn't be left unprotected. No, Ada couldn't come and have lunch with them. All right, Charles, send her a sandwich. If you insist. It really isn't necessary.

They were back in their room at the hotel before Evelyn shucked off the newspapers and Charlie got a look as the treasure. He gaped. It was pink, ugly as hell, and so heavy that Evelyn could barely hold it waist high. She stood framed by the French doors open on the pearl-blue lake, proud, victorious, radiant, smartly dressed in a navy silk suit and a flower-trimmed Lily Daché hat. Her blue eyes sparkled. Her rosy lips were curved in an angelic smile.

'*What is it?* Really, Charles! It's a Mayan sculpture. Nobody we know has one. You're forbidden to take them out of this country. But I'll manage. Come out on the balcony and see it before it's before it's too dark.'

It happened like that.

She was there and then she wasn't.

Her hat floated like a wreath on water, with not even a ripple or a bubble to show where she had gone in.

Ada blamed herself. She had discovered the treasure. She had told Evelyn it was taboo. So Evelyn had to have it. Charlie blamed himself. He hadn't warned his wife against their shaky balcony.

Was it premeditated? Or were the Indians right? The Indians knew about the treasure—Indians always know everything—and they knew that the American woman had been spirited into the lake because she had tried to own a Mayan god.

Everything that Charlie's money could do about Evelyn was done. Drawn together by grief, guilt, love and admiration for Evelyn—and an increasing pleasure in each other's company—Charlie and Ada waited by the lake. Every morning there were fresh flowers in the local markets. The hotel had an excellent bar.

Another baby moon was cradled in that same old crater before Charlie admitted, only to himself, that Evelyn would never let her treasure go and so was forever in the lake. Charlie and Ada spoke often now of Evelyn's face those last moments, saying it was almost saintlike. Evelyn had been blissfully happy. So they shipped the yard goods, tablecloths, lunch cloths and napkins to the peegees, and they were happy.

Was it premeditated? Was it murder? Or were the Indians right?

THE PURSUIT OF MR BLUE

by G. K. Chesterton

A long a seaside parade on a sunny afternoon, a person with the depressing name of Muggleton was moving with suitable gloom. There was a horseshoe of worry in his forehead, and the numerous groups and strings of entertainers stretched along the beach below looked up to him in vain for applause. Pierrots turned up their pale moon faces, like the white bellies of dead fish, without improving his spirits; niggers with faces entirely grey with a sort of grimy soot were equally unsuccessful in filling his fancy with brighter things. He was a sad and disappointed man. His other features, besides the bald brow with its furrow, were retiring and almost sunken; and a certain dingy refinement about them made more incongruous the one aggressive ornament of his face. It was an outstanding and bristling military moustache; and it looked suspiciously like a false moustache. It is possible, indeed, that it was a false moustache. It is possible, on the other hand, that even if it was not false it was forced. He might almost have grown it in a hurry, by a mere act of will; so much was it a part of his job rather than his personality.

For the truth is that Mr Muggleton was a private detective in a small way, and the cloud on his brow was due to a big blunder in his professional career; anyhow it was connected with something darker than the mere possession of such a surname. He might almost, in an obscure sort of way, have been proud of his surname; for his came of poor but decent Nonconformist people who claimed some connection with the founder of the Muggletonians; the only man who had hitherto had the courage to appear with that name in human history.

The more legitimate cause of his annoyance (at least as he himself explained it) was that he had just been present at the bloody murder of a world-famous millionaire, and had failed to prevent it, though he had been engaged at a salary of five pounds a week to do so. Thus we may explain the fact that even the languorous singing of the song entitled, 'Won't You Be My Loodah Doodah Day?' failed to fill him with the joy of life.

For that matter, there were others on the beach, who might have had more sympathy with his murderous theme and Muggletonian tradition. Seaside resorts are the chosen pitches, not only of pierrots appealing to the amorous emotions, but also of preachers who often seem to specialize in a correspondingly sombre and sulphurous style of preaching. There was one aged ranter whom he could hardly help noticing, so piercing were the cries, not to say shrieks of religious prophecy that rang above all the banjos and the castanets. This was a long, loose, shambling old man, dressed in something like a fisherman's jersey; but inappropriately equipped with a pair of those very long and drooping whiskers which have never been seen since the disappearance of certain sportive Mid-Victorian dandies. As it was the custom for all mountebanks on the beach to display something, as if they were selling it, the old man displayed a rather rotten-looking fisherman's net, which he generally spread out invitingly on the sands, as if it were a carpet for queens; but occasionally whirled wildly round his head with a gesture almost as terrific as that of the Roman Retiarius, ready to impale people on a trident. Indeed, he might really have impaled people, if he had had a trident. His words were always pointed towards punishment; his hearers heard nothing except threats to the body or the soul; he was so far in the same mood as Mr Muggleton, that he might almost have been a mad hangman addressing a crowd of murderers. The boys called him Old Brimstone; but he had other eccentricities besides the purely theological. One of his eccentricities was to climb up into the nest of iron girders under the pier and trail his net in the water, declaring that he got his living by fishing; though it is doubtful whether anybody had ever seen him catching fish. Worldly trippers, however, would sometimes start at a voice in their ear, threatening judgement as from a thundercloud, but really coming from the perch under the iron roof where the old monomaniac sat glaring, his fantastic whiskers hanging like grey seaweed.

The detective, however, could have put up with Old Brimstone much better than with the other parson he was destined to meet. To explain this second and more momentous meeting, it must be pointed out that Muggleton, after his remarkable experience in the matter of the murder, had very properly put all his cards on the table. He told his story to the police and to the only available representative of Braham Bruce, the dead millionaire, that is, to his very dapper secretary, a Mr Anthony Taylor. The Inspector was more sympathetic than the secretary; but the sequel of his sympathy was the last thing Muggleton would normally have associated with police advice. The Inspector, after some reflection, very much surprised Mr Muggleton by advising him to consult an able amateur whom he knew to be staying in the town. Mr Muggleton had read reports and romances about the Great Criminologist, who sits in his library like an intellectual spider, and throws out theoretical filaments of a web as large as the world. He was prepared to be led to the lonely château where the expert wore a purple dressing-gown, to the attic where he lived on opium and acrostics, to the vast laboratory or the lonely tower. To his astonishment he was led to the very edge of the crowded beach by the pier to meet a dumpy little clergyman, with a broad hat and a broad grin, who was at that moment hopping about on the sands with a crowd of poor children; and excitedly waving a very little wooden spade.

When the criminological clergyman, whose named appeared to be Brown, had at last been detached from the children, though not from the spade, he seemed to Muggleton to grow more and more unsatisfactory. He hung about helplessly among the idiotic side-shows of the seashore, talking about random topics and particularly attaching himself to those rows of automatic machines which are set up in such places; solemnly spending penny after penny in order to play vicarious games of golf, football, cricket, conducted by clockwork figures; and finally contenting himself with the miniature exhibition of a race, in which one metal doll appeared merely to run and jump after the other. And yet all the time he as listening very carefully to the story which the defeated detective poured out to him. Only his way of not letting his right hand know what his left hand was doing, with pennies, got very much on the detective's nerves.

'Can't we go and sit down somewhere,' said Muggleton impatiently.

'I've got a letter you ought to see, if you're to know anything at all about this business.'

Father Brown turned away with a sigh from the jumping dolls, and went and sat down with his companion on an iron seat on the shore; his companion had already unfolded the letter and handed it silently to him.

It was an abrupt and queer sort of letter, Father Brown thought. He knew that millionaires did not always specialize in manners, especially in dealing with dependants like detectives; but there seemed to be something more in the letter than mere brusquerie.

DEAR MUGGLETON,

I never thought I should come down to wanting help of this sort; but I'm about through with things. It's been getting more and more intolerable for the last two years. I guess all you need to know about the story is this. There is a dirty rascal who is a cousin of mine, I'm ashamed to say. He's been a tout, a tramp, a quack doctor, an actor, and all that; even has the brass to act under our name and call himself Bertrand Bruce. I believe he's either got some potty job at the theatre here, or is looking for one. But you may take it from me that the job isn't his real job. His real job is running me down and knocking me out for good, if he can. It's an old story and no business of anybody's; there was a time when we started neck and neck and ran a race of ambition—and what they call love as well. Was it my fault that he was a rotter and I was a man who succeeds in things? But the dirty devil swears he'll succeed yet; shoot me and run off with my—never mind. I suppose he's a sort of madman, but he'll jolly soon try to be some sort of murderer.

I'll give you £5 a week if you'll meet me at the lodge at the end of the pier, just after the pier closes tonight—and take on my job. It's the only safe place to meet—if anything is safe by this time.   J. BRAHAM BRUCE

'Dear me,' said Father Brown mildly. 'Dear me. A rather hurried letter.'

Muggleton nodded; and after a pause began his own story; in an oddly refined voice contrasting with his clumsy appearance. The priest knew well the hobbies of concealed culture hidden in many dingy lower and middle class men; but even he was startled by the excellent choice of words only a shade too pedantic; the man talked like a book.

'I arrived at the little round-house at the end of the pier before there was any sign of my distinguished client. I opened the door and went inside, feeling that he might prefer me, as well as himself, to be as inconspicuous as possible. Not that it mattered very much; for the pier was too long for anybody to have seen us from the beach or the parade, and, on glancing at my watch, I saw by the time that the pier entrance must have already closed. It was flattering, after a fashion, that he should thus ensure that we should be alone together at the rendezvous, as showing that he did really rely on my assistance or protection. Anyhow, it was his idea that we should meet on the pier after closing time, so I fell in with it readily enough. There were two chairs inside the little round pavilion, or whatever you call it; so I simply took one of them and waited. I did not have to wait long. He was famous for his punctuality, and sure enough, as I looked up at the one little round window opposite me I saw him pass slowly, as if making a preliminary circuit of the place.

'I had only seen portraits of him, and that a long time ago; and naturally he was rather older than the portraits, but there was no mistaking the likeness. The profile that passed the window was of the sort called aquiline, after the beak of the eagle; but he rather suggested a grey and venerable eagle; an eagle in repose; an eagle that has long folded its wings. There was no mistaking, however, that look of authority, or silent pride in the habit of command, that has always marked men who, like him, have organized great systems and been obeyed. He was quietly dressed, what I could see of him; especially as compared with the crowd of seaside trippers which had filled so much of my day; but I fancied his overcoat was of that extra elegant sort that is cut to follow the line of the figure, and it had a strip of astrakhan lining showing on the lapels. All this, of course, I took in at a glance, for I had already got to my feet and gone to the door. I put out my hand and received the first shock of that terrible evening. The door was locked. Somebody had locked me in.

'For a moment I stood stunned, and still staring at the round window, from which, of course, the moving profile had already passed; and then I suddenly saw the explanation. Another profile, pointed like that of a pursuing hound, flashed into the circle of vision, as into a round mirror. The moment I saw it, I knew who it was. It was the Avenger; the murderer or would-be murderer, who had trailed the old millionaire for so long across land and sea, and had now tracked him to this blind-alley of an iron pier that hung between sea and land. And I knew, of course, that it was the murderer who had locked the door.

'The man I saw first had been tall, but his pursuer was even taller; an effect that was only lessened by his carrying his shoulders hunched very high and his neck and head thrust forward like a true beast of the chase. The effect of the combination gave him rather the look of a gigantic hunchback. But something of the blood relationship that connected this ruffian with his famous kinsman showed in the two profiles as they passed across the circle of glass. The pursuer also had a nose rather like the beak of a bird; though his general air of ragged degradation suggested the vulture rather than the eagle. He was unshaven to the point of being bearded, and the humped look of his shoulders was increased by the coils of a coarse woollen scarf. All these are trivialities, and can give no impression of the ugly energy of that outline, or the sense of avenging doom in that stooping and striding figure. Have you ever seen William Blake's design, sometimes called with some levity, "The Ghost of a Flea," but also called, with somewhat greater lucidity, "A Vision of Blood Guilt," or something of that kind? That is just such a nightmare of a stealthy giant, with high shoulders, carrying a knife and bowl. This man carried neither, but as he passed the window the second time, I saw with my own eyes that he loosened a revolver from the folds of the scarf and held it gripped and poised in his hand. The eyes in his head shifted and shone in the moonlight, and that in a very creepy way; they shot forward and back with lightning leaps; almost as if he could shoot them out like luminous horns, as do certain reptiles.

'Three times the pursued and the pursuer passed in succession outside the window, treading their narrow circle, before I fully awoke to the need of some action, however desperate. I shook the door with rattling violence; when next I saw the face of the unconscious victim I beat furiously on the window; then I tried to break the window. But it was a double window of exceptionally thick glass, and so deep was the embrasure that I doubted if I could properly reach the outer window at all. Anyhow, my dignified client took no notice of my noise or signals; and the revolving shadow-pantomime of those two masks of doom continued to turn round and round me, till I felt almost dizzy as well as sick. Then they suddenly ceased to reappear. I waited; and I knew that they would not come again. I knew that the crisis had come.

[153]

'I need not tell you more. You can almost imagine the rest; even as I sat there helpless, trying to imagine it; or trying not to imagine it. It is enough to say that in that awful silence, in which all sounds of footsteps had died away, there were only two other noises besides the rumbling undertones of the sea. The first was the loud noise of a shot and the second the duller noise of a splash.

'My client had been murdered within a few yards of me, and I could make no sign. I will not trouble you with what I felt about that. But even if I could recover from the murder, I am still confronted with the mystery.'

'Yes,' said Father Brown very gently, 'which mystery?'

'The mystery of how the murderer got away,' answered the other. 'The instant people were admitted to the pier next morning, I was released from my prison and went racing back to the entrance gates, to inquire who had left the pier since they were opened. Without bothering you with details, I may explain that they were, by a rather unusual arrangement, real full-size iron doors that would keep anybody out (or in) until they were opened. The officials there had seen nobody in the least resembling the assassin returning that way. And he was a rather unmistakable person. Even if he had disguised himself somehow, he could hardly have disguised his extraordinary height or got rid of the family nose. It is extraordinarily unlikely that he tried to swim ashore, for the sea was very rough; and there are certainly no traces of any landing. And, somehow, having seen the face of that fiend even once, let alone about six times, something gives me an overwhelming conviction that he did not simply drown himself in the hour of triumph.'

'I quite understand what you mean by that,' replied Father Brown. 'Besides, it would be very inconsistent with the tone of his original threatening letter, in which he promised himself all sorts of benefits after the crime . . . there's another point it might be well to verify. What about the structure of the pier underneath? Piers are very often made with a whole network of iron supports, which a man might climb through as a monkey climbs through a forest.'

'Yes, I thought of that,' replied the private investigator; 'but unfortunately this pier is oddly constructed in more ways than one. It's quite unusually long, and there are iron columns with all that tangle of iron girders; only they're very far apart and I can't see any way a man could climb from one to the other.'

'I only mentioned it,' said Father Brown thoughtfully, 'because that queer fish with the long whiskers, the old man who preaches on the sand, often climbs up on to the nearest girder. I believe he sits there fishing when the tide comes up. And he's a very queer fish to go fishing.'

'Why, what do you mean?'

'Well,' said Father Brown very slowly, twiddling with a button and gazing abstractedly out to the great green waters glittering in the last evening light after the sunset. 'Well . . . I tried to talk to him in a friendly sort of way; friendly and not too funny, if you understand, about his combining the ancient trades of fishing and preaching; I think I made the obvious reference; the text that refers to fishing for living souls. And he said quite queerly and harshly, as he jumped back on to his iron perch, "Well, at least I fish for dead bodies." '

'Good God!' exclaimed the detective, staring at him.

'Yes,' said the priest. 'It seemed to me an odd remark to make in a chatty way, to a stranger playing with children on the sands.'

After another staring silence, his companion eventually ejaculated: 'You don't mean you think he had anything to do with the death?'

'I think,' answered Father Brown, 'that he might throw some light on it.'

'Well, it's beyond me now,' said the detective. 'It's beyond me to believe that anybody can throw any light on it. It's like a welter of wild waters in the pitch dark; the sort of waters that he . . . that he fell into. It's simply stark staring unreason; a big man vanishing like a bubble; nobody could possibly . . . Look here!' He stopped suddenly, staring at the priest, who had not moved, but was still twiddling with the button and staring at the breakers. 'What do you mean? What are you looking like that for? You don't mean to say that you . . . that you can make any sense of it?'

'It would be much better if it remained nonsense,' said Father Brown in a low voice, 'Well, if you ask me right out—yes, I think I can make some sense of it.'

There was a long silence, and then the inquiry agent said with a rather singular abruptness. 'Oh, here comes the old man's secretary from the hotel, I must be off. I think I'll go and talk to that mad fisherman of yours.'

'*Post hoc propter hoc?*' asked the priest with a smile.

'Well,' said the other, with jerky candour, 'the secretary don't like me and I don't like him. He's been poking round with a lot of questions that didn't seem to me to get us any further, except towards a quarrel. Perhaps he's jealous because the old man called in somebody

[155]

else, and wasn't content with his elegant secretary's advice. See you later.'

And he turned away, ploughing through the sand to the place where the eccentric preacher had already mounted his marine nest; and he looked in the green gloaming rather like some huge polyp or stinging jelly-fish trailing his poisonous filaments in the phosphorescent sea.

Meanwhile the priest was serenely watching the serene approach of the secretary; conspicuous even from afar, in that popular crowd, by the clerical neatness and sobriety of his top-hat and tail-coat. Without feeling disposed to take part in any feud between the secretary and the inquiry agent, Father Brown had a faint feeling of irrational sympathy with the prejudices of the latter. Mr Anthony Taylor, the secretary, was an extremely presentable young man, in countenance as well as costume; and the countenance was firm and intellectual as well as merely good-looking. He was pale, with dark hair coming down on the sides of his head, as if pointing towards possible whiskers; he kept his lips compressed more tightly more most people. The only thing that Father Brown's fancy could tell itself in justification sounded queerer than it really looked. He had a notion that the man talked with his nostrils. Anyhow, the strong compression of his mouth brought out something abnormally sensitive and flexible in these movements at the sides of his nose, so that he seemed to be communicating and conducting life by snuffling and smelling, with his head up, as does a dog. It somehow fitted in with the other features that, when he did speak, it was with a sudden rattling rapidity like a gatling-gun, which sounded almost ugly from so smooth and polished a figure.

For once he opened the conversation, by saying: 'No bodies washed ashore, I imagine.'

'None have been announced, certainly,' said Father Brown.

'No gigantic body of the murderer with the woollen scarf,' said Mr Taylor.

'No,' said Father Brown.

Mr Taylor's mouth did not move any more for the moment; but his nostrils spoke for him with such quick and quivering scorn, that they might almost have been called talkative.

When he did speak again, after some polite commonplaces from the priest, it was to say curtly: 'Here comes the Inspector; I suppose they've been scouring England for the scarf.'

Inspector Grinstead, a brown-faced man with a grey pointed beard, addressed Father Brown rather more respectfully than the secretary had done.

'I thought you would like to know, sir,' he said, 'that there is absolutely no trace of the man described as having escaped from the pier.'

'Or rather not described as having escaped from the pier,' said Taylor. 'The pier officials, the only people who could have described him, have never seen anybody to describe.'

'Well,' said the Inspector, 'we've telephoned all the stations and watched all the roads, and it will be almost impossible for him to escape from England. It really seems to me as if he couldn't have got out that way. He doesn't seem to be anywhere.'

'He never was anywhere,' said the secretary, with an abrupt grating voice, that sounded like a gun going off on that lonely shore.

The Inspector looked blank; but a light dawned gradually on the face of the priest, who said at last with almost ostentatious unconcern:

'Do you mean that the man was a myth? Or possibly a lie?'

'Ah,' said the secretary, inhaling through his haughty nostrils, 'you've thought of that at last.'

'I thought of that at first,' said Father Brown. 'It's the first thing anybody would think of, isn't it, hearing an unsupported story from a stranger about a strange murder on a lonely pier. In plain words, you mean that little Muggleton never heard anybody murdering the millionaire. Possibly you mean that little Muggleton murdered him himself.'

'Well,' said the secretary, 'Muggleton looks a dingy down-and-out sort of cove to me. There's no story but his about what happened on the pier, and his story consists of a giant who vanished; quite a fairy-tale. It isn't a very creditable tale, even as he tells it. By his own account, he bungled his case and let his patron be killed a few yards away. He's a pretty rotten fool and failure, on his own confession.'

'Yes,' said Father Brown. 'I'm rather fond of people who are fools and failures on their own confession.'

'I don't know what you mean,' snapped the other.

'Perhaps,' said Father Brown, wistfully, 'it's because so many people are fools and failures without confession.'

Then, after a pause, he went on: 'But even if he is a fool and a failure, that doesn't prove he is a liar and a murderer. And you've forgotten that there is one piece of external evidence that does really support his story. I mean the letter from the millionaire, telling the

[157]

whole tale of his cousin and his vendetta. Unless you can prove that the document itself is actually a forgery, you have to admit there was some probability of Bruce being pursued by somebody who had a real motive. Or rather, I should say, the one actually admitted and recorded motive.'

'I'm not quite sure that I understand you,' said the Inspector, 'about the motive.'

'My dear fellow,' said Father Brown, for the first time stung by impatience into familiarity, 'everybody's got a motive in a way. Considering the way that Bruce made his money, considering the way that most millionaires make their money, almost anybody in the world might have done such a perfectly natural thing as throw him into the sea. In many, one might almost fancy, it would be almost automatic. To almost all it must have occurred at some time or other. Mr Taylor might have done it.'

'What's that?' snapped Mr Taylor, and his nostrils swelled visibly.

'I might have done it,' went on Father Brown, '*nisi me constringeret ecclesiae auctoritas*. Anybody, but for the one true morality, might be tempted to accept so obvious, so simple a social solution. I might have done it; you might have done it; the Mayor or the muffin-man might have done it. The only person on this earth I can think of, who probably would not have done it, is the private inquiry agent whom Bruce had just engaged at five pounds a week, and who hadn't yet had any of his money.'

The secretary was silent for a moment; then he snorted and said: 'If that's the offer in the letter, we'd certainly better see whether it's a forgery. For really, we don't know that the whole tale isn't as false as a forgery. The fellow admits himself that the disappearance of his hunch-backed giant is utterly incredible and inexplicable.'

'Yes,' said Father Brown; 'that's what I like about Muggleton. He admits things.'

'All the same,' insisted Taylor, his nostrils vibrant with excitement. 'All the same, the long and the short of it is that he can't prove that his tall man in the scarf ever existed or does exist; and every single fact found by the police and the witnesses proves that he does not exist. No, Father Brown. There is only one way in which you can justify this little scallywag you seem to be so fond of. And that is by producing his Imaginary Man. And that is exactly what you can't do.'

'By the way,' said the priest, absentmindedly, 'I suppose you come from the hotel where Bruce had rooms, Mr Taylor?'

Taylor looked a little taken aback, and seemed almost to stammer. 'Well, he always did have those rooms; and they're practically his. I haven't actually seen him there this time.'

'I suppose you motored down with him,' observed Brown; 'or did you both come by train?'

'I came by train and brought the luggage,' said the secretary impatiently. 'Something kept him, I suppose. I haven't actually seen him since he left Yorkshire on his own a week or two ago.'

'So it seems,' said the priest very softly, 'that if Muggleton wasn't the last to see Bruce by the wild sea-waves, you were the last to see him, on the equally wild Yorkshire moors.'

Taylor had turned quite white, but he forced his grating voice to composure: 'I never said Muggleton didn't see *Bruce* on the pier.'

'No; and why didn't you?' asked Father Brown. 'If he made up one man on the pier, why shouldn't he make up two men on the pier? Of course we do know that Bruce did exist; but we don't seem to know what has happened to him for several weeks. Perhaps he was left behind in Yorkshire.'

The rather strident voice of the secretary rose almost to a scream. All his veneer of society suavity seemed to have vanished.

'You're simply shuffling! You're simply shirking! You're trying to drag in mad insinuations about me, simply because you can't answer my question.'

'Let me see,' said Father Brown reminiscently. 'What was your question?'

'You know well enough what it was; and you know you're damned well stumped by it. Where is the man with the scarf? Who has seen him? Whoever heard of him or spoke of him, except that little liar of yours? If you want to convince us, you must produce him. If he ever existed, he may be hiding in the Hebrides or off to Callao. But you've got to produce him though I know he doesn't exist. Well then! Where is he?'

'I rather think he is over there,' said Father Brown, peering and blinking towards the nearer waves that washed round the iron pillars of the pier; where the two figures of the agent and the old fisher and preacher were still dark against the green glow of the water. 'I mean in that sort of net thing that's tossing about in the sea.'

With whatever bewilderment, Inspector Grinstead took the upper hand again with a flash, and strode down the beach.

'Do you mean to say,' he cried, 'that the murderer's body is in the old boy's net?'

Father Brown nodded as he followed down the shingly slope; and, even as they moved, little Muggleton the agent turned and began to climb the same shore, his mere dark outline a pantomime of amazement and discovery.

'It's true, for all we said,' he gasped. 'The murderer did try to swim ashore and was drowned, of course, in that weather. Or else did he really commit suicide. Anyhow, he drifted dead into Old Brimstone's fishing-net, and that's what the old maniac meant when he said he fished for dead men.'

The Inspector ran down the shore with an agility that outstripped them all, and was heard shouting out orders. In a few moments the fishermen and a few bystanders, assisted by the policemen, had hauled the net into shore, and rolled it with its burden on to the wet sands that still reflected the sunset. The secretary looked at what lay on the sands and the words died on his lips. For what lay on the sands was indeed the body of a gigantic man in rags, with huge shoulders somewhat humped and bony eagle face; and a great red ragged woollen scarf or comforter, sprawled along the sunset sands like a great stain of blood. But Taylor was staring not at the gory scarf or the fabulous stature, but at the face; and his own face was a conflict of incredulity and suspicion.

The Inspector instantly turned to Muggleton with a new air of civility.

'This certainly confirms your story,' he said. And until he heard the tone of those words, Muggleton had never guessed how almost universally his story had been disbelieved. Nobody had believed him. Nobody but Father Brown.

Therefore, seeing Father Brown edging away from the group, he made a movement to depart in his company; but even then he was brought up rather short by the discovery that the priest was once more being drawn away by the deadly attractions of the funny little automatic machines. He even saw the reverend gentleman fumbling for a penny. He stopped, however, with the penny poised in his finger and thumb, as the secretary spoke for the last time in his loud discordant voice.

'And I suppose we may add,' he said, 'that the monstrous and imbecile charges against me are also at an end.'

'My dear sir,' said the priest, 'I never made any charges against you. I'm not such a fool as to suppose you were likely to murder your master in Yorkshire and then come down here to fool about with his luggage.

All I said was that I could make out a better case against you than you were making out so vigorously against poor Mr Muggleton. All the same, if you really want to learn the truth about this business (and I assure you the truth isn't generally grasped yet), I can give you a hint even from your own affairs. It *is* rather a rum and significant thing that Mr Bruce the millionaire had been unknown to all his usual haunts and habits for weeks before he was really killed. As you seem to be a promising amateur detective, I advise you to work on that line.'

'What do you mean?' asked Taylor sharply.

But he got no answer out of Father Brown, who was once more completely concentrated on jiggling the little handle of the machine, that made one doll jump out and then another doll jump after it.

'Father Brown,' said Muggleton, his old annoyance faintly reviving: 'Will you tell me why you like that fool thing so much?'

'For one reason,' replied the priest, peering closely into the glass puppet-show. 'Because it contains the secret of this tragedy.'

Then he suddenly straightened himself and looked quite seriously at his companion.

'I knew all along,' he said, 'that you were telling the truth and the opposite of the truth.'

Muggleton could only stare at a return of all the riddles.

'It's quite simple,' added the priest, lowering his voice. 'That corpse with the scarlet scarf over there is the corpse of Braham Bruce the millionaire. There won't be any other.'

'But the two men—' began Muggleton, and his mouth fell open.

'Your description of the two men was quite admirably vivid,' said Father Brown. 'I assure you I'm not at all likely to forget it. If I may say so, you have a literary talent; perhaps journalism would give you more scope than detection. I believe I remember practically each point about each person. Only, you see, queerly enough, each point affected you in one way and me in exactly the opposite way. Let's begin with the first you mentioned. You said that the first man you saw had an indescribable air of authority and dignity. And you said to yourself, "That's the Trust Magnate, the great merchant prince, the ruler of markets." But when I heard about the air of dignity and authority, I said to myself, "That's the actor; everything about him is the actor." You don't get that look by being President of the Chain Store Amalgamation Company. You get that look by being Hamlet's Father's Ghost, or Julius Caesar, or King Lear, and you never altogether lose it. You couldn't see enough of his clothes to tell

[161]

whether they were really seedy, but you saw a strip of fur and a sort of faintly fashionable cut; and I said to myself again, "The actor." Next, before we go into details about the other man, notice one thing about him evidently absent from the first man. You said the second man was not only ragged but unshaven to the point of being bearded. Now we have all seen shabby actors, dirty actors, drunken actors, utterly disreputable actors. But such a thing as a scrub-bearded actor, in a job or even looking round for a job, has scarcely been seen in this world. On the other hand, shaving is often almost the first thing to go, with a gentleman or a wealthy eccentric who is really letting himself go to pieces. Now we have every reason to believe that your friend the millionaire was letting himself go to pieces. His letter was the letter of a man who had already gone to pieces. But it wasn't only negligence that made him look poor and shabby. Don't you understand that the man was practically in hiding? That was why he didn't go to his hotel; and his own secretary hadn't seen him for weeks. He was a millionaire; but his whole object was to be a completely disguised millionaire. Have you ever read "The Woman in White"? Don't you remember that the fashionable and luxurious Count Fosco, fleeing for his life before a secret society, was found stabbed in the blue blouse of a common French workman? Then let us go back for a moment to the demeanour of these men. You saw the first man calm and collected and you said to yourself, "That's the innocent victim"; though the innocent victim's own letter wasn't at all calm and collected. I heard he was calm and collected; and I said to myself, "That's the murderer." Why should he be anything else but calm and collected? He knew what he was going to do. He had made up his mind to do it for a long time; if he had ever had any hesitation or remorse he had hardened himself against them before he came on the scene — in his case, we might say, on the stage. He wasn't likely to have any particular stage-fright. He didn't pull out his pistol and wave it about; why should he? He kept it in his pocket till he wanted it; very likely he fired from his pocket. The other man fidgeted with his pistol because he was as nervous as a cat, and very probably had never had a pistol before. He did it for the same reason that he rolled his eyes; and I remember that, even in your own unconscious evidence, it is particularly stated that he rolled them *backwards*. In fact, he was looking behind him. In fact, he was not the pursuer but the pursued. But because you happened to see the first man first, you couldn't help thinking of the other man as coming up behind him. In mere mathematics and mechanics, each of them was running after the other — just like the others.'

[162]

'What others?' inquired the dazed detective.

'Why, these,' cried Father Brown, striking the automatic machine with the little wooden spade, which had incongruously remained in his hand throughout these murderous mysteries. 'These little clockwork dolls that chase each other round and round for ever. Let us call them Mr Blue and Mr Red, after the colour of their coats. I happened to start off with Mr Blue, and so the children said that Mr Red was running after him; but it would have looked exactly the contrary if I had started with Mr Red.'

'Yes, I begin to see,' said Muggleton; 'and I suppose all the rest fits in. The family likeness, of course, cuts both ways, and they never saw the murderer leaving the pier—'

'They never looked for the murderer leaving the pier,' said the other. 'Nobody told them to look for a quiet clean-shaven gentleman in an astrakhan coat. All the mystery of his vanishing revolved on your description of a hulking fellow in a red neckcloth. But the simple truth was that the actor in the astrakhan coat murdered the millionaire with the red rag, and there is the poor fellow's body. It's just like the red and blue dolls; only, because you saw one first, you guessed wrong about which was red with vengeance and which was blue with funk.'

At this point two or three children began to straggle across the sands, and the priest waved them to him with the wooden spade, theatrically tapping the automatic machine. Muggleton guessed it was mainly to prevent them straying towards the horrible heap on the shore.

'One more penny left in the world,' said Father Brown, 'and then we must go home to tea. Do you know, Doris, I rather like those revolving games, that just go round and round like the Mulberry-Bush. After all, God made all the suns and stars to play Mulberry-Bush. But those other games, where one must catch up with another, where runners are rivals and run neck and neck and outstrip each other; well—much nastier things seem to happen. I like to think of Mr Red and Mr Blue always jumping with undiminished spirits; all free and equal; and never hurting each other. "Fond lover, never, never, wilt thou kiss—or kill." Happy, happy Mr Red!

He cannot change; though thou hast not thy bliss,
For ever wilt thou jump; and he be Blue.

Reciting this remarkable quotation from Keats, with some emotion, Father Brown tucked the little spade under one arm, and giving a hand to two of the children, stumped solemnly up the beach to tea.

LOVE COMES TO
MISS LUCY

by Q. Patrick

T hey sat around the breakfast table, their black coats hanging sleevelessly from their shoulders in the Mexican tourist fashion. They looked exactly what they were — three middle-aged ladies from the most respectable suburbs of Philadelphia.

'*Más café*,' demanded Miss Ellen Yarnell from a recalcitrant waitress. Miss Ellen had travelled before and knew how to get service in foreign countries.

'And *más* hot — *caliente*,' added Mrs Vera Truegood who was the oldest of the three and found the mornings in Mexico City chilly.

Miss Lucy Bram didn't say anything. She looked at her watch to see if it was time for Mario to arrive.

The maid dumped a tin pot of lukewarm coffee on the table.

'Don't you think, Lucy,' put in Ellen, 'that it would be a good idea if we got Mario to come earlier in the morning? He could take us out somewhere so we could get a nice hot breakfast.'

'Mario does quite enough for us already.' Miss Lucy flushed slightly as she spoke of the young Mexican guide. She flushed because her friends had teased her about him, and because she had just been thinking of his strong, rather cruel Mexican legs as she had seen them yesterday when he rowed them through the floating gardens of Xochimilco.

Miss Lucy Bram had probably never thought about a man's legs (and certainly not at breakfast time) in all her fifty-two years of polite,

[164]

Quakerish spinsterhood. This was another disturbing indication of the change which had taken place in her since her cautious arrival in Mexico a month before. The change, perhaps, had in fact happened earlier, when the death of an ailing father had left her suddenly and bewilderingly rich, both in terms of bonds and a release from bondage. But Miss Lucy had only grown aware of it later, here in Mexico—on the day when she found Mario in Taxco.

It had been an eventful day for Miss Lucy. Perhaps the most eventful of all these Mexican days. Her sense of freedom, which still faintly shocked her sedate soul, had awakened with her in her sunny hotel bedroom. It had hovered over her patio breakfast with her two companions (whose expenses she was discreetly paying). It had been quenched neither by Vera's complaints of the chill mountain air nor by Ellen's travel-snobbish remark that Taxco was sweet, of course, but nowhere near as picturesque as the hill towns of Tuscany.

To Miss Lucy, with only Philadelphia and Bar Habor behind her, Taxco's pink weathered roofs and pink, feathery-steepled churches were the impossible realization of a dream. 'A rose-red city half as old as time . . . .'

The raffish delight of 'foreignness', of being her own mistress, had reached a climax when she saw The Ring.

She saw it in one of the little silversmith shops below the leafy public square. It caught her attention while Vera and Ellen were haggling with the proprietor over a burro pin. It wasn't a valuable ring. To her Quaker eyes, severely trained against the ostentatious, it was almost vulgar. A large, flamboyant white sapphire on a slender band of silver. But there was something tempting in its brash sparkle. She slipped it on her finger and it flashed the sunlight back at her. It made her mother's prim engagement ring, which was worth certainly fifty times as much, fade out of the picture. Miss Lucy felt unaccountably gay, and then self-conscious. With a hurried glance at the stuffy black backs of Vera and Ellen, she tried to take it off her finger.

It would not come off. And while she was still struggling Vera and Ellen joined her, inspecting it will little cries of admiration.

'My, Lucy, it's darling.'

'Pretty as an engagement ring.'

Miss Lucy flushed. 'Don't be foolish. It's much too young for me. I just tried it on. I don't seem to be able . . .'

She pulled at the ring again. The Mexican who owned the shop hovered at her side, purring compliments.

'Go on, Lucy,' said Ellen daringly. 'Buy it.'

'Really, it's annoying. But since I can't seem to get it off, I suppose I'll have to . . ..'

Miss Lucy bought the white sapphire ring for a sum which was higher than its value, but which was still negligible to her. While Ellen who handled all the financial aspects of the trip because she was 'so clever' at those things, settled with the proprietor, Miss Lucy said to Vera:

'I'll get it off with soap and water back at the hotel.'

But she didn't take it off. Somehow her new disturbing happiness had become centred in it.

In Taxco Miss Lucy's energy seemed boundless. That evening, before dinner, while Vera and Ellen were resting aching feet in their rooms, she decided upon a second trip to the Church of Santa Prisca which dominated the public square. Her visit had been marred by the guidebook chatter of her companions. She wanted to be alone in that cool, tenebrous interior, to try to get the feeling of its atmosphere, so different from the homespun godliness of her own Quaker meeting-house at home.

As she stepped through the ornate wooden doors, the fantastic churrigueresque altar of gold-leaf flowers and cherubs gleamed richly at her. An ancient peasant woman, sheathed in black, was offering a guttering candle to an image of the Virgin. A mongrel dog ran past her into the church, looked round and ran out again. The splendour and the small humanities of the scene had a curious effect upon Miss Lucy. This stood for all that was 'popish' and alien and yet it seemed to call her. On an impulse which she less than half understood, she dropped to her knees, in imitation of the peasant woman, and crossed herself, the sapphire ring flashing with some of the exotic quality of the church itself.

Miss Lucy remained kneeling only a short time, but before she rose she was conscious of a presence close to her on the right. She glanced around and saw that a Mexican youth in a spotless white suit had entered the church and was kneeling a few yards away, the thick black hair shining on his reverently bent head. As she got up, his gaze met hers. It was only a momentary glance, but she retained a vivid impression of his face. Honey-brown skin and the eyes—particularly the eyes—dark and patient with a gentle, passive beauty. Somehow that brief contact gave her the sensation of seeing a little into the mind of this strange city of strange people. Remembering him, her

[166]

spontaneous genuflection seemed somehow the right thing to have done. Not, of course, that she would ever speak of it to Vera and Ellen.

She left the church, happy and ready for dinner. The evening light had faded, and as she passed from the crowded Xocalo into the deserted street which led to the hotel, it was almost night. Her footsteps echoed unfamiliarly against the rough cobblestones. The sound seemed to emphasize her loneliness. A single male figure, staggering slightly, was coming up the hill now toward her. Miss Lucy was no coward, but with a tingle of alarm she realized that the oncomer was drunk. She looked around. There was no one else in sight. A weak impulse urged her to return to the Xocalo, but she suppressed it. After all, she was an American, she would not be harmed. She marched steadfastly on.

But the seeds of fear were there, and when she came abreast of the man, he peered at her and swung toward her. He was bearded and shabby and his breath reeked of tequila. He started a stream of Spanish which she couldn't understand. She knew he was begging and, trained to organized charities, Miss Lucy had no sympathy for street beggars. She shook her head firmly and tried to move on. But a dirty hand grabbed her sleeve, and the soft whining words continued. She freed her arm more violently than she intended. Anger glinted in the man's eyes. He raised his arm in an indignant gesture.

Although he was obviously not intending to strike her, Miss Lucy recoiled instinctively and as she did so, caught her high heel in the uneven cobbles and fell rather ungracefully to the ground. She lay there, her ankle twisted beneath her while the man stood threateningly, it seemed, over her.

For a moment, Miss Lucy felt panic—blind overwhelming terror completely unjustified by the almost farcical unpleasantness of the situation.

And then from the shadows, another man appeared. A slight man in a white suit. Miss Lucy could not see his face but she knew that it was the boy from the church. She was conscious of his white-sleeved arm flashing toward the beggar and pushing him away.

She saw the beggar reel backwards and shuffle mutteringly off. Then she was aware of a young face close to her own, and a strong arm was helping to rise. She could not understand all her rescuer said, but his voice was gentle and concerned.

'Qué malo,' he said, grinning in the direction of the departing beggar. *Malo mexicano.*' The teeth gleamed white in the moonlight. 'Me Mario, from the church, yes? Me help the *señora*, no?'

He almost carried Miss Lucy, who had twisted her ankle painfully, back to the hotel and right to her room where she was turned over to the flustered administrations of Vera and Ellen.

As Mario hovered solicitously around, Ellen grabbed at her pocketbook with a whispered: 'How much, Lucy?'

But here Miss Lucy showed a will of her own. 'No. Money would be an insult.'

And Mario, who seemed to understand, said '*Gracias, Señora.*' And after several sentences, in which Miss Lucy understood only the word *madre*, he picked up Miss Lucy's left hand—the one with the new sapphire ring—kissed it and then bowed himself smilingly out.

That was how Mario had come into their lives. And having come in, it was apparent that he intended to stay. Next morning he came to the hotel to inquire for Miss Lucy and she saw him squarely for the first time. He was not really handsome. His long-lashed eyes were perhaps a shade too close together. His slight moustache above the full-lipped mouth was perhaps too long. But his figure, though slight, was powerful, and there was something about him that inspired both affection and confidence.

He was, he explained, a student anxious to make a little money on vacation. He wanted to be a guide to the *Señoras*, and since Miss Lucy could not walk with her twisted ankle, he suggested that he hire a car and act as their chauffeur. The fee he requested was astonishingly small and he stubbornly refused to accept more.

The next day he hired a car at a low price which more than satisfied even the parsimonious Miss Ellen and from then on he drove the ladies around to points of interest with as much care and consideration as if they had been his three *madres*.

His daily appearances, always in spotless white, were a constant delight to Miss Lucy—indeed, to all three of them. He was full of plans for their entertainment. One day he drove them around the base of Mount Popocatepetl and for several hours they were able to rhapsodize over what is certainly one of the most beautiful and mysterious mountains in the world. And for a moment when they happened to be alone together, staring at the dazzling whiteness of the mountain's magnificent summit, Miss Lucy felt her hand taken in Mario's firm brown one and softly squeezed.

It was, of course, his way of telling her, despite the difficulties of language, that they were sharing a great Mexican experience and he was glad they were sharing it together. Under his touch the large sapphire in the ring pressed into her finger painfully, but another feeling, different from pain, stirred in her.

After the Popocatepetl trip, Miss Lucy decided that it was time to leave Taxco and take up their quarters in Mexico City.

She instructed Ellen to dismiss Mario—to give him an extra hundred pesos and to let him know politely and yet firmly that his services were terminated. But Ellen might as well have tried to dispel Popocatepetl or bid it remove itself into the sea. Mario just laughed at her, waved away the hundred pesos, and referred himself directly to Miss Lucy. There were bad Mexicans in Mexico City. He threw out his strong, honey-gold hands. He would take care of them. No, of no importance was the money of *Señora* Ellen (the other two women were always *Señora* to him, Miss Lucy alone was *Señorita*). The important thing was that he should show them everything. Here the strong arms waved to embrace the sun, the sky, the mountains, all of Mexico. And the dark eyes with the too thick lashes embraced Miss Lucy too.

And Miss Lucy, against some deeply rooted instinct, yielded.

Mario went with them to Mexico City.

It was the second week of their stay in Mexico City and they had decided upon a trip to the Pyramids at Teotihuacán. As usual Miss Lucy sat in front with Mario. He was an excellent driver and she loved to watch his profile as he concentrated on the road; loved his occasional murmurs to himself when something pleased or displeased him. She liked it less when he turned to her, flashing his dark eyes caressingly on her face and lowering them to her breast. His gaze embarrassed her and today something prompted her to say to him laughingly in English:

'Mario, you are what in America we call a flirt. I imagine you are very popular with the girls here in Mexico.'

For a moment he did not seem to understand her remark. Then he burst out:

'Girls—*muchachas. Para me, no.*' His hand went into breast pocket and he brought out a small battered photograph. '*Mi muchacha.* My girl, *mi única muchacha . . . Una sola . . .*'

Miss Lucy took the photograph. It was of a woman older than herself with grey hair and large sad eyes. There were lines of worry and illness in her face.

'Your mother?' said Miss Lucy gently. 'Tell me about her.'

Mario rattled on, not in the slow careful Spanish which he generally reserved for the ladies, but in a rapid monologue of which Miss Lucy understood but part. She gathered that Mario's mother was terribly poor, that she had devoted her life in a tiny Guerrero village to raising fatherless children, and was a saint on earth. It was obvious that Mario felt the almost idolatrous love for his mother that is so frequent in young Mexican males.

While he talked excitedly, Miss Lucy reached a decision. Somehow, before her vacation was over, she'd get from Mario his mother's address and she'd write and send her money, enough money to finance Mario at college. A mother surely would accept it even though her son might be too proud to yield to persuasion.

'Is that one of the pyramids?' It was Ellen's disappointed voice that broke the chain of Miss Lucy's thought. 'Why, it's nothing compared to the pyramids in Egypt!'

Miss Lucy was thrilled, however, by the pyramids of the Sun and the Moon. And as she gazed at their sombre, ancient magnificence, she felt that strange inner elation, which she had felt on the morning when she had genuflected and crossed herself in the church at Taxco.

'I'm not going to climb up all those crumbly steps,' said Ellen peevishly. 'I'm too old and it's too hot.'

And Vera, though never too hot, was far too old. She stood at the foot of the pyramid, her coat hanging sleevelessly over her shoulders, the inevitable cigarette in her claw-like hand. 'You go, Lucy—you're young and active.'

Lucy went.

With Mario's help she climbed to the very top of the Pyramid of the Sun and she was hardly out of breath when she reached the summit, so great was her sense of mystic exaltation.

They sat alone and close together on the summit, this cultivated woman past fifty with a degree from Bryn Mawr, and this almost ignorant boy from an adobe hut in the hinterland of Guerrero. They looked over the vast design of the square where the ancient village had been with its Temple of Quetzalcoatl of the Plumed Serpents, gazing down at the Road of the Dead which led from the Temple to the Pyramid of the Moon.

Mario started to tell her of the sacrificial rites of the feast of Toxcatl which, in ancient days, took place once a year.

As he talked, Miss Lucy half-closed her eyes and visualized the scene: the assembled public hushed in the huge square beneath them;

the priests, each in his appointed place on the steps of the Pyramid;
the spotless youth who was, of course, Mario.

And because it was Mario who was being sacrificed in her mind,
sacrificed to the futility of life and beauty, she felt a warm human pity
for him and instinctively her hand went out—the hand with the
cheap sapphire ring that would not come off—and it found his, and
was held fast in his warm brown fingers.

Miss Lucy was hardly aware of it when Mario's arm slipped round
her, and his dark head dropped against her breast. It was not until she
became conscious of a smell like warm brown sugar, which was his
skin, and a smell of flowery oil which he used on his hair, that all
Philadelphia came rushing back. She jumped up hastily—jumping out
of the centuries to this practical moment when two friends would be
waiting at the base of the pyramid, hungry for lunch—and there were
a great many steps to descend.

On the way home Miss Lucy decided that she and Vera would take
the back seat, so Ellen sat in front and argued with the sulky Mario.

When they reached the pension, Miss Lucy said quickly:

'It's a Sunday tomorrow, Mario. You'd better take a holiday.' He
began to protest. When Lucy repeated 'No, not tomorrow, Mario,' his
face fell like a disappointed child's. Then his expression changed, and
his dark eyes looked squarely, challengingly into hers.

As she turned into the house, Miss Lucy felt her heart pounding.
The intimacy of that glance had brought into the open the thing
which she had not dared to contemplate before. She was quite certain
of it now.

Somehow—for some reason that she did not understand in some
way that her simple mind had never dreamed of—Mario desired her.

He desired her physically.

That night, before she went to bed, Miss Lucy did something she
had never done in her life before. She stood in her plain cotton
nightgown for several minutes before the long Venetian mirror in the
sumptuous room and took stock of herself as a woman.

She saw nothing new or startling—nothing external to balance the
startling changes which were going on inside her. Her face was not
beautiful. It never had been, even in youth, and now it was
uncompromisingly middle-aged. Her hair was almost white but not
white enough. It was soft and plentiful and sat rather prettily on her
forehead. Her eyes were clear and pleasing in themselves, but
surrounded by the lines and shadows natural to her age. Her breasts

were firm beneath the cotton nightgown but her figure was in no way remarkable. In fact, there was nothing externally desirable either about her face or her body. And yet she was desired. She knew it. For some reason a handsome Mexican youth found her desirable. Miss Lucy was sure of that.

There was no nonsense about Miss Lucy and she knew that young men often make up to rich older women in the hopes of eventually obtaining money from them. But Mario, apart from the fact that he'd refused all financial offers, did not even know that Miss Lucy was by far the richest of the three ladies. Only a Philadelphia lawyer or a member of their old Quaker family could possibly know how rich Miss Lucy really was. No, if Mario had wanted money, he would have concentrated on Ellen who held the purse strings and never for a moment let it be known to anyone that it was Miss Lucy's money she was dispensing.

There was nothing about Miss Lucy, drab, black-clad Miss Lucy, to suggest wealth. True, her mother's engagement ring had a rather valuable diamond in it. But only an expert jeweler would recognize that. As for the flashy white sapphire ring, that wasn't worth anyone's time or energy and Miss Lucy would have gladly given it to Mario out of gratitude if only she could have got it off her finger.

No, there were thousands of other women in Mexico City with far more obvious signs of wealth. There were young, beautiful women and any one of them might have been pleased and proud to have Mario as an escort and—yes, Miss Lucy faced it uncompromisingly— as something else.

And yet . . . suddenly Miss Lucy became frightened at the illogicality of it all.

Some virginal instinct stirred in her and warned her of—danger.

And because there was no nonsense about Miss Lucy, she decided that she must do something final about it. Lying there quietly beneath the sheets, she came to her great resolution.

Miss Lucy and Vera were waiting at the bus station. Both of them hugged their coats around them as if cold. Vera was always cold, of course. But today Miss Lucy was cold, too, despite the splendid warmth of the spring sunshine. Her eyes—and her nose were red.

They were waiting for Ellen who had been left behind to deliver the final *coup de grâce* to Mario. The bus for Patzcuaro was leaving in twenty minutes.

At last Ellen appeared. Her nose was red too.

'You shouldn't have done it, Lucy,' she snapped. 'It was cruel.' She thrust two one-hundred-peso bills into Lucy's hands. 'I thought he was going to hit me when I gave him these.' She sniffed. 'And he burst into tears like a child when he read your letter.'

Miss Lucy did not speak. In fact, she spoke very little during the entire length of the tiring bus journey to Patzcuaro.

The three women had been sitting since dinner around their table on the veranda overlooking the serene expanse of Lake Patzcuaro. Ellen, restlessly voluble, was discussing possible plans for the next day. Miss Lucy was, apparently, paying no attention. Her eyes studied the evening grey-green waters of the lake with its clustering islands and its obscene bald-headed vultures that squawked and fought greedily over scraps of carrion on the lake shore.

After a short time she rose, saying: 'It's getting a bit cold. I think I'll go up to my room. Good night.'

Miss Lucy's room, with its small veranda, commanded a view of the lake from another angle. Below her, in the growing darkness, the fishermen were pottering with their boats, talking in low, sibilant voices or singing snatches of Michoacán songs.

Miss Lucy sat watching them. She was thinking of Mario, missing him with an intensity that was almost painful. She had thought of him constantly since she left Mexico City and now was appalled at her harshness in dismissing him by proxy through Ellen. She should have spoken to him herself. She would hate to have him think . . . The thoughts went on with a goading persistence. She had done him a wrong, hurt him. . . .

At some indeterminate stage of her reverie she became conscious of a white-clad figure moving among the fishermen below. Miss Lucy's gaze rested on him and then her heart turned over. She strained forward and peered into the darkness. Surely, surely, there was something familiar about those light, graceful movements — that small, compact form.

But it couldn't be Mario! She had left him hundreds of miles away in Mexico City, and Ellen had been particularly instructed not to tell him where they were going.

The figure in white moved away from the lake shore towards her window. He passed through a shaft of light from an open door. There was no doubt about it now.

It was Mario.

She bent over the balcony, her heart fluttering like a foolish bird.

[173]

He was only about fifteen feet below her.

'Oh, Miss Lucy, I have found you.' He spoke in the slow careful Spanish which he reserved for her. 'I knew I would find you.'

'But, Mario, how . . . ?'

'The bus company told me you had come here. I got a ride and I have been waiting.'

She saw his teeth gleaming as he smiled at her. 'Miss Lucy, why did you go away without saying *adiós*?'

She did not answer.

'But I am back now to take care of you. And tomorrow you and I— we will go on the lake. Before the other two ladies are up. You and I alone together. There will be a moon and then the sunrise.'

'Yes . . .'

'At five o'clock in the morning I come. I will have a boat. Before even the birds awake I will be waiting here.'

'Yes, yes . . .'

'Good night, *carissima*.'

Miss Lucy went back into her room. Her hands were trembling as she undid her dress and slipped into bed.

And she was still trembling when—in the middle of the night, it seemed—a low whistle beneath her window told her that Mario had come for her.

She dressed swiftly, patted her soft grey hair into place, threw a coat over her shoulders and hurried downstairs. The hotel was very quiet. No one saw her as she made her way through the deserted lobby and no one saw her as she went down the slope to where Mario was waiting for her with the boat.

He took her hand and pressed it to his lips. Then he drew her gently towards the boat.

She did not resist. It was as though he were Destiny leading her onwards toward the inevitable.

Mario had been right. There was a moon—full and lemon-white, it shed a weird light on the opaque waters of the lake.

Miss Lucy was in the bottom of the boat, lying on her coat. It was cold, but she did not seem to notice it. She was watching Mario as he stood up in the boat, guiding it skilfully past the other craft into the deep waters of the lake. He had rolled his trousers up beyond his knees and his legs looked strong and somehow cruel in the moonlight. He was singing.

Miss Lucy had not realized before what a beautiful voice he had.

The song seemed sweet and ineffably sad. Mario's eyes caressed her as his gaze travelled downwards from her face and rested on her hands which lay impassive on her lap. The cheap sapphire sparkled in the moonlight.

Miss Lucy was not conscious of time or place as the boat moved slowly toward the secret heart of the lake with its myriad islets. She was not conscious of the dimming stars and the moon paling before the dawn. She felt only a deep, utter tranquillity, as though this gentle almost imperceptible motion must go on forever. She started at the sound of Mario's voice:

'Listen, the birds.'

She heard them in the cluster of small islands that were all around her, but she could see only the vultures that hovered silently overhead.

Mario rested from his rowing and produced a parcel. It contained *tortas*, butter, and goat cheese. He also brought out a bottle of red Mexican wine.

He spread butter on a *torta* with his large clasp knife and handed it to Miss Lucy. Suddenly she realized that she was very hungry. She ate wolfishly and drank from the bottle of the sweet Mexican wine. It went to her head and made her feel girlish and happy. She laughed at everything Mario said and he laughed too while his eyes still caressed her.

And so they breakfasted like honeymoon lovers, as a sunrise splashed red gold over the lake, miles away now from anyone, with only the visible vultures and the invisible songsters to witness them.

When the last *torta* was eaten and the bottle drained, Mario took up his paddle again and propelled the boat deeper into the heart of the lake, on and on without speaking.

As soon as she saw the island, Miss Lucy knew it was the one Mario had chosen. It looked more solitary, more aloof than the rest of them, and there was a fringe of high reeds around its edges.

He steered the boat carefully through the reeds which were so tall that they were completely hidden in a little world of their own. When they reached the shore, he took her hand and raised her gently with the one word:

'Come.'

She followed him like a child. He found a dry spot and spread out her coat for her. Then, as she lay down, he sat with her head in his lap. She could see his face above hers very close; could see those dark eyes set a little too close together; could feel the warm breath, wine-scented, that came from his lips.

She closed her eyes knowing that this was the moment to which everything had been leading—ever since the day in the church of Santa Prisca when she had first met Mario. She could feel his hands caressing her hair, her face, gently, gently. She felt him take her hand, felt him touch the sapphire ring.

The moment he touched the ring, she knew. She could feel it in his fingers, an outflowing, obsessive desire. The whole pattern which had seemed so complex was plain.

His hands moved upward. His fingers, still gentle, reached her throat. She didn't scream. She wasn't even frightened.

As his hands tightened their grasp, the full mouth came down upon hers, and their lips met in their first and only kiss.

Mario threw the bloodstained knife away. He hated the sight of blood and it had disgusted him that he had had to cut off a finger to get the ring.

He hadn't even bothered about the engagement ring that had belonged to Miss Lucy's mother. It was a plain, cheap affair, and for weeks now the great beauty of the sapphire had blinded him to anything else.

He spread the coat carefully over Miss Lucy's body. For a moment he considered putting it in the reeds, but it might float away and be discovered by the fishermen.

Here, on the island, it could be years before anyone came, and by that time—he glanced up at the vultures hovering eternally overhead. . . .

Without looking back Mario went to the boat and rowed toward the deserted mainland shore. There he landed, overturned the boat, and pushed it free so that it would drift into deep water.

An American woman had gone out in a boat on the lake with an inexperienced boatman. They had both been drowned. The officials would never drag so big a lake to find the bodies.

Mario made his way in the direction of the railroad track. He could board a freight car and tomorrow perhaps he would be in Guerrero.

He was sure his mother would like the ring.

FOOD FOR THE SHARKS

by Vincent Starrett

From the rail of the promenade deck, while hundreds of our fellow passengers hustled around us, Jimmie Lavender and I watched the colorful uproar of departure. Shrieks, whistles, and shouted messages filled the wintry evening air. Forty feet below, on the dock, swam a sea of upturned faces, brandished hats, and fluttering handkerchiefs. Shrill admonitions and farewells were screamed between the groups that lined the sides of the great liner and the greater throng that struggled against the barricades below. It was as if every triviality of intercourse had been saved for this last twenty minutes of contact between the liner and the land.

'One would think these hoodlums were leaving the country for years instead of weeks,' said Lavender. His eyes roved over the spectacle of heaving humanity beneath us. 'I almost wish *we were*, Gilly,' he added.

He was frankly tired and fed up with the thing called civilization.

'More passengers arriving,' I commented. 'Somebody of importance this time.'

A small man, briskly pompous, in the uniform of the navigation company, was pushing through the tangle of relatives and friends, forcing an open lane to the gang-plank. At his heels walked a taller man of distinguished appearance; he was bearded like a pard and wrapped in a long ulster, and he swung a heavy stock vigorously as he

[177]

walked. As I looked at him he turned to assist a woman from whom, for a moment, he had been separated by the crush.

There was still another member of the party: immediately behind the tall man shuffled a group of porters carrying a burdensome object, the nature of which became suddenly clear to me.

'By Jove, Jimmie,' I said, 'it's a stretcher. They're bringing somebody up on a stretcher!'

'So they are,' said Lavender. 'Some poor devil who needs the sea or the tropics, I suppose. I almost need a wheel chair myself!'

It wasn't exactly true, but I knew what he meant. Lavender was really tired. His activities for many months had been strenuous. It had been a relief to me when he accepted my suggestion that we make a winter cruise. The bracing air of the Atlantic and, later, the balmy breezes of the Caribbean, I thought, would be just the thing for him.

The crowd on the pier fell back good naturedly and left a passage through which the stretcher-bearers could advance. A uniformed steward ran forward to assist the porters. With only a little difficulty the stretcher and its burden was guided up the runway onto the liner. . . .

A whistle began to blow in short, staccato blasts, and the uproar on the dock redoubled.

'Visitors ashore,' said Jimmie Lavender. 'It won't be long now, Gilly. As an excellent bar is part of our normal equipment, shall we toss a cocktail or two into the vacuum before dinner?'

It seemed an admirable idea and we put it into execution. Leaving the mob below to shout and struggle, we began a slow march along the littered deck of the *Caromantic* in the direction of the smoking room. As we passed a doorway giving onto the main staircase, however, it occurred to Lavender that he would like to wash up, and we descended one deck and sought our stateroom. It was this change of plan that gave us a closer glimpse of the man on the stretcher. . . .

He was carried past us, as we reached the stairfoot, into one of the swanky forward compartments that are proverbially occupied by rich men, diplomats, and other citizens of importance.

We looked down at him as he went past on his pallet, with a steward at every corner and his companions walking ahead. The fellow certainly looked haggard and defeated; but his eyes were open and he made a courageous effort to smile as he caught our sympathetic glances. The face was that of a man about forty. He wore a small mustache of reddish color—the color of his hair—and I noted that one

[178]

eyebrow was distinguished by a small scar, a minute spot where no hair grew. It gave the eye a faintly rakish look that was incongruous considering the man's condition. The face was further distinguished by a broad stain on the opposite temple—a stain the color of red grapes. The thing fascinated me, not because I am a student or collector of birthmarks, but because its outline seemed to me almost precisely that of the North American continent. In miniature, of course!

'Taking the voyage with his wife and his physician,' was Lavender's comment as we resumed our journey. 'The tall man with the beard and glasses is pretty sure to be a doctor.'

In this he was correct, it developed. Anything is gossip on an ocean liner, and in the course of a few hours we learned that the sick man was a certain Davenport, presumably wealthy, that the woman was his wife, and that their companion was the famous Dr Sylvanus Kroll of New York and Paris.

The next day we saw the doctor in the dining room, a hearty fellow with a booming voice and fine teeth that flashed between his careful mustache and his well-trimmed yellow beard. His dark-rimmed spectacles failed to hide the quizzical humor of his blue eyes, and instinctively I felt he was a man to like and trust. He sat alone at a table laid for three, so it seemed obvious that Davenport and his wife were having their meal in their compartment.

We sat at the purser's table—Lavender and I—a table made up exclusively of men, and it was the purser who volunteered our next bit of information. Somebody mentioned the doctor, wishing we might have him at our table, and the ship's officer shrugged and smiled. It was the way the physician had ordered things himself, he explained.

'His patient will be out in a day or two, as soon as we pick up some warm weather. He's still a little weak. Influenza! It leaves a man that way for a time, you know.'

'Who is Davenport?' I asked. 'Somebody I ought to know?'

'Don't know myself,' answered the purser, whose name was Harrap. 'He's got money, obviously. Something in banking, I think. His wife—between ourselves—is a pip!'

For a couple of days the weather continued coldish, with a lashing rain the second day; then almost suddenly it moderated. 'The gulf stream!' all the wise guys said. The doctor from New York and Paris continued to breakfast, lunch and dine alone, although on deck he was affable enough. His deck chair wasn't far from ours, and he used to nod in passing and say the usual things. He didn't encourage conversation, but on the other hand he wasn't too snobbishly aloof. I liked his looks and when I encountered him in the pool, one morning, I talked a bit about the islands we were going to see.

His knowledge was surprising and fascinating. We even got around to West Indian *voodoo*, at one point, and he offered to lend me a book on the subject that he was reading. There was a sort of night club on board—there always is—and we agreed entirely about the souses who went on holiday criuses and spent their time doing the same things they did at home.

Then the weather became warmer, as I say, and the passengers began to dig out their linen suits and try to look like planters. The usual shipboard romances began to be noticeable. There was one pair that had fallen hard for each other. . . .

'I step on them in the most unlikely places,' said Jimmie Lavender. 'Perhaps I should say the most *likely* places! All the odd, obscure corners I should like to occupy myself! It's hard to achieve any privacy on a liner.' He laughed. 'And always whispering together like a pair of conspirators! They are positively annoyed when anybody comes near them.'

'Maybe they're conspirators, at that,' I answered idly. 'I can't imagine a better rendezvous for a couple of crooks wanting to talk things over away from the police.'

He slapped me on the shoulder. 'You warned me, yourself, Gilly, that shop talk was forbidden!'

For the rest, the passenger list was fairly typical. School teachers on holiday; affluent bounders and their families, to whom Christmas and New Year's Day in the home meant nothing; brokers, lawyers, a third-rate novelist looking for copy, bond salesmen, window-trimmers, a clergyman or two, a wealthy meat packer and his snooty collection of half-grown children, and—I have no doubt—a dozen gangsters temporarily removing themselves from circulation. The usual layout. Put all the men except the clergymen in tuxedos of an evening, and it would have been hard to tell the decent citizens from the indecent. The women, however, preponderated.

Always excepting ourselves, Dr Sylvanus Kroll of New York and Paris seemed to me the most attractive fellow on board. I wished we might know him better. . . .

As it turned out, we got to know him very well indeed.

2

Our second view of the man called Stanley Davenport was memorable. He was brought on deck along in the late afternoon of the third day, with a bright sun still shining in the ship's path and everything happy and serene. With his wife on one side and his doctor on the other he walked slowly toward the deck chair labeled with his name. . . . And just before he reached it he crumpled like a leaf and collapsed on the deck!

One couldn't blame his companions, they were obviously taken by surprise. They half caught him as he went down, and they *did* manage to break his fall, so that he didn't actually crash.

Dr Kroll's face was grave as he bent over him, and the face of Mrs Davenport was something breath-taking to look at. The doctor felt Davenport's heart and didn't like the situation at all. He shook his head. Then he gestured frantically for the deck steward, and for several minutes there was more scrambling around than at any time since the ship sailed.

The stretcher made its appearance at last and Davenport was gently hoisted onto it; them away he went again—back to his compartment —the stewards scattering the passengers ahead of them.

Well, that was that. . . . At dawn we were anchored in the harbor of Kingston, Jamaica, or somewhere outside, waiting for a pilot or somebody to come aboard. I peered out of my porthole and saw, in the gray half-light of morning, a narrow peninsula of land set with one thatched dwelling and a fringe of waving palm trees.

It was very early, but I slid into some garments and started for the deck; and, as luck would have it, I ran into Dr Kroll in the passage, near the grand staircase. . . . He looked worn and discouraged.

'How is your patient?' I asked him.

He shook his head wearily. 'Just gone,' he told me. 'Not five minutes ago!'

'Good Lord!' I said. 'Not dead?'

He nodded, and I never saw a man look more broken about anything in my life.

It was a foolish question but I asked it: 'Is there anything I can do?'

'Nothing,' he answered. 'Thanks, all the same.'

He turned abruptly and went back into the Davenport compartment; and after a moment of hesitation I continued on my way to the upper deck. After all, it was no affair of mine; but I felt sorry for the woman and the doctor.

[181]

When Lavender joined me, a little later, I gave him the news. He looked startled, then sympathetic. 'What a pity!' was his only comment.

'What will they do?' I asked, after a moment. The magnificent view of the great island from the promenade, as the sun crept up over the horizon, seemed a fantastic backdrop for the tragedy.

'With the body? I don't know. Take it back with them, I suppose.'

'Can they?'

'Oh, yes,' said Lavender. 'There are—ways! They won't broadcast their intention, of course; it might cause a certain squeamishness. It may be nothing will be said about the death—though, after all, the doctor mentioned it himself.'

I had sense enough not to spread the news. There were few on board, in any case, with whom I cared to talk. And, I'm bound to say, Jamaica wasn't spoiled for me by the unexpected tragedy of Stanley Davenport. . . . With Lavender I went ashore when we had docked, and passed a very pleasant day in Kingston and its environs. I even bought myself a white helmet and greatly admired myself in the haberdasher's mirror. . . .

The way Lavender's health and spirits had picked up was inspiring. I congratulated myself on my happy thought.

Everybody was back on the ship for the evening meal—nearly everybody—and about ten o'clock we sailed again, steaming southward across the Caribbean for Panama. Nothing was said about the death of Davenport at the purser's table that night, but I noted that the table at which Dr Kroll had sat alone was now vacant. Presumably he was spending his time in the dreary forward compartment with the grief-stricken widow.

I was curious, I confess; but Lavender seemed indifferent. 'Let the poor devils alone, Gilly,' he admonished. 'It's a hell of a vacation for them now.'

Of course I stopped talking about Davenport; but, as it happened, the sequel to the episode came up the following morning. . . .

I am an early riser, and again I found myself in the long passage leading to the grand staircase, at an hour when most of the passenger list was still snoring. I had been at great pains not to waken Lavender—by his own request.

This time I met not only Dr Sylvanus Kroll but a surprising group of others. First and foremost, there was the captain of the liner in person, in full uniform; then the first officer, a clergyman, four seamen, and the pale-faced widow. And on a sort of tea-cart there was, fairly obviously, the body of Stanley Davenport. It was well wrapped; indeed it was quite thoroughly wrapped. Among other things it was wrapped in canvas and the canvas was sewed. . . .

I had blundered onto a burial at sea.

The doctor nodded pleasantly enough. 'Good morning, Mr Gilruth,' he said. 'It was not our wish to distress anybody by this spectacle; but as you have already heard of Mr Davenport's death perhaps it doesn't matter. It was his wish that—if he died at sea—he should be buried at sea. We are carrying out his wish. May I hope,' he asked, drawing me aside, 'that you won't talk about this with any of the other passengers? After all, there are those who might not be so happy about their holiday, if they realized—'

I understood perfectly, I told him, interrupting. He nodded gravely, the elderly captain smiled his approval, and the widow thanked me by a gentle touch of her hand on my arm.

Then the solemn procession started along the passage toward the aft staircase, and as I had nothing better to do I followed. I had never seen a burial at sea, but I had read about them, there was an awesome fascination about them that always stirred me. I didn't accompany the cortege into the depths of the vessel; but from an upper deck, a little later, I looked down on the little knot of mourners in the stern and watched the ceremony. It was brief. The captain obviously said something, and the clergyman read from a prayerbook, and the widow wept. Then there was a stooping and hoisting movement by the bare-headed seamen, a sort of gray *sliding* in the dim light of morning, and a faint splash as the gruesome mummy I had seen went over the side and entered its final resting-place. I am not sure that I really heard the splash, but I felt it all up and down my spine. . . .

Lavender was astonished when I told him what had happened. Then he smiled.

'By Jove, Gilly, you *are* an opportune sort of person, aren't you? Positively *fortuitous!* Well, it was a sensible enough thing to do. I mean to bury him at sea, since that was his wish.'

'It was very solemn,' I said; 'almost sinister, in the gray light, with all this background of restless, rolling water, and—you know?'

He nodded. 'They chose an hour when nobody would be up to be shaken by it. Nobody, that is, but my friend Gilruth, who is on hand, at all hours, for births, deaths, christenings, weddings, and what not?'

[183]

'And breakfasts,' I added. 'It hasn't spoiled my appetite, I'm glad to say. Let's go down.'

The lovers, whom I have earlier mentioned, were already at breakfast when we entered; they made up part of a table not far from our own. Their names, I had learned, were Osgood and Hamilton, Miss Osgood being the female half of the combination. I had nodded once or twice and even spoken a few casual good-mornings, but there hadn't been anything approaching conversation.

I was surprised therefore when, as we passed their table, the young woman spoke to me.

'Good morning, Mr Gilruth,' she burbled. 'You were an early riser, this morning, weren't you?'

I bowed and smiled. 'I didn't know I was observed,' I told her. 'You must have been an early bird yourself.'

'A little,' she confessed; then she added: 'I saw you leaning against the rail like a lost soul. You seemed so sad and lonely that I almost spoke to you.'

Hamilton too smiled at me. What the devil did this friendliness portend, I wondered. But once more I nodded my brightest nod. 'Be sure to speak, next time,' I said idiotically. 'Yes, I was thinking of home and Mother—actually pining for a chance to weep!'

As I seated myself and picked up the ship's newspaper—a mimeographed broadside of events brought to the liner every morning by radio—I murmured to Jimmie Lavender: 'Now what does *that* mean?'

'Likes the way your hair curls,' said Lavender with a grin. He too picked up one of the little broadsheets from the table and lost himself in its contents.

After a few moments he spoke: 'This is interesting, Gilly. The third item down—under a New York dateline. An old friend of ours!'

I read the item. 'Well, well,' I said. 'Andy Nevert!'

We had once exchanged pistol shots with the gentleman, in Chicago, shortly before his capture in the state of New York, during a flight from justice.

Nevert, according to the news flash, had escaped from the penitentiary at Auburn, some days before. The tidings had just leaked out, and the police of all the Eastern states were looking for him earnestly.

3

A curious change came over Lavender that day. It puzzled me, accustomed as I was to his moods. There was a peculiar light in his eye, and something on his mind. If we had been at home, at work on a case, I would have guessed that something significant had occurred to him—that he had smelled a rat. However, we were not at home and we were not at work on a case.

He was obviously turning something in his mind, and after a time I thought I knew what it was. In a quiet corner of the lounge, I taxed him with it.

'So you think he may be on board?' I said.

He looked faintly surprised. 'Who?'

'Andy Nevert?'

'Dear, dear.' smiled Jimmie Lavender. 'What put that into your head?'

'Principally your abstraction—ever since you read that squib in the paper.'

He shrugged and looked out of the window at the strollers passing and repassing on the deck. 'It crossed my mind,' he admitted. 'I suppose it's possible. We don't know when the fellow escaped—the paper didn't say. But it was several days ago. Of course there's all America for him to hide in. For that matter, several other ships left New York about the same time we did—before us and after us. However, it would be a smart thing for him to do. A jolly little cruise in the West Indies while all trains across the continent were being watched!'

'You think he's on board,' I accused.

'We know him by sight,' Lavender pointed out. 'Have you seen anybody who resembles him?'

'No, I haven't.'

'Neither have I.'

'Then what's on your mind?'

'When you spoke, a moment ago, I was thinking of your little friend—Miss What's-her-name? Osgood! I had just remembered something. Shortly after she spoke to you at breakfast I saw her on the after deck in intimate converse with—whom do you think?'

'Hamilton, I suppose.'

'No, Kroll! The doctor himself.'

'Hmph,' I said. 'She is beginning to get friendly, isn't she? First me, then the doctor!' But an idea struck me forcibly while I was speaking. 'I'll bet she saw that burial, Lavender! She saw *something*, anyway; and she's curious about it.'

'It's possible,' he agreed.

'Did they seem quite friendly?'

'Oh, quite!'

I thought it over. 'And you think they may have known each other? What *do* you think?'

'I don't really know. It was my impression that the doctor began the conversation—not Miss Osgood. I came up just as it was beginning. I may be wrong, of course.'

It seemed to me he was being unnecessarily mysterious. 'Well, why not?' I demanded. 'He's had enough to worry him lately, God knows!'

'That's true,' agreed Jimmie Lavender. 'I thought of that—all by myself.' He grinned. 'It's just that I have a suspicious mind.'

'Suspicious of what?'

'Everything, I'm afraid—once I get started. But your suggestion about Nevert is a good one. I wonder if the radio has queried us about him. It would be interesting to find out.'

He got to his feet with remarkable alacrity, and I followed him to the office of the chief purser.

'Mr Harrap,' he began briskly, 'I suddenly find it necessary to introduce myself. When I'm at home, in Chicago, I'm what is known as a private detective—usually a filthy profession, but in my own case not all you might imagine.'

The purser looked up smiling. 'Am I under arrest?' he asked. 'I know your reputation very well, Mr Lavender. I read the crime news as often as I read my Bible. Naturally, I haven't talked about it at the table—your business is your own—but I imagine there are plenty of others on board who know you.'

Jimmie Lavender stared for a moment. Then he laughed. '*Touché!*' he said. 'Don't think me a smug ass—but it really hadn't occurred to me that you knew anything about me.'

'What can I do for you?' asked Harrap genially.

'I'm curious about a man named Nevert. He's a murderer, and I'm wondering if he's on this ship!'

The purser raised his eyebrows. 'The hell you are!' he said.

'You haven't read your little paper, this morning?'

'What little paper?'

Jimmie Lavender produced the morning newspaper. 'You really

should read your own paper, Harrap,' he chided. 'Now don't get excited, for I may be all wrong.' He indicated the paragraph and waited for the purser to read it. . . . 'All I'm saying is, there's a possibility the man may be on board. You can see that for yourself. It would be a clever escape. I suppose you'd have heard if there had been any inquiry from New York.'

'Radio? Oh, yes! There has not been.'

'As it happens,' said Lavender, 'I know the man by sight.'

'Good Lord, Mr Lavender, you haven't *seen* him, have you?'

'No, I haven't; but I think some sort of search should be made—don't you?'

The purser was dubious. 'A sort of "show-up" of the passengers, you mean?' he questioned nervously. 'I'm sure the company wouldn't like it.'

'You mean the passengers wouldn't like it, and the company wouldn't like *that*. You're right, of course. No, if he's among the passengers he's well disguised. Leave that to me—I'll keep my eyes open. What I'm really wondering is whether he isn't hidden away someplace.'

'*Stowed away!*' Harrap was incredulous. 'If he were hiding in any of the cabins one of the stewards would be sure to report it.'

'There are other hiding-places, I suppose.'

Harrap shook his head. 'He'd have been found before this. He may be a member of the crew, of course. We took on a few new men, in New York, for this trip.'

'That's a possibility.' agreed Lavender. 'I'll have a look at them, if you like. Now how about the boat deck?'

The purser grinned. 'We had a boat drill the second day out, Mr Lavender—you took part in it!'

'I know! We stood beside the boats for a minute or two, then went back to our cabins. No canvasses were removed.'

'Some were,' said the purser; but he got to his feet. 'Look here, have you any real reason to think this man may be hiding on board? Or is it just a hunch?'

Lavender hedged. 'I think I have,' he answered, after a moment.

'Then we'll see the captain right away." said Harrap. 'Will you come along?'

And that's how it came about that our stowaway was discovered.

Lavender and I stood by, with the captain and the purser, while the first officer—a husky rascal—and a group of seamen dragged a squirming, apologetic young man out of a canvas-covered lifeboat on the boat deck and asked him what the hell he thought he was doing there.

He was a tousled-looking specimen, but not at all pugnacious. Indeed, he was very meek, although husky enough to have put up a fight if he had wanted to. His face was pretty dirty and his hair was a sight; but I suppose it's hard to keep your face clean and your hair combed while half-sitting, half-lying in a small boat.

He was taken to the captain's quarters promptly, while a group of sun-bathers on the sport deck above wondered what had happened.

'Who are you?' asked the captain, not too ferociously.

'Hooper,' answered the culprit, with a slight stammer. 'George H-h-hooper. S-s-sorry I was caught! I intended to slip ashore in Panama, you know,' he explained in friendly fashion. 'Out of a j-j-job in New York. Thought I might g-g-get something to do on the C-c-canal.'

'And you've been in that boat ever since we left New York?' asked Harrap incredulously. 'It's a wonder you didn't freeze to death—or starve!'

'I'm pretty t-t-tough,' said the stowaway, grinning amiably. 'Had some s-s-sandwiches in my pocket for the first three d-d-days.'

'You're lying,' said the captain suddenly. 'Somebody on this ship has been taking care of you—feeding you!'

The stowaway shook his head without malice. 'No.' he replied. 'J-j-just myself.'

Harrap and the captain turned and looked at Jimmie Lavender. The same thought was suddenly in the mind of each; for a moment they had forgotten the detective's suspicions.

Lavender shook his head. 'I was mistaken, Captain,' he confessed. 'This man is not Andy Nevert.' He hesitated, then asked a question of his own. 'What do you intend to do with him?'

'We'll have to see about that,' said the captain gruffly. 'I may turn him over to the American authorities at Panama.'

A look of pleasure crossed the young man's face. 'I'd l-l-like that,' he said. 'Then when I got out of j-j-jail I'd be where I want to be.'

An odd conviction was growing in my mind. I couldn't put a name to it. Somewhere, I was sure, I had seen this man before. There was something about his face that was familiar. Yet it was unfamiliar too. I looked at Jimmie Lavender; but he was calmly lighting a cigarette and being very leisurely about it. After a time he spoke, tossing away his match.

'Plenty of time to think it over,' he shrugged. 'Sorry I raised a false alarm, Harrap!'

'Not at all,' said the purser heartily. 'I'm glad you did. You were right about the stowaway, anyway.'

It was at that instant that the shocking truth flashed over me, and for a moment I guess I reeled. I mean it! My head swam. I tottered toward Lavender, gesticulating feebly. The thing seemed impossible, and yet it was true.

Lavender took me by the arm. 'Steady, boy,' he said. 'I'm afraid the sun is getting you.' He led me outside while the others stared. In a few moments the giddiness had passed.

'Not a word, Gilly,' said Jimmie Lavender sharply. 'Wait till we are out of sight and hearing.'

In an obscure corner of the afterdeck he released me. 'Yes?' he questioned.

'That man,' I said. 'He's—My God, Jimmie, didn't you see his eyes?'

'His eyebrows, you mean,' he corrected me. 'I saw them. One of them is scarred.'

'He's Stanley Davenport,' I said. 'The man they buried this morning!'

Jimmie Lavender nodded. 'Minus his birthmark,' he agreed. 'Washed it off, I suppose, before he took his place in the boat last night. His hair is the right color too, but he's shaved his mustache. It makes him look much younger. A clever make-up, Gilly. I'm annoyed with myself for not seeing through it earlier.'

'What does it mean?' I asked. And suddenly, in the little silence that followed, another thought rose up and shook me. . . . '*Jimmie!*' I said.

'I thought of that too, Gilly,' said Jimmie Lavender. 'You're right. If this man is Stanley Davenport, who was it—or *what* was it—they dropped overboard?'

4

Was it an insurance hoax? I wondered.

I saw that Lavender was struggling with a little smile of satisfaction. For once, at least, my intelligence functioned.

'You *knew* that fellow wasn't Nevert before you saw him,' I accused. 'You never thought Andy Nevert was on board!'

He nodded. 'That's true. Nevert's not a fool. Before taking passage he would have looked over the passenger list. He'd have found my name—and yours—and wouldn't have sailed.'

'Then what—?'

'I think the plot is fairly clear at last. It's murder.'

I thought of that grisly ceremony in the dawn—and my flesh crawled. Were there still sharks abroad in the Caribbean?

'Come on,' said Jimmie Lavender. 'We've got to see the doctor—not Kroll, the other one.'

In a few minutes we were closeted with the ship's doctor and Lavender had tossed his bomb.

'Of course I saw the body,' protested the indignant medico. 'The man was obviously dead—and naturally I accepted Dr Kroll's assurances.'

'*Quite* obviously dead,' said Lavender. 'He had been dead, Doctor—and *embalmed*—since Saturday at least! It's now almost Thursday noon.'

The doctor's face expressed emotions beyond description. 'Good God, Mr Lavender, what are you saying?' he cried at last.

'I'm thinking of murder,' answered Lavender gravely. Then he took pity on the stupefied officer. 'I'm not blaming you, Doctor. I can imagine how it happened. Kroll told you the man was dead. You assumed him to be a reputable physician. He took you to the room and showed you a corpse. Probably you didn't touch it, or even go very near it. How did that happen?'

The doctor's eyes were popping.

'Mrs Davenport was in the room,' he answered, after a moment. 'She was lying across the body—crying!' He made futile motions with his hands, trying to express his feelings. 'But what you tell me is impossible!'

'It was staged with great cleverness,' said Lavender. 'At all times either Kroll or the woman was between you and the corpse. You stood inside the door and saw a dead face on the pillow. It was a face clearly marked with Davenport's birthmark, a deep red stain. The curtains were drawn across the portholes; the room was half-lighted by one of those damned bed-lamps in the wall. That's the way it *must* have been.'

The doctor struggled for utterance. 'You're right about—about the conditions,' he stammered at last. 'But even so—'

'Come, come, Doctor, I've been a little slow and stupid about this case myself,' Lavender interrupted. 'Naturally, you took Kroll's word for everything. I'm not blaming you. But we must rectify our errors. I'm a detective, if the information interests you.'

The ship's doctor came upright slowly. 'What do you want me to do?' he asked. 'Prove what you say and I'll do anything you suggest.'

'We are all going to the compartment now—and I warn you we may be going into considerable danger!'

We picked up Harrap on the way and tried to make him understand the situation. 'My God!' was all he said.

It was Harrap, however, who tapped gently on the Davenport door.

'Who is it?' asked a woman's voice, and the door opened the merest crack and showed a woman's eye. 'Oh—I'm sorry, Purser, but I'm dressing. The doctor isn't here. What was it you wanted?'

Jimmie Lavender pushed the door wide open and walked in, followed nervously by Harrap and the doctor. I was last, and I closed the door behind me and shot the bolt.

The woman had fallen back before our advance and now stood clutching at the footrail of her bed. Her mouth was open for a scream, but Lavender stopped her with a gesture.

'I'm sorry, Mrs Davenport, if we are making a mistake,' he said, 'but I really don't think we are. I think this trunk is the answer to our questions.'

With dramatic suddenness he indicated a trunk of giant size and strength, which stood in a corner of the stateroom. It was partly open for all the world to see, half filled with a variety of garments, both masculine and feminine.

'It is the only thing around here that might conceivably hold a dead body,' added Jimmie Lavender in a low voice.

That did it. The woman screamed and fell back across the bed.

'Why was Mr Davenport murdered?' asked Lavender quietly.

But rapid footsteps were now sounding along the passage. Then a hand was on the doorknob and it was shaken furiously. 'What is it?' asked the voice of the missing doctor, suddenly anxious. And then: 'Damn it, what's the matter with this door!'

Lavender tried to lay a hand across the woman's mouth, but he was too late. . . . She dashed the hand aside and screamed her lungs out.

'Go back!' she screamed. 'Go back, Sylvanus! They've got me—and they've found the trunk! Run, Sylvanus, run!'

I have often wondered where, in the middle of the Caribbean, she expected him to run.

The footsteps of the doctor retreated hurriedly along the passage as

Lavender sprang forward and snapped back the door-bolt.

What followed was like part of a wild nightmare. . . .

Kroll, as we reached the end of the passage, had already reached the stairhead and was plunging toward the deck. Closest to him was Lavender, but he was yards behind. After Lavender ran the purser and I, neck and neck and jostling each other, with the stout little ship's doctor loping in the rear. It hadn't occurred to any of us to stay with Mrs Davenport!

But it was a hopeless chase. The speeding doctor was half the deck ahead when we emerged on the promenade; he was running like a deer. As we took after him, we saw him brush aside a startled steward and spring up an iron stairway leading to the upper regions. Two passengers were picking themselves up from the boards and two hundred others were staring, stupefied, at the spectacle.

The pursuit ended on the boat deck. In almost our last glimpse of him, the murderer was climbing swiftly to the canvas-shrouded top of one of the great lifeboats. There for a moment he stood, outlined against the sea and the sky, clinging to a davit. Then his arm went back and something glittered in his hand. A shot sounded, half lost in the throbbing rush of the liner through the water, and Jimmie Lavender stepped back with a look of surprise in his gray eyes.

'Close!' he said appreciatively.

But it was Kroll's last gesture of defiance. With a powerful leap he sprang forward and outward. For an instant his body seemed to hang motionless in the air; then it dived swiftly to the blue-green waters of the Caribbean.

I looked around, but there was no sign of land as far as the eye could see. From horizon to horizon there were only miles and more miles of rolling ocean. . . .

'The easiest way out,' said Jimmie Lavender. 'Did anybody think to stay with Mrs Davenport?'

5

There was a note beside the woman's body. Surprisingly, it was in the doctor's hand. . . .

'If this is ever read,' it said in part, 'it will be because we have failed, and because we have no wish to try our case before a jury. Who is now reading this note, I wonder. Is it Mr Lavender? Congratulations,

Mr Lavender! Be easy with the boy you found in the lifeboat—for if you are reading this it will be after you have found him. He was Mrs Davenport's chauffeur, and he owed a lot to her. If it had not been for his red hair he would not have been let in for this mess at all. We are not sorry about anything. Davenport was a tiresome animal, and he simply *wouldn't* die a natural death. He's better off—perhaps we all are.'

'You see, Gilly, there was only one reasonable explanation,' said Jimmie Lavender. 'After we recognized the stowaway the plot was clear. He was impersonating someone, someone with a red birthmark, a little mustache, and a scarred eyebrow. It was the eyebrow that betrayed him; he was caught before that little matter could be adjusted by nature. The chances were strong that he was impersonating the man he pretended to be. Therefore, the real Davenport was dead— had been brought dead onto the ship—and it was the real Davenport who was buried in the sea. In short, a murder had been committed ashore, and an effort was being made to make it appear a natural death at sea.'

The afternoon was broiling. The ship was still hurrying across the Caribbean toward Panama.

'After your picturesque account of the burial, I began to wonder at the haste indicated. The doctor's explanation was plausible, but there were other possibilities. I wondered, too about your friend Miss Osgood—just a little. Why was she suddenly interested in *you*, and later why was the doctor suddenly interested in *her*? It seemed clear to me that the lady also had been up early that morning—even earlier than you perhaps. What might she have seen that would interest Kroll? Not just the burial—you knew all about that, and the doctor wasn't worried.'

I was fascinated.

'I recalled the fondness of the Osgood female and her sappy friend for obscure corners of the boat deck; and then I had a hunch. I remembered that last night—quite late—well after midnight, in point of fact—the doctor himself had been on the boat deck; I saw him coming down. But what had been happening? Was it a *liaison*? In view of everything—including Hamilton—I didn't think so. Nor could I believe Miss Osgood and Dr Kroll to be in cahoots. It seemed possible that some little mystery might center about the boat deck. If Miss Osgood had blundered onto something not intended for her eyes— well, you see how my mind worked.'

[193]

I nodded. 'The stowaway!'

'It was possible at least; and if there *was* a stowaway, why, then, the puzzle pieces began to fall into place. A body had been substituted for that of the supposed dead man and the supposed dead man had become a stowaway. Your idea about Nevert was a godsend—I used it for purposes of search.'

'I was stupid,' I contributed. 'And the real Davenport has been dead since Saturday—it sounds impossible.'

'It took nerve. You can imagine the details, I suppose. They're fairly nasty. Davenport's body was in the trunk—preserved with exquisite attention, we may be sure, when no one was around.'

'Pretty grim,' I commented.

'Well, yes, and there are other words! Kroll was an expert in all branches of his profession. Since the body wouldn't precisely fit—yet must of necessity be horizontal for the funeral—he would temporarily remove the lower—'

'I understand you perfectly,' I said. 'Did you notice the label on the trunk? It said, "Wanted on the Voyage," My God!'

'But it was clever. Make no mistake about that. The trunk was delivered at the ship and placed in their compartment, where they rejoined it—carrying the imposter on a stretcher—just before the ship sailed. That's *genius*, Gilly! If that chauffeur hadn't been caught—if he had been allowed to escape at Panama come Saturday—'

'Why Panama, I wonder! Why not Jamaica? It would have been that much earlier.'

'Because Jamaica is strictly British territory, I think. If he was caught, and had no passport—well, there might have been difficulties that could be avoided in an American protectorate. His story that he was looking for a job at the Canal was very plausible.'

We looked up. A steward was standing beside us with a wireless message. . . .

'Undoubtedly Stanley Davenport,' said the New York police department. 'No relations we can trace. Neighbors say he left Saturday with wife and physician for West Indies cruise. Kroll unknown to police. Physicians say he is a specialist of doubtful reputation and ability.'

'They're wrong about his ability anyway,' said Jimmy Lavender. 'Well, Gilly, the motivation seems fairly clear at last. Kroll practically confessed it. Davenport was an invalid who refused to die. His physician—presumably a distinguished quack—persuaded his wife to fall in love with himself, with a view to making her a wealthy widow. How's that?'

'I've no doubt you're right,' I agreed.

'Nor I—and I have to thank you, Gilly, for a very successful holiday. I never felt better in my life!'

'But what about Miss Osgood?' I asked. 'What was her part in all this mystery?'

'My blushes, Gilly! I hate to tell you—but I think I know the answer to that one, too. I couldn't ask her, of course—that would have been indelicate. Well, the doctor, like myself, had seen her on the boat deck frequently. I think he saw her there again, early this morning, and suspected her of knowing about the young fellow in the lifeboat. She *didn't*, as it happens. But the reason she was interested in *you*, this morning, was another matter. I think she was afraid you had spotted her and Hamilton.'

'Spotted them?'

'Now don't be obtuse, Gilly, and don't be shocked. Such things do happen in an imperfect world. Your Miss Osgood was a brazen hussy, I'm afraid. It was pretty warm when we left Jamaica, and—well, I think she and Hamilton spent the night on deck.'

The little doctor, strolling past a minute later, asked me what the devil I was laughing at.

PETRELLA'S
HOLIDAY

by Michael Gilbert

T he constable on point duty in St. Andrew's Circus always has
an exasperating time. And this is aggravated when the sun
shines, since most of the traffic on the A.2 coastal road passes
through the Circus, heading into it by three different routes, then
squeezing out through the inadequate width of Vigo Street before
attaining the comparative freedom of the Old Kent Road.

Constable Whitty was not only hot. He was rankling under the
underserved rebuke of Sergeant Mortimer. 'Keep 'em moving,' he
muttered to himself. 'How the hell can anyone keep 'em moving when
there's nowhere for 'em to move to? If this was Russia, now, or
America—' He visualised himself, revolver in holster waving a stream
of limousines down a four-track highway. 'A hundred years out of
date. That's what's wrong with this country. I *ask* you.'

A small cart, drawn by a depressed pony, clattered slowly across the
intersection, followed by a lorry with an articulated trailer, six girls on
bicycles, and a hearse. Time to switch, thought Whitty. Roll on two
o'clock.

He raised a hand to halt the oncoming car, turned and beckoned
forward the head of the traffic waiting in St. Andrew's Road. A
delivery van and an open car got smartly off the mark, followed by a
saloon car. The van on the near side of the car stayed put. Whitty
beckoned even more imperiously. The van failed to respond.

[196]

'Engine failure,' diagnosed Whitty, 'near the head of a line of traffic on a day like this. Why does everything happen to me?'

He strode up to the offending vehicle, which was an old, open-backed, Army fifteen-hundredweight truck, and thrust his head into the driver's compartment. 'If you can't start her, you'll have to push her,' he said.

Then he stopped. The man in the driver's seat was leaning across over the wheel, an empty look on his face, and a neat hole in the side of his forehead framed by a rim of fresh, bright blood.

Inspector Petrella, although he did not realise it at the time, had passed St. Andrew's Circus just before the shooting.

He had not gone through it, but had walked down Dunraven Street, which is separated from the Circus by a large blitzed site. As he went by, he had noticed a line of South Borough Secondary School boys hanging over the wall, and he had observed a game of cricket in progress. The players, as he saw out of the corner of his eye, were young men—indeed, not all that young—probably from the local printing works.

The bowler, who had a shock of red hair, looked up, and it crossed Petrella's mind that he recognised him. He was on his way to an urgent appointment and had no time to stop, but he determined to have a word with Mr Wetherall, who was the headmaster of South Borough Secondary School, and occupied the flat above Petrella's in Brinkham Road. Some of the blitzed sites were unsuitable playgrounds.

Petrella was on his way to a rendezvous with a man called Roper, who spent his mornings driving a delivery van, his evenings selling newspapers, and the whole of his time keeping his eyes and ears open. For he was a police informer, and one of the most valuable on Petrella's list. His charges were high, but his information was usually accurate.

Petrella waited, with professional patience, for a full hour, and when he stepped out again into the hot street a cruising police car located him and whipped him back to Gabriel Street. There he found his own superior, Superintendent Benjamin, and Benjamin's superior, Chief Superintendent Thom, in possession.

'I believe,' said Thom—who was half an inch below the minimum height for a policeman, and known to every criminal south of the Thames as Pussy—'that you were using Roper yourself.'

'That's right, sir. I was meeting him this lunch-time. He stood me up.'

'He had some information for you?'

'He *said* he knew where the Borners kept their bank. He hadn't actually got round to talking terms.'

'He'll not talk any more, now,' said Thom. 'He got an airgun bullet through the side of his head just before two o'clock. A right neat job. I don't know when I've seen a neater. We've got Roper. We've got his van. And about a thousand people to question. And that's all we have got.'

'It'll be in all the evening papers,' said Benjamin, who had a long solemn face, and hated publicity of any sort. 'It's probably on the streets by now.'

'It's no bad thing if it is,' said Thom. 'We shall have to appeal for members of the public to come forward. We'll draft an announcement for the BBC.'

'Where are you going to take the statements?' asked Petrella.

'I think we'll use this station,' said Thom. 'It's handiest, and the best place to see people will be in your office.'

Petrella had feared as much.

Stimulated by appeals in the newspapers and on the wireless, the people of south-east London converged on Gabriel Street, for two whole days, in a steady stream. Some of them were cranks, some were liars, and a few of them had actually been in St. Andrew's Circus at the moment of the shooting.

Sergeant Shoesmith, whose methodical habits were invaluable in a crisis of this sort, produced a plan on an enormous scale, which he fastened to the wall, and on it he plotted, in distinctive colours, the position of every witness. In black, if their presence was unsupported; in green if they had been seen by one other person; in red if seen by two or more.

It was late in the afternoon on the first day that a young man arrived, produced an envelope, and tipped out of it a dozen photographs. 'I'm from *The Clarion*,' he said. 'My editor thought you might like to see these. Interesting, aren't they?'

'I'll say they're interesting,' said Petrella. 'Where did you get them?'

'*The Clarion's* running a series. Black Spots in London's Traffic. We did Charing Cross last week. This week it was St. Andrew's Circus. Rather a coincidence, really.'

'Are these actually—?'

'The time of the shooting? Yes. We took one lot between twelve and two. Another lot between five and seven. The last one of the first series would be the one you'd want, I should think. Isn't that your chap, in fact?'

Petrella and Sergeant Shoesmith and Constable Wilmot crowded round the photograph. It was extraordinary. Like having a dream, and then seeing it all in the newspapers next morning. They carried the photograph across to the plan.

'There's that saloon car,' said Petrella. 'And you can see the nose of the bus, behind. That's Whitty. He's just signalling on the other line of traffic. Looks a bit hot, doesn't he?'

Sergeant Shoesmith said, 'I always thought that man with the beard was a liar. He said he was standing under the clock from half past one to half past two. He isn't in any of the photographs at all. There's the little woman who thought it was Communists. And the man with the four dogs.'

'Isn't that a bicycle?' said Petrella. 'Look, you can just see the front of the mudguard.' He looked at the plan. 'That must be the schoolgirl. The one who thought she heard a shot. Just exactly where did you take these from? Can you show me on this plan?'

'It was an office,' said the young man. 'Our chaps usually work from windows. If you stand about on the pavement taking pictures you get a crowd round you. Just about there, I should say. It's a window on the first floor. He used a telescopic attachment. That's why the background's sharp but the foreground's a bit blurred.'

'I think they're excellent photographs,' said Petrella. 'Can we hang on to them?'

'Certainly. We had these copies made for you. Only thing is, if you do get anything out of it, you might let us in on it.'

Petrella promised to do that.

While Petrella, assisted by Sergeant Shoesmith and Detective Constable Wilmot, was sorting out the eye-witnesses, Superintendent Benjamin was inquiring into the movements of the Borners.

'Curly and me,' said Maurice Borner, a handsome, dark-haired, young man with an arrogant Assyrian nose, 'was playing snooker at Charley's. Copper was there, too. We started about one, and wasn't finished much before three.'

'A long game?' suggested the Superintendent.

'That's the way it is,' said Maurice, 'when you get interested in a thing.'

'Anyone else see you?'

'You know Charley's, Superintendent. It's sort of private. A few of us use it. I believe Sammy did look in.'

Sam Borner, fatter than his brother and superficially jollier, agreed readily that he had looked in at Charley's. He had spent most of the lunch-hour in his flat with Harry and Nick. They had been having a quiet game of cards. They often had a quiet game of cards at lunch-time.

'It's as clear as the nose on Maurice's face,' said Benjamin. 'That's the lot that did it. It's not going to be easy to prove. No one's going to be keen on giving evidence against them. They carry too much weight.'

'I know the two Borners,' said Petrella. 'Nick Joel and Harry Hammanight—he's the big ex-sailor, isn't he? Who are the others?'

'Curly's one of the Bassets—the only one out at the moment. Copper's a redhead. He used to be quite a nice boy, and a promising boxer before they got hold of him.'

Something in Petrella's memory stirred, but died.

'And it's all very fine,' went on Benjamin, 'for us to say we know the Borners did it because they'd got their knife into Roper and because they've got an alibi which is so watertight that it sticks—that's not going to cut much ice in Court. First thing we've got to find out is how it was done. What the hell are you grinning at?'

'I was just thinking,' said Petrella, 'that that's one of the finest mixed metaphors I've ever heard.'

'Tchah,' said Benjamin.

By the second evening Petrella and his assistants were contemplating a dwindling number of possibilities.

'I think,' said Petrella, 'that we could rule out anyone on the pavement. It would be much too risky.'

'Suppose,' said Wilmot, who was young and read detective stories, 'they had this airgun disguised as an umbrella.'

'Why would anyone carry an umbrella on a day like that?'

'Well, a walking-stick.'

'It's no use supposing,' said Petrella. 'We *know* that no one was doing anything of the sort. We know everyone who was on the pavement, on both sides of the road, their names and addresses, and where they came from, and where they were going to. Do you suppose that any of them could have got away with pointing a walking-stick at Roper without half a dozen people noticing it?'

'I agree with you, sir,' said Sergeant Shoesmith. 'Our investigations have definitely ruled out the possibility of any of the passers-by being implicated, and the owners of all windows overlooking the scene have been checked and crosschecked.'

'Suppose someone got on the roof, went up the fire escape—'

'And shot Roper through the top of the driver's seat without leaving a hole in it?'

'Roper could have been leaning out of the cab.'

'He could have been,' said Petrella patiently, because he liked Wilmot, 'but how could the man on the roof know that he was going to lean out of the cab at just that place and time?'

'I'm inclined to think, sir,' said Sergeant Shoesmith, 'that it must have been a man in one of the other vehicles. We have established that Roper followed the same route almost every day on the way from his shop to the depot where he picked up his evening papers. And it was inevitable that he would be held up at St. Andrew's Circus. All he had to do was to draw up behind Roper, or beside him, shoot at the moment the traffic was signalled forward, and rely on getting away in the confusion.'

'Splendid,' said Petrella. 'Splendid. Now tell me which of the vehicles you had in mind. We have succeeded in identifying them all, I think.'

'Well,' said Sergeant Shoesmith. 'I admit that's a bit more difficult.'

'There were only three possibles,' said Petrella. 'Unless the killing was done on the spur of the moment, the car *must* have been in the same stream of traffic as Roper. No one coming into St. Andrew's Circus from another direction could possibly guarantee to be at the head of one line at the precise moment Roper was near the head of the other. Right?'

'Right,' said Wilmot. He enjoyed seeing Sergeant Shoesmith put in his place.

'And he must have been beside him or in front of him. The shot couldn't have been delivered from behind. That brings us down to the delivery van immediately in front, the open car to the right front, or the saloon car, level with Roper on the right. We know who they are. They've all come forward, none of them has the faintest connection with Roper, and none of them looks in the least like a murderer. Apart from that—' Petrella prodded a document on the table in front of them—'we've now got the results of the laboratory tests, which show that the bullet went into Roper from the lefthand side, either on the level, or from very slightly above—it would depend on how he was holding his head at the moment of impact. Which makes complete nonsense of the idea that he was shot from a van in front, or from a car much lower than he was and on his right.'

'That's right,' said Wilmot again. 'Real tricky, this one.'

'It's no good just saying it's tricky,' said Petrella crossly. 'We've got to find the answer to it. There's no arguing away the fact that someone put a bullet into Roper's head. He didn't shoot himself.'

It occurred to Petrella afterwards that the reason they couldn't see the answer was because they were too near the problem. He took all the photographs home with him that night, and propped them round the teapot while he ate the evening meal he had cooked for himself. And when he went upstairs afterwards to chat with Mr Wetherall, he took the photographs with him.

Mr Wetherall, the reigning headmaster of the South Borough Secondary School, was a neat, grizzled man, with a nose reminiscent of the great Duke of Wellington and an all-embracing knowledge of the characters and habits of the south Londoners whom he had taught, as boys, for thirty years, and successive generations of whom he had watched grow up into tough, unpredictable, cheerful, amoral citizens.

'I have no faith,' he said, 'in amateur detectives who step in where the professional has failed, but if you wouldn't mind handing me that magnifying glass—it is rather a fine one, isn't it? Young Simmonds gave it to me when he left. You may know his father.'

Petrella knew Mr Simmonds well: he was the second most eminent receiver of stolen goods in South Borough.

'This is the photograph that was taken at the moment of the shooting? And the others at short intervals before it?' Mr Wetherall pored over the photographs, occasionally chuckling to himself as he recognised an ex-pupil in the crowd.

Then he straightened up and said, 'Well, really. I'm quite sure you've noticed it for yourself, but that young lady—the one in the final photograph, she appears to be smoking a cigarette. Odd, don't you think, that she isn't doing so in any of the earlier ones? Significant, perhaps?'

'Which young lady?'

'No. Not in the crowd. I mean the young lady in the advertisement on the hoarding. The one advertising SUDDO. *Make Monday Fun-day.*'

Petrella snatched the glass, and focused it. Then, with fingers that fumbled, he grabbed the other photographs and concentrated on each in turn.

What Mr Wetherall had said was absolutely true. The young housewife, holding aloft a snowy-white garment, and announcing with a dazzling smile that Monday was Fun-day had, between her teeth, *in the final photograph only*, a thin, cylindrical object not unlike a large cigarette.

Early next morning he sought out Mr Cooper, who was agent for the owner of the bombed side which fronted on St. Andrew's Circus, masked at that side by hoardings, and which ran clear back, behind the hoardings, to Dunraven Street.

'I put this barbed wire up a day or two ago,' said Mr Cooper. 'I heard people had been getting down into the site, at the back, playing cricket. We've never had any trouble before. Do you want to go down yourself? It's a bit of a climb.'

'See if you can borrow a ladder,' said Petrella, 'while I shift some of this wire.' Half an hour later, with the assistance of a signpainter's ladder, they were standing on what had once been the basement floor of a large building.

'If you don't mind,' said Petrella, 'I'll do this bit alone. I don't want any unnecessary footprints.'

Mr Cooper looked at him curiously, and said, 'This something to do with the shooting the other day?'

'It might be,' said Petrella. 'Why?'

'I did wonder why anyone would want to climb down here just to play cricket. You can see for yourself. It'd be an awkward place to get at, even without the wire. I suppose I ought to have said something before.'

'Yes,' said Petrella. 'But don't blame yourself. I actually saw them playing, and it didn't occur to me, either. Hold the ladder, would you mind?'

He climbed on the back wall, and made his way across a weed-grown ground floor. Then there was a girder to cross. It had originally been two buildings, he guessed, back to back; one fronting on Dunraven Street, the other on St. Andrew's Circus. He was now in what was left of the larger one. The line of hoardings was above him, their footings at eye level.

Behind them ran the wall which the local authority had put up immediately after the bombing, to prevent people falling into the hole. Petrella looked at the wall cautiously. There was no obvious way up on to it, but there was a pile of rubble at one end which would offer a starting place. And, at the base of the rubble, faint but still distinct, a footprint. Petrella regarded it as lovingly as Robinson Crusoe gazed at the print of Man Friday.

Lucky we haven't had any rain, he thought. Get something to cover it. And have a cast made quick. Better tackle the wall from the other end.

He went back the way he had come, pulled up the ladder, and returned with it to the hoarding. Using a ladder, it was possible to avoid setting foot on the coping at all. He tried to visualise the photographs. Which had been the Suddo advertisement? There was the beer poster on the left. Then the petrol hoarding. Was Suddo next, or next but one?

It was such a neat job that, even knowing what he was looking for, it took Petrella five minutes to find it. A section, twelve inches long by four inches high, had been cut from the woodwork of the hoarding—and cut so neatly that it fitted without any sort of fastening. Petrella prised it out with his fingernails. The space in front of it was blocked by the back of the poster, but a narrow slit had been cut in the paper and pasted over from the back.

Petrella opened it with the tip of his finger, and found himself looking at the face of a bus driver, fifteen feet away and almost exactly on a level with his own.

'It was an ambush,' said Petrella to Benjamin. 'They knew he went through the Circus every day about that time. Of course, they were bound to be seen getting into the site at the back. They covered that by five of them playing lunch-hour cricket while Maurice did the shooting.'

'Bit risky,' said Benjamin. 'Suppose a policeman had gone by and recognised them.'

Petrella was still young enough to blush.

He said, 'One did. I actually saw them playing, and thought I recognised the one I looked at—it was Copper Dixon, the redhead. I'd seen him once before, in Court. It should have clicked, but it didn't.

'I see,' said Benjamin. 'All the same, you should be able to identify him when the time comes. What about the boys?'

'In the ordinary way, I don't expect they'd be keen to give evidence at all, but Mr Wetherall—he's their headmaster—tells me that one of them is an Irish boy called O'Connor. The South Bank Irish don't like the Borners. It's a piece of local politics. I don't know the ins and outs of it, but he thinks that O'Connor will give evidence. And if he does, the other boys will follow his lead.'

'And they saw Maurice actually climbing down, out of the back part of the building?'

'That's what O'Connor says. And we've got one clear footprint in the rubble he stepped on to get up. And three fairly clear ones on the ledge. That could be useful.'

'Unless he's thrown that pair of boots into the river,' said Benjamin. 'But he may not have done. Even professional criminals make mistakes.'

He was turning it all over as he spoke. Petrella would make a good witness, but he had seen only one man. The boys had seen all six, but were dangerous people to put into the box. Scientific evidence of the shoe marks. That might be conclusive. Juries love a bit of science.

'I'll try it on the Director of Public Prosecutions,' he said at last. 'And see what he thinks.'

The case of the Queen against Borner and Others was news at all its stages. The ingenious and cold-blooded killing had caught the public attention. Even the hearing in the Magistrates' Court produced its quota of sensations.

Such proceedings are often a mere formality, a skirmish preliminary to the main battle at the Old Bailey. But in this case it was clear that the opposition meant to fight the whole way. Maurice Borner was defended by Mr Walter Frenchman, Q.C., who was old, fat, and experienced; the remaining five by Mr Michael Harsch, an up-and-coming young criminal advocate of considerable ability.

Thinking things over afterwards, Petrella came to the conclusion that, although he disliked young Mr Harsch with all his heart, it was old Mr Frenchman who had done the damage. Mr Harsch had been too open in his dislike of the police. He had played too obviously to the public gallery. But some of the mud that he slung had seem to stick.

It had not, for instance, taken him long to ferret out the fact that Petrella occupied the flat below Mr Wetherall, from whose school most of the witnesses came, and he had built upon this fact an impressive edifice of falsehood and collusion.

'And now, Inspector,' said Mr Harsch, when he had exhausted this agreeable topic. 'Now we come to the occasion—the remarkable occasion—on which you failed to recognise one of my clients, Mr Dixon, when you saw him, as is alleged, indulging in a game of cricket, but yet had no difficulty in recognising him afterwards, when it suited your superior officers that you should do so.'

This did not appear to need an answer but, as Mr Harsch had paused for breath, Petrella said, 'Yes.'

'You agree that it was extraordinary?'

'Do I agree that what was extraordinary?'

'That you failed to recognise this man when you first saw him.'

'I recognised him,' said Petrella, 'but failed to place him.'

'Just what do you mean by that?'

'I mean that I recognised his face, but failed to recall his name—at the time.'

'When had you seen him before?'

This was a fast one. If Petrella had said, as he very nearly did, 'In this Court, a month before,' it would have been a grave technical error. He blocked it by saying, 'I had seen him some time before.'

'And how did you recognise him afterwards?'

'Afterwards I was shown certain photographs, and saw the accused himself, and recognised him as the man I had seen.'

'In fact, you conveniently recognised him when pressed to do so later.'

'Certainly not.'

'And you are quite sure that the man you saw, and failed to recognise, was the same as the man you saw later and succeeded in recognising?'

'Oh yes.'

'You have, if I may say so, a conveniently selective memory.'

Petrella was glad to recall, however, that Mr Harsch had not had things all his own way. Next in the witness box was Mr Wetherall, called to speak to the character of the boys concerned.

It was, perhaps, rash of Mr Harsch to cross-examine, but he had not yet learnt when to let well alone. 'I suggest, Mr Wetherall,' he said, 'that in a natural desire to speak well of your boys, you have been inclined to somewhat over-estimate their truthfulness and powers of observation.'

'I'm sorry, Harsch,' said Mr Wetherall, 'that you should so soon have forgotten the elementary rules of grammar which I tried for four years to drum into your head. There is no excuse, even in a court of law, for splitting an infinitive.'

The press had liked this—COUNSEL REBUKED BY OWN HEADMASTER. They had liked it a good deal more than Mr Harsch himself. Most of his friends at the Bar believed he had been to Marlborough.

Petrella was told that he had behaved himself quite well. In retrospect he was glad of it. There were moments that afternoon when he had despised, in the person of the sleek, young advocate, the whole British judicial system. He had been forewarned what to expect, and was tolerably equipped to deal with it. At the worst it had been a wasted and frustrating afternoon.

But what was a young policeman, whose talents lay in the physical apprehension of criminals, to make of the dialectical hair-splitting of men like Mr Harsch? And why, in the name of sanity, did the newspapers invariably select for their headline every point made *against* the police—DETECTIVE HAD CONVENIENT MEMORY, SAYS BARRISTER—and as invariably omit the occasions on which the Magistrate concluded the case by exonerating the officer concerned of the suggestions made against him?

Was it because the insults were news and the compliments were not? Or was it, perhaps, because the reporter concerned had been fined forty shillings for a parking offence the month before, and now saw an easy chance of getting his own back?

But these matters were not important. They were pinpricks in comparison with the disaster that had followed.

At the conclusion of the prosecution's case the Magistrate had, with apparent reluctance, committed the six men for trial at the Central Criminal Court, but had then been guilty of the outrageous folly, at Mr Frenchman's request and in the face of the strongest police pressure, of releasing all but Maurice Borner on bail. Useless to point out, as Benjamin did, his long face white with fury, that the backbone of the prosecution's case, so far as the five were concerned, was likely to be the evidence of schoolboys. And that if the gang was allowed to go free between the preliminary hearing and the trial of the case, there would very likely be no case at all. The Magistrate had listened, but with a shut mind.

'I might as well have been talking to the backside of my own car,' said Benjamin. 'If he wants every one of those boys to tell a different story—or no story at all—by the time they get to the Old Bailey, he's going the right way about it.'

'Curse the lot of them,' said Petrella, sitting on the edge of his bed on a fine September morning, and swinging pyjama'd legs. It was ten o'clock. But somehow he felt disinclined to get up at all. Nor was there any need for him to get up if he did not want to. For he was on holiday.

It was not a holiday that he had sought, for he had no wish to leave Gabriel Street until the Borner affair was settled, but two days earlier Superintendent Benjamin had given him a direct order.

'We've got a bit of a breathing space,' he said, 'before the case comes on at the Bailey. It can't be in the calendar before October. You're to go off and treat yourself to a holiday.'

When Petrella looked mutinous, he had added, 'I'm not thinking of you. I'm thinking of myself. If you don't take a breather now, you won't last out the winter. We're too understaffed for me to allow you more than ten days, but ten days you'll take, whether you like it or not.'

Petrella had not even the excuse that there was nowhere for him to go. Colonel Montefiore, an aged relative of his mother, had given him an open but explicit invitation to stay at his home in the Chilterns whenever Petrella felt inclined. 'Bring old clothes. I can lend you a gun. And you can have your breakfast in bed every day,' wrote the Colonel. 'And forget about criminals. The only criminals we have round here are poachers, and they're all my friends.'

Two days ago the prospect had been attractive. Now, somehow, Petrella was not sure. He felt tired and irritable. At the same time restless, but disinclined for action. He pulled on a dressing-gown, and wandered across to the window.

Summer was still to all appearances in full swing. The trees were heavy with leaves, and the sky was blue. A warm summer wind was driving ice-cream cartons and scraps of paper along the pavement. In spite of the sun Petrella shivered. His mouth was dry and his feet were cold. He felt disinclined for food, but thought that a cup of strong coffee might do him good.

He was to take the afternoon train, and a bag, half packed, lay on the floor beside his bed. It occurred to him that he was ill-equipped for a visit to the country. It was all very well for the Colonel to talk about old clothes. There were standards to be observed. He would have to do some shopping.

An hour later he left the house. It was a glorious day, and the sun struck down through the leaves. He thought that a gentle walk might do him good, and he set off along Brinkman Road.

He stopped at Spinks', in the Broadway, and bought himself half a dozen handkerchiefs, but thought that Spinks' widely-advertised line in Gent's Genuine Norfolk Jackets was hardly what the Chilterns would expect. He would have to visit the West End to get what he wanted. He decided that the quickest way, at that time of day, would be to cut across to the Surrey Docks Underground Station.

Childers Street is a long an uninspiring thoroughfare. Towards its far end it swings sharply to the right into River Street. Petrella had an idea that, if he kept straight on, there was a back way which must bring him out somewhere near the Docks Station. He realised that he was wrong when the tiny street he was using degenerated into a passage between walls of houses, and ended in a pair of heavy gates which were standing open.

Out of obstinacy he went on through the gates, and found himself on a triangular, cobbled quay which sloped down to the bank of the Surrey Union Canal. The edge of the quay was equipped with a line of iron bollards, and sitting on one of the bollards, smoking a short pipe, was a brown-faced, white-bearded man, whom Petrella recognised.

'Why, hullo, Doctor,' said Petrella, 'this is a pleasant surprise.'

'Good morning, Inspector,' said the old man. 'Come to inspect my boat?'

'I don't know that I ought—'

The old man looked at him and said, 'You look as if a drink wouldn't do you any harm.'

His barge, the Journey's End, was tied up, fore and aft, to the quay. They stepped on to her iron-plated deck, and made their way astern to the scuttle, which led down into the owner's living-quarters, sleeping-quarters, and tiny galley. It looked beautifully snug. Petrella sat down on the spare bunk and watched the doctor pottering about with a percolator, a packet of sugar, a saucepan of milk, and two mugs.

It all took a long time, and before the coffee was ready it seemed to Petrella that he must have slept and woken again. He looked up to see the doctor standing in front of him, a china mug in one hand and a puzzled look on his face.

'You all right, son?'

'Of course I'm all right,' said Petrella.

His own voice sounded thick and faraway. 'A bit tired, that's all. But I'll be all right. I'm starting my holiday today.'

'Let's see you on your feet.'

Petrella started to get up. Then the barge was no longer tied up. It tilted alarmingly. He reached out, and caught the edge of the table to steady himself. There was a heavy sea running. And a curtain of mist floated in front of his eyes. Odd that the weather should change so quickly. At that moment he lost hold of the edge of the table, and before he could steady himself the whole barge had tilted back again, and deposited him on the bunk. Then the mist dropped down.

The owner of the *Journey's End* stood for a moment, peering at this young man who had called to drink a cup of his coffee and had passed out on his spare bunk. Up and down the waterfronts, docksides, and canals of south London, people called him 'Doctor'. In twenty years it had grown to be a sort of courtesy title. Few people realised that he was, in fact, a qualified doctor, and a man of considerable, if curious, attainments.

He laid his hand on Petrella's forehead, which was damp and hot, felt his pulse, and listened for a moment to his breathing. Then he unlaced Petrella's shoes and took them off, removed his coat and waistcoat, collar and tie, pulled a pillow from his own bunk and put it under the young man's head, and covered him with a couple of rugs.

Minutes, or hours, later Petrella opened his eyes and tried to sit up. The old man jumped up out of his chair and came across.

'See if you can drink this,' he said. It was a tumbler of water, into which he dropped a couple of white tablets. 'I didn't try to push 'em down your throat when you were out. I've seen people choke that way.'

'What is it? What's up?' said Petrella. 'Did I pass out?'

'My guess is you've got flu, and a high temperature,' said the old man. 'Did you say you were starting a holiday?'

'That's right,' said Petrella. 'Ten days' holiday.' He drank up the glass, and went to sleep again. It was a hot, black-and-red sleep, a sleep of aching bones and bad dreams, in which he was endlessly cross-examined by a crocodile in a stuff gown who alternately snapped its yellow teeth and wept over him.

When he finally opened his eyes and started on the slow and difficult job of working out where he was, the first thing he noticed was that they really were afloat. No wild and illusory lurching this time, but a gentle, pleasant pitching of the great, iron coffin in which he lay. He sat up in the bunk too quickly. And lay back again while the world stopped spinning.

Then he propped himself up more cautiously on his elbow and looked round. On the fixed table, in reach of his arm, was a tumbler of water. He picked it up, drained it, was conscious of a bitter, not unpleasant taste, and fell asleep again almost before his head was on the pillow . . .

When he woke next it was night. The cabin was lit by the warm and cosy glow of a paraffin lamp. As he stirred, the doctor got up from behind the table and came over to him.

Petrella found that his head was quite clear. 'I'm afraid,' he said, 'I've been a bit of a nuisance.'

'Far from it. I've never had a more docile patient.'

'How long have I been here?'

The doctor counted on his fingers. 'Two days,' he said. 'And a little over ten hours.'

'Good God.' It is always startling when a tiny segment of life goes by default.

'You said you were starting a holiday. I saw no reason why you shouldn't have it on my barge, under the care of a medical practitioner. Qualified, if a bit rusty.'

'It's very kind of you,' said Petrella. 'I was going to stay with my mother's cousin. He'll be having a fit.'

'We'll send him a telegram first thing tomorrow morning.'

'Where are we? And how did we get here?'

'If you ask too many questions.' said the doctor, 'you'll put your temperature up again. We're in a stretch of water called the Long Neck, just below Walton. We came here via Greenland Dock, Russia Dock, Lavender Pond, and the open river. Now go to sleep.'

When Petrella woke next morning, he felt ravenously hungry and knew that he was well again. After breakfast the doctor went ashore to dispatch a telegram to Colonel Montefiore, at Blagdens Wake, Nettlebed. He wrote it out and handed it, with some misgiving, over the counter of a tiny village shop which called itself a sub post office. His misgivings were entirely justified, for it never reached its destination, though a Colonel Mount-ferry of Nettlebed House, Bannockburn, did receive, some weeks later, a telegram which said:

Taken ill suddenly. Will write. Patrick.

The six days that followed were, without any exception, the best that Petrella could remember.

He was steady on his feet by the evening of the first day, and strong enough next morning to help the doctor about the simple manoeuvres of his craft.

He learnt to operate lock gates with a handle like a huge grandfather clock-key which lived in the barge's engine-room, to steer for long, slow miles through a forgotten waterway, where they might not see a house for hours at a stretch, and their only visitors would be the bullocks who would gallop to the hedges when they heard the *Journey's End* coming, and stand, breathing hard and rolling their frightened, curious eyes until her iron bulk vanished round a bend or under one of the low, stone bridges which had so little headroom that it seemed impossible she should squeeze through them at all.

He learnt to tend the wants of the Diesel engine which drove them forward, to trim and fill the paraffin lamps, and to peel potatoes. But it was the evenings he enjoyed most. When the barge was safely tied up, and the lamps were lit; when supper had been eaten and washed up and stacked away, and they settled down to talk before going to bed.

He heard from the doctor something of his curious life. 'I was fifty,' said the old man. 'It was actually my fiftieth birthday, when I stopped being a doctor and became a bargemaster. I'd made quite a lot of money. Those were days when your patients came to you because they liked and trusted you, not because the Government told them to, and a man who was successful in his line could make a reasonable amount of money. I was unmarried, and I calculated that I had enough banked away to keep a man of my frugal habits in comfort for the best part of a century.

'That day I was called to the house of a man I knew well. He was a businessman. Not a tycoon, you understand, just a pleasant person who worked and worried from morning to night to support an expensive wife and three gold-plated children.

'When I reached the house he was dead. Thrombosis. A less fashionable complaint then than it is now. I shut my surgery that very day, sold my practice, and bought the *Journey's End*.

'It's the only decision in my life I've never regretted. I make enough by doing odd jobs to cover running expenses. Sometimes I hear from my stockbroker that my investments have gone up again. I never touch them. When I die they'll go to my old medical school.'

It wasn't until the evening of the fourth day that Petrella thought to inquire where they were going. He discovered that their destination was some miles short of Basingstoke, where they were delivering a grand piano, and some harvesting machinery, and picking up two ponies.

It was on the way back that Petrella told the doctor the whole story of the Borners and Roper from beginning to end, and the old man listened in absorbed and judicious silence. He interrupted only once to say, 'I knew Copper. He helped me with the barge. He was a nice boy, but too easily led.' And at the end of it all he said, 'You sound bitter about it. Why?'

'I did feel bitter about it,' said Petrella. 'I'm all right now. It was just that in the police we do a lot of work, and take a few risks and a few knocks in the interests of law and order, and one would think the law would be on our side.'

'The law's on no one's side,' said the doctor. 'Once it's on anyone's side, it stops being law at all and becomes something cooked up by the politicians.'

'Yes, but—' said Petrella.

'If you had the law behind you in the sense that it supported you whatever you did, right or wrong, you'd degenerate into a state security force. Like the Gestapo.'

Petrella said mutinously, 'I bet when the Gestapo caught half a dozen dangerous thugs the magistrate didn't let *them* out on bail.'

Unknown to Petrella, while the *Journey's End* was nosing her calm path among the water lilies of the Basingstoke and south-western Canal, in South Borough events were on the move.

On the morning following Petrella's departure, Mr Wetherall called on Superintendent Benjamin.

'Patrick and I are great friends,' he said. 'And I knocked on his door this morning to see if he'd gone. To tell you the truth, I wouldn't have been surprised to find him laid up. He hasn't been looking at all well lately. His room was empty, but there was a suitcase, which he'd obviously been meaning to take with him, on the floor, half packed.'

Benjamin had troubles of his own. He said, 'He may have been short of time. Suppose it was a question of coming back for his bag or catching the train? Or something like that.'

'It desn't sound like him,' said Wetherall. 'The breakfast things weren't washed up, either.'

'If you're really worried,' said Benjamin, 'I could get in touch with the people he's meant to be staying with. He left a telephone number.'

'If it wouldn't be too much trouble,' said Mr Wetherall.

However, no one was put to any trouble. For at that moment, Colonel Montefiore came through himself.

'Mistake?' he said. 'Of course there's no mistake. Patrick told us exactly which train he would catch. I assumed, when he failed to arrive, that he must be ill in bed at home. I think someone should go and see.'

[213]

Benjamin said he would do what he could, and turned a now worried face to Mr Wetherall. 'There's quite a few things *might* have happened,' he said. 'His holiday's his own affair. He could have changed his mind about where he was going. I'll have inquiries made, but we don't want to start a fuss about nothing. Things are rather upset round here as it is.'

Mr Wetherall swears that he said nothing. On the contrary, he asserts that it was one of his own boys that told *him* the news.

'You know that Inspector,' said Martin, who was head of the school that year, and a privileged character. 'The young one—Petrella. I heard the Borners done him. They coshed him the night before last. And dropped his body in the canal.'

'Where on earth did you hear that?'

'Everyone knows it,' said Martin. 'What we reckon is, they'll be after Mike and Terry and the others next. Bound to be. After all, *they're* witnesses, too, aren't they? Some of the boys are forming a vigilant committee—a sort of escort—to protect them till the trial comes on. A good idea, I think, don't you, sir?'

'Good heavens,' said Mr Wetherall. 'It's a terrible idea.' He cast his mind over the names of the boys concerned. Of the six who had come forward, the leaders had been Mike O'Connor and Terry Shane, both Irish boys, and both members of the large Irish colony which centred on Stafford Street, Latimer Street, and Cutaway Lane.

He remembered hearing that there had been bad blood, even before the Roper killing, between the Borners and the Irish. Something that someone had said in a pub, which had ended in broken glass and blood, and had been stored in the retentive Irish memory. If the Borners and their supporters got it into their heads that O'Connor and Shane were giving evidence out of spite—and if the school got involved—he pictured a battlefield strewn with South Borough Secondary School corpses, and hurried round once again to the Police Station.

He found that the news had run ahead of him.

'I can't get anything reliable,' growled Benjamin. 'There's talk of him being seen in Childers Road, and I'm having the bank of the canal there searched. As a precaution, you understand.'

'But it's four days now,' said Mr Wetherall. 'And he's not what you'd call an inconsiderate young man. Even if he'd gone off—'

Then he saw that Benjamin was as worried as he was.

[214]

That afternoon a police constable picked up a paper bag, with six new handkerchiefs in it, on the wharf at the end of Childers Road. The handkerchiefs were new, and there was an invoice with them, and the invoice had a number on it which indicated the assistant at Spinks' who had made the sale. She remembered Petrella and described him with an accuracy which suggested she had looked at him more than once. 'Dark black hair, young-looking, a brown face, very deep blue eyes.' She also remembered the raincoat he was wearing; and the fact that he had looked a bit under the weather.

Benjamin gave orders for a search of that section of the Surrey Canal. And sent an urgent message to Chief Superintendent Thom at District. Dragging operations were carried on by arc lamp all that night; and the next morning a team of frogmen was called in.

More than a hundred South Borough boys were late for school that morning, having stopped to watch the operation, and in the first break O'Connor addressed a mass meeting of his school-fellows. He was a thick, stocky, snub-nosed boy with sun-bleached hair, and like all Southern Irishmen he had a grasp of the essentials of mob oratory.

Mr Wetherall read the portents, and telephoned Superintendent Benjamin, who was even then in conference with his superiors.

'There'll likely be trouble,' said Dory, a slow-spoken man, who was in charge of the whole of the Division, both uniformed and detective branches. 'We'll need a few extra men to carry out a proper search for Petrella. I think I'll ask for them now, just in case.'

'It's the boys,' said Benjamin. 'They've got it into their heads that the Borners have knocked off Petrella to stop him giving evidence. It's a short step from that to the idea that they're planning to knock off the other witnesses too.'

'And you don't believe it?' said Thom.

'No, I don't,' said Benjamin. 'It's out of character. I'm afraid something may have happened to Petrella. He was looking pretty rotten. Supposed he passed out and slipped into the canal. Or he may just have lost his memory. But I don't believe anyone, even that gang, would be silly enough to knock off a witness, in cold blood. And remember, to make sense of it they've got to get rid of seven or eight boys as well.'

He wondered, afterwards, if he had been arguing to convince himself.

It was on the following evening, the sixth after Petrella's disappearance, that the fight occurred in Basset Street. No one quite knew how it started. The fact that it was half past nine suggested that Copper Dixon and Curly had been drinking, but the provocation seemed to have come from a group of schoolboys who had no business to be out at that hour. It ended in Copper losing two teeth from a thrown milk bottle and Terry Shane breaking his wrist in the scuffle that followed. A car load of policemen cleared the streets.

Terry Shane's father was not the person to allow an assault on his son to go unanswered. Micky Shane had had a distinguished career in the all-in wrestling ring, where his speciality had been bouncing his opponents on their heads. He was now growing fat, and a little out of training, but he commanded a considerable following in the Stafford Street area, and on the following evening a party consisting of eight or ten Irishmen paid a visit to the Six Bells, in Carver Street, which was known to be a stronghold of the Borners. Copper, who was the only one of the gang present, got out by a back door, and the Irishmen spent a pleasant ten minutes wrecking the Saloon Bar.

It is just possible that, left to themselves, the two factions might have felt honour was now satisfied, and called it a day.

The Borners and their mob of followers were beginning to show signs of nervousness. As long as the mob was in being, a powerful and flourishing entity, people had touched their hats to it out of fear of reprisals. Under the stress of circumstances, it was beginning to fall apart.

Had the boys of South Borough Secondary School been prepared to let the matter drop, it might have simmered down.

But they were not. On the contrary. Like harbingers of strife, the black-and-red caps blew before the storm, and where they went, fresh trouble was born.

The ninth evening after Petrella's disappearance was warm, even for September. Quiet, overcast, and still. Sammy Borner thought that he would pass the time with a game of snooker with the boys at Charley's. He left his car in the back street outside the entrance to the club, which was in a basement, and approached by a flight of iron steps. When he came out an hour later he found that all his tyres were flat. Not just one, but all four. He also observed five or six boys, one of them a chunky youth with light hair, standing on the pavement, their hands in their pockets, looking at nothing in particular.

'You do this?' he inquired.

'That's right,' said the chunky boy, and added, 'bloody murderer.'

Sammy hesitated for a moment, but the arrival of his friends, Harry, Curly, Copper, and Nick, who were leaving the club at the same time, gave him a feeling of solidarity.

The opposition, after all, was only five schoolboys. They had earned a lesson. Sammy ducked into the back of the car, picked up a jack handle, and moved forward. The chunky boy whistled shrilly, and the next moment the street was full of boys and men.

The riot call reached Dory at Borough High Street Police Station, where he was in conference with Benjamin.

'The Irish have got Sammy Borner and his friends holed up in a snooker cellar in Parton Street,' he said. 'There's been a bit of bloodshed. If they get their hands on them, in their present temper, they'll finish them.'

'And that,' said Benjamin, 'would break my heart.'

Dory was already giving his orders.

Two squad cars and a tender reached the corner of Parton Street together. The air was full of the noise of battle and breaking glass.

'Sounds quite a party,' said Dory. He marshalled his forces. 'Ben, you stay here with four men, and keep them away from the cars.' And when Benjamin protested, 'In a mess-up like this, a uniform's worth more than a good character.' He arranged the eight men he had chosen into careful formation. 'Front two link arms with me,' he said. 'Use your feet if you have to. And keep together.'

They went round the corner like a human tank. It took them sixty highly-coloured seconds to reach the billiard saloon, to push aside the table which was up-ended against the door, and to replace it behind them.

They found four badly-frightened men, and a fifth lying on his face in a pool of blood.

'We're in,' said Dory. 'But that's not to say we'll get out again. They'll be expecting us this time. Wainwright, go and see if you can find a back door or a window or something. Who's this?'

'It's Curly,' said Sammy Borner. He looked as if he had been crying. 'They've killed him. You've got to do something.'

'We're none of us dead yet,' said Dory.

There was a splintering crash from the street. The crowd had tipped Sammy's car up on to one side and over into the mouth of the area. The smell of spilt petrol filled the air.

'There *is* a window, sir,' said Wainwright. 'But it opens into a sort of little closed yard.'

[217]

'I don't care if it opens into the back of beyond,' said Dory. 'So long as it leads somewhere. Hughes and Gavigan, carry this man. And don't drop him. We want him in one piece. Now let's get going.'

The window was barely large enough. As they manhandled Curly through, there came from the room they had left a muffled explosion followed by the white glare of detonated petrol.

Dory reformed his force in the courtyard. 'Soon as we get round the corner,' he said, 'we'll be in sight. Make straight for the cars, and don't stop for anything.'

Once again the power of united effort, and the drive of a man who knew his own mind, prevailed against disorganised numbers. They tumbled into the cars.

'Make for Gabriel Street,' said Dory. 'It'll give them farther to go if they come after us.'

'They're coming all right,' said Benjamin. 'So's the Fire Brigade.' As they rounded the corner, they heard the bells of the first fire engine.

The *Journey's End* tied up at the Camberwell basin and Petrella climbed ashore. The sky was coal-black and threatening.

'Lucky you've got a mackintosh,' said the doctor. 'Rain soon, and plenty of it, if I'm any judge.'

'I don't know how to thank you,' said Petrella. 'It's been the finest holiday I've ever had.'

'Nothing to thank me for,' said the doctor. 'I've enjoyed having you along. Come again soon.'

Petrella said he would; but he knew, even then, that no other trip would be quite like that first one.

He climbed the steps from the dockside up to the level of the Camberwell Road. His first idea was to take a bus home. When he saw the glow in the sky to the north-west, and heard the sound of the fire bells, he changed his mind. He thought he would make first for Gabriel Street, to pick up the news. It was less than ten minutes' quick walk.

He had covered half the distance when, with spectacular suddenness, the heavens were opened and the rain came down. Petrella buttoned up the neck of his mackintosh, and broke into a jog trot . . .

Benjamin and Dory were standing in the first-storey window of Gabriel Street, looking out at the crowd which filled the short approach road. The crowd was mostly men, with a scattering of boys. It was not doing anything in particular.

[218]

'I hope they don't try to get in,' said Dory. 'That'd mean calling for reinforcements. We've handled them ourselves so far. I'd like to keep it that way.'

'They don't know what they want,' said Benjamin. 'It wouldn't take very much to move them in either direction.'

'Thank God it's raining. That'll wash the whisky out of them. What the hell are you laughing at?'

Superintendent Benjamin did not often laugh. Now his long face was wrinkled into folds of genuine merriment.

'I was thinking,' he said, 'that the Borners have—what's the legal word?—surrendered to their bail.'

'They've surrendered to their bail, all right,' said Dory. He thought of them as he had left them ten minutes before: Curly still unconscious, being worked on by the police doctor; the other four, white-faced, jumpy even when the cell doors had shut on them.

'Do you think we ought to tell Whitcomb?'

Dory said something uncomplimentary about the Stipendiary Magistrate and went over again to look at the crowd.

'Count your blessings,' said Benjamin. 'If we can get through without any more broken heads, we'll come out the right side of the ledger. Think of the evidence those boys are going to give after tonight.'

Dory said, 'I fancy they're moving.'

'Moving?' said Benjamin. 'They're running away.'

There was a disturbance at the mouth of the street. More than a disturbance, a turmoil.

The crowd, which had already started to thin out, was thrown back on itself, as a stream is thrown when it meets a more powerful current. Men moved back on either side, leaving a clear lane in the middle. And down the lane was advancing—

'Good God,' said Benjamin. He leaned forward and jerked the window open.

It was hardly Petrella's fault that his long, black hair should have been flattened by the rain over his skull, or that his face, under the neon light, should have taken on a peculiar bluish-white tinge.

Benjamin took a grip of himself. He reminded himself of the unlikelihood—indeed, the impropriety—of the ghost of a Detective Inspector revisiting his old station; and he jumped for the stairs, ran down, and pushed through the crowd.

'Open the door,' he said to the Station Sergeant.

'What about them outside?'

'I don't think we shall have much trouble with them now. Help me with these bolts.'

Petrella advanced diffidently into a hushed room. 'Good evening, sir,' he said. 'Good evening, Sergeant. What's up?' He gazed in blank astonishment at the dozen and more uniformed men sitting round on benches. 'Why the reception committee?'

'You'd better come upstairs,' said Benjamin. And to the Sergeant, 'You can send 'em all home, except normal duty men.'

Upstairs Petrella found Chief Superintendent Dory lighting a cigarette. He observed that he had a split ear and a black eye.

'Now that you are back,' said Dory grimly, 'perhaps you'll be good enough to explain what you've been up to.'

But Petrella, for once, was unperturbed. He was triple-armed in his own unassailable rectitude.

'I don't know what's been going on around here,' he said. 'But it can't be anything to do with *me*. I've been on holiday.'

THE HOUSE BY THE HEADLAND

by Sapper

'Y ou'll no get there, zurr. There'll be a rare storm this night. Best bide here, and be going tomorrow morning after 'tis over.'

The warning of my late host, weather-wise through years of experience, rang through my brain as I reached the top of the headland, and, too late, I cursed myself for not having heeded his words. With a gasp I flung my pack down on the ground, and loosened my collar. Seven miles behind me lay the comfortable inn where I had lunched; eight miles in front the one where I proposed to dine. And midway between them was I, dripping with perspiration and panting for breath.

Not a breath of air was stirring; not a sound broke the death-like stillness, save the sullen lazy beat of the sea against the rocks below. Across the horizon, as far as the eye could see, stretched a mighty bank of black cloud, which was spreading slowly and relentlessly over the whole heaven. Already its edge was almost overhead, and as I felt the first big drop of rain on my forehead, I cursed myself freely once again. If only I had listened to mine host: if only I was still in his comfortable oak-beamed coffee-room, drinking his most excellent ale . . . I felt convinced he was the type of man who would treat such trifles as regulation hours with the contempt they deserved. And, even as I tasted in imagination the bite of the grandest of all drinks on my parched tongue, and looked through the glass bottom of the tankard at the sanded floor, the second great drop of rain splashed on my face.

For a moment or two I wavered. Should I go back that seven miles, and confess myself a fool, or should I go on the further eight and hope that the next cellar would be as good as the last? In either case I was bound to get drenched to the skin, and at length I made up my mind. I would not turn back for any storm, and the matter of the quality of the ale must remain in the lap of the gods. And at that moment, like a solid wall of water, the rain came.

I had travelled into most corners of the world, in the course of forty years' wandering; I have been through the monsoon going south to Singapore from Japan, I have been caught on the edge of a water-spout in the South Sea Islands; but I have never known anything like the rain which came down that June evening on the south-west coast of England. In half a minute every garment I wore was soaked; the hills and the sea were blotted out, and I stumbled forward blindly, unable to see more than a yard in front of me. Then, almost as abruptly as it had started, the rain ceased. I could feel the water squelching in my boots, and trickling down my back, as I kept steadily descending into the valley beyond the headland.

There was nothing for it now but to go through with it. I couldn't get any wetter than I was; so that, when I suddenly rounded a little knoll and saw in front a low-lying, rambling house, the idea of sheltering there did not at once occur to me. I glanced at it casually in the semi-darkness, and was trudging past the gate, my mind busy with other things, when a voice close behind me made me stop with a sudden start. A man was speaking, and a second before I could have sworn I was alone.

'A bad night, sir,' he remarked, in a curiously deep voice, 'and it will be worse soon. The thunder and lightning is nearly over. Will you not come in and shelter? I can supply you with a change of clothes if you are wet?'

'You are very good, sir,' I answered slowly, peering at the tall, gaunt figure beside me. 'But I think I will be getting on, thank you all the same.'

'As you like,' he answered indifferently, and even as he spoke a vivid flash of lightning quivered and died in the thick blackness of the sky, and almost instantaneously a deafening crash of thunder seemed to come from just over our heads. 'As you like,' he repeated, 'but I shall be glad of your company if you cared to stay the night.'

It was a kind offer, though in a way the least one would expect in similar circumstances, and I hesitated. Undoubtedly there was little pleasure to be anticipated in an eight-mile tramp under such conditions, and yet there was something—something indefinable, incoherent—which said to me insistently: 'Go on; don't stop. Go on.'

I shook myself in annoyance, and my wet clothes clung to me clammily. Was I, at my time of life, nervous, because a man had spoken to me unexpectedly?

'I think if I may,' I said, 'I will change my mind and avail myself of your kind offer. It is no evening for walking for pleasure.'

Without a word he led the way into the house, and I followed. Even in the poor light I could see that the garden was badly kept, and that the path leading to the front door was covered with weeds. Bushes, wet with the rain, hung in front of our faces, dripping dismally on to steps leading up to the door, giving the impression almost of a mosaic.

Inside the hall was in darkness, and I waited while he opened the door into one of the rooms. I heard him fumbling for a match, and at that moment another blinding flash lit up the house as if it had been day. I had a fleeting vision of the stairs—a short, broad flight—with a window at the top; of the two doors, one apparently leading to the servants' quarters, the other opposite the one my host had already opened. But most vivid of all in that quick photograph was the condition of the hall itself. Three or four feet above my head a lamp hung from the ceiling, and from it, in every direction, there seemed to be spiders' webs coated with dust and filth. They stretched to every picture; they stretched to the top of all the doors. One long festoon was almost brushing against my face, and for a moment a wave of unreasoning panic filled me.

Almost did I turn and run, so powerful was it; then, with an effort, I pulled myself together. For a grown man to become nervous of a spider's web is rather too much of a good thing, and after all it was none of my business. In all probability the man was a recluse, who was absorbed in more important matters than the cleanliness of his house. Though how he could stand the smell—dank and rotten—defeated me. It came to my nostrils as I stood there, waiting for him to strike a match, and the scent of my own wet Harris tweed failed to conceal it. It was the smell of an unlived-in house, grown damp and mildewed with years of neglect, and once again I shuddered. Confound the fellow! Would he never get the lamp lit? I didn't mind his spiders' webs and the general filth of his hall, provided I could get some dry clothes on.

[223]

'Come in.' I looked up to see him standing in the door. 'I regret that there seems to be no oil in the lamp, but there are candles on the mantelpiece, should you care to light them.'

Somewhat surprised I stepped into the room, and then his next remark made me halt in amazement.

'When my wife comes down, I must ask her about the oil. Strange of her to have forgotten.'

Wife! What manner of woman could this be who allowed her house to get into such a condition of dirt and neglect? And were there no servants? However, again, it was none of my business, and I felt in my pockets for matches. Luckily they were in a watertight box, and with a laugh I struck one and lit the candles.

'It's so infernally dark,' I remarked, 'that the stranger within the gates requires a little light, to get his bearings.'

In some curiosity I glanced at my host's face in the flickering light. As yet I had had no opportunity of observing him properly, but now as unostentatiously as possible I commenced to study it. Cadaverous almost to the point of emaciation, he had a ragged bristly moustache, while his hair, plentifully flecked with grey, was brushed untidily back from his forehead. But dominating everything were his eyes, which glowed and smouldered from under his bushy eyebrows, till they seemed to burn into me.

More and more I found myself regretting the fact that I had accepted his offer. His whole manner was so strange that for the first time doubts as to his sanity began to creep into my mind. And to be alone with a madman in a deserted house, miles from any other habitation, with a terrific thunderstorm raging, was not a prospect which appealed to me greatly. Then I remembered his reference to his wife, and felt more reassured . . .

'You and your wife must find it lonely here,' I hazarded, when the silence had lasted some time.

'Why should my wife feel the loneliness?' he answered, harshly. 'She has me—her husband . . . What more does a woman require?'

'Oh! Nothing, nothing,' I replied hastily, deeming discretion the better part of veracity. 'Wonderful air; beautiful view. I wonder if I could have a dry coat as you so kindly suggested?'

I took off my own wet one as I spoke, and threw it over the back of a chair. Then, receiving no answer to my request, I looked at my host. His back was half towards me, and he was staring into the hall outside. He stood quite motionless, and as apparently he had failed to hear me,

I was on the point of repeating my remark when he turned and spoke to me again.

'A pleasant surprise for my wife, sir, don't you think? She was not expecting me home until tomorrow morning.'

'Very,' I assented . . .

'Eight miles I have walked, in order to prevent her being alone. That should answer your remark about her feeling the loneliness.'

He peered at me fixedly, and I again assented.

'Most considerate of you,' I murmured, 'most considerate.'

But the man only chuckled by way of answer, and swinging round, continued to stare into the gloomy, filthy hall.

Outside the storm was increasing in fury. Flash followed flash with such rapidity that the whole sky westwards formed into a dancing sheet of flame, while the roll of the thunder seemed like the continuous roar of a bombardment with heavy guns. But I was aware of it only subconsciously; my attention was concentrated on the gaunt man standing so motionless in the centre of the room.

So occupied was I with him that I never heard his wife's approach until suddenly, looking up, I saw that by the door there stood a woman—a woman who paid no attention to me, but only stared fearfully at her husband, with a look of dreadful terror in her eyes. She was young, far younger than the man—and pretty in a homely, countrified way. And as she stared at the gaunt, cadaverous husband she seemed to be trying to speak, while ceaselessly she twisted a wisp of a pocket handkerchief in her hands.

'I didn't expect you home so soon, Rupert,' she stammered at length. 'Have you had a good day?'

'Excellent,' he answered, and his eyes seemed to glow more fiendishly than ever. 'And now I have come home to my little wife, and her loving welcome.'

She laughed a forced, unnatural laugh, and came a few steps into the room.

'There is no oil in the lamp, my dear,' he continued, suavely. 'Have you been too busy to remember to fill it?'

'I will go and get some,' she said, quickly turning towards the door. But the man's hand shot out and caught her arm, and at his touch she shrank away, cowering.

'I think not,' he cried, harshly. 'We will sit in the darkness, my dear, and—wait.'

'How mysterious you are, Rupert!' She forced herself to speak

[225]

lightly. 'What are we going to wait for?'

But the man only laughed—a low, mocking chuckle—and pulled the girl nearer to him.

'Aren't you going to kiss me, Mary? It's such a long time since you kissed me—a whole twelve hours.'

The girl's free hand clenched tight, but she made no other protest as her husband took her in his arms and kissed her. Only it seemed to be that her whole body was strained and rigid, as if to brace herself to met a caress she loathed . . . In fact the whole situation was becoming distinctly embarrassing. The man seemed to have completely forgotten my existence, and the girl so far had not even looked at me. Undoubtedly a peculiar couple, and a peculiar house. Those cobwebs: I couldn't get them out of my mind.

'Hadn't I better go and fill the lamp now?' she asked after a time. 'Those candles give a very poor light, don't they?'

'Quite enough for my purpose, my dear wife,' replied the man. 'Come and sit down and talk to me.'

With his hand still holding her arm he drew her to a sofa, and side by side they sat down. I noticed that all the time he was watching her covertly out of the corner of his eye, while she stared straight in front of her as if she was waiting for something to happen . . . And at that moment a door banged, upstairs.

'What's that?' the girl half rose, but the man pulled her back.

'The wind, my dear,' he chuckled. 'What else could it be? The house is empty save for us.'

'Hadn't I better go up and see that all the windows are shut?' she said, nervously. 'The storm makes me feel frightened.'

'That's why I hurried back to you, my love. I couldn't bear to think of you spending tonight alone.' Again he chuckled horribly, and peered at the girl beside him. 'I said to myself, "She doesn't expect me back till tomorrow morning. I will surprise my darling wife, and go back home tonight." Wasn't it kind of me, Mary?'

'Of course it was, Rupert,' she stammered. 'Very kind of you. I think I'll just go up and put on a jersey. I'm feeling a little cold.'

She tried to rise, but her husband still held her; and then suddenly there came on her face such a look of pitiable terror that involuntarily I took a step forward. She was staring at the door, and her lips were parted as if to cry out, when the man covered her mouth with his free hand and dragged her brutally to her feet.

'Alone, my wife—all alone,' he snarled. 'My dutiful, loving wife all

[226]

alone. What a good thing I returned to keep her company!'

For a moment or two she struggled feebly; then he half carried, half forced her close by me to a position behind the open door. I could have touched them as they passed; but I seemed powerless to move. Instinctively I knew what was going to happen; but I could do nothing save stand and stare at the door, while the girl, half fainting, crouched against the wall, and her husband stood over her motionless and terrible. And thus we waited, while the candles guttered in their sockets, listening to the footsteps which were coming down the stairs . . .

Twice I strove to call out; twice the sound died away in my throat. I felt as one does in some awful nightmare, when a man cries aloud and no sound comes, or runs his fastest and yet does not move. In it, I was yet not of it; it was as if I was the spectator of some inexorable tragedy with no power to intervene.

The steps came nearer. They were crossing the hall now—the cobwebby hall—and the next moment I saw a young man standing in the open door.

'Mary, where are you, my darling?' He came into the room and glanced around. And, as he stood there, one hand in his pocket, smiling cheerily, the man behind the door put out his arm and gripped him by the shoulder. In an instant the smile vanished and the youngster spun round, his face set and hard.

'Here is your darling, John Trelawnay,' said the husband quietly. 'What do you want with her?'

'Ah!' The youngster's breath came a little faster, as he stared at the older man. 'You've come back unexpectedly, have you? It's the sort of damned dirty trick you would play.'

I smiled involuntarily: this was carrying the war into the enemy's camp with a vengeance.

'What are you doing in this house alone with my wife, John Trelawnay?' Into the quiet voice had crept a note of menace, and, as I glanced at the speaker and noticed the close clenching and unclenching of his powerful hands, I realized that there was going to be trouble. The old, old story again, but, rightly or wrongly, with every sympathy of mine on the side of the sinners.

'Your wife by a trick only, Rupert Carlingham,' returned the other hotly. 'You know she's never loved you; you know she has always loved me.'

'Nevertheless—my wife. But I ask you again, what are you doing in this house while I am away?'

[227]

'Did you expect us to stand outside in the storm?' muttered the other.

For a moment the elder man's eyes blazed, and I thought he was going to strike the youngster. Then, with an effort, he controlled himself, and his voice was ominously quiet as he spoke again.

'You lie, John Trelawnay.' His brooding eyes never left the other's face. 'It was no storm that drove you here today; no thunder that made you call my wife your darling. You came because you knew I was away; because you thought—you and your mistress—that I should not return till tomorrow.'

For a while he was silent, while the girl still crouched against the wall staring at him fearfully, and the youngster, realizing the hopelessness of further denial, faced him with folded arms. In silence I watched them from the shadow beyond the fireplace, wondering what I ought to do. There is no place for any outsider in such a situation, much less a complete stranger; and had I consulted my own inclinations I would have left the house there and then and chanced the storm still raging outside. I got as far as putting on my coat again, and making a movement towards the door, when the girl looked at me with such an agony of entreaty in her eyes that I paused. Perhaps it was better that I should stop; perhaps if things got to a head, and the men started fighting, I might be of some use.

And at that moment Rupert Carlingham threw back his head and laughed. It echoed and re-echoed through the room, peal after peal of maniacal laughter, while the girl covered her face with her hands and shrank away, and the youngster, for all his pluck, retreated a few steps. The man was mad, there was no doubt about it: and the laughter of a madman is perhaps the most awful thing a human being may hear.

Quickly I stepped forward; it seemed to me that if I was to do anything at all the time had now come.

'I think, Mr Carlingham,' I said firmly, 'that a little quiet discussion would be of advantage to everyone.'

He ceased laughing, and stared at me in silence. Then his eyes left my face and fixed themselves again on the youngster. It was useless; he was blind to everything except his own insensate rage. And, before I could realize his intention, he sprang.

'You'd like me to divorce her, wouldn't you?' he snarled, as his hand sought John Trelawnay's throat. 'So that you could marry her. . . . But I'm not going to—no. I know a better thing than divorce.'

The words were choked on his lips by the youngster's fist, which crashed again and again into his face; but the man seemed insensible to pain. They swayed backwards and forwards, while the lightning, growing fainter and fainter in the distance, quivered through the room from time to time, and the two candles supplied the rest of the illumination. Never for an instant did the madman relax his grip on the youngster's throat: never for an instant did the boy cease his sledge-hammer blows on the other's face. But he was tiring, it was obvious; no normal flesh and blood could stand the frenzied strength against him. And, suddenly, it struck me that murder was being done, in front of my eyes.

With a shout I started forward—somehow they must be separated. And then I stopped motionless again: the girl had slipped past me with her face set and hard. With a strength for which I would not have given her credit she seized both her husband's legs about the knees, and lifted his feet off the ground, so that his only support was the grip of his left hand on the youngster's throat and the girl's arms about his knees. He threw her backwards and forwards as if she had been a child, but still she clung on, and then, in an instant, it was all over. His free right hand had been forgotten . . .

I saw the boy sway nearer in his weakness, and the sudden flash of a knife. There was a little choking gurgle, and they all crashed down together, with the youngster underneath. And when the madman rose the boy lay still, with the shaft of the knife sticking out from his coat above his heart.

It was then that Rupert Carlingham laughed again, while his wife, mad with grief, knelt beside the dead boy, pillowing his head on her lap. For what seemed an eternity I stood watching, unable to move or speak; then the murderer bent down and swung his wife over his shoulder. And, before I realized what he was going to do, he had left the room, and I saw him passing the window outside.

The sight galvanized me into action; there was just a possibility I might avert a double tragedy. With a loud shout I dashed out of the front door, and down the ill-kept drive; but when I got to the open ground he seemed to have covered an incredible distance, considering his burden. I could see him shambling over the turf, up the side of the valley which led to the headland where the rain had caught me, and, as fast as I could, I followed him, shouting as I ran. But it was no use— gain on him I could not. Steadily, with apparent ease, he carried the girl up the hill, taking no more notice of my cries than he had of my presence earlier in the evening. And, with the water squelching from my boots, I ran after him—no longer wasting my breath on shouting, but saving it all in my frenzied endeavour to catch him before it was too late. For once again I knew what was going to happen, even as I had known when I heard the footsteps coming down the stairs.

I was still fifty yards from him when he reached the top of the cliff; and for a while he paused there silhouetted against the angry sky. He seemed to be staring out to sea, and the light from the flaming red sunset, under the black of the storm, shone on his great, gaunt figure, bathing it in a wonderful splendour. The next moment he was gone . . . I heard him give one loud cry; then he sprang into space with the girl still clasped in his arms.

And when I reached the spot and peered over, only the low booming of the sullen Atlantic three hundred feet below came to my ears . . . That, and the mocking shrieks of a thousand gulls. Of the madman and his wife there was no sign.

At last I got up and started to walk away mechanically. I felt that somehow I was to blame for the tragedy, that I should have done something, taken a hand in that grim fight. And yet I knew that if I was called upon to witness it again, I should act in the same way. I should feel as powerless to move as I had felt in that ill-omened house, with the candles guttering on the mantelpiece, and the lightning flashing through the dirty window. Even now I seemed to be moving in a dream, and after a while I stopped and made a determined effort to pull myself together.

'You will go back,' I said out loud, 'to that house. And you will make sure that that boy is dead. You are a grown man, and not an hysterical woman. You will go back.'

And as if in answer a seagull screamed discordantly above my head. Not for five thousand pounds would I have gone back to that house alone, and when I argued with myself and said, 'You are a fool, and a coward,' the gull shrieked mockingly again.

'What is there to be afraid of?' I cried. 'A dead body: and you have seen many hundreds.'

It was as I asked the question out loud that I came to a road and sat down beside it. It was little more than a track, but it seemed to speak of other human beings, and I wanted human companionship at that moment—wanted it more than I had ever wanted anything in my life. At any other time I would have resented sharing with strangers the glorious beauty of the moors as they stretched back to a rugged tor a mile or two away, with their wonderful colouring of violet and black, and the scent of the wet earth rising all around. But now . . .

With a shudder I rose, conscious for the first time that I was feeling chilled. I must get somewhere—talk to someone; and, as if in answer to my thoughts, a car came suddenly in sight, bumping over the track.

There was an elderly man inside, and two girls, and he pulled up at once on seeing me.

'By Jove!' he cried, cheerily, 'you're very wet. Can I give you a lift anywhere?'

'It is very good of you,' I said. 'I want to get to the police as quickly as possible.'

'The police?' He stared at me surprised. 'What's wrong?'

'There's been a most ghastly tragedy,' I said. 'A man has been murdered and the murderer has jumped over that headland, with his wife in his arms. The murderer's name was Rupert Carlingham.'

I was prepared for my announcement startling them; I was not prepared for the extraordinary effect it produced. With a shriek of terror the two girls clung together, and the man's ruddy face went white.

'What name did you say?' he said at length, in a shaking voice.

'Rupert Carlingham,' I answered, curtly. 'And the boy he murdered was called John Trelawnay. Incidentally, I want to get a doctor to look at the youngster. It's possible the knife might have just missed his heart.'

'Oh, Daddy, drive on, drive on quick!' implored the girls, and I glanced at them in slight surprise. After all, a murder is a very terrible thing, but it struck me they were becoming hysterical over it.

'It was just such an evening,' said the man, slowly; 'just such a storm as we've had this afternoon, that it happened.'

'That what happened?' I cried a trifle irritably; but he made no answer, and only stared at me curiously.

'Do you know these parts, sir?' he said at length.

'It's the first time I've ever been here,' I answered. 'I'm on a walking tour.'

'Ah! A walking tour. Well, I'm a doctor myself, and unless you get your clothes changed pretty quickly, I predict that your walking tour will come to an abrupt conclusion—even if it's only a temporary one. Now, put on this coat, and we'll get off to a good inn.'

But, anxious as I was to fall in with his suggestion myself, I felt that that was more than I could do.

[231]

'It's very good of you, doctor,' I said; 'but, seeing that you are a medical man, I really must ask you to come and look at this youngster first. I'd never forgive myself if by any chance he wasn't dead. As a matter of fact, I've seen death too often not to recognize it, and the boy was stabbed clean through the heart right in front of my eyes—but . . .'

I broke off, as one of the girls leaned forward and whispered to her father. But he only shook his head, and stared at me curiously.

'Did you make no effort to stop the murder?' he asked at length.

It was the question I had been dreading, the question I knew must come sooner or later. But, now that I was actually confronted with it, I had no answer ready. I could only shake my head and stammer out confusedly:

'It seems incredible for a man of my age and experience to confess it, doctor—but I didn't. I couldn't . . . I was just going to try and separate them, when the girl rushed in . . . and . . .'

'What did she do?' It was one of the daughters who fired the question at me so suddenly that I looked at her in amazement. 'What did Mary do?'

'She got her husband by the knees,' I said, 'and hung on like a bulldog. But he'd got a grip on the boy's throat and then—suddenly—it was all over. They came crashing down as he stabbed young Trelawnay.' Once again the girls clung together shuddering, and I turned to the doctor. 'I wish you'd come, doctor: it's only just a step. I can show you the house.'

'I know the house, sir, very well,' he answered, gravely. Then he put his arms on the steering-wheel and for a long time fidgeted restlessly, and the girls whispered together. What on earth was the man waiting for? I wondered: after all, it wasn't a very big thing to ask of a doctor . . . At last he got down from the car and stood beside me on the grass.

'You've never been here before, sir?' he asked again, looking at me fixedly.

'Never,' I answered, a shade brusquely. 'And I'm not altogether bursting with a desire to return.'

'Strange,' he muttered. 'Very, very strange. I will come with you.'

For a moment he spoke to his daughters as if to reassure them; then, together, we walked over the springy turf towards the house by the headland. He seemed in no mood for conversation, and my own mind was far too busy with the tragedy for idle talk.

But he asked me one question when we were about fifty yards from the house.

'Rupert Carlingham carried his wife up to the headland, you say?'

'Slung over his shoulder,' I answered, 'and then . . .'

But the doctor had stopped short, and was staring at the house, while, once again, every vestige of colour had left his face.

'My God!' he muttered, 'there's a light in the room . . . A light, man; don't you see it?'

'I left the candles burning,' I said, impatiently. 'Really, doctor, I suppose murder doesn't often come your way, but . . .'

I walked on quickly and he followed. Really the fuss was getting on my nerves, already distinctly ragged. The front door was open as I had left it, and I paused for a moment in the cobwebby hall. Then, pulling myself together, I stepped into the room where the body lay, to halt and stare open-mouthed at the floor . . .

The candles still flickered on the mantelpiece; the furniture was as I had left it; but of the body of John Trelawnay there was not a trace. It had vanished utterly and completely.

'I don't understand, doctor,' I muttered foolishly. 'I left the body lying there.'

The doctor stood at the door beside me, and suddenly I realized that his eyes were fixed on me.

'I know,' he said, and his voice was grave and solemn. 'With the head near that chair.'

'Why, how do you know?' I cried, amazed. 'Have you taken the body away?'

But he answered my question by another.

'Do you notice anything strange in this room, sir?' he asked. 'On the floor?'

'Only a lot of dust,' I remarked.

'Precisely,' he said. 'And one would expect footprints in dust. I see yours going to the mantelpiece; I see no others.'

I clutched his arm, as his meaning came to me.

'My God!' I whispered. 'What do you mean?'

'I mean,' he said, 'that Rupert Carlingham murdered John Trelawnay, and then killed himself and his wife, five years ago . . . during just such another storm as we have had this evening.'

THE MURDER ON THE GOLF LINKS

by M. McDonnell Bodkin

'Don't go in, don't! don't! please don't!'

The disobedient ball, regardless of her entreaties, crept slowly up the smooth green slope, paused irresolute on the ridge, and then trickled softly down into the hole; a wonderful 'put'.

Miss Mag Hazel knocked her ball impatiently away from the very edge. 'Lost again on the last green,' she cried petulantly. 'You have abominable luck, Mr Beck.'

Mr Beck smiled complacently. 'Never denied it, Miss Hazel. Better be born lucky than clever is what I always say.'

'But you are clever, too,' said the girl, repentantly. 'I hear everyone say how clever you are.'

'That's where my luck comes in.'

He slung the girl's golf bag over a broad shoulder, and caught his own up in a big hand. 'Come,' he said, 'you will be late for dinner, and every man in the hotel will curse me as the cause.'

They were the last on the links. The western sky was a sea of crimson and gold, in which floated a huge black cloud, shaped like a sea monster with the blazing sun in its jaws. The placid surface of the sea gave back the beauty of the sky, and in the clear, still air familiar objects took on a new beauty. Their way lay over the crisp velvet of the seaside turf, embroidered with wild flowers, to the Thornvale Hotel in the valley a mile away.

'How beautiful!' the girl whispered half to herself, and caught her breath with a queer little sigh.

Mr Beck looked down and saw that the blue eyes were very bright with tears. She met his look and smiled a wan little smile.

'Lovely scenery always makes me sad,' she explained feebly. Then after a second she added impulsively: 'Mr Beck, you and I are good friends, aren't we?'

'I hope so,' said Mr Beck, gravely. 'I can speak for myself anyway.'

'Oh, I'm miserable! I must tell it to someone. I'm a miserable girl!'

'If I can help you in any way,' said Mr Beck, stoutly, 'you may count on me.'

'I know I oughtn't to talk about such things, but I must, I cannot stop myself; then perhaps you could say a word to father; you and he are such good friends.'

Mr Beck knew there was a confession coming. In some curious way Mr Beck attracted the most unlikely confidences. All sorts and conditions of people felt constrained to tell him secrets.

'It's this way,' Miss Hazel went on. 'Sit down there on that bank and listen. I'll be in lots of time for dinner, and anyhow I don't care. Father wants me to marry Mr Samuel Hawkins, a horrible name and a horrible man. I didn't mind much at the time he first spoke of it. I was very young, you see; I lived in a French convent school until father came back from India, and then we lived in a cottage near a golf links. Oh! such a quiet golf links, and Mr Hawkins came down to see us, and he first taught me how to play. I liked him because there was no one else. So when he asked me to marry him, and father wished it so much, I half promised—that is, I really did promise, and we were engaged, and he gave me a diamond ring, which I have here—in my purse.'

Mr Beck smiled benignly. The girl was very young and pretty and innocent—little more than a child, who had been playing at a make-believe engagement.

'How long is it since you changed your mind?' he asked.

'Well, I never really made it up to marry Mr Hawkins. I only just agreed to become engaged. But about a week or ten days ago I found I could not go on with it.'

'I see; that was about the time, was it not, that the young electrical engineer, Mr Ryan, arrived?'

She flushed hotly.

'Oh! it's not that at all—how hateful you are! Mr Ryan is nothing to me, nothing. Besides, he was most rude; called me a flirt, and said I led him on and never told him I was engaged. Now we don't even speak, and I'm so miserable. What shall I do?'

'Don't fret,' said Mr Beck, cheerily; 'it will come all right.'

'Oh! but it cannot come all right. Father will be bitterly disappointed if I don't marry Mr Hawkins. He's awfully rich, carries diamonds about loose in his waistcoat pocket. He has fifty thousand pounds' worth of diamonds getting brightened up in Amsterdam; that's where they put a polish on them, you know. He showed father the receipt for them mixed up with bank-notes in his pocket-book. His friend, Mr Bolton, who is in the same business, says Mr Hawkins is a millionaire.'

'And Mr Ryan has only his brains and his profession,' said Mr Beck, cynically.

'Now you are just horrid. I don't care twopence about Mr Hawkins' diamonds or his millions. But I love father better than anyone else.'

'Except?' suggested Mr Beck, maliciously.

'There is no exception—not one. You come second-best yourself.'

'Oh, do I? Then I will see if I cannot find some diamonds and cut out Mr Hawkins. Meantime, let us get on to our dinner. You need not be in any hurry to break your heart. You are not going to marry Mr Hawkins to-morrow or the day after. Something may happen to stop the marriage altogether. Come along.'

Something did happen. What that awful something was neither Miss Hazel nor Mr Beck dreamt of at the time.

It was the fussy half hour before dinner when they arrived at the veranda of the big Thornvale Hotel that had grown out of the Thornvale golf links. As Miss Mag Hazel passed through the throng every eye paid its tribute of admiration; she was by reason of her golf and good looks the acknowledged queen of the place.

A tall, handsome young fellow near the porch gave a pitiful look as she passed, the humble, appealing look in the eyes of a dog who has offended his master.

'How handsome he is; what beautiful black eyes he has!' her heart whispered, but her face was unconscious of his existence.

She evaded a small, dark man with a big hooked nose who came forward eagerly to claim her. 'Don't speak to me, Mr Hawkins, don't look at me. I have not five minutes to dress for dinner.'

A tall, thin man with a grey, drooping moustache stood close by her left in the central hall. To him she said: 'I will be down in a minute, dad. I want you to take me in to dinner, mind. You are worth the whole lot of them put together.'

Colonel Hazel's sallow cheek flushed with delight, for he loved his daughter with a love that was the best part of his life.

Big, good-humoured, smiling Tom Bolton, as the girl went in to dinner on her father's arm, whispered a word in the ear of his friend, Sam Hawkins, and the millionaire diamond merchant cast a scowling glance at handsome Ned Ryan, who gave him frown for frown with interest thereto.

At Thornvale Hotel the company lived, moved, and had their being in golf. They played golf all day on the links, and talked golf all the evening at the hotel. All the varied forms of golf lunacy were in evidence there. There was the fat elderly lady who went round 'for her figure', tapping the ball before her on the smooth ground, and throwing it or carrying it over the bunkers. There was the man who was always grumbling about his 'blanked' luck, and who never played what he was pleased to think was his 'true game'.

There was the man who sang comic songs on the green, and the man whose nerves were strained like fiddle-strings and tingled at every stir or whisper, whom the flight of a butterfly put off his stroke. There was a veteran of eighty-five, who still played a steady game. He had once been a scratch man, and though the free, loose vigour of his 'swing' was lost, his eye and arm had not forgotten the lesson of years. His favourite opponent was a boy of twelve, who swung loose and free as if he were a figure of indiarubber with no bones in his arms.

Mr Hawkins and Mr Bolton were a perfect match with a level handicap of twelve; each believed that he could just beat the other, and the excitement of their incessant contests was intense.

But Miss Mag Hazel reigned undisputed queen of the links. None of the ladies, and only one or two of the men, could even 'give her a game'. Lissom as an ash sapling, every muscle in her body, from her shoulder to her ankle, took part in the graceful swing which, without effort, drove the ball further than a strong man could smite it by brute force. Her wrist was like a fine steel spring, as sensitive and as true.

Heretofore only one player disputed her supremacy—Mr Beck, the famous detective, who was idling a month in the quiet hotel after an exciting and successful criminal hunt half way round the world. Mr Beck was, as he always proclaimed, a lucky player. If he never made a brilliant stroke, he never made a bad one, and kept wonderfully clear of the bunkers. The brilliant players found he had an irritating trick of plodding on steadily, and coming out a hole ahead at the end of the round.

[237]

He and Mag Hazel played constantly together until young Ned Ryan came on the scene. Ryan was a brilliant young fellow with muscles of whipcord and whalebone, whose drive was like a shot from a catapult. But he played a sporting game, and very often drove into the bunker which was meant to catch the second shot of a second-class player. Mag Hazel found it easier to hold her own against his brilliance than against the plodding pertinacity of Mr Beck.

It may be that the impressionable young Irishman could not quite play his game when she was his opponent. He found it hard to obey the golfer's first commandment: 'Keep your eye on the ball.' He tried to play two games at the same time, and golf will have no divided allegiance.

The end of a happy fortnight came suddenly. It was a violent scene when, in a grassy bunker wide of the course, into which he had deliberately pulled his ball, he asked her to marry him, and learnt that she was engaged to the millionaire diamond merchant, Mr Hawkins. Poor Ned Ryan, with Irish impetuosity, raved and stormed at her cruelty in leading him to love her, swore his life was barren for evermore, and even muttered some very mysterious, meaningless threats against the more fortunate Mr Hawkins.

Tender-hearted Mag had been very meek and penitent while he raved and stormed, but he was not to be appeased by her meekness, and flung away from her in a rage.

Then it was her turn to be implacable when he became penitent. All that evening he hovered round her like a blundering moth round a lamp, but she ignored him as completely as the lamp the moth and shed the light of her smiles on Mr Beck.

So those two foolish young people played the old game in the old, foolish fashion, and tormented themselves and each other. The two men concerned in the matter, Mr Ryan and Mr Hawkins, scowled at each other on the golf links and at the bridge table, to the intense amusement of the company, who understood how little golf or cards had to do with the quarrel.

At last Ned Ryan had an open row with Mr Hawkins on the golf links, and told him, quite unnecessarily, he was no gentleman.

Then suddenly this light comedy deepened into sombre tragedy. The late breakfasters at the hotel were still at table when the thrilling, shocking news came to them that Mr Hawkins had been found murdered on the links.

Perhaps it is more convenient to tell the dismal story in the order in which it was told in evidence at the coroner's inquest.

Mr Hawkins and Mr Bolton had arranged a round in the early morning before breakfast, when they would have the links to themselves. They had a glass of milk and a biscuit, and started off in good spirits, each boasting he was certain to win.

They started some time between half-past six and seven, and about an hour afterwards Mr Bolton returned hastily, saying that he had forgotten an important letter he had to send by that morning's post, and that he had left Mr Hawkins grumbling at having to finish his round alone. Mr Bolton then went up to his own room, and five minutes later came back with a letter, which he carefully posted with his own hand just as the box was being cleared.

At half-past seven Colonel Hazel, strolling across the links, specially noticed there were no players to be seen. Ned Ryan went out at a quarter to eight o'clock to have a round by himself, having first asked Mr Bolton to join him. He had, as he stated, almost completed his round, when in the great, sandy bunker that guarded the seventeenth green he found Mr Hawkins stone dead.

He instantly gave the alarm, and Mr Beck and Mr Bolton were among the first on the scene. The detective, placid and imperturbable as ever, poked and pried about the body and the bunker where it lay. Mr Bolton was plainly broken-hearted at the sudden death of his life-long friend.

Beyond all doubt and question the man was murdered. There was a deep dint of some heavy, blunt weapon on the back of his head, fracturing the skull. But death had not been instantaneous. The victim had turned upon his assassin, for there were two other marks on his face—one an ugly, livid bruise on his cheek, and the other a deep, horrible gash on the temple from the same blunt-edged weapon. The last wound must have been instantly fatal. The weapon slew as it struck.

It was plain that robbery was not the motive of the crime. His heavy purse with a score of sovereigns and his pocket-book full of bank-notes were in his pockets, his fine diamond pin in his scarf, and his handsome watch in his fob.

The watch had been struck and smashed, and, as so often happens in such cases, it timed the murder to a moment. It had stopped at half-past eight. It was five minutes after nine when Mr Ryan had given the alarm.

While all the others looked on in open-eyed horror incapable of thought or action, Mr Beck's quick eyes found a corner of the bunker where the sand had been disturbed recently. Rooting with his hands as a dog digs at a rabbit burrow with his paws, he dug out a heavy niblick. The handle was snapped in two, and the sand that clung damply round the iron face left a dark crimson stain on the fingers that touched it.

No one then could doubt that the murderous weapon had been found.

Mr Beck examined it a moment, and a frown gathered on his placid face. 'This is Mr Ryan's niblick,' he said slowly.

The words sent a quiver of excitement through the crowd. All eyes turned instinctively to the face of the young Irishman, who flushed in sudden anger.

'It's a lie,' he shouted, 'my niblick is here.' He turned to his bag which lay on the sward beside him. 'My God! it's gone. I never noticed it until this moment.'

'Yes, that is mine,' he added, as Mr Beck held out the blood-stained iron for inspection. 'But I swear I never missed it till this moment.'

Not a word more was said.

The crowd broke up into groups, each man whispering suspicions under his breath. The whisperers recalled the recent quarrel between the men, and in every trifling circumstance clear proof of guilt was found. Only Mr Bolton stood out staunchly for the young Irishman, and professed his faith in his innocence.

Like a man in a dream Ned Ryan returned alone to the hotel, where an hour later he was arrested. On being searched after arrest a five-pound note with Hawkins' name on the back of it was found in his pocket, and his explantion that he had won it at golf provoked incredulous smiles and shrugs amongst the gossipers. Two days later a coroner's jury found a verdict of wilful murder against the young engineer.

There was a second sensation, in its way almost as exciting as the first, when it was found that the murdered man had willed the whole of his huge fortune unconditionally to Miss Margaret Hazel.

But the girl declared vehemently she would never touch a penny of it, never, until the real murderer was discovered. She had a stormy interview with Mr Beck, whom she passionately charged with attempts to fix the guilt on an innocent man. She made no secret now of her love for the young Irishman, to the horror of the respectable and proper people at the hotel, who looked forward with cheerful assurance to her lover's execution.

But the distracted girl cared for none of those things. She poured the vials of her wrath on Mr Beck.

'You pretended to be my friend,' she said, 'and then you did all in your power to hang the innocent man I love.'

Mr Beck was soothing and imperturbable. 'Nothing of the kind, my dear young lady. It is always my pleasant duty to save the innocent and hang the guilty.'

'Then why did you find out that niblick?'

'The more things that are found,' said Mr Beck, 'the better for the innocent and the worse for the guilty.'

'Oh! I'm not talking about that,' she cried, with a bewildering change of front. 'But here you are pottering about doing nothing instead of trying to save him. I will give you every penny poor Mr Hawkins left me if you save him.'

Mr Beck smiled benignly at this magnificent offer. 'Won't you two want something to live on,' he asked, 'when I have saved him, and before he makes his fortune?'

She let the question go by. 'Then you will, you promise me you will!' she cried eagerly.

'I will try to assist the course of justice,' he said, with formal gravity, but his eyes twinkled, and she took comfort therefrom.

'That's not what I want at all.'

'You believe Mr Ryan is innocent?' asked Mr Beck.

'Of course I do. What a question!'

'If he is innocent I will try to save him—if not—'

'There is no "if not". Oh! I'm quite satisfied, and I thank you with all my heart.'

She caught up the big, strong hand and kissed it, and then collapsed on the sofa for a good cry, while Mr Beck stole discreetly from the room and set out for a solitary stroll on the golf links, every yard of which he questioned with shrewd eyes.

He made one small discovery on the corner of the second green. He found a ball which had belonged to the murdered man. There was no doubt about the ownership. Mr Hawkins had a small gold seal with his initial cut in it. This he used to heat with a match to brand his ball. The tiny black letters, 'S.H.', were burnt through the white skin of the new 'Professional' ball, which Mr Beck found on the corner of the second green. He put the ball in his pocket and said nothing about his find.

But about another curious discovery of his he was quite voluable that evening at dinner. He found, he said, a peculiar-looking waistcoat button in the bunker that guarded the second green. It seemed to him to have been torn violently from the garment, for a shred of the cloth still clung to it.

'If I had found it in the bunker where the murder was committed,' said Mr Beck, 'I would have regarded it as a very important piece of evidence. Anyhow it may help. I will examine young Ryan's waistcoats to see if it fits any of them.'

Then for a few days nothing happened, and excitement smouldered. People had no heart to play golf over the scene of the murder. The parties gradually dispersed and scattered homewards. Colonel Hazel, who had been completely broken up by the tragedy, was amongst the first to go.

Mag gave her address to Mr Beck, with strict injunctions to wire the moment he had good news.

'Remember, I trust you,' were the last words she said as they parted at the hotel door.

Mr Bolton and Mr Beck were almost the two last to leave. The diamond merchant was disconsolate over the death of his old friend and comrade, and the detective did all in his power to comfort him.

One morning Mr Bolton had a telegram which, as he explained to Mr Beck, called him away on urgent business. He left that afternoon, and Mr Beck went with him as far as Liverpool, when they parted, each on his respective business.

The next scene in the tragedy was staged in Holland.

Two men sat alone together in a first-class railway carriage that slid smoothly through a level landscape intersected with canals. They had put aside their papers, and talked and smoked. One of the men was plainly a German by his dress and manner—the other a Frenchman.

The Frenchman had tried vainly to stagger through a conversation in German and the German in French until they had found a common ground in English which both spoke well though with a strong foreign accent.

There had been an account of a big diamond robbery in the papers, and their talk drifted on to crimes and criminals of all countries—a topic with which the Frenchman seemed strangely familiar. He did most of the talking. The German sat back in his corner and grunted out a word or two of assent, to all appearance deeply interested in the talk. Now and again a silver flask passed between the two men, who grew momentarily more intimate.

'Herr Raphael,' said the Frenchman, 'I am glad to have met you. You have made the journey very pleasant for me. You are a man I feel I can trust. I am not, as I told you, Victor Grandeau, a French journalist. I am plain Mr Paul Beck, an English detective, at your service.'

With a single motion the shiny, sleek, black wig and the black moustache disappeared into a small handbag at his side. The whole character, and even the features of the face, seemed to change as suddenly, and the broad, bland, smiling face of our old friend Mr Beck presented itself to the eyes of the astonished German, who shrank back in his corner of the seat in astonishment at the sudden revelation. But Mr Beck quietly ignored his astonishment.

'As you seem interested in this kind of thing,' he said, 'I will tell you the story of one of the most curious cases I have ever had to deal with. You are the very first to hear the story. Indeed, it is so new that it hasn't yet got the right ending to it. Perhaps you have heard of the Thornvale murder in England? No! Then I'll begin at the beginning.'

He began at the beginning and told the story clearly and vividly as it was told at the inquest. The German listened with most flattering interest and surprise.

'When I found that golf ball,' Mr Beck went on, 'it gave me an idea. Do you know anything of golf?'

'I play a little,' the other confessed.

'Then you will understand that from the place where I found his ball I knew that the murdered man—I told you his name was Hawkins—Samuel Hawkins—never got as far as the second green. If he had, his ball would not have been lying where I found it. He would have holed it out and gone on.

'It was plain, therefore, he must have been murdered just after he played that shot—murdered somewhere between the tee and the green of the second hole. I went back to the deep bunker I told you of that guarded the second green, and I found there traces of a struggle.

'They had been cunningly obliterated, but to a detective's eye they were plain enough. The sand was smoothed over the footprints, but here and there the long grass and wild flowers had been torn away by a desperate grasp. I even found a faint bloodstain on one of the stones. Then, of course, I guessed what had happened. The man had been murdered in the bunker of the second green and carried under cover of the ridge to the bunker of the seventeenth. That, you see, disposed of the alibi of Mr Bolton, who had left him early in the game.'

'Oh, no!' interrupted the German, with eager interest in the story, 'you told me that Mr Bolton was at the hotel from half-past seven, and the watch of the murdered man showed the murder had been committed at half-past eight.'

Mr Beck looked at the German with manifest admiration. 'Forgive me for mentioning it. You would have made a first-class detective if you hadn't gone into another line of business. I should have told you that the evidence of the watch had been faked.'

'Faked!' queried the other, with a blank look on his face.

'Oh! I see. Being a German, of course you don't understand our slang phrases. I examined the watch, and I found that though the glass had been violently broken, the dial was not even scratched. The spring had been snapped, not by the blow but by overwinding. It was pretty plain to me the murdered had done the trick. He first put the hands on to half-past eight and then broke the spring, and so made his alibi. He got the watch to perjure itself. Neat, wasn't it?'

The German merely grunted. He was plainly impressed by the devilish ingenuity of the murderer.

'Besides,' Mr Beck went on placidly, 'to make quite sure, I laid a trap for Mr Bolton which worked like a charm. The night of the murder I went into his room and tore one of the buttons out of his waistcoat. The next day I mentioned at dinner that I had found a button in the second bunker where, if I guessed rightly, he and only he knew the murder was really committed. It was a lie, of course. But it caught the truth. That same evening Mr Bolton burnt the waistcoat. It was a light cotton affair that burnt like paper. The glass buttons he cut off with a knife and buried. That looked bad, didn't it?'

'Very bad,' the German agreed. He was more deeply interested than ever. 'Did you arrest the man, then?'

'Not then.'

'But why?'

'I wanted to make quite sure of my proofs. I wanted to lay my hands on the receipts for the diamonds which I believed he had stolen. I told you of those, didn't I?'

'Oh, yes, you told me of those. Did you search for them?'

'Yes, but I couldn't find them. I searched Mr Bolton's room, and searched his clothes carefully, but I couldn't find a trace of the papers.'

Again the German grunted. He seemed somehow pleased at the

failure. Possibly the quiet confidence of this cocksure detective annoyed him.

'But,' Mr Beck went on, placid as ever, 'I tried a guess. You may remember, Herr Raphael, that when Mr Bolton came back from the golf links he posted a letter immediately. I had a notion that he stuck the receipts in the envelope and posted it addressed to himself at some post-office to be left till called for. Wasn't a bad guess, was it?'

'A very good guess.'

'Then I did a little bit of forgery.'

'You what?'

'Did a little bit of forgery. I forged the name of Mr Bolton's partner to a telegram to say that five thousand pounds were urgently needed. That, I knew, was likely to make Mr Bolton gather up the receipts and start for Amsterdam. We went to Liverpool together and I changed to an elderly lady. I saw him as an able-bodied seaman pick up his own letter at the Liverpool Post-Office. I came over with him in the boat to Rotterdam. As a French journalist I saw him as a stout German get into this very carriage and—here I am!'

It was a very lame ending to an exciting story. The stout German plainly thought so. He had listened with flattering eagerness almost to the end; now he leant back in the corner of his seat suppressing a yawn.

'It is a very amusing story,' he said slowly. 'But, my friend, you must be thirsty with much talking. I in my bag have a flask of excellent schnapps, you shall of it taste.'

A small black bag rested on the seat beside him. He laid his hand on the fastening.

'It is no use,' Mr Beck interrupted, 'no use, Mr Bolton. I have taken the revolver out of the bag and have it with my own in my pocket. The game is up, I think. I have put my cards on the table. What do you say?'

Suddenly Mr Bolton broke into a loud, harsh laugh that ended in a sob. 'You are a fiend, Beck,' he shouted, 'a fiend incarnate. What do you mean to do?'

'To take you back with me to London. I have a man in the next carriage to look after you. No use worrying about extradition. You have a return ticket, I suppose; so have I. There will be a train leaving as we arrive. Meanwhile, if you don't mind—' He took a neat pair of handcuffs from his pocket and held them out with an ingratiating smile.

Mr Bolton drew back a little. For a moment it seemed as if he would spring at the detective's throat. But the steady, fearless eyes held him. He put his hands out submissively and the steel bracelets clicked on his wrists.

They had only to cross the platform to reach the return train that was just starting. But Mr Beck found time to plunge into the telegraph office and scribble three words to Mag Hazel's address: All right—BECK.

ACKNOWLEDGEMENTS

The Publisher has made every effort to contact the Copyright holders, but wishes to apologise to those he has been unable to trace. Grateful acknowledgement is made for permission to reprint the following:

'Perfect Honeymoon' by Robert Barnard. Copyright © 1987 by Davis Publications, Inc. First appeared in *Ellery Queen's Mystery Magazine*.

'The Summer Holiday Murders' by Julian Symons. From *Some Like it Dead* copyright © Julian Symons 1960 reproduced by permission of Curtis Brown Ltd, London.

'Triangle at Sea' by Anna Clarke. Copyright © 1984 by Davis Publications, Inc. First appeared in *Ellery Queen's Mystery Magazine*.

'Kill and Cure' by Guy Cullingford. Courtesy the Author.

'The Beach House' by Norman Daniels. Courtesy the Author.

'The Old Shell Collector' by H.R.F. Keating. Courtesy the Author.

'Cottage for August' by Thomas Kyd. Courtesy Alfred B. Harbage, Jr, Executor of the Estate of Thomas Kyd, Severna Park, Maryland, USA.

'Love Comes to Miss Lucy' by Q. Patrick. Copyright © 1947 by Q. Patrick. Reprinted by permission of Curtis Brown Ltd, New York.

'Petrella's Holiday' by Michael Gilbert. Courtesy the Author.

[247]